RUTH MOHRMAN

The Oak People

Cadoc Publishing

For my parents, Les and Eileen Mohrman, to whom I grow ever more grateful

Contents

Foreword

Ancient Egyptian sailors, sailing close to modern-day Israel's Mediterranean coast, became familiar with the shape of the Carmel mountain range as it appeared to them from the sea, and gave it the name of the Antelope's Nose or the Gazelle's Nose. There are a number of caves on the Carmel and, on its western slopes, currently some 3km from the sea, lies the entrance to Kebara cave. During the Middle Paleolithic or stone-age period (200,000 to 40,000 years ago) and the Upper Paleolithic (40,000 to 10,000 years ago) the cave is known to have been occupied at different times by Neanderthals and by early humans of our own lineage. There is evidence that these different branches of humanity coincided along this coast in prehistory, hunting wild deer and gazelles and foraging for plant foods. Recent research indicates that Neanderthals and homo sapiens people did interact more than was once thought and even interbred, meaning that modern-day people from European or Asian backgrounds have 1-2% Neanderthal DNA.

At times during the Paleolithic, lower sea levels meant that there was a wider expanse of plain between the mountain slopes and the Mediterranean than there is today. Nevertheless, mollusc shells found in the Carmel caves indicate that the cave inhabitants probably travelled to the seashore from time to time, perhaps for food, as the Oak People do in the story that follows. The slopes of the Antelope Nose are today green all year round, covered with pines, carob, almond and terebinth trees, as well as groves of Palestinian oaks (quercus calliprinos). Plant remains found in Kebara cave suggest that the inhabitants were gathering and processing acorns, pistachios, wild legumes and vetches as well as fruit, at least 40,000 years ago. Animal bones found reveal that they ate tortoises and hunted larger animals for food: gazelles (small antelope), deer of various kinds and occasionally wild boar.

Early modern humans are thought to have lived in small bands of, perhaps, twenty-five people, probably based on one or two extended families. They would have links with other groups from whom sexual partners could be found, as their young matured. Little is known for certain about the culture of hunter-gatherer bands but music seems to have played a part in their lives. Primitive drums are generally thought to have been used from very early in human history and bone or ivory flutes have been found, dating from the Paleolithic period. Numerous paintings and engravings have been found in caves occupied in prehistory. It is becoming clear, too, that art and music may not have been a feature solely of the lives of our own homo sapiens ancestors. A flute has been unearthed in a cave occupied by Neanderthals in the Middle Paleolithic and cave drawings in Spain have been dated to 20,000 years before homo sapiens arrived in Europe. Story-telling, too, is probably as old as the earliest forms of human society. Like the San Bushmen story of the mantis and his son, which I have woven into the story that follows, early stories and myths probably centred on the animals and the natural environment which was so crucial to human survival and of which they felt themselves to be a part.

Just how stone-age people related together is clearly impossible to know. However, it is an interesting feature of the small hunter-gatherer groups that still survive in isolated parts of Africa, Asia and South America that social relations are egalitarian and based on co-operation. The particular skills of each group member are recognized and valued. Perhaps because small groups made up of interdependent individuals cannot afford violence and feuding, considerable effort is expended to make sure that decisions are consensual and no one individual tries to become dominant. Perhaps the hierarchical style of leadership with which we are most familiar only emerged when groups become larger, co-operation became less feasible and consensus became more difficult to maintain. What does seem likely is that early humans felt affection and pity for each other, much as we do. There is evidence of individuals living for years after sustaining injuries which would have rendered them unable to hunt or forage for food, and therefore a burden to the group. The only explanation for their survival is that other group members fed and cared for them.

The religious or spiritual practices of early modern humans must remain a matter for conjecture. Alongside the animal drawings in the Lascaux caves in France, produced by Paleolithic humans, are curious markings thought to be the earliest lunar code, suggesting the importance of the Moon to the cave-dwellers who made them. The Oak People in the novel reverence Balqa (the Moon) and conceive of him as male. Many cultures have associated the Moon with femininity but not all. The Phrygian culture of Western Asia

Minor has a male lunar god called Mên, who is associated with fertility, healing and punishment.

Evidence has been found of early modern humans burying their dead with artifacts including flints and shells and pieces of ochre as early as 92,000 years ago, which might suggest a belief in an afterlife. It is becoming increasingly likely that Neanderthals, too, intentionally buried their dead, although whether they only learned this behaviour from modern humans with whom they came into contact is unclear.

The ethnic religions of many peoples around the world include the tradition of seers or shamans, individuals who act as messengers between the human and the spirit world. They are those who seem able to travel to other worlds or dimensions and bring back messages or healing for the group. Itzal, the shaman of the Painted People in the novel, is one such individual, though in his case the spiritual knowledge he claims access to is corrupted by the all too human traits of dominance and violence. Ansa, the main protagonist of the novel, enters a different kind of transcendental state when she comes close to death in childbirth and has what is commonly called a near death experience. Near death experiences have been reported throughout recorded history but as medical techniques become more effective in prolonging life for those who experience heart attacks, for example, many more near death experiences are being reported, across cultures, and studied. Often the divine figures who appear will be interpreted through the lens of the religious or social context of the individual concerned. But there are some features of the experience that seem to crop up regularly and cross-culturally: the famous tunnel with light at its end, the sensation of looking down from above on your own body, the apprehension of knowledge and wisdom that is beyond normal human capability. Perhaps the most striking feature of many profound near death experiences is the long-lasting change it brings about in the experiencer and the way that death is never again feared.

Preface

THE OAK PEOPLE

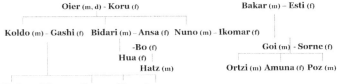

Oier (m, d) - Koru (f)   Bakar (m) – Esti (f)

Koldo (m) - Gashi (f) Bidari (m) – Ansa (f) Nuno (m) – Ikomar (f)

-Bo (f)

Hua (f)   Goi (m) - Sorne (f)

Hatz (m)   Ortzi (m) Amuna (f) Poz (m)

Tipi (m) – Lilura (f) Iban (m) Ula (f) Loza (f)

OTHER CHARACTERS

PAINTED PEOPLE
Lotz (m) – Nahia (f)
Odol (m)
Zorion (Headman)
Itzal (Seer)

DESERT PEOPLE
Garoa (Ansa's stepmother)
Zeru (d, Ansa's brother)
Elori (m)

MARSH PEOPLE
Apal (m)
Eneko (m)
Gutshi (m)

GLOSSARY

ama	mother
Balqa	the Moon
Balqa stone	pearl
blood spider	venomous redback spider
chukar	a kind of partridge
earthnut	a plant with almond-flavoured edible tubers (*lathyrus tuberosus*)
Eshtu	the Sun
firestone	iron pyrite, a mineral used for making fire, when struck by a flint
gaat	qat (khat), drug found in the leaves of a wild shrub, *catha edulis*, which contains a central nervous stimulant called cathinone
grass peas	the edible seeds of chickling vetch (*lathyrus sativus*)
ita	father
kep	head
khamsin	hot wind blowing from the desert
kho	ochre, natural clay earth pigment, used for painting
nama	yarrow plant (*achillea millefolium*), used for medicinal purposes
nefafa	sea snails
nut grass	a kind of sedge (*cyperus rotundus*) with edible nut-shaped tubers
puti	vagina
qartam	sea-holly (*eryngium maritinum*), used for medicinal purposes
Red Balqa	the Hunter's or Blood Moon in October, when the full moon rises soon after sunset and appears larger than usual and an orange colour
sakaitz	neanderthals
Salt Water	the ocean
ta-uma	gathering of small groups, to make a larger one
thornfruit	edible fruit of the hawthorn

Acknowledgement

I would like to acknowledge the close attention and encouragement provided by the Edgeworks Writers Group over the years which saw the gestation of this book. Engaging with a story set so far back in prehistory was quite an ask, but the members of the group (Deborah Kay Davies, Norman Schwenk, Jane Blank and Claire Syder) set about it with enthusiasm and were unfailingly helpful in their comments. Special thanks are due to Norman Schwenk, who died in early 2023 after a lifetime of writing, teaching and fostering other writers, for agreeing to read through the complete novel and to Anne Griffith, more recently, for reading the final version and providing much-appreciated support and friendship.

Thanks are also due to my husband, Andrew, for his ever-present support and simply for being himself.

Chapter 1

Ansa

Ansa squats by the stream to wash, being careful to wet between her legs like the women told her. The fingers of Eshtu play hot on her shoulders as she walks back to the camp. Soon the tents come into view, the summer grass long since trampled down around them. Her heart drops like a stone in water when she sees wood being heaped up for the feast tonight and thinks of what must follow. In the morning, the camp will be broken up.

Garoa is by the shelter, watching. 'What took you so long?' There is no trace of softness in the voice of her father's wife. 'Get over to the fire. They're mixing the kho.'

Ansa turns obediently towards the nearest hearth, where some of the Oak women are squatting around a flat pounding stone. She is glad to see that the wrinkled one who will be her mother-in-law is among them. Koru has kind eyes and the stories she tells around the fire fill Ansa with wonder.

The women look up, excited to see the bride approaching. She kneels in the space they have made, folding her long legs beneath her like an antelope. She keeps her head down.

'You needn't look so scared,' one of the women says. 'We'll make you beautiful for him.'

1

'That's why she's frightened!' There is shrill laughter. 'Or maybe she knows what to expect – maybe she's done it before.'

Ansa feels the warm colour rising up and spreading over the dark skin of her face. There is no real malice in the words of the women but their curiosity is like a blade scraping her skin. Then comes an older voice and she risks a fleeting upward glance.

'Leave the child in peace,' says Koru.

The others settle down to their pounding. Closing her eyes, Ansa thinks about what is to come. Though she tries to grasp and hold them, the thought pictures pass overhead like a flock of birds, out of her reach. *Women taking down the shelters in the early morning light. Her own people with packs on their backs, turning to wave. Ita putting his hand on her head, then walking away with Garoa and the children. He does not look back.*

She tries to picture herself trekking across the plain with these Oak People to their mountain range - the Nose of the Antelope. Climbing up to their cave. What can it be like to sleep in the dark nostril of a mountain? With strangers? To gather food with those women? One by one, the thoughts dip down then race up, away from her grasp. Only one thought remains, still and glowering, like a waiting vulture. After tonight's Balqa feast and the joining, she must lie down under a skin with the gap-toothed man, Bidari.

She looks up to see Koru peering short-sightedly at the red heap on the flat stone, feeling the smoothness of the powder between her fingers. Ansa has never seen kho of such a red before. When it is mixed with water, the bowl looks as if it is full of blood. It is so beautiful that she forgets her fear.

'Where did you find it?' she whispers.

The woman who is mixing the paste smiles. 'So you do

have a tongue.' She bends over, her mouth close to Ansa's face. She smells strange. 'The kho comes from a place high up on our mountain.'

High up on the mountain. Isn't that where the wild men live? Ansa's heart beats faster as she remembers all she has heard around the fire. The Sakaitz are pale, with huge gaping nostrils - the offspring of men and she-boar. They are no taller than children but they are very strong. One old man said they can climb for a whole day, without stopping. She shivers, glad that they keep to the high places and are only seen when Balqa is in the land of death and the nights are dark.

The women form a circle around Ansa, to hide her from prying eyes. The heat of their bodies, the unfamiliar smell of them, is overwhelming. A young woman starts to paint her chest with a brush made of goat hair: unseen others are painting her back, her arms. She submits to the soft stroking and soon her breath starts to come more easily. Though their hands are pulling her this way and that, the women demand nothing from her. When they speak it is not to her, but to each other. 'Isn't she thin?' 'See how long her neck is!'

She looks with wonder at the red lines curving along her arm. Is it their rivers the women are painting, or perhaps the patterned bark of their oaks? A wind begins to blow up. Ansa looks across the plain at the red circle on the horizon, dipping further and further out of sight. Someone grasps hold of her chin and she closes her eyes as they start to paint her face. Behind her eye-lids the half-face of Eshtu still shines, no longer red but green.

Ansa cannot remember a time when she didn't know the story of Eshtu. *The Skyfather withdrew beyond sight into the*

3

high heavens, and wept. A hot tear of rage fell from his eye and became Eshtu, who toils up through the sky and down again each day, shedding his fierce heat and light. The Skymother sat with her husband to soothe him. When his anger had cooled, the Skyfather began to weep once more, this time with sadness. A cold tear of mourning fell from his eye and became Balqa, who gives his soft light to the night sky. Balqa is not fierce like his older brother Eshtu, but he has greater wisdom. He knows the secret of death.

She thinks of all the dark nights back in her desert home, when Balqa was in the land of death. She would watch the sky with the other children, each one wanting to be the first to see him born again, the thinnest blade of light. Tonight, he will be swollen with life, huge and round. This is the time for a man and a woman to be joined.

'Just your eyelids now and then it will be done,' says the voice of the young woman.

Night has come and the plain is basking in a pale light, reflected back by the Crocodile River, as it slides smoothly towards the Salt Water. In the space between the shelters, the men sit in a circle, to watch the women dance. Huddling close together, the women spring up and down, competing to see who can jump the highest. They form a gliding snake of bodies, pulsing in and out of the ring of men and boys. The men's singing, a low murmur at first, grows louder.

Ansa watches from beside her father's tent, the sick fear in the pit of her belly turning to excitement as the rhythm of the drums becomes more insistent. The coiling snake twists in and out, curving back on itself, the women's legs shining in the light of the flames. The men are clapping their knees, swaying in time to the drums. Ansa's mouth waters as the

4

aroma of roasting meat reaches her.

Dragging her eyes away from the dance, Ansa stares up at Balqa, so huge and bright on this magic night that even the Nose of the Antelope seems small beneath him. The singing and the drumming drop away and she is alone. The ripe, fat face of Balqa seems to swell, drawing her up through the darkness. She sucks comfort from him greedily, as if he were the breast of her mother. Longing to be able to gaze at the luminous face forever, she traces every shadow, every feature, until the old, nameless terror creeps up on her once more.

Trembling, Ansa brings her eyes back to the plain. The drum beat is faster still, more insistent. Alone by the shelters, she springs to her feet. Fever crackles like lightning on the evening air as the women whirl more wildly, till Balqa reaches the highest point in his night's journey and a voice rises above the others, calling out the words they have been waiting for. One after another the men get to their feet, their voices shivering away into silence. The dancing snake glides to a halt. Only the one, big drum is left now, sounding a slow, steady beat. Each face is turned up to the sky. Ansa feels the magic ripple the length of her neck and over her scalp as, one with all the others, she lifts her arms to the light above. The roar of greeting goes up then fades away, leaving the plain still and silent, as if the world were holding its breath.

Now it is over, the children squeal and run in circles, their hands in the air. People are gathering around the big cooking fire, the sweet smell of boar meat everywhere. When the hunters came back this morning with a fat male boar, everyone said it was a good omen for the joining. Ansa begins to tremble. They will come for her soon.

She crawls back into the tent, her skin stiff with paint, and watches through a gap in the goatskin. The people are sitting now in a big circle and becoming quiet – even the children are still. A figure emerges from the shadows on the far side and walks into the centre of the circle. When the light from the flames falls on his face, Ansa sees that it is Bidari and her belly tightens with fear. The blood seems to drain from her head and she feels light and strong, as if she could spring away like a goat into the safe darkness of the vast plain. She could run all night, like the wild men with the flat faces. They would never catch her.

But no, she is still crouching in the stuffy heat of the shelter, her eyes on the figure by the hearth. Another man gets to his feet and she recognizes the slope of his shoulders – her father. He leaves the circle and walks towards the tent where she is cowering. The soft white light of Balqa falls now on his face, now on his hair. The night itself seems to hang, waiting with her, still and full of dread. Ita bends down, pulling back the goat hide. In the darkness, Ansa cannot see his face. He reaches in to help her up and tears come to her eyes at his touch but when he speaks, it is only to grumble, as always.

'What are you hiding for? Don't bring shame on me.'

As she follows him towards the waiting circle a thought lands on her like a fly, almost unnoticed. *Tomorrow is the last time I will see my father.* She waits but no sting of pain comes and she brushes the thought away.

Bidari

Passing inside the circle, Bidari feels a slap on the calf and looks down to see his brother, Nuno, grinning and gesturing with his middle finger. The men sitting nearby laugh and Bidari laughs with them. For once, they are all watching him, even Koldo, his older brother. He searches among the women for the face of his mother. There she is, looking small among them but holding herself upright.

Ansa is walking into the firelight behind her father and Bidari gasps at the beauty of the girl's taut, smooth skin, with its tracery of red. Amid clapping and calling, he goes to stand beside her. He finds Koldo's face in the circle and is gratified to see the lust in his brother's eyes, as he stares at the bride.

The people are impatient for the succulent meat, but when Bidari's mother gets up and walks stiffly over to the hearth, they fall silent. Remembering the other joinings he has witnessed, Bidari clasps his hands behind his back but Ansa stands motionless, like a cornered antelope, and her father has to pull her into place. Turning them to face each other, the parents take the hands of the couple and bring them together. A din of calling starts up. It is the first time Bidari has touched Ansa. Her hands feel small in his, like those of a child. She is shaking. He smiles, eager to show her there is nothing to fear.

A long strip of the boar meat is brought to Bidari, dripping with fat. Hot from the fire, he juggles it from hand to hand to make everyone laugh. Someone shouts out for him to get on with it because the others can't eat till he and Ansa have eaten. Bidari tears off some meat to give her, then bites into the rest. Fat trickles down his chin and he grins at Ansa, pale beneath the kho and trembling. Her throat is working as she swallows the food and he feels himself become hard, aching to be inside her.

The Oak People and the Desert People crowd around the cooking hearth, children pushing their way to the front. The men gather round Bidari, laughing and cuffing the top of his head and wishing him fruit from Ansa. Both his brothers, Koldo and Nuno, already have wives and Koldo's wife has given birth four times. Bidari glances over at Ansa. She is tall but very thin. Is she too young to become a mother? He likes to think of her flat belly swelling with the child he will place there.

The women will be busy with Ansa for a time yet. He goes to find his mother and squats down in front of her. She looks tired but he can tell that she is happy.

She puts out her hand and touches his face. 'Bidari – be patient with her.'

He waits, puzzled, but she says nothing else. A solitary male voice rises above the hubbub and the drums - the men are starting the goat song. He brushes the top of his mother's head with his lips and leaps up to join them.

Ansa

At first, Ansa can see nothing in the sweltering darkness. She is alone, listening to the chatter of the women outside. They brought her here, to Bidari's tent, and pushed her inside, but they show no sign of going away. The sick cramps in her belly still come and go and now that she is away from curious eyes, tears come. She is kneeling on something soft they have laid on top of the itchy grass. She drops her head and starts to rock to and fro. The pictures are still there, even behind her closed eyes. *Standing next to Bidari in the firelight. The eyes of the people on her body. The clapping. The shouting.*

Outside the shelter, the women's voices grow louder with excitement. The hide is drawn back and a face appears in the grey of the night. A figure crawls into the shelter. She stops rocking but sickness is pulsing through her body in waves and when she tries to move, there is a painful throbbing in her forehead. She dare not open her eyes but waits, helpless, for what is to come.

She can smell Bidari and feel the heat of his body as he squats down in front of her. He is not a big man; when they stood together in the circle, he was only a little taller than her. His warm breath is playing on the top of her head. When he takes her hand, his feels damp, unfamiliar.

'Ansa.'

She keeps her head down, listening to the women outside, whispering and laughing. She longs to be outside in the cool air with them.

'Lie down with me,' he says and pulls her onto the ground beside him. Another wave comes and she tries not to retch. She is lying on her back on the soft skin. It is painful to move her head.

She can feel the unknown hands on her body, stroking and probing all over, even between her legs, in her puti. She finds herself tapping his words on the ground, one finger at a time. *Lie-down-with-me; Lie-down-with-me; Lie-down-with-me.*

What he is doing does not hurt, not yet. She has not taken a breath since he began and she feels faint. Taking a gulp of air, she presses down hard to feel the earth under the soft covering. His breath is coming more quickly and she can feel his body, tense and hot, as he leans over her. There is no pain. Why did the women warn her it would hurt? He mutters something and climbs right on top of her. Now there is pain! Something hard is pushing into her soft, secret flesh. She shrinks away from him but she is pinned down. The weight and the heat of his body make it hard to breathe and now the sickness rises up from her belly into her throat. She retches.

For half a breath, he stops moving on top of her. Then, when she is still and quiet, he begins again, rocking up and down, pushing into her. His face is right above hers, his mouth open, showing the small gap between his top teeth. She turns her head so that his hot breath is on her neck. The weight of his chest bears down heavily onto her and there is a burning soreness between her legs and inside her body. Squashed under him, her guts are cramping. Boar fat and bitter bile come up into her mouth and she retches again. This time he is moving so urgently that he doesn't seem to notice. Another wave of sickness comes. She cannot hold it in much longer. At last, his frenzy comes to an end. With a groan, he pulls away from her and rolls over onto the ground. She just has time to get to her knees before spewing the contents of her belly onto the ground.

The relief is immediate but when she moves her head, there is a stabbing pain above her eyes. The secret place between her legs throbs painfully. She kneels by the mess of vomit, unable to move. She should get some ash to cover it but she is frightened and now, suddenly, so tired. The tears begin to flow silently down her cheeks and she flinches as Bidari's hand touches her arm. He seems angry.

'What's the matter? Do I disgust you?'

She begins to sob and now he is squatting in front of her, looking puzzled. He starts to wipe the tears from her face with his thumbs.

'Are you sick? Come and lie down,' he says. 'You can sleep now.'

He helps her onto her side on the soft skin and she draws up her knees, hugging herself with her arms. Still, the tears are coming and she cannot stop them, even though her crying seems to disturb him. He is kneeling beside her, stroking her hair, and there is a smell of kho as her tears soften the dried-on paint. The patterns on her face will be ruined.

'Did I hurt you?' he says, but she doesn't know how she should answer.

After a while, he leaves her and she can hear him moving about the shelter. Then he is gone. There are voices outside but it is like a dream. All she wants is to be alone, to rock herself on the soft skin till sleep comes.

When she wakes, it is still dark. Bidari is lying beside her, motionless. She rolls over onto her back and he stirs. Without a word, he gets to his feet and disappears, coming back with water.

She sits up and drinks it down in one long draught. 'Thank you,' she whispers. It is the first time she has spoken to him.

He seems relieved and goes away but soon he is back, holding something. Kneeling, he takes one of her hands and places the object in her palm. It is too dark in the shelter to see what it is. He crawls towards the entrance, motioning to her to follow. Her puti is wet, but the soreness is beginning to ease. When he pulls back the goat skin, there is Balqa, hanging bright and low in the sky.

'Now look,' Bidari whispers.

The plain is still and there is only the creaking of the cicadas. Two men are dozing by the night fire. Ansa opens her fingers and there is something soft in her hand, like the skin of a baby animal. It is a tiny bag, strung through near the top with a long, fine thong of the same skin.

'Open it,' he repeats.

She can tell by his voice that he is smiling. When she pulls the thong loose and feels inside, there is something small, the

11

size of a baby's tooth. It glimmers a soft white as she holds it up to catch the light. Is it a shell? She rolls it between her fingers but it is too smooth and round to be a shell. She holds it up again and, at last, she knows.

'A Balqa stone!' she breathes, still unbelieving. She has never even seen such a precious and powerful thing.

'Do you like it?' There is eagerness in his voice.

Ansa doesn't reply. She is peering at the shiny ball, transfixed. She has heard that sometimes people who fish in the Salt Water prise open a shell and find Balqa there, gleaming and milky, smooth and round. But she has never dreamed that she would hold him in her hand.

'Is it for me, to keep?' She dares not believe it yet.

'Yes.' He chuckles at her, but there is no unkindness in his laugh.

They crawl back into the shelter and lie down on the skin. Ansa turns on her side and draws up her knees. Bidari lies behind her, his hand resting on her belly, and soon his breathing slows into sleep. She clasps the bag tightly to her chest. In the morning, she will tie it to her belt but tonight she will sleep with Balqa in her hand. The well-worked hide that has been placed on the ground feels comforting beneath her aching body and the cramping in her guts is all but gone. Already, there is a tingling in her fingertips as she grasps the Balqa stone through its soft kidskin covering.

Chapter 2

Ansa

Ansa is lying back on the rocky slope, her head cushioned by a tuft of dry summer grass. She puts one end of the dull black pod in her mouth and nibbles at it, letting the sweetness slowly fill her mouth. Bo is close by, her arms clasped around her knees, looking out across the parched plain, towards the Salt Water.

'Ansa.'

'What?' Ansa's eyes are closed. The shadow thrown by the oak protects her head from Eshtu's fierce heat.

'What is it like?' Bo asks.

Ansa opens her eyes but she is too comfortable to move.

'What does it feel like? To have a child growing in your belly?'

The girl spins round and crawls over to place her palm on Ansa's stomach.

Ansa sits up. 'There's nothing to feel,' she says, moving Bo's hand away.

Before long, the girl is up and busying herself, turning the pods so that they dry more evenly in the midday heat. Ansa watches her. She is like the long-legged flies, never resting in one place for long.

It was Bo who befriended her when she first came to the mountain, who showed her the springs and the places where tortoises scrape a hole for their eggs. It is Bo who whispers in her ear when the others use a word she doesn't understand. With the grown women, Ansa still feels like a stranger, but never with this girl.

Bo takes one of the pods to chew and sits but she is soon up again, spitting out the floury seeds. At last she seems to settle. Ansa closes her eyes and listens to the buzzing of the cicadas. The wind plays on her legs: a hot wind from the desert, from her home. She begins to feel drowsy but Bo's voice drags her back from sleep.

'Ansa – are you glad you came to the cave?' Bo's voice is almost pleading.

Ansa sighs and sits upright; she will get no rest till she has answered. Is she glad? She thinks of that day when she saw the dark shape of the cave mouth for the very first time. The men went inside first, on their guard, but it was empty except for the bones of a hyena's kill. The Oak People lit fires all through the cave, to smoke out the biting flies. Even on that first day, when everything was so strange, she knew that the green mountain was welcoming her, offering her shelter. She looks out now at the wide plain with its rivers and, in the distance, the gleam of the Salt Water.

'I like it here.'

Bo has taken her hand and is batting it to and fro between her own palms. She speaks again, almost in a whisper. 'But what about Bidari – do you like sitting with him?'

All at once, Ansa understands what is troubling Bo. Before too long, the girl will begin to bleed and then she will have to leave the cave and go to live with strangers herself. Ansa remembers that first painful coupling with Bidari.

'Bidari is kind to me - not like my father and his wife. There is nothing to be afraid of.'

Bo laughs and a blush creeps over her face. 'Your father's wife?' she says, after a while. 'Isn't Garoa your mother?'

'No – my father joined with her when I was small.'

Bo twists right round to face Ansa, her brown eyes bright and alive. 'What happened to your mother? Did she die, like mine? Do you have any brothers or sisters?'

Ansa shifts her buttocks against the hard rock. She is suddenly tired of Bo's questions. Always more questions. 'I had a brother,' she says and gets to her feet, stretching her arms above her head and yawning. She scans the horizon for any sign of cloud. If the rains come too early, the pods will rot.

'You *had* a brother? What happened to him?' Bo asks.

Ansa looks back up the winding path, shielding her eyes. The others will be back soon, with more pods. She hears Bo behind her, feels the tug on her arm. The girl will not let go – she is like a hyena with her kill.

'Tell me, Ansa.'

Fighting to part the mist that has come down over her thoughts, Ansa tries to picture her home in the desert. She sees her mother, smiling down on the baby in her arms. The baby has finished feeding and crawls away across the sand. Ansa feels the old fear begin to stir and the picture fades. She is back on the mountain and Bo's face is close, her eyes like spear points.

'Did your mother die when your brother was born?'

More than anything, Ansa wants to be left alone, so she just nods her head but now the girl's arms are around her and

15

she shrinks back. She wants to push the girl away but Bo has started sobbing.

'Don't,' Ansa says. 'It was a long time ago.'

It makes no difference. Bo is crying for her own mother now and once she starts, there is no way to stop her.

Ansa climbs up, crawls through the opening, and the mountain swallows her. After the glare of Eshtu, she can see nothing at first, but she is not frightened. She is never frightened here in this place that no-one knows about, not even Bo. It is no more than a deep gash in the cliff, high above the path, but wide enough to crawl through and to sit alone, out of the heat or the rain: to sit and not be seen.

Ansa feels for the bag by her belt and takes out the Balqa stone. With her finger she gently rolls it round and round on the palm of her hand, her eyes fixed on the bright, empty sky.

She is back in the desert, squatting with the other children, the breath of Eshtu hot on her head. Her friend Fede is drawing in the sand with a stick. She is the only one to guess what it is, even though Fede has drawn the snake coiled up! She gets up and skips across the scorching sand.

'Ama!' She bursts into the tent. 'Ama!'

When Ama turns round, her face is angry. 'Shh,' she whispers sharply. 'Your brother has just gone to sleep.'

She looks at the way Ama is cradling the baby's head, so carefully, so gently. His eyes are closed and, for once, he is quiet.

She goes back out and sits down behind the tent, in her special place. She squeezes her hands together till they hurt. What would happen if she squeezed her brother's head as hard as that? Would his eyes pop out, like a lizard's?

There is a tiny sound, or perhaps a movement, and the

memory is gone as quickly as it came. The Balqa stone has fallen from her hand. Ansa feels around with her fingers. It is there, under her leg. Releasing her breath, she replaces it in the bag and crawls to the mouth of the shelter. Eshtu is low in the sky. She clambers down to the path and starts back for the cave. No-one will have missed her.

Bidari

Bidari walks on ahead with his elder brother, brushing the flies from his face. They keep to the path that winds between patches of bog, marked by reed grass taller than their heads. This part of the plain is riddled with swamp and they test the ground with their sticks. The others are following on behind, keeping to the tracks they have made.

A breeze bends the tips of the dry seed stems, breathing a tang of salt onto their faces, and Bidari feels the old excitement grow in him. He breaks off a stalk of reed grass and chews, the sweet liquorice flavour reminding him of trips to the shore when he was a boy. He used to roll the sweet gum into balls between his fingers.

'I remember the first time I saw the water,' he says.

'Yes.' Koldo laughs. 'You ran straight in, before anyone could stop you. I've never heard such squealing.'

'I thought it was just like the Crocodile River, but it chased me and sucked me in!'

Bidari laughs out loud at the memory. He is happy to be walking beside Koldo, just the two of them. He cannot wait to see Ansa's face when she sees the waves for the first time. He cannot wait to dive beneath the water and taste the salt in his mouth.

But Koldo has gone quiet and his face is clouded. 'I wish

our father was with us,' he says, at last.

Bidari looks up at his brother, taller than him by almost a head. 'Why? The Marsh People won't attack - they let us use their path.'

Koldo shakes his head but says nothing more. Bidari starts jabbing at the ground savagely with his stick. Why must he spoil this bright day with his dark thoughts?

'What are you doing?' Koldo's voice is sharp. 'If your stick breaks, you won't get another here, on the marshes.'

He stops at once. When Koldo is roused, his anger is like the bite of a snake. Bidari's happiness is beginning to drain away.

'What's wrong, then, if it's not the Marsh People?'

Koldo frowns. 'I'm thinking of when our father was alive – when we were boys. There was always meat then. Don't you remember?'

Bidari thinks back. He remembers playing on the mountain, close to their mother. Koldo is right. The men were always coming back with deer or antelope, swinging from a branch. Most times, now, they come back from the hunt empty-handed.

'But we don't often sleep hungry, do we?' Bidari rummages in the bag strung over his shoulder. He holds out some scraps of dried meat to his brother as evidence. Koldo snorts in disdain.

'Tortoise, lizard - that's child's food. When was the last time you had fat meat, as much as you could eat? It was at the Balqa feast.'

Bidari knows that what he says is true, but Eshtu is high in the sky and the smell of salt comes more powerfully than ever on the wind. He strides ahead, chewing his meat.

'Watch where you're walking!' Koldo calls.

Bidari turns to face him and laughs. He starts to walk backwards, to show he doesn't care. 'What's the matter with you, big brother? The antelope will come back to the mountain. And tonight we'll eat nefafa, as many as you like.' Bidari pokes his stick at Koldo's chest and, at last, sees a smile hovering around his brother's mouth.

Cupping his hands, Bidari whistles to Nuno and Goi, behind. The women and the children are following, leaving only the old ones back at the cave with the babies. He will take some nefafa home for his mother. Koru loves to chew the salty morsels of flesh.

He searches the sky but there is no sign yet of the rains. Turning back, he can just see the figure of Ansa on the path. Who is that woman with her? Could it be Bo? He catches up with Koldo in a few quick strides.

'Look at Bo,' he says. He begins to mimic how the women walk: taking small steps, swinging his hips and cupping his hands around imaginary breasts, till Koldo laughs.

'How big do you think her tits will be?' he goes on.

Koldo shakes his head, but he is still laughing. 'Keep your eyes to yourself – you have a wife.'

They walk in silence for a while.

'It'll be a few winters yet, but then a man will have to be found for Bo,' Koldo says. 'Ansa's Desert People don't have any boys the right age. Bakar wants me to go to the marshes – perhaps something can be arranged with them.'

'What happened to Bo's people?' Bidari asks.

Koldo slows his pace and cocks his head to one side. 'They died of that river sickness, so Bakar and Esti took her in. Don't you remember?'

19

Bidari is quiet for a few breaths. 'Ansa will miss Bo, when the time comes for her to go. They are always together.'

'But soon Ansa will have a child to care for,' Koldo reminds him.

Bidari grins, his joy returning at the thought of Ansa's swelling belly. 'Yes. Surely she will be happy once she has a child.'

Ansa

Everything is new to Ansa and different: the lush green bog, the taste of the reed grass Bo gave her, the smell of salt on the air. They pass a pool of brackish water and she stops to watch a wading bird: the spindly red legs beneath the plump white body, the black bill like a digging stick, darting down into the water.

Koldo's wife, Gashi, is behind them and she keeps calling to Ansa and Bo to wait. Ansa turns to see her weaving reeds around a stout stem and pushing it into the soft ground beside the path.

'Why is she doing that?'

'It's a waysign,' Bo replies. 'For when we go back – to show us where to dig.'

Now Ansa sees that Gashi is marking the youngest patches of reed grass, those that will have the most succulent roots.

'Koru wants us to take back some leaves too, for her cough,' Gashi says.

After a time, the reeds are left behind and the ground under their feet changes. Spikes of dry grass are forcing their way up through sand now, rather than red earth, and Bo points out a long, low hill of sand ahead. As they come closer, Ansa can taste salt on her lips. Her ears catch the sound of the water, like a huge hunting cat, breathing in and out. The birds here are different too, shrieking loudly and wheeling down close to the ground, their white wings spread wide.

At the foot of the dunes, Bidari is waiting for her. Grasping her hand, he pulls her, laughing, up the incline. Her feet sink down into the soft sand and by the time they reach the top, both of them are panting for breath. What she sees in front of her takes the last of the wind from her lungs. Ahead, and as far as she can see to each side, is water, an unbroken expanse of moving water, bluer than the summer sky. It rushes towards her across the sand, each wave an angry foaming white, which is then sucked back into the blue expanse. Ansa watches, transfixed, clinging tightly to Bidari's hand.

He gives a great whoop of delight and runs down the hill, dragging her with him. She is terrified, but finds herself keeping pace with him. Suddenly, there is the shock of cold water under her toes and a strange dragging sensation around her ankles. She is frightened to go on, but too terrified to let go of Bidari's hand. Laughing, he wades in and she goes with him, her legs slowed by the weight, her breath snatched by the cold, till the salty water is surging around their bellies. There are shrieks of delight from the others. She is pushed up as a wave thumps into her back and speeds past her, cresting into a bank of white foam and spray. Her feet can no longer find the sand and she begins to panic; the water is trying to pull her away from Bidari. Hearing the fear in her cry, he fights his way towards her and holds her steady till she can regain her footing. Ansa clings to him and hears herself laughing as another wave tries to knock them both over. His face is close to hers and he is laughing too, and then he is kissing her and his mouth is cold and tastes of salt.

The water swirling around her, Ansa opens her mouth to Bidari. He begins to kiss her again, more forcefully. He pulls her close and says something in her ear but the words are lost in the roar of the waves. Suddenly she remembers the Balqa stone and reaches for her belt, where it hangs in its skin bag. Battling with a new wave surging across her chest, her numb fingers search but find nothing. Letting out a wail of anguish, Ansa turns away from Bidari and begins to wade back towards the sand. Soon the waves are slapping harmlessly at the backs of her knees. Frantically, she feels for the bag with her wet, numbed fingers only to find it at last behind her back, still knotted to her belt.

Bidari is beside her, his wet hair dripping onto her shoulder. Hands twisted behind her, she struggles with the wet knot. Bidari tries to help but she pushes his hands away. At last, she manages to untie the thong and pull the sodden bag apart. She rolls the Balqa stone out onto her palm where it sits, gleaming softly, untroubled by the Salt Water. Tears gather in Ansa's eyes. She is shaking with relief and turns to show Bidari, but now his face is dark and closed. He says nothing, just turns and walks away from her towards the others.

Chapter 3

Bo

Bo wakes to the purring of the Salt Water and sand in her wet hair. After swimming in the waves they had all fallen asleep, and now the day is growing old. A low bank of cloud hangs on the horizon and they still have to find the place where the dark rocks lie littered on the sand like huge discarded flints. All along the shoreline, the Salt Water is drawing back, leaving a smooth wet expanse.

Bo's belly is complaining but there is nothing to eat. They set off in the direction Koldo is pointing and soon they see the first of the black humps, shining wet in the waning light. Her tiredness forgotten, Bo breaks into a run. The first rock is bare but there is another further on that looks hopeful. She shouts to the others.

This rock is like a dark breast, clustered with grey shell nipples. Bo drops to her knees and feels inside her bag for the scraper. She sets to work at once, knocking the nefafa from the rock, one by one, and tossing them into the bag. The snail creatures cling to the rock with surprising strength but the sharp lip of the tool breaks the suction between rock and soft flesh.

Bo stops to rest. Koldo's wife, Gashi, is coming across the

sand to join her. They work together steadily, moving from rock to rock, till their bags are full. By now, Eshtu is a huge red ball, disappearing into the Salt Water.

Bo looks around in the failing light. The others are still working. 'Shall we go back?'

Gashi nods and stands up to stretch. She is tall like Ansa, but heavier and stronger, from carrying children. They hoist the bags once more over their shoulders and set off back to the camp. An ache is spreading across Bo's back and the wet, sandy bag rubs a sore on her bare skin, but she tries to keep up.

'You are strong, for a girl your age,' Gashi says, and Bo feels the flush of pleasure rising up her neck. 'Any man will be glad to take you, when the time comes.'

In the failing light, it is hard to make out the place in the dunes they had chosen for their camp.

'Can you see any smoke?' Gashi asks.

Bo spots a thin grey wisp rising from behind the sandy ridge. She crosses the beach and, with the last of her strength, toils up the sandhill, her feet sinking deep at each step. She is dizzy, the nefafa heavy on her shoulder. Soon now, she will be able to eat.

But there is only one figure in the hollow. Ansa is lying curled up, asleep, against the far slope. A small fire is burning in a makeshift hearth on the sandy floor, but it is almost spent. Where is the wood, to feed the fire? Where are Gashi's boys?

Bo dumps her bag down – disappointment flooding through her body. There is no ashpit for cooking the shellfish. There is hardly even a cooking fire and Ansa is lying asleep. What has she been doing?

Running down the slope and dropping onto her knees, Bo

prods Ansa hard. 'Wake up! Gashi's coming!'

Ansa opens her eyes and sits up slowly, her mouth widening in a slow yawn.

'Where are the boys? Have you sent them to get more wood?'

The urgency in Bo's voice seems to haul Ansa back from the land of sleep. 'I made a fire,' she says.

Bo looks at the hopelessly small blaze. 'That's no good. We need a heap of ash. Get up!'

Before Ansa has time to move, they hear the sand sighing as it gives way around Gashi's feet. She is standing on the crest of the dune, a dark shape against the pale blue of the evening sky. She says nothing but half runs, half slides down the slope. Crossing to the meagre hearth, she lays down her bag, then turns to Ansa.

'Where are Tipi and Iban?' she asks, her voice like ice.

'I expect they've gone to get more wood,' Bo intervenes, breathless. She turns to Ansa: 'haven't they?'

Ansa hangs her head. 'They wanted to swim again.'

Gashi just stares as Ansa gets to her feet and stumbles over to the fire. Taking up a stick, she tries to coax the small flames into life.

'They are only children,' Gashi says, her voice low but full of contempt. 'You cannot let yourself be ruled by them.'

'I'll go and get some wood,' Bo blurts out, hardly able to bear Ansa's humiliation.

Just then, they hear squealing laughter and the boys appear, out of breath, at the top of the sandhill. They are dripping wet.

'Ama!' the younger one cries, stumbling down the hill to his mother. 'I beat Tipi! I got back first!'

Gashi smiles and brushes the hair back from her son's face. Then she turns to his brother. 'Tipi - you should have known better – there's no wood for the fire.'

Bo grabs the smaller boy's hand and begins to climb out of the hollow, calling to the other. 'Come on, let's see how much wood we can find before the others get back.'

Ansa

Her face burning with shame, Ansa stumbles around in the twilight, looking for wood. Here, by the Salt Water, there are only spindly trees with sharp thorns and soon her arms are covered with scratches. When she has gathered as much as she can carry she heads back to the camp, heavy with dread. Voices reach her on the wind; the men are back from the water's edge with more shellfish. They will see that there is no fire.

She drags herself on, only to find that Bidari is waiting for her on the ridge. He runs down to meet her, grains of sand spurting up into the air.

'Give me that,' he says. He takes the brushwood from her, cursing as the thorns prick his fingers.

His voice is harsh; Gashi must have told him that she neglected the fire. The thought comes that he might punish her as Garoa used to, but he only walks on ahead with the firewood. Just when it seems that he is not going to say anything, he turns back, his voice like a sulky child's.

'Hadn't you better check? You might have lost your precious Balqa stone in the bushes.'

Ansa's hand flies quickly to her waist, but the bag is where it should be. Her forefinger and thumb easily find the tiny sphere, through the kidskin covering. Relieved, she looks up and catches the hard grin on Bidari's face, a grin with no laughter in it. He strides ahead now and does not look back. Why did he ask about the Balqa stone?

Ansa stumbles blindly back towards the camp, weighed down by the events of the day. Bo and the boys have brought more wood and now the fire is blazing. The nefafa lie in heaps and, for once, they will all sleep with full bellies. But Ansa crouches on the ridge, trying to find the courage to face the stares and the whispers.

Someone is teasing Bidari about the branches he has just added to the haul. 'Look! Bidari has taken to women's work now.'

Bidari laughs with the others but then Gashi's voice comes out of the darkness, sharp as a blade. 'He will have to get used to collecting wood: his wife can't seem to do it.'

The hollow becomes quiet and Ansa shrinks back, away from the light of the flames.

Bidari sounds startled. 'What do you mean? Ansa gathered that wood herself.'

Ansa keeps out of sight, confused. Doesn't he know that she fell asleep? That it's her fault there was no fire?

The contempt is still there in Gashi's voice. 'We knew she wouldn't be able to collect nefafa. That's why we left her with the boys - to build the fire. But instead, she just slept.'

Gashi buries more nefafa in the bed of ash, then turns to the others. 'Anyway, it's done now – come and eat.'

Ansa kneels in the darkness beyond the firelight, watching the others rake shells from the ashpit, then sit on the sand to eat. Hot tears are rolling down her face. How can she join them in the hollow now? Behind her lies the lonely expanse with its dark, hidden dangers. She searches the sky but there is no comfort there; Balqa is nowhere to be seen.

She watches as Bidari leaves the fire's light and warmth to climb up out of the hollow. He doesn't see her at first but then he is dropping down onto his heels beside her. He lifts her chin roughly and peers closely into her face. Even in the dark, Ansa can feel the turmoil behind his eyes. She saw a look like that on her father's face once, when they came upon an injured goat in the wadi. He was standing, spear in hand, his teeth clenched for the kill, staring into the eyes of the animal.

Ansa tries to turn her head, away from his gaze. But then he is touching her wet cheek more gently, the same Bidari who ran shrieking and laughing into the water with her. Was it only today? She begins to sob and he sinks down into the sand beside her, sighing heavily. He embraces her, making soothing noises as if she were a child. When her crying has come to an end, Bidari helps her up and together they climb down to join the others.

It is very dark. Among the sleeping forms Ansa stirs, half woken perhaps by the rousing of the wind. The cloud is dropping away to reveal a sky crowded with blinking, jostling stars, but the face of Balqa is still absent. Troubled, she turns over, the sand giving way beneath her, then sleep comes padding silently and takes her once more. This time, she is carried away and set down on a beach, near the water's edge.

It is morning and each wave sparkles as it surges towards her over the sand. She hears a voice, calling. Bo is waist high in the Salt Water. She is laughing and jumping with each wave.

'Ansa! Come and play with me!'

The salty breeze plays with her hair, teasing and tempting her. She wants so much to run into the water, to feel the cold slapping at her legs, but there is something she should be doing. What is it? She walks along the beach, searching, searching, but there are no trees for firewood. She looks down and, with a pang of dread, sees that her hands are empty.

The sand beneath her feet has changed. The Salt Water is gone and now she is back home in the desert. There is the akazia tree. Out of the corner of her eye, she catches sight of the bad rock, lying flat on the desert floor and she turns away so as not to see the mean black slit where it meets the ground.

The bitter smell of smoke comes wafting through the heat and now the old familiar voices. Home! There is Ama, sitting on the ridge. She runs to curl up in the nest between Ama's legs, but what is that wailing? There are tears on Ama's cheeks. In her lap lies the baby - still and quiet. He is the wrong colour. Ama is looking at her but she doesn't seem to see.

'Ama! Ama!'

She doesn't answer – just keeps on staring through her. Now Ama has the face of Gashi and her eyes are angry and cold. When she speaks, she is looking past Ansa, at someone else.

'Look after Zeru for me,' she says to Bo, 'Ansa cannot be trusted.'

Ansa wakes with a small cry. She is trembling. *Zeru.* That was her brother's name. How could she have forgotten? Rolling over onto her back, she opens her eyes and stares at the stars, busy about their night-time work. They are calling to one another but their voices are swallowed up in the vastness of the sky.

Her brother was named Zeru, after the sky. Now she can remember Ama singing his name when she fed him, and how Ama cried after he had gone, and how she did not want Ansa

29

near her after that.

A heavy dew has fallen and Ansa's whole body is chilled. She lies still, remembering, and though Bidari's body is warm beside her, it is a long time before the trembling stops.

Chapter 4

Ansa

Ansa arches her head back against the birthing rock, to relieve the aching low down in her spine. After the icy winds of winter, spring has come at last to the mountain and with it have come her pains. Before they left, the women tucked a skin around her but the nights are still cold and she is shivering. The wind slows now, breathing a silent calm over the plain below. She searches the sky but there is no sign of Balqa. This is the fourth night since he slipped into the land of death. It is the time of waiting. Waiting for Balqa to return, bringing flowers that shoot up amid the long grass. Bringing food for their bellies. Bringing new life.

The pain comes tearing again, like the teeth of a cat busy with her kill. Ansa's huge belly grows tight and hard under her hand. She pushes her elbows against the rock, as the women showed her. When it passes, she leans back, breathing heavily. Thirsty, she climbs to her feet, and stumbles towards the spring. It is slippery underfoot. She loses her footing and grabs at a tuft of grass, sprouting from between the rocks. Ansa drinks greedily and straightens up, the night air drying the sweat from her forehead. She makes her way back to the birthing rock.

At the next tearing she shakes with the effort of keeping silent. The pains are growing more fierce. The first one surprised her at dusk, as she was climbing back up to the cave in the wind. The women saw at once that the baby was coming. They brought her here to the rock and showed her what she must do. They were kind but she can't forget the anxious look in Gashi's eyes, nor her words. *If you cry out, the baby will be born twisted.*

She knows there is worse to fear than that. Once, when she was a child in the desert, one of the women screamed and screamed till the men covered their ears and went off far away, past the wadi. Then everything went quiet and, later, she saw them digging a hole in the sand.

Ansa's whole body is a gaping fear. The next pain is stalking her, waiting for the moment to attack, and there is nowhere for her to run. She scrabbles around on the damp ground till her fingers find the small skin bag. Shaking, she unties it and drops the Balqa stone into her cupped palm. As her belly hardens with the next pain, it seems to her that the power of Balqa pulses from the stone into her hand and up through her body. The mist of fear begins to lift, revealing a calm certainty that lay beneath it all along. Just as the winter is coming to an end, so Balqa will be born again in the sky. There will be food again on the mountain. A child will leave her body in the morning – a living child. Her belly softens and Ansa's lips form a smile in the dark. The next tightening comes – more powerful than ever – but she is no longer frightened. When it has passed, Ansa replaces the tiny sphere in its bag and ties the bag tightly.

The night wears on and the pains are stronger than she could have thought possible. Her lip is bleeding where she has bitten it to stop from crying out, but still the calm of Balqa hangs over her. The women are close by, in the cave, waiting. They will come as soon as they hear the baby crying. Meanwhile, she is alone on the welcoming mountain, alone with a task which belongs only to her.

Ansa can scarcely feel her feet and hands but her belly is on fire, moving with a rhythm all of its own: first hardening into a monstrous rock of pain, then slackening and leaving her exhausted. How can there be so much pain? Even the thought of that grave in the sand is not enough, now, to stop her screaming out.

She can no longer smell smoke from the cave and tears begin to form, running down her cheeks. What if they have forgotten? What if they don't hear the baby crying? What if the baby will not come out? With the next pain comes a wave of sickness, as if she has eaten sour fruit, and a great weight inside her body, pressing down and down.

Bo

Charged with the task of listening, Bo is curled up near the cave mouth, dozing, when she hears it. She gets up at once and, skirting the dying embers of fire in the hearth, crosses to where Gashi lies sleeping. She touches her arm and Gashi is instantly awake.

'What did you hear? Was it Ansa or the baby?'

'It was the baby – I know it was. Listen!'

The shrill rattling cry starts up again, like the call of the birds who fly over the Salt Water. Gashi springs to life. 'You go to her. I'll wake Koru and the others.'

Bo runs along the path to the spring in the growing light. The air is cool, the grass wet from yesterday's rain. Ansa

33

is propped motionless against the birthing rock, her head slumped forward, and Bo is terribly frightened until she sees Ansa look up with a smile of greeting.

Bo drops to her knees and embraces her friend, her tears making brown tracks through the white ash dust on her cheek. 'What was it like? Was it terrible?'

Ansa pulls back the ibex skin. The slippery new creature lies quietly now on the mound of her belly, its dark skin smeared with something white, eyes tight shut, limbs weaving slowly. Bo looks up into Ansa's face - suddenly different, the face of a stranger, a grown woman. Envy twists inside her.

She longs to pick the baby up and cradle it in her arms but perhaps she should wait for Koru and the others. Bringing her face close, she watches, entranced, as the baby's mouth opens and closes, like a fish. There is a bloody smudge on its forehead and Bo licks her finger and tries to wipe it away. Suddenly, a thought comes to her.

'Is it a boy or a girl?' She moves the blue belly rope out of the way so that she can see. 'It's a girl!' She looks up into Ansa's face. Does she mind?

'A girl,' Ansa repeats, and Bo can tell she is not disappointed. In fact, it seems a shadow is lifting from Ansa's face.

Bo's gaze is drawn back to the baby. She puts her finger inside one of the hands, astonished at how strongly the tiny fingers grasp her own.

They hear voices and Bo gets to her feet, uncertain what she should do. She has never been with the women after a birth before. Ikomar and Sorne appear, with Esti close behind.

'It's a girl!' she calls to them.

Old Koru comes into sight, leaning heavily on Gashi's arm. The others fall silent and stand back to make way for them.

The cloud has cleared during the night, leaving a vast, clear sky that speaks of the coming of spring. The only sounds are running water and the call of the birds high overhead. All around, the slopes of the mountain roll down into the plain, a green sky beneath their feet. A new rush of flowers, white and yellow and red stars, has been coaxed from the ground by the last rains. Bo feels the everyday quietness of the morning shift, sliding into a magic silence.

Koru is weak from the chest sickness that comes to her every winter and Gashi has to help her down to the ground. When she is settled on her haunches, the old woman pulls back the ibex skin. Without a word, she lifts the baby off Ansa's belly, the tiny arms and legs startling out into space. A shrill wailing sets up as Koru places her carefully on the ground. Ignoring the cries, Koru slowly feels the baby all over with practised hands, then traces the belly rope its whole length to the dark afterbirth which lies between Ansa's legs. She lifts the liver-like mass and carefully feels all around the edges.

The baby's cries become more frantic, yet no-one is picking her up. Bo watches as the old woman turns her attention to Ansa. Her wrinkled fingers probe Ansa's belly, pressing with apparent force. Taking no notice of the new mother's groan, Koru continues her examination. She grasps Ansa's teats and pulls on them, again and again. Now someone passes her a blade and Bo gasps as the rope is cut, but the baby does not seem to feel any pain; her crying becomes less shrill and urgent. Koru presses some nama leaves against the bleeding stem, then she wraps the baby tightly in a cured kid skin and lays her back on the ground. The warmth of the skin seems to soothe her and she becomes quiet at last. Koru sits

35

stiffly back on her heels, resting, but still no one moves. At last, Koru brushes her palms together, one after the other, to signal that everything is completed. The magic is fading but Bo holds back, watching to see what the others will do. One by one, the women touch Koru's forehead in respect and then it is over and they crowd round, eager to get a first look at the new child.

Bidari

Nuno is lower down the slope, calling up to Bidari to hurry, but it is hopeless. They will never get back down to the cave in time. Balqa is in the land of death and even the stars will be lost in this thick cloud. When darkness falls, they will not be able to see their own feet. Bidari is exhausted. He has been fighting the wind on the mountain top all day and now does he have to fight his younger brother too?

It seems so long since he woke this morning to the sound of cursing. The rain had blown into the cave, putting the fires out. Worse still, Bakar's precious stash of firestone had got wet and it was ruined. There was nothing to be done but go to the quarry for more.

At first, when the day was new, it felt good to be climbing the mountain with Nuno, like starting on a hunt. But a cool wind had been whipping rain into their faces all day, the sudden gusts forcing them to cling to whatever they could find. It was well after midday before they reached the place. Chiselling deep into the wet face of the rock, he had found it first – a dull yellow layer. They had hacked the firestone out together, the uneven lumps glinting darkly in their hands. Bidari had stowed them quickly away from the light, so they would not lose their power.

'Dari!' Nuno's voice from below is fainter now. 'Come on!'

Bidari curses. Nuno is a fool if he thinks they can get back to the cave in the waning light. He surveys the slopes, unfamiliar shapes under their lush green winter cover. Perhaps if they can find the path that leads to the pear trees, they could sleep in that place where the rock overhangs the path. He pictures the space. It's safe, but will there be room for them both?

He calls to his brother and waits till Nuno appears, bent double from climbing back up. 'I know a place where we can sleep.' Bidari says. 'It's not far.'

Nuno is impatient. 'What's the matter with you? We can get back before dark.'

Bidari begins to waver. If they don't get back with the firestone, how will the others start the night fire? As he peers out into the gathering darkness, he hears a low growling, coming from below them on the mountain. Both men freeze, listening intently. The sound does not come again. Without a word, Bidari starts back up in the direction of the shelter and Nuno follows him.

Bidari wakes in the early light. Nuno is curled beside him in the small space under the overhang, snoring. Shuffling on his buttocks towards the opening, Bidari's fingers touch something hard and cold: a hand axe – more than one. They are sharp enough but roughly struck. He picks one up but it feels too small for his palm. The tools puzzle him. How did they get here?

He climbs down to the path from the ledge and starts to piss. Before he has finished, the crack of a falling stone comes from behind. He spins round. Something is moving, higher up the slope. The mountain cat they heard last night? He calls out to Nuno, then searches around for something to defend himself with. He waits and watches, but there is no further movement on the mountainside. Instead, Nuno's eyes are peering at him from the gap, his hair sticking out in every direction. Bidari bursts out laughing and now Nuno is shinning down and jumping on top of him and they are fighting like they used to when they were boys.

For the first time in days, Eshtu is climbing joyfully in a clear blue sky. In the light the walk down to the cave is easy and Nuno goes on ahead, singing. Bidari's belly is empty and he thinks of what food is left in the cave. Acorn meal. He screws up his nose; however long the acorns are soaked, they still taste bitter. He makes a detour to the nearest spring and drinks, then searches carefully in the vegetation nearby. Squatting down, he loosens the roots of some charlock from the moist red soil, cleans them under the flow of cold water and bites into their fresh sharpness with relish. Ansa comes into his thoughts. Is she getting enough to eat? She has carried the child all through the wet, cold winter, when food was scarce. He must catch her something. The lizards will be out basking again soon, when the days grow warmer.

After the rain and the wind, he is grateful for the touch of Eshtu's fingers on his back, but something else is different too. The birds are singing as if they have a glad secret. Bidari looks up into the sky and lifts his arms in welcome. There, almost too weak to make out against the blue of the morning sky, is the sharpest blade of white. The familiar thrill courses through his body. Balqa has returned to them and, this time, he brings the summer with him.

Bidari breaks into a run and now he can see Nuno, below, at

the place where the tracks cross. Ikomar, his wife, has come
to meet them and she's holding something in her hands. They
look up and Nuno begins to wave and shout. The bundle
Ikomar carries is wrapped in leaves, dark with blood. There
has been a kill!

He bounds down the path and now Nuno is embracing
him, his face full of excitement. Ikomar pulls back the leaves
to show him. There has been no kill. It is an afterbirth - the
cord still attached. No wonder Ikomar is cradling the meat
so carefully. She will cook it to eat and then, perhaps, she
will grow a child at last.

'It's a girl. Come and see!' Ikomar cries, tugging at his arm.

All at once, Bidari understands. While he was up on the
mountain, Ansa has given birth! Dropping his bag on the
ground, Bidari takes the short cut, scrambling down the slope,
zig-zagging between the outcrops of rock. Old Esti is sitting
at the cave entrance with blind Bakar, minding the smaller
children.

'Bidari! You've got a daughter!'

She struggles to her feet, eager to be the one to show him,
but her husband holds her back. He peers, unseeing, in
Bidari's direction and calls out in his cracked voice: 'Where
is it? Did you get it?'

Bidari looks at the blind man blankly, then remembers the
firestone.'Yes, Uncle. It's safe – Nuno has it.' He turns to Esti.
'Where is Ansa? Has my mother finished with her?'

'Yes, yes, they're inside!'

Bidari bends his head and passes into the cool of the cave.
A buzz of talk reaches him from over by the wall. The others
move back, leaving only his mother, kneeling beside Ansa.
Koru is holding the baby in the crook of her arm, and she

beckons to him.

As his eyes become accustomed to the dim light, he can see the change in Ansa's belly. He squats down in front of her, grasping both her hands. Her skin feels warm and dry. Relieved, he peers into her face. She smiles at him shyly and then leans back against the rock. The birth has exhausted her.

Leaving her to rest, Bidari turns to his mother. Her eyes are wet with tears and she pulls his head to her wrinkled breast and kisses it, like she used to when he was a boy. Then she gently pushes him away, wiping her eyes with the flat of her hand.

'You must name the baby.'

Bidari kneels down on the ground and Koru places the baby in his arms, showing him how to hold the child's head. The bundle feels surprisingly heavy. Bidari pulls back the goat skin and peers at the child. A girl, they said. The baby's movements seem strong as she wriggles in his arms and her little legs and arms are fat. But it is her eyes that hold him. She is looking straight into his face, but she doesn't seem to see him.

He looks up anxiously to his mother. 'Is she blind?'

'No, no. Her eyes are weak now, but they will become strong.'

Koru smiles at his ignorance and he notices new lines in her weathered face, drawn there by the pain of her winter illness. *One day I will lose her.* With the thought comes a crushing in Bidari's chest. Although he has Ansa, it is not the same. She never opens her heart to him.

He pushes the dark thoughts away. This baby has been born at a good time - after the winter cold and before the heat of summer brings the fevers. More than likely, she will survive and grow strong. And she has come from his own body. He remembers, too, what he saw in the sky and his face opens into a smile. This child has been born on the day of Balqa's return. Bidari carefully places the baby back in Ansa's arms. Lifting his arm and wiping his fingers across his armpit, he smears the baby's forehead with his own sweat.

'Hua. A new day. Her name will be Hua,' he announces.

Ansa

Now that she has eaten, more than anything Ansa longs to lie down and sleep, but the women say she must try to put the child to the breast. Gashi brings the baby and squats beside her.

'Lift your knees up.' She obeys. 'Higher than that – that's right, or her mouth will not reach.'

Ansa holds the head close to her breast but the baby is tired too and her eyes keep closing.

'Try stroking her cheek.' Gashi shows her what to do. It works. The tiny mouth opens. 'Now – quickly – put her to the teat.'

The baby's wet mouth slides one way then another, till suddenly the tiny lips close around her nipple and set up a rhythmic sucking. The pulling is much stronger than she had expected. Ansa looks up in triumph to find that Gashi is smiling.

All at once, the cat begins tearing at her belly again and blood seeps out from her puti onto the bedding leaves.

'That's right,' says Gashi, pleased. 'It's good for you to bleed now.'

She slides her little finger beside Ansa's breast and gently

41

into the sucking mouth, to break its firm grip on the nipple, then helps Ansa put the baby to the other breast. The pain dies down and the regular pull of the baby's sucking is comforting: like a heartbeat - gentle but steady.

It is night and she is tired and hungry. She is sitting on Ama's lap and Ama is trying to force some food into her mouth. She doesn't like the taste and spits it out, even though she can tell that Ama is getting angry. The smoke from the fire blows into her face and she begins to cough. Ama wipes her mouth, roughly, then puts more of the horrible food onto her tongue.

'Eat, Ansa. You must eat.'

She begins to cry, spluttering food everywhere. Ama pats her back and she burrows her face into Ama's neck and sobs. Slowly, she slides her mouth down to Ama's nipple.

'No, Ansa!' Ama pulls her away. 'You must learn to eat meat. The baby will need my milk.'

She looks down at Ama's rounded belly and the tears start up again.

Ansa opens her eyes to find Gashi beside her. The sucking has stopped. Gashi takes the baby from her and helps her to lie down.

'Sleep now,' she whispers.

Chapter 5

Ansa

Ansa stirs in her sleep and opens her eyes. Eshtu has woken too and is reaching in through the mouth of the cave with his fingers of light. She feels a hand on her breast and stiffens; Bidari likes to couple with her when they are both warm from sleep. But, to her relief, the bedding leaves are cold and it is Hua who is clambering across her stomach and reaching for her nipple. Ansa grasps the small firm body and lifts it so that Hua's face is level with her own. She rubs her nose against Hua's but the little girl only squirms to be free. Ansa sits up, wrapping the deerskin more tightly around them both as Hua stuffs the nipple in her mouth. She drinks for a while, swallowing noisily, then begins to play with Ansa's coarse hair till there are strands caught around her finger. Irritated, Ansa stares into the darkness, trying to free her hair from Hua's grasp. The little girl gurgles with laughter, but then grabs at her mother's hair again.

Hua begins sucking from the other breast and Ansa leans back, feeling her muscles relax. The sleeping space she shares with Bidari is away from the mouth of the cave, up a rough slope. It is always the same here – cool and dark and quiet. And the walls here do not drip, even in winter. Alone and hidden, Ansa is happy.

She listens to the familiar sounds of the cave. The gash of light at the cave mouth reveals the figure of Esti, crouching over the cooking hearth. She calls for help with the fire and the small shape of a child appears. He picks up a bark tray, full of ash, and then disappears again into the darkness. From outside comes the dull repeated striking of stone on bone.

Suddenly, she lets out a screech of pain. Hua's grinding teeth are pushing through her gums and she is chewing Ansa's nipple. Ansa pulls the child away and taps her, hard, on her arm. Hua begins to wail, struggles from her mother's grasp and waddles away.

Ansa sits for a while, then crawls away from the wall. Hua is nowhere to be seen but there is a pile of soft turds, where she has emptied her bowels. Ansa is angry; the child is old enough to go to the dunghill. Scooping up the mess with bedding leaves, she makes her way towards the light. Hua is sitting on Bo's lap, by the cave mouth. Her cheeks are still wet but now she is laughing.

Peering out into the morning, Ansa sees old Bakar bent low over the tool he is shaping, but there is no sign of the younger men. She slips out and down the slope to empty the mess onto the dunghill. She squats to piss, then runs along the path that winds around the bluff, to the watching place. Her eyes run over the steep slopes below, dotted red, white and yellow with flowers. The men are visible, a trail of ants, already down on the plain. They must have sighted prey because they are making for the oak thicket. She counts the figures: a whole hand of fingers, so Koldo's boy, Tipi, must have gone with them, to make his first hunt. Ansa drops down to a squat and gazes out for a while, across the plain, towards the great

Salt Water.

Ansa's fingers are busy picking grass peas, but her thoughts are full of the hunt. It is many days since they made a big kill. She pictures how it will be if the men succeed. *Dusk. The sound of singing. Everyone running out to watch them climb up, the branch across their shoulders bent by the weight of the carcass. Children watch as the men skin and butcher the kill. Later, the big cooking fire hissing with fat from the meat. Gorging until they are full. Leaning back, bellies full, listening to the story of how Tipi became a man.*

It is past midday and Ansa's gathering bag bulges out from her waist. Shading her eyes, she scans the higher slopes. Ikomar is working at a patch higher up, and there is someone higher still, who might be Bo. Ansa bends again, searching among the straggly foliage, but she has picked all the ripe pods. She spots another clump just above her.

She cannot reach up there with Hua tied to her back – the slope is too steep. She unties the sling, lays the sleeping child in the shade of a bush, then climbs up. Picking the curved, black pods is much easier now. She spots more higher up the slope and looks back, but Hua is still sleeping. Clambering up, she follows the trailing stems to find the pods. Some of them are over-ripe and break open in her hand, scattering mottled white grass peas over the ground. At last, her bag is full.

As Ansa straightens up she feels a tingling in her full breasts. She must wake Hua and suckle her before starting back to the cave. The afternoon wind is blowing across the plain, from the great Water. She starts to climb down, but now fear catches her by the throat. There is the bush, the grass beside it flattened by the weight of the little body, but no sign of Hua. How can she be gone? Ansa spins round, looking in every direction. Nothing. The sky presses down on her – a vast empty weight. She scrambles down to the bush, calling out Hua's name again and again. Nothing but the flapping of birds' wings as, disturbed by her shouting, they swoop down from the thicket of terebinth and then up into the sky.

She scans the mountain slopes desperately, making the danger call. The shrill warbling sound carries a long way, but it's growing late and the other women have gone back. She tries to steady her thoughts. Hua can't have climbed up the slope - she would have seen her. Which way then? She shudders, thinking of the Crocodile River, flowing full and fast. In terror she calls again, but there is no answering cry, no movement in the grass. She rips off her gathering bag, spilling the pods on the grass, and runs toward the terebinths.

A movement in the branches draws her eye upward and she slows to a halt. A vulture, his head the colour of egg yolk and crested with white hair like an old man, his face turned to one side, his cruel beak curving downward, is watching her intently. Ansa cries out but the bird does not move, just continues to fix her with his unblinking stare. Something about the bird's cold scrutiny is familiar. *Ama.* Could it be that her mother has come back, after all these years, to punish her? Just then, slowly and gracefully, the vulture opens his white wings and glides from his branch, down to the grass. He alights beside a gap amid the glossy leaves and seems to stare straight at Ansa. She gasps as her ears pick up a familiar sound, soft at first but then louder, unmistakable: Hua's gurgling laugh.

Ansa runs to the thicket and there, hidden from sight under

the spreading leaves, is Hua. She is sitting on the grass, her back straight and her chubby legs stretched out in front of her. She is holding a blue-white tortoise egg in each hand and two more broken ones are lying on the ground beside her. When she sees Ansa, she chuckles again and holds out one of the eggs.

'Ama!'

Shaking, with tears running down her face, Ansa wraps Hua up in her arms, crushing the tortoise egg. She stumbles out onto the open plain just as the vulture gains soaring height –the black fingers of his wingtips reaching down from the afternoon sky.

Bidari

In the oak thicket, hidden from the glare of daylight, Bidari and the other men squat around the circle. In this magic place, the growth underfoot is sparse and now Bidari's younger brother, Nuno, is pulling out the young green shoots which have pushed through the earth since the last hunt, till the perfect circle of red earth gapes - an open mouth, ready to speak. He has collected a pile of small sticks and stones and the men watch in silence as he passes his hands over the bare earth three times, then takes up a stick and uses it to trace the outline of the mountain slopes with their intersecting paths. Twigs and white stones mark the special places. Bidari watches Nuno in wonder, the dappled light playing on his hands as they confidently create the hunt picture.

Goi is rocking from side to side on his heels, impatient to be moving. Next to Goi squats the slight form of Tipi, silent and nervous. Bidari remembers his own first hunt, the fear and the pride woven together like the strands of a rope. His father was still with them then. In those days, the deer and the antelope would freely offer themselves but it is different now. Often the men stand in the watching place from dawn until Eshtu is high in the sky and see nothing moving on the plain.

But this morning, in the early light, they had seen him, a lone, fully grown male antelope, grazing the lush grass where the mountain's feet stand on the plain. Winding their way down the slopes in the fierce heat, the men's excitement had been something you could taste in the air. But now Bidari's nephew, Tipi, is staring with fear, as Nuno's deft hands give shape to the hunt. Although the boy has been playing at hunting ever since he learned to walk, this tight, magic silence is new to him. He keeps darting glances at his father, but Koldo's eyes are fixed on the red earth. The silence must not be broken.

Nuno begins to sound a long single note, low down in his throat. The hunters close their eyes and try to search in the darkness for the sandy brown face of the antelope, the soft snout, the deep liquid eyes. Bidari can feel the strain building in his aching thighs. The thicket is alive with the ticking of insects and the sound of Nuno's voice. Again and again, Bidari tries to search out the antelope's spirit but, for him, there is only darkness.

At last, the humming ceases and Bidari opens his eyes. Nuno is bending forward over the red earth. Inside the circle, a shape is beginning to form from the tip of his stick: front legs, a belly, back legs bent at the knee, a smooth rump, a long neck and small head, ears pointing up. Goi laughs with relief. Nuno has seen the antelope in the dark land. The hunt will be successful.

Bidari leans in closer to watch and takes a sharp breath in. Nuno is not drawing the long, ringed horns of the big male antelope they saw this morning, but short horns, barely reaching past the beast's ears. He has drawn a female. Koldo turns to him with a questioning look.

'It was a doe who showed herself to me,' Nuno replies.

The hunters exchange glances. The buck they saw must be travelling with a mate. Reaching for their spears, the men get to their feet and come out, blinking, into the bright daylight. They walk in single file to the edge of the plain. Goi drops down to a squat. The grass is disturbed where they saw the antelope in the early light. Bending low, his eyes to the ground, he beckons to the others.

The small spear tip-shaped marks are clearly visible in the soft earth and Goi points to the tracks of the male, then those of a female crossing them. The urge to give chase passes between the men like lightning. Goi runs toward the lower slopes, dropping down again and again to scan the ground. The animals will have found a shady place to rest, now that Eshtu is high in the sky. Without a backward glance, Koldo and Nuno follow.

'Keep behind me,' Bidari instructs Tipi. 'Go like a snake. Don't let the mountain feel your feet on her.'

As they climb, the ground becomes rocky and the story it is telling them becomes muddled. At last, the tracks disappear altogether and the men squat down to catch their breath. Koldo licks his finger and holds it up. The afternoon wind is beginning to blow and they must decide what to do.

Nuno speaks first. 'They can't be far away and they will need to drink. We should go to the quarry spring and wait.'

But Goi wants to keep searching for their tracks. 'What if

they don't come to the spring? The daylight will be wasted.'

Koldo holds his finger up again and then sides with Nuno. 'The wind will hide our scent,' he says. 'Let's take our chance at the spring.'

They follow the path that leads to the quarry, Tipi jogging along beside Bidari. 'Why didn't you speak, Uncle?' he asks.

Bidari just grins, but the boy's question is like a troublesome insect, buzzing around him all the way to the spring. Why *is* it that Koldo and Nuno never ask for his thoughts?

Bidari yawns, sleepy after the climb and now the waiting. A long drink from the spring has stilled the rat-gnawing hunger in his belly. Goi and Tipi are slumped against the rocky outcrop behind the cover of thornbush, dozing. His two brothers, Koldo and Nuno, are huddled close together, keeping watch for the antelope.

Closing his eyes, a picture of Koru comes. She is sitting with the other women at the cave mouth, bent over the hide she is working on. Bidari feels calm. His mother has been coughing all through the winter, but now she seems stronger.

There is a pricking pain on his shoulder. He slaps at the biting fly but now there are more, fussing around his face and his matted hair. He brushes them away. The movement reminds him of the waving game he plays with Hua and he smiles. She is learning to talk now. He likes to see her playing with the other children, or with Bo. Bidari's forehead creases into a frown. Why does Ansa never play with the child? The only time he sees her in her mother's lap is when she is suckling.

Bidari shifts his position, taking care to stay screened by the thornbush. Ansa makes him uneasy. Why does he never hear her laughing with the women? Why does she keep herself apart? She was happier for a while, after Hua was born. She even began to tease him when they were on their own, away from the others. *Ansa, her long neck arching back, laughing at him.* He wants to mate with her just as much as ever. It's like a bite he needs to scratch, even though her body never seems to welcome him. He thinks of the dream he keeps having. *Ansa is with him in the forest, under a pine tree. They mate on a bed of needles and he pulls out from her. He is sweating. He rolls over onto his back and his body brushes against her. He shudders with the shock. Her skin is as cold as ice, her legs frozen and stiff.* It is always the same and he wakes up frightened, but excited.

A soft, urgent hiss from Nuno and Bidari opens his eyes, suddenly alert. He crawls silently over to rouse Goi and Tipi, his finger to his lips, then joins his brothers. From their position on a ledge above the spring, screened by the thorny vegetation, they can hear water spurting from the belly of the mountain just below. Now Bidari begins to hear the sound that alerted Nuno – a clipping and scraping of hoof on rock. Koldo listens, his head cocked to one side. He holds up two fingers to the others, crouching behind him. There are two beasts coming to drink. The hunters spread out along both wings of the ledge, the scuffling sounds of their movement masked by the voice of the water. Each armed with his spear, they wait for Koldo's signal. Bidari's heart is beating fast. He glances at Tipi. His skinny face is slick with sweat and his knuckles are white, clenching the wooden stave of his spear.

The male comes into view first, nimbly picking his way among the rocks to reach the cool water. Then the female follows, more slight than the male, stick-thin white legs splayed among the stones. The buck lowers his head and drinks gratefully from the pool, then tosses his horns and ears in the running water. The men remain still and silent, hardly daring to breathe. Magic ripples down Bidari's neck. An eagle calls, circling overhead, and the female lifts her slender neck and looks up, her snout twitching.

Still the men wait, spear arms raised, for Koldo's signal. It will come when she lowers her head to drink. Bidari feels a nudge next to him and gestures to Tipi. *Wait.* Suddenly, everything is wrong. There is a loud crack as the head of Tipi's spear hits the rocky ground, short of the target. The antelope jump and spring away from the pool at once, back along the rough path. Goi is on his feet. He takes aim and hurls his spear at the retreating haunches of the female, but he is too late. The animal disappears from view down the slope.

They are walking to the cave, in single file along the narrow path. The antelope will not come back to the spring today. Eshtu is dropping down towards his home and the wind breathes cool, salty air on their backs. Tipi walks just ahead of Bidari, his head down. Back by the running water, Koldo had turned on Tipi, his voice like thunder.

'Why didn't you wait for the signal?'

Bidari had tried to say it was not the boy's fault but his brother had spun round, his face hard. 'The boy may be young but he has to learn.'

A chasm of anger had opened up in Bidari's chest. 'Then why don't you teach him – you're his father!'

Koldo had cursed. Then, he seemed to soften and let the boy alone. But Bidari knows, as they all do, that the loss of the doe is a sore disappointment. The people need meat.

The path fades as the hillside descends more steeply, becoming clothed with dense stands of buckthorn, yellow-green flowers clustering now amidst the glossy leaves. The men snake their way down between the shrubs, their practised feet finding the easier places. The gnawing hunger starts again in Bidari's belly. He wonders if the women have found earthnuts - anything that will sit heavy in his gut and satisfy him. They walk in silence. If there had been meat to carry home, they would be singing now.

Bo

It is getting late but the fingers of Eshtu still play warm on the nape of Bo's neck as she twists her head under the spring to drink. Thirsty after the climb with her bag full of pods, she takes long, satisfying gulps. The water that misses her mouth splutters in tiny cataracts over her shoulder and down the new valley that has opened up between her breasts. She moves her head from side to side under the cold flow, until her hair is a heavy wet rope, hanging down her back.

She hears a sound and pulls her head away, wiping the water from her eyes. Bidari is on the path. That means the hunters are back! But he is alone and the droop of his shoulders answers her question before she has even asked it.

'Did you make meat?'

He shakes his head. There is nothing more to be said. Still Bidari stands, looking at her. Water is trickling down her face, over her chin and onto her breast. Bo goes to wipe it away but finds that she doesn't want to touch herself in front of him.

At last, Bidari speaks. 'Where's Hua? I thought she'd be with you.'

'No – Ansa took her. To pick grass peas.' Bidari turns away and now she can begin to squeeze the water from her hair. 'Isn't she back yet?'

He shakes his head and Bo begins to feel uneasy. It is getting late. Where is Ansa? She and the other women have been back a long time. The blank disappointment of the hunt has left Bidari's face, and now it is coming alive with fear. They go to the watching place, the sky a soft green-blue, with wisps of flame. There is just enough light to scan the slopes below. Bo's young eyes are sharper than Bidari's.

'There! Look!' She grabs Bidari's arm, pointing.

A figure vanishes behind a stand of buckthorn but then reappears – it is Ansa climbing up on the easier path, a dark silhouette against the reddening sky. They go to meet her. Hua is slung to her front and as soon as she hears Bo's voice, the little girl cries to be put down. She toddles unsteadily towards Bo's outstretched arms, her face breaking into a huge smile. Bo clasps the soft, warm weight of the child to her chest.

'Have you missed me?' Hua's face is sticky and streaked with yellow. 'Did Ama find you an egg?'

'Where have you been?' asks Bidari.

Ansa doesn't answer, just stares down at the ground. All at once, Bo realizes what is missing. 'Where are the peas?'

Silence. When Ansa looks up, her face seems pale and her eyes are red. 'I didn't find any,' she mumbles.

'Yes you did!' Bo replies. 'I saw you picking them.'

Ansa's cheeks flush red and she turns away from them both, towards the cave. She breaks into a run but Bidari follows. He catches up with her and they walk together, his arm around her waist. Bo stands watching, bouncing Hua on her hip.

Chapter 6

Ansa

Ansa crawls under the overhang of the sleeping place, away from the sharp tongues, the probing eyes, but she finds no respite from the old terror. It crouches over her, darkening her thoughts. Behind her closed eyes she sees the bush, the flattened grass, the empty plain. It reminds her of something from long ago, in her desert home. Clenching her fists, Ansa tries to remember but it is like grasping a river fish with her hands. The terror is on her chest now, a malicious weight, bearing down. She strains to take in breath.

Suddenly, she remembers the Balqa stone and her fingers struggle with the bag at her belt. Rolling the cool, smooth orb between her fingertips, her breath begins to come more easily. Balqa might grow thin and die but he always comes back to her. Even on that day when she found Ama lying stiff and cold on the sand, the women clustered around, wailing. She thought, then, that nothing would ever be the same but when darkness fell, Balqa appeared in the sky as usual, smiling down on her.

The shadow of fear passes, leaving her bone tired. Soon, sleep will come for her, she thinks, but instead it is Bidari who comes, carrying Hua. She makes a small sound as he lays her down on the bedding but she doesn't wake. Bidari makes no move to lie down. He sits, his back against the wall, staring into the darkness.

'Ansa.'

His voice jabs at her, keeping her awake. If she doesn't answer, maybe he will think she is asleep. Then comes a fearful thought – he knows she left Hua under the bush. But how could he know? Hua could not tell him, she is too young.

'It was my fault,' Bidari says.

Ansa lies rigid, not understanding.

'I thought he was going to throw his spear too early, so I signed to him.'

She lets her breath go. The hunt. He is talking about the hunt. She turns toward him. 'What happened?'

Bidari settles himself down between her and Hua. Glad not to hear the child's breathing any more, she will listen to him talk and lose herself in the hunt. He will talk about what really happened, not just the story they tell around the fire. A secret smile plays around her mouth. Bidari tells her things that even Gashi doesn't know.

'We were going to take her at the spring, by the quarry,' Bidari begins, 'and we would have – we were downwind - but Tipi moved. I told him to keep quiet. The next thing I knew, he was taking aim. He thought I was giving him the signal.'

Ansa closes her eyes, trying to picture the spring, the hunters crouching, their spears poised.

'It was Tipi's first hunt.' Bidari sounds bitter. 'His father should have taught him what to do! But he was too busy whispering with Nuno.'

'Wait,' Ansa breaks in. 'You said *her*. Wasn't the antelope a male?'

'Yes – the one we saw feeding on the plain was a buck. But in the circle, Nuno drew a female.'

Ansa's breath catches in her throat, her scalp prickling as she thinks of the men, making hunt magic. She is not supposed to know what they do under the oaks, but she begged Bidari once and he told her.

'That's another thing.' Bidari's body is tight with anger. 'Nuno was wrong - the antelope got away. Why do we listen to him?'

Ansa lies silent in the smoky darkness, waiting for Bidari's anger to pass and his body to relax.

'We can try again – they won't leave the mountain yet,' he says, at last.

His hand begins to stroke her belly, his fingers reaching under her belt. He rolls her over and she closes her eyes and lets him do what he wants, but her thoughts stay with the hunters and with the antelope, hooves clattering against the stone as they make their escape.

She is running, her heart drumming, the cool wind on her head. The grass is lush under her feet but it hides the stones from her and she falls, twisting her foot. She gets up and runs on, hardly noticing the pain. A thicket of trees lies ahead, nestling at the toes of the mountain. The harder she runs, the further away the trees seem to grow. She flies on and on, without stopping. A vulture is circling above her, covering great distances with each sweep. She feels the danger like a spear thrust. There is no time to lose – she must find Hua.

The thicket of terebinth is closer now, the leaves fresh after the winter rains and dense enough to hide anything that shelters among them. The vulture is still circling overhead. She runs on till at last she hears what she has been waiting for – the sound of Hua's laugh. Hua's smell is coming from inside the thicket. Ansa crashes through the leaves, blundering from the heat of the plain into cool shadow. Before her eyes have become accustomed to the dark, she feels a searing pain in her leg and hears something thudding to the ground beside her. She looks down and sees the dark blood on her stick thin leg. Her leg is the colour of sand, covered with smooth hair. A noise and then another terrible pain – but in her flank. This time the spear does not fall to the ground, but works deep into her flesh. Another flame of pain flies toward her, then another. She thrashes around, uncertain, smelling her calf and hearing his cries. The air carries no terrifying scent of human and yet there they stand in the glade. One of them is holding her calf close to his chest.

Ansa wakes to feel Bidari's breath on her cheek. His arms are round her but still she twists and turns, trying to reach the calf. There are tears flowing down her cheeks.

'Shh,' Bidari is saying, 'it's just a dream.'

Slowly, she comes back to the cave and Bidari, back to herself. She lies down again on the bedding leaves but her thoughts will not stay still. After a while, she reaches out for Bidari's arm.

'What?'

'The antelope that got away – the female – was she in calf?'

'Why? No – I don't think so,' he answers. 'Go back to sleep.'

Bidari turns over, but then remembers something. 'But we found their dungsite on the way back and Goi says there must be a pregnant female running with them. Why?'

'I don't know.'

Bidari's breath is soon coming slowly and evenly in her ear, but Ansa lies awake the whole night, her thoughts like the river in winter.

It is morning and the women are busy with the grass peas they brought back yesterday. There is a space next to Bo but Ansa moves on to sit beside Goi's wife, Sorne, instead. Sorne is quiet and she never asks questions. Ansa picks up a thornbrush to rake hot ash over the pods. Gashi and Ikomar are at the higher hearth, splitting the first batch. She can hear popping as the parched grass peas jump into the basket.

Ansa looks down, trying not to let the others sense the churning in the pit of her stomach. She hears something outside and cranes her neck to see, but it is only Goi coming back with more brushwood. Bidari is outside, hunched over the tool hearth, blowing onto the tinder.

Disappointment at the failed hunt hangs in the air like stale smoke and there is not the usual chatter. Sweat trickles down Ansa's face, dripping with a tiny hiss onto the hot ashes. *Where is he?* She longs to go to the path and look out for him, but the women will ask why. At last, there comes the sound of someone running. Tipi appears at the cave mouth, a slight dark shape against the brilliant sky. He is panting from the climb, his face alive with excitement.

'It's there!' he shouts. 'Only a baby – it can't move!'

He bends double, trying to get his breath back. Ansa can feel the skin on the back of her neck prickling. The others stare at Tipi blankly.

'What do you mean?' his mother asks. 'Where have you been?'

The words tumble out. 'Down on the plain – under the

59

terebinth.'

The women look at one another – puzzled. Is it a game? Tipi glances at Ansa but she looks away.

'What have you found?' Gashi asks.

'A calf – an antelope! It's new-born – hiding under the branches on its own. I don't think it can move.'

Hearing Tipi's raised voice, Goi appears at the mouth of the cave, the spear he had been mending still in his hand. Bidari is close behind.

'Did you kill it?' asks Goi.

Tipi shakes his head. He looks uncertainly towards Ansa.

'Why not, you fool? A calf would be better than nothing.'

Tipi is stung by the reproach in Goi's voice. 'Yes, but it would be stupid to only take the calf!' he shouts back.

Bidari cuffs him across the head. 'Have respect for your cousin! And what did you mean – about the calf?'

Tipi's face comes alight. 'We could use the calf to lure his mother, and then we'd have her too!'

Goi chuckles. The boy is beginning to think like a hunter but he is ignorant. 'The mother will be close by – she'll smell us before we get anywhere near,' he explains more gently.

Tipi's face falls. Then he looks up again. 'But tonight, when the light fades, she'll go and graze again. She'll have to leave him alone then.' Tipi spins round to the hearth, where the women are sitting. 'That's what Ansa said,' he blurts out.

Ansa can feel the heads turning towards her. She stares at the grass peas on her lap, the seeds a row of raised lumps inside each curved pod. Her fingers search for the little bag at her belt, the Balqa stone inside the kidskin.

'Ansa?' It is Goi's voice, high with surprise. 'What has Ansa got to do with this?'

'She told me,' comes Tipi's reply. 'About the calf. She said to go and look for it there.'

Ansa hears the click of disapproval coming from Gashi's throat and she longs to be away from the cave, safe in her rockshelter.

Bidari has been listening and now he walks across to her, excited. 'When did you find the calf, Ansa?'

Then Bo's voice: 'Why didn't you tell us you'd seen it?'

She looks up at last, knowing that she must say something. 'I didn't see it. It wasn't there, then ...' She stumbles over her words, knowing how stupid they sound.

'Well then, how did you know it would be there?' Gashi asks.

The confusion is like a mist. What can she say? How can she answer them? 'I saw it in a dream,' she says at last. They can't blame her for that.

No one speaks. She rubs the kidskin bag between her fingers, again and again. Still no-one says anything.

'We should take the calf,' Goi says to Bidari at last, turning as if to go. 'Before it finds its feet.'

'No!'

Ansa no longer cares about staring eyes. She is back in the dream, feeling the fear, the pain, the confusion of the antelope. The mother has given herself and her calf to the people for food. Why else would she have visited Ansa in her sleep? They must not refuse her gift. Ansa scrambles to her feet, scattering pods on the floor. She pleads with Bidari.

'The mother will go to graze again when the day ends – go and wait in the thicket with the calf! She will come back to him,' she says, holding him with her eyes, willing him to listen. She can feel how unsettled the others are by her words.

61

'But she will pick up our scent – she won't come back to the thicket.' Bidari sounds puzzled, even frightened.

'Not if you cover your smell!' she insists. 'Use the calf's own piss. Rub it on yourselves. Then she won't know you're there!'

Bo

In the far distance, where the land meets the Salt Water, the sky is aflame with colour. Bo stands, with Hua in her arms, staring out across the plain. She watches the red disc slip silently down behind the water.

'Shh … shh…' she repeats softly, rocking the little girl. Hua cut her foot – not deeply – but her head is nestled into Bo's neck, every now and then a sob rippling through her little body. Bo is lost in thought. Where did Ansa go, after her strange outburst? At last, Hua lifts her head and begins to look around.

'Let's go and see who's coming,' Bo says.

They walk at the little girl's pace. Bo is relieved to see that she is able to put weight on her injured foot. By the time they reach the vantage point, Eshtu has disappeared completely. Soon, all daylight will be gone. Bo picks Hua up again and scans the lower path.

'Look!' She points down the slope. 'I think they're coming!'

'Co-ming!' Hua copies her, 'co-ming!'

Bo laughs and kisses the top of her head. She squints, trying to make out the path in the twilight. The men are climbing in single file, the last rays falling on their spears. And between them, a bulky shape, swinging from side to side. Even in the poor light, there is no mistaking what that means.

Bo runs back to the cave as quickly as she can, Hua bumping

against her hip. She calls out as soon as she is within earshot. 'They're coming back! They've made meat!'

The children hear and come running. Sorne appears in the mouth of the cave, then Nuno's wife, Ikomar. 'Are you sure?' she asks.

'Yes – I saw it!'

'Quickly!' Ikomar beckons to the older children. 'We'll need more firewood.' They run off, eager to get a first glimpse of the returning hunters.

Bo peers around, but there is no sign of Ansa. Seeing Gashi's broad shoulders by the hearth, she goes to help. 'What can I do?' she asks.

'Clear the last of these peas out of the ash, then we can start the fire.' It is not Gashi's way to show it but the excitement is there, in her eyes. They have not eaten fat meat for a long time. 'We'll need a deep pit – and the big stones.'

'It might only be the calf,' Bo says, 'I couldn't tell in the dark.'

The fire is beginning to give out a fierce heat by the time they hear Iban's voice, shouting. 'Ama! They're coming!'

The half-face of Balqa is visible above the mountain top as Bo runs out of the cave. She can hear singing, growing steadily louder as the men draw closer. The successful hunter will walk ahead and come in first. Unmistakable among the other voices, Bo hears Hua's cry and feels tugging at her knees. She picks the child up and peers around in the flickering firelight, but still there is no sign of Ansa.

At last, a figure appears at the bend in the path, emerging into the light. It is Tipi, breathing hard, his face shining with pride. He is carrying a branch, or perhaps it is his spear, and the body of an antelope calf hangs from it, the small head with its soft ears lolling backwards. The women let out a high trill of welcome. The other men come into view and the light falls on two faces –Bidari and Goi. They are carrying their spears upright, a stout branch lashed between them to form a crosswise pole. A cry goes up. Hanging from the branch, her front and back legs tied, is a fully grown female antelope, her haunches sleek and fat.

The women and the children crowd around. Bidari unties the legs of the female, letting the children stroke her smooth flanks. He and Goi will skin her because it was their spears that took her life. Koldo goes to help Tipi with his kill. He takes a blade and shaves one end of Tipi's spear to a sharp point.

Bo runs over to them, excited. 'Did it turn out as Ansa said?'

Koldo pauses, looking up at her blankly.

'Ansa found the calf – it was her idea,' Bo reminds him. She turns to Tipi. 'Didn't you tell him?'

The boy looks away and starts to untie the calf.

'Leave it on the pole – it'll be easier to pull the skin off,' Koldo says. He turns to Bo. 'What has Ansa to do with it? Tipi found the calf,' he explains, 'among the terebinth trees, down on the plain.' There is pride in his voice. 'And now look what Balqa has sent. The mother as well!'

Koldo thrusts the sharp point of the stake into the ground and gives Tipi a hammer stone to knock it in with. With each blow, the body of the calf bounces against the stake.

'But it was Ansa …' Bo insists.

Koldo is testing the pole and he takes no notice. He gives Tipi the sharp blade and turns the calf's body so that the underside of its belly is exposed.

'Wait for the hunt song,' Koldo calls to Bo as he traces a line downwards from the calf's neck with his finger, showing

Tipi where to cut. Then he turns and Bo can see the white of his teeth in the firelight, as he smiles. 'You'll hear all about it then.'

Bo takes Hua over to see the mother antelope. Her body lies on the ground and the children are counting how many times the spears pierced her hide. She leaves Hua there and wanders back into the cave, her eyes smarting from the smoke. The women are squatting around the large cooking hearth. Sorne is laying more stones around the edge of the flaming fire, squealing as sparks fly up into her face.

Bo catches sight of someone, sitting in the shadows by the far wall. Her legs almost buckle beneath her, with relief. She runs over to Ansa. 'Where have you been? They've taken the calf and the mother!'

The light falls on Ansa's face; she seems anxious.

'What's wrong?' Bo's voice is loud with surprise. Sometimes, understanding Ansa is like trying to make out tracks that cross in every direction.

'Shh …' Ansa hisses.

Bo squats down beside her. 'What's the matter? They made meat just like you said! Koldo doesn't know. He thinks …'

'Don't tell him!' Ansa whispers urgently. 'There's nothing to tell, anyway.'

'But you found the calf, Ansa, and you told Tipi what to do! How did you know?'

'Shh…' Ansa says again, 'Gashi will hear you.'

'But Gashi knows!' Bo springs up and strides towards Gashi. 'You heard what Tipi said! He said it was Ansa's idea to use the calf to lure the mother.'

The women stop what they are doing and the cracking and spitting of the fire is suddenly loud in the silence. They stare

65

at her and Bo feels the blood rising up her neck.

'You were there,' she pleads, turning to Sorne, 'and Ikomar. You must remember.'

There are tears at the back of Bo's eyes. She hears a sound behind her and turns to see Ansa creeping quietly towards the mouth of the cave, keeping beside the wall, in the shadows.

Gashi breaks the silence at last. 'It was Tipi who found the calf,' she says firmly. 'And it is men who know the ways of hunting.' There are murmurs of assent from the others. 'Come and help us move the stones!'

Bo disobeys and runs to the mouth of the cave but Ansa is nowhere to be seen. Bo feels a hand on her back and turns to find Koru beside her.

'Leave her. There's nothing you can do,' Koru says gently.

Bo can no longer hold back the tears. 'They heard Ansa – they know it was her idea!'

Koru lets out a long sigh. 'They know,' she agrees quietly. 'Now, go and help them.'

Bo wipes her face and goes back to the hearth. Gashi moves along, making a space for Bo next to herself.

Chapter 7

Ansa

The summer has come and gone. The men have been high up the mountain, tracking deer and quarrying stone, sometimes away for many days at a time. Ansa is glad to lie alone at night, with only Hua asleep by her side. Hua has grown taller and stronger and she is full of questions. There have been other changes too. Bo works as one of the women now. Like the pears beside the path, her breasts have swelled and ripened but she is still waiting for her first blood.

The days are growing cool again and the first rains have fallen. It is morning and the wind is shooting wet spears into the cave mouth but Ansa sits by the entrance. She doesn't mind the rain. At least here the whispers don't reach her and she doesn't see the bent heads, the shoulders turned away from her. They have given her the knobbly roots of reeds to work on and she is struggling to tug out the fibres. Hua toddles across, wanting milk.

As soon as she has drunk her fill, the little girl wanders away again. Ansa peers over her shoulder into the dark interior of the cave, to see Hua climbing back onto the lap of her second mother, Bo. Bo is sitting by Gashi again, where she has sat all summer, like the older woman's shadow.

Ansa feels a warm caress on her arm and looks up to see that the wind has blown the clouds across the sky, clearing a path for Eshtu. She stares out at the scudding clouds, wishing that the wind would turn in his tracks, scoop her up from the cave and carry her away. She is startled by the sound of a cough and turns to see Koru picking her way slowly across the uneven floor, towards the entrance. Soon she is at Ansa's side.

'The rain has stopped,' she says.

Ansa nods, feeling the tightness in her chest that comes now, whenever the others speak to her. Mostly, they leave her alone.

'Ikomar tells me the thornfruit are ripe,' Koru goes on, undeterred by Ansa's silence. 'I would like to taste something sweet, before the winter comes.'

There is a wistfulness in the cracked voice and Ansa risks an upward glance. Bidari's mother is staring out into the brightness.

She turns to Ansa.'Will you come and pick them for me?'

Ansa's whole body feels stretched tight, like the skin of a drum. She gets to her feet and goes over to the wall, where the gathering bags are kept.

'We won't need those,' Koru says. 'Just pick enough for the two of us.'

It seems to Ansa as if this must be a dream. She glances back, towards the other women. Did they hear? Perhaps they did, because Gashi is staring at her. It is always Gashi or Ikomar who tend to Koru's needs, though Ansa is the old woman's daughter by marriage, just like the others. Now Koru's words keep tripping through her thoughts: *pick enough for the two of us. The two of us.*

The hawthorns grow lower down, on the exposed edge of a patch of carob woodland. It is past midday and, after the rain, Ansa is grateful for the comfort of Eshtu's touch. Away from the path, the ground is sodden. They walk under cover of the carobs, raindrops falling onto their shoulders.

Under the hawthorns, Koru sinks down to the grass, a rasping sound accompanying each breath. Leaving her to rest, Ansa finds a branch dotted with ripe fruit, the colour of dried blood. She bends the branch and picks the small fruits carefully, between the thorns. She takes a handful to Koru and turns back to pick more.

'Sit down,' Koru says, when she comes back the third time. 'Eat some with me.'

Reluctantly, Ansa obeys. Ikomar was right; the fruit is just ripe, fragrant and sweet but not yet mealy. She spits out the clump of seeds and takes another.

Koru sits in silence, taking fruit after fruit and sucking the flesh with great pleasure. The intent look on Koru's lined face takes Ansa back to the morning after Hua's birth. Koru had looked the same when her fingers were probing Ansa's body. She remembers the taut, magic silence and begins to feel frightened. But then, satiated, Koru leans back against the trunk of the carob, just an old woman after all, tired from her walk.

They sit for a time, Koru's eyes closed, but there is no change in her breathing to suggest that she has fallen asleep. Ansa waits, listening to the kyok-kyok of the red-necked bird on the branch way above.

Koru opens her eyes at last and when she speaks, her words seem to cut through the air. 'Do you still have the Balqa stone?'

69

At first, Ansa is too shocked to move, then her fingers creep towards the small bag at her belt. It seems as if Koru is able to look inside her, to see everything.

'You haven't lost it?'

'No.'

Ansa gets to her feet, troubled. The Balqa stone is not something to talk about. She has almost forgotten that there was a time when it did not hang close to her body.

'Wait,' Koru says. 'Will you show it to me?'

A surge of anger pushes up into Ansa's throat. How dare she ask that? A picture flashes in front of her eyes: Koru snatching the bag with her clawed hand, Ansa tugging at it in panic. She watches herself lifting a heavy boulder and dropping it onto Koru's head, sees the thin old bone of the skull, a crushed mess amid the brains.

'Come and sit by me.' Koru's voice is gentle.

Ansa swallows down the rage. With an effort, she comes back to herself and to the harmless old woman. Sitting down, she unties the bag, emptying the contents onto Koru's waiting palm.

'I'd forgotten its beauty,' Koru says, fingering the Balqa stone reverently. 'See how it shines, even here under the trees?'

'Forgotten?' Ansa is confused. 'When have you seen it before?'

'It was mine,' Koru replies simply.

Mine? For one whole breath, no thoughts will come and then Ansa starts to be terribly afraid. Afraid that Koru will reclaim the Balqa stone. But Koru is smiling and replacing the magic stone in her palm, closing her fingers over it.

'I gave it to Bidari for a joining gift for you. I wanted you to have it.'

Ansa looks up, searching Koru's face for any sign of malice or cruel laughter. Since the day she sent Tipi to find the calf, the other women have tricked her many times; she is sure of it. But there is only kindness in the old woman's face.

'May it bring you comfort,' Koru says.

She is looking straight into Ansa's eyes and, at first, Ansa squirms under her gaze. Koru's fingers are still enclosing her own. Slowly she becomes aware of jagged, painful memories of the hot summer just gone scattered all around her, like discarded stone chippings. *A harsh word from Gashi. Bidari turning his head away from her questions. The chatter of the women dying away when she comes close. The love on Hua's face when she looks up at Bo.*

Koru seems to be in no hurry to move. Ansa is aware of warmth spreading from the Balqa stone to her hand, her wrist and along her arm. After a time, her breathing slows and the tightness in her chest begins to ease. Now, when she thinks of Gashi, of Bidari, of Hua, the pain is less. There is a space around her now, the debris cleared away.

Koru releases Ansa's fingers and leans back, resting her head against the tree. When she starts to speak again, her voice has taken on the lilt of story-telling.

'I am going to tell you about one of the old people from long ago. This is the story of Mina and Askone, the honey badger.'

Ansa's heart starts to beat faster. Story-telling is for the night, for sitting around the fire together, not for one person alone. But Koru is clearing her throat, as she always does before a story. Ansa closes her eyes to listen.

'One morning, Mina woke up, thinking of her mother and

71

her brothers. She decided to go and visit them. All morning she walked and, when Eshtu was high in the sky, Mina heard a shrill voice from high up in a tree.'

'"Tya, tya, tya," came the chattering of the honeybird. Looking up, Mina could just see the rounded belly, through the branches. The honeybird fanned out her tail feathers, showing the white spots underneath. "Tya, tya, tya," she said again. Mina listened carefully and, sure enough, she began to hear the faint humming of the bees.'

'How good it would be to take honey to my mother and my brothers, thought Mina.'

'She started to climb the tree. Half way up, she fell to the ground and the hand on her heart side was broken. Mina thought of the sweet honey and began to climb again. This time she almost reached the top before she fell, breaking the foot on the other side of her body. But still the honeybird called - "tya, tya, tya" – and still came the humming of the bees. She climbed once more and, this time, she reached the top. With her digging stick in her good hand, she poked inside the tree trunk. The bees buzzed around Mina's face, stinging her, but she hooked out a big piece of honeycomb, thanked the bees, and slithered down the tree.'

'Mina limped on her way, leaving a trail of blood on the path. Once, twice, three times, she thought she heard the sound of someone following. When she stopped to look, there was no-one.'

'It was winter and Mina began to grow cold. She was tired and her mother's people were still far off. The sound came again and Mina turned quickly. There, behind a rock, she spied a white head, a blunt black snout, a pair of small eyes. It was fierce Askone, who loves to gather honey. He began to

72

growl and to scrape at the ground with his sharp claws.'

'Mina looked around for brushwood to make a fire that would keep Askone away but then stopped dead in her tracks. She had only one good hand. To pick up the wood, she would have to lay down the honey.'

'Mina heard Askone growling, right behind her. His strong body was curling round her legs. He began to paw at her, his sharp claws tearing her skin, his jaws snapping at the honey. Mina cried out but she held tight to the honeycomb and lifted it up above her head.'

'Way up in the heavens, the Skymother sneezed and stars flew from her nostrils, shooting out into the darkness. Hearing Mina's cry and seeing the gift held up towards her, the Skymother at once began to journey through the sky, stopping only to throw over herself the coat of a she-leopard.'

'Mina caught sight of the leopard, loping towards her through the darkness. She screamed and dropped the honeycomb on the ground. As everyone knows, Askone is not frightened of anything, not even of leopard. He snatched up the honey at once and sauntered away behind a rock, to eat it.'

'Mina cried out again. She could not run but only hop along, waiting for the she-leopard to pounce. She could almost feel the hot breath on her back, the sharp teeth tearing her skin. But to her astonishment, what came was not pain but comfort. The Skymother had taken off her leopard coat and was wrapping Mina in it to keep her warm. She took Mina in her arms and rocked her, to and fro, till she fell asleep.'

Ansa opens her eyes. The story is over and Koru is getting to her feet. It is time to go back.

Bidari

While there is still light, the men sing as they walk and Bidari hardly notices the ache of the long hunt in his muscles. Two mountain goats hang from their poles, promising good meat at last. It was worth the heavy climb up the mountain and another day's trek along the heights, on empty bellies. This will be their last trip before winter sets in.

An uneasy quiet begins to settle over them, as the last colour leaches from the sky. Until Balqa appears there will be a time of deepening darkness, and they are far from home, and this mountain does not belong to them.

Bidari is relieved when Koldo signals to stop and make camp, just below the path, on a plate of rock which juts out from the mountainside. Scrubby bushes grow around the edge, promising them some shelter from the wind. They spread out to gather wood for a fire, leaving Goi and Tipi to guard the meat.

Among the pines on the ridge, firewood is easy to find. His arms full of dead branches and cones, Bidari is entranced to see Balqa appear, smiling on those alien flat lands on the far side of the mountain, just as he does on their own gentle slopes. The face hangs huge; it is only two nights since the women danced for Balqa's fullness. Not Ansa, of course, because her blood has come again, the first time since Hua's birth. Bidari shivers. It is bad luck to bleed at the time of fullness and when the men are on a hunt. Bidari turns back to the hollow and the reassuring sight of the goats, swinging in the wind.

Goi squats down low, hunched over a ball of tinder, while Tipi stands in front of him as a wind break. He strikes the firestones together, again and again, till a spark falls in the right place. Goi bends closer, blowing gently till the bunch of moss bursts into flame. He beds it carefully amongst the branches and soon the fire is burning strongly.

Koldo wants to butcher the goats straight away but Nuno says no. 'The blood will draw the hyenas. Wait for daylight.'

To stay their hunger, Koldo breaks open the skulls with a few skilful blows, and scoops out the brains.

'We should take the brains back, for curing skins,' Goi protests, but he eats all the same.

The hunters sit around the fire, warmth spreading through their tired bodies. They are silent. Not even Bidari feels like singing here, in this unknown place. Earlier they had found a spring and now Bidari sees that Nuno has placed a bowl of water on the ground, beside the goats. The face of Balqa shines white on the water's skin.

Goi begins to bank up the fire and Bidari settles down onto the ground, pulling his bed skin close around him. Koldo has climbed up onto the exposed path. Before long, he is back.

'It's quiet now,' he says, 'but we need to keep watch for hyenas.'

Bidari catches the look that passes between his brothers and fear stirs in the pit of his belly. Koldo is not saying what they all know: here on the heights, there are worse dangers than hyena. This is where Sakaitz have been seen.

Koldo is motionless, listening and thinking. At last he turns to Bidari. 'You watch first. When Balqa has climbed as far as the Scorpion star, wake Nuno. I will take over from Nuno, then Goi.'

'No! I'll watch first,' Nuno breaks in. 'Bidari will go straight to sleep. He always does. It's a wonder he kept awake long enough to put a child in Ansa's belly.'

The sound of the men's laughter is comforting in this alien place and even Koldo joins in. 'That's why I said he should keep first watch. Once he's gone to sleep, no-one can wake him.'

The others settle, leaving Bidari to rouse himself and move over to the fire. For protection, he chooses a stout branch from the pile and places one end in the fire to catch alight. Then he sits cross-legged, where he can see up to the path.

Far from being drowsy, Bidari is wide awake, his senses now sharpened by anger. How dare they laugh at him? Even Tipi. Bidari tightens his grip on the torch till the knuckles are white, letting his rage flow into the wood. Ever since the spring, when Ansa shamed him by showing her knowledge of hunting, Nuno has been merciless.

He thinks about Ansa and feels uneasy. How *did* she know about the calf? Sometimes she seems more like a man than a woman. She does not behave like a mother to Hua. And now, at the wrong time, when the men are hunting on the high mountain, she begins to bleed. And yet, thinking of her body makes him itch with lust. The more she shames him, the more he seems to want her.

A low growling alerts Bidari, but it is only Goi beginning to snore. The anger has drained away and his exhaustion is returning but he will not fall sleep, not after what they said. He gets to his feet to do a circle around the fire and it is then he hears the noise. He stands motionless, but there is only the cracking and spitting of the flames. The sound comes again and the back of his neck prickles with fear. Did it come from above or below? A mountain leopard, crouching above him, ready to pounce? He goes to wake the others but stops short. What if there is nothing and he looks foolish? He picks up the torch and goes to look, but there is no movement on the path. It is quiet – nothing but the ordinary night sounds. He holds his breath: silence.

By now, the water in Nuno's bowl will be full of the power of Balqa. To give himself courage, he drinks from it and as he does so the sound comes again, from above and along the path. He recognizes the chuckle of a hyena and breathes with relief. The sound is high-pitched, the call of a cub. When the answering cackle comes, it is fainter still and Bidari is not troubled. He adds more wood to the fire; they will not come close while the fire burns bright.

But then the whooping begins, not so distant now and louder. They are grouping. Bidari climbs up to the path again. In the light of his flaming torch, he can make out the hyenas' eyes, small glowing stones advancing towards him in the darkness. When the creatures see the fire, they become quiet, the points of light hanging motionless in the night. An impatient lowing starts up. Bidari runs at them, holding the burning stick high. The animals cravenly turn and run. When they are gone, Bidari climbs back down, only to find Nuno sitting bolt upright, listening.

'It was only hyena,' Bidari says. 'I've frightened them off.'

'Shh…' Nuno hisses. 'There's something there! Can't you feel it? It's not hyena. Nor leopard either.'

Fear comes creeping back onto Bidari's neck but he can hear nothing, feel nothing wrong.

Nuno is on his feet now. 'Give me the torch,' he whispers. Nuno's hand is stretched out, waiting, and Bidari senses his contempt. Bidari makes no attempt to pass the burning branch. Get your own weapon, he thinks.

Suddenly, everything becomes confused. Nuno is shouting

77

for Koldo, who wakes and stumbles up from the ground. There is a movement near the fire and a goat swings and bumps against the pole. It falls to the ground with a thud and then Bidari sees its hind legs disappearing into the shadows. Before he can understand what is happening, Nuno is running into the bushes after the goat, empty-handed.

Bidari looks around for Koldo but instead another figure emerges from the darkness. He is shorter than Nuno, shorter even than Bidari. Tipi? The figure turns into the bushes after Nuno, and Bidari catches sight of his large, squashed nose, the bulging muscle on his upper arm. He has something in his pale hand – a club or a short thrusting spear. Bidari aims his burning stick at the back of the squat man and hurls it with the strength of fear. The torch thuds to the ground in a shower of sparks but the man is gone.

Koldo appears, spear in hand, shouting. 'Where did they go? Which way?'

Bidari points to the bushes and, in an instant, Koldo is crashing into the foliage, with Goi close behind him. Stopping to pick up his torch, Bidari runs after them. The ground beneath him falls sharply and he finds himself sliding, reaching out in the darkness to grasp at branches, boulders, anything he can hold on to. From below, he hears the crashing of torn undergrowth, twigs cracking, the calling of outlandish voices.

Bidari manages to break his fall, landing on his buttocks on stony ground. His shoulder is grazed and there is a dull ache in his wrist but he is able to stand. He hears a familiar voice and calls out in the darkness.

'Down here!' Koldo shouts back.

He finds a path for his feet, slipping and sliding down the

slope. Nuno is lying sprawled under a bush, not moving. Koldo is kneeling beside him, examining his brother's scalp under the matted hair. He holds his hand close to Nuno's mouth.

'He's breathing!'

They spin round at the sound of breaking twigs, but it is only Goi, stumbling towards them.

'Where's Tipi?' Koldo asks.

He cups his hands around his mouth and calls – a high sound, dropping suddenly low. They wait, but there is no answer to the danger call. All they can hear is the muffled crack of dislodged stones, way below them. Koldo signals again and now the answer comes faintly, from above.

'That's Tipi,' Bidari says. 'That's his call.'

Koldo props Nuno up into a sitting position and he begins to moan quietly. There is blood shining dark on Koldo's fingers, where he touched his brother's head. The three men help Nuno to his feet and he stands, swaying, one arm round the neck of each of his brothers. They follow Goi, who has gone on ahead to search out the easier ground, but Nuno's legs keep buckling under him. At last, the figure of Tipi appears on the ledge above them, dark against the light of the flames.

They lay Nuno down by the fire, and cover him with a skin. The fire still burns strongly. Tipi must have been tending it, thinks Bidari, even in all the confusion. He is proud of his nephew, who is becoming a man.

The mountain is tranquil now, as if her peace had never been disturbed, only where there had been two goats for them to take back, now there is only one. Bidari examines the empty pole, the lengths of sinew that had bound the goat hanging loose. Something down on the ground catches his eye. It is a small handaxe but not one of theirs: roughly struck, its edge unevenly sharp. He has seen a tool like this before, but he cannot remember where.

Nuno drinks from the bowl of Balqa water and soon he is asleep. In the light of the flames, Koldo probes the wound with his fingers. The blood is drying. Bidari has been dreading the questions that must come and now, at last, Koldo turns to him, cursing under his breath.

'Did you go to sleep?'

'No!' Bidari stares at his brother defiantly.

'What happened then?' asks Goi.

Bidari shakes his head. 'They were too quick…' He shifts uneasily. 'I saw one of them - he was no taller than Tipi. He was pale-skinned.'

There is silence and then comes Goi's whisper. 'Sakaitz? Was it Sakaitz?'

Tipi gasps, his eyes on his father's face. 'But you said they only come out when the nights are dark.'

Koldo does not reply, but gets up to feed the fire. Horror and fear hang over them in the cold mountain air. It is hard to think.

'Lie down and try to sleep. I'll watch,' Koldo says at last.

'They won't come back,' Bidari murmurs to Tipi. 'Not now they've got meat.'

Bidari cannot sleep; every part of his body is tight and alert. He lies awake, watching Tipi's shoulders tremble beneath his bed skin. It is a long time before the boy becomes still.

Chapter 8

Bo

Bo spots the clump of mallow first. She calls to Gashi and begins scrambling down the hillside. The soil is dark after yesterday's rain, cold and wet between her toes. The mallow buds are tight green teardops, not yet ready to be shed. Soon, Gashi is beside her. Rubbing one of the leaves between her fingers, she peers underneath.

'This one is good. 'Can you feel? It's smooth. Some of them have hairs that itch your hands.'

Bo picks some of the circular leaves, bigger than her palm.

'We'll steep them in hot water for Koru,' says Gashi. 'Now help me with this.'

They probe the stony soil with their sticks, feeling for the base of the root.

'Will it will cure her cough?' Bo asks.

Gashi sits back on her heels, looking out across the plain. 'Maybe,' she says.

She begins digging again. When they have exposed the long white root, Gashi chops away the stems and stashes it in her bag. It is time to go back.

'Wait,' says Bo. 'Is there anything that will help Nuno?'

'We can spread some of the mallow on the wound, but it

seems to be healing well.' Gashi's voice is low and sad.

Bo looks up sharply. 'That's good, isn't it, if the wound is healing?'

'Yes,' answers Gashi, but her face says something different.

Bo is puzzled. Why is Gashi so miserable? Is she frightened? Esti says that Sakaitz never come down to the plain and she has lived a long time – she must be right.

Bo follows Gashi up the path. The sky is blue and clear after the heavy rain. Gashi turns back, brighter now, a mischievous smile on her face.

'If you want to make more medicine – dig up some whitespear for yourself.'

'Why? I'm not sick.'

'Whitespear brings on a woman's bleeding.'

Bo feels the warmth rising up her neck. She squirms, thinking of how the women gave her some of the goat's blood to drink. With the men watching too! She only pretended to drink and then poured it away. She doesn't want to become a woman. When that happens, she'll have to leave the cave and go to be with strangers.

When they get back, the others are out gathering food and they find Koru near the cave mouth, her head bent low over something. When she looks up, they see drops of sweat on her lined forehead.

'What are you doing, Ama?' Gashi demands. 'You should be resting.'

She tries to take the work from Koru, but the old woman objects. It is a tiny tortoiseshell bowl and Koru is painting a pattern on it with kho. She takes up her brush again.

'It's for Hua,' she whispers. 'It's almost finished.' Bo can hear the wheezing in her chest.

Gashi says nothing, then turns away to start stripping the fibres from the mallow root. She gives Bo a piece to chew; it tastes unexpectedly sweet.

'Koru never made anything for my daughter,' Gashi grumbles. 'What's so special about Hua?'

Bo doesn't know what to say and she goes outside. Esti is walking back along the path, leading Bakar. He cannot see the ground any longer and has to grasp the shoulder of his wife. Today they look old and, suddenly, Bo is full of gratitude for them. If they hadn't brought her here as a child, what would have happened? When Esti tells her to fetch some water, Bo goes willingly for once.

When Koru's drink is ready, Gashi strains out the pulp and takes an eggshell of the warm liquid to the old woman. She is resting against the wall, the patterned bowl lying finished beside her. Leaning forward to drink, a fit of coughing overcomes her. When the spasm is over at last and she has taken a sip, Bo sees blood on the rim of the shell.

Gashi tests the wall behind Koru's head with her palm and clicks her tongue in disapproval.

'It's wet here,' she says to Bo. 'We must move her.' She helps the old woman to her feet. 'You should sleep where it's dry – in Bidari's place,' she says, leading Koru across the floor of the main cavern.

There is an odd, rasping sound to Koru's breathing. 'The bowl – Hua's bowl,' she manages to say.

Bo takes the bowl and goes on ahead, climbing the slope to the place where Bidari and Ansa sleep. She piles up bedding leaves and tests the wall with her fingers. It is dry.

When Koru is settled, she swallows more of the medicine, nodding her head in approval.

'How is Nuno?' she asks.

'The wound is closing well,' Gashi replies. 'There's no poison in it.'

'Does he remember what happened?'

'No. Maybe when he has had more rest...'

Gashi's voice trails away and Bo stares at her. Why all the whispering? The cut on Nuno's head is healing. He has no fever.

Koru's eyes are closed, her head dropping onto her chest. Gashi and Bo start quietly down the slope, leaving her to sleep, but then comes a child's voice, calling. Hua is scrambling across the uneven floor in Bo's direction. Ansa is behind her, watching.

'Koru needs somewhere dry,' Gashi says quietly. 'We've given her mallow water. She'll sleep now.' She continues down the slope, shooing Hua in front of her. 'Hush now.'

But the little girl's cry seems to have woken Koru. 'Ansa! Is that you? Come here.' There is something of the old strength in her voice.

Gashi sighs, then stands back to make room for Ansa to climb the slope.

'Bring Hua with you,' Koru calls.

Gashi strides across the wide floor of the cave and out into the light. Bo follows her and sees tears on the older woman's cheek.

'What is it? Is it Koru?' Bo touches Gashi's arm and she begins to cry more openly.

'She's going to die,' whispers Gashi.

Bo is frightened; Gashi never cries. 'But Koru has a cough every winter,' she protests.

Gashi swallows back the tears but doesn't answer.

'The drink has helped her. We could get more leaves – I can go every day!'

'No.' There is a weary certainty in Gashi's voice. 'She's getting ready to die, or she would not have chosen someone to pass on her knowledge to.'

'What do you mean? Who has Koru chosen?'

'Don't you remember? When Koru wanted thornfruit – who did she take with her?'

Bo thinks back. 'Ansa.'

'Now she is too sick to talk but who does she want beside her?' Gashi's tone is growing bitter and she turns away, speaking more to herself than to Bo. 'Ansa. Why Ansa?'

Ansa

Ansa's heart is beating fast. Koru motions to her to sit down under the rock overhang and takes hold of her hand. The old woman's fingers are clammy. For some days, Ansa has been waiting, hoping that Koru will ask her to go again to the hawthorns. But to be here with Koru, alone, is even better. *Perhaps she will tell another story and cradle me, as if she were my own mother.* If only Koru would settle, but instead she keeps peering over Ansa's shoulder.

'Come, Hua,' the old woman calls. 'Come and sit in your mother's lap.'

Ansa turns in surprise to see the little girl, quiet for once, her thumb in her mouth. She had forgotten about Hua. What does Koru want with her? She moves closer, trying to block the old woman's view of the child.

Koru is reaching for something in the bedding beside her. She gives Ansa the tortoiseshell bowl and Ansa holds it up to the light, where the intricate design is revealed. It is beautiful and Ansa's eyes fill with tears. Now Koru takes it back and drops in a handful of tiny things that roll about, click-clacking against the sides of the bowl. Rummaging around in the bedding has made her cough again. When the spasm is over, she pulls Ansa close and whispers in her ear.

'It's for Hua.'

Hua? Koru beckons and the little girl goes to sit in her grandmother's lap but Koru directs her to Ansa. 'Go to your Ama – she's got a present for you.'

Hua hesitates but then curiosity overcomes her. She takes her thumb out of her mouth.

'What is it?' she asks, clambering over her mother's legs. She has seen the bowl in Ansa's hand.

'Close your eyes! Sit with Ama and you can have it,' Koru says, her drawn face alive with pleasure. Hua settles herself in the space between Ansa's legs. 'That's it! Now close your eyes!'

Hua screws up her face and covers it with her hands. She begins to giggle.

'Ready? Now open!'

Hua grabs at the bowl. She flashes a look at Ansa – eyes wide with excitement.

'Look inside!' Koru chants.

Hua tips the contents of the bowl onto the floor. She bends low over them and picks one up. 'Shells!'

Ansa takes one of the shells and holds it up to catch the best of the dim light. It has the shape and the dotted markings of a tiny coiled snake. Fascinated, she picks up another and sees that it is like a flower with layers of star-shaped petals. Hua hands her another, with a pointed tip, like a spear head. This one is round and smooth and it reflects the light, just like the

Balqa stone. Ansa starts putting them back into the bowl, but Hua insists on emptying them out again.

'Take them outside,' Ansa says sharply, an urge to be rid of the child squirming inside her.

But Koru intervenes. 'No – let her play here.'

Ansa tries once more to collect the shells and, this time, Hua thinks it's a game. She tips them all out of the bowl and fixes her eyes on Ansa's face, laughing, waiting. Ansa stares hard at the little girl. *Why is she laughing at me? Could it be that she wants to play?* The tight places inside Ansa begin to relax. As quickly as she can pick the shells up and put them back in the bowl, Hua tips them out again. Koru is laughing and so is Hua and now Ansa finds herself joining in. Hua grabs her mother's hands to stop her picking up the shells. Her fingers are tiny but they are strong.

At last, Hua turns the bowl upside down and begins to play a game on her own, chattering to the shells and hiding them inside the tortoiseshell mountain.

'Didn't you play with your Ama, when you were small?' Koru asks.

Ansa tries to picture Ama's face but it seems so long ago and so far away. All she can remember are hard, cold eyes.

'My mother was too busy to play,' she says at last.

'Did she have many other children?'

Ansa shifts uncomfortably on the rock floor. Hua looks up but then returns to her game.

'She had a boy. His name was Zeru,' she manages to say. Koru returns her look steadily.

'So you have a brother.'

'No. He died.'

Koru takes Ansa's hand. 'Your mother must have been glad

that you were strong,' she says, so gently that tears begin to form at the back of Ansa's eyes.

'No – she wasn't glad!' The words run from Ansa's mouth. 'She was angry.'

'Angry? Why?'

Ansa forces herself to remember the look that was always on Ama's face after her brother died: the terrible questions she couldn't answer.

'I don't know.'

Koru leans back against the wall and closes her eyes for a while.

'I'm going to tell you another story from the time of the old ones,' she says. 'This one is from the days before our people began to wander, when the Skyfather would appear to men in the shape of animals. It is the story of the mantis and his son.'

Koru takes a few deep breaths that seem to cause her pain but when she begins to speak, her voice is strong enough.

'The mantis knew that soon he must fight with the cruel and quarrelsome people who sit on their heels – that is the baboon people.'

'What is a baboon?' Ansa breaks in.

'Baboon has fur and a tail and a pointed face,' Koru replies. 'And he sits back and finds fault with everyone and everything. Now, don't ask questions but only listen.'

Hearing Koru's story-telling voice, Hua stops playing with the shells and leans against Ansa to listen. Her thumb goes back into her mouth.

'The mantis knew that he would need many spears so he sent his son to collect stout branches. Before long, the baboon people noticed what he was doing and they began to chatter among themselves, asking what this might mean.'

'The youngest baboon spoke to the mantis boy and asked him why he was gathering branches. Because he was young and ignorant, the son of the mantis told the truth.'

"My father has sent me to gather branches to make spears."

"What will he do with the spears?" asked the baboon boy.

"He will take aim at the people who sit on their heels," came the answer.

'Then the young baboon turned to his brother and told him what the boy had said and his brother told their cousin and their cousin went to an old, grey baboon and told him.'

Koru pauses, her breath catching in her throat, making her cough. While Ansa is waiting for the fit to pass, Hua's head drops against her chest; the little girl is fast asleep. Feeling the warm weight of Hua's body nestling into her own, Ansa is suddenly happy. A few strands of her hair are caught tight in Hua's fist and Ansa gently releases them, holding the small hand in hers. Hua stirs, but does not wake.

'What did the baboon elder say?' Ansa prompts, when Koru has recovered.

'He said, "Why – the mantis means to attack us – we are the people who sit on our heels!" Then he said "Take the child and kill him!"'

So the cruel baboon people began to strike the son of the mantis with their fists – again and again till they broke his head. The boy's eye came out and rolled away. Then the baboon people began to play with the eye, throwing it to one another. Soon they were fighting over it, saying, "the eye is mine" – "no, the eye is mine". While they played and quarrelled, the son of the mantis lay dying.'

'Meanwhile the mantis himself was resting in the heat of

the day – waiting for his son to return. Sleep took him far away and showed him what was happening to his son. When he woke, the mantis took up his spear at once and ran to the place where the baboons live. The baboon people did not know who he was.'

"Throw the eye to me!" he called to them, but they would not and kept passing it between themselves. The mantis stood between them and, at last, he managed to catch it. Quickly, he anointed the eye with sweat from his armpit, then he stowed it in his skin bag.'

'At this, the baboons realized who he was. They jumped on him and began to strike him. He was wounded and bleeding but he managed to escape with his son's eye safe in the bag.'

'The mantis travelled to the green place of reeds by the water's edge and he tenderly withdrew his son's eye from the darkness where it lay. He dropped it gently into the water and left. Each day, for many days, the mantis came back to the water's edge, watching carefully from behind the reeds.'

'The heart of the mantis leapt with joy to see his son grow again, just as Balqa grows again in the sky. At last he was fully grown and his father came upon him as he slept by the water's edge. The mantis woke the boy. He was startled but the mantis anointed the child with his arm scent and said:

"Why are you afraid of me?"

He took the boy in his arms and rocked him to and fro, saying again and again, "don't be afraid. I am your father. You are my son."

He dressed the boy in the skin he had prepared and took him home.'

The story is finished and Koru leans back, exhausted. Without another word to Ansa, she turns onto her side, lays her head down on the bedding and covers herself. Soon she is asleep. Ansa sits listening to Hua's soft breathing and the rasping breath of Koru for a long time, the tears rolling slowly, silently, down her cheeks.

Ansa climbs up to the shelter and crawls in. She sits, rocking herself from side to side, feeling again Koru's hand in hers, Hua's body snuggled against her. She thinks of the mantis cradling his son in his arms and a warm stillness steals over her. The tears begin to fall again, a slow, steady trickle like the spring in summer. Could it be that Hua does not hate her, after all?

The light is fading; she must go back to the others, to Koru. Ansa edges her way to the entrance and turns to begin the climb back down. It is then that she sees it. *A dark line of shadow between the rock and the sand.* The last rays of the day's warmth are draining away and she begins to shiver. That sand, that rock, sit in the desert, many days' walk away. She is safe on the mountain, the Nose of the Antelope. She takes a long breath and drops her leg, feeling for a foothold. *The dark line of shadow between rock and sand.*

Ansa begins to understand that she is not seeing with her eyes, but with her thoughts. Shaking, she crawls back into the shelter, feeling for the bag at her belt. She grasps the Balqa stone and rolls the smooth orb between her fingers till she is calm again. As soon as she dares to replace the stone, there it is again. *The sand. The shimmering heat. The akazia tree.* She closes her eyes, but the memory only grows stronger and more vivid.

Eshtu is high in the sky and she's on the sand, in the shade of the akazia tree. She can hear the other children calling to her but

Ama told her to watch him while he sleeps. If she leaves him alone, Ama will slap her.

She looks around for something to do, and hops over the hot sand to pick up a handful of small stones. She throws one at a rock but misses. She tries another and this time the cracking sound tells her it has hit home. She scampers across the sand and kneels by the boulder, looking for her lucky stone. Where did it go? Could it be under?

'No!'Ansa's cry echoes against the walls of the shelter. She must never think about that rock. It is not safe. She covers her eyes with her hands, but the pictures only seem to grow clearer.

She kneels by the rock, squinting into the black line of shadow. She runs her fingers along the sand. Nothing. The boulder rolls a little at her touch. She moves it forwards and backwards. This is better than throwing stones – maybe she can roll it right over.

It's heavy and hurts her hands. No – wait – she can push it like this. It begins to rock from side to side, further each time – it's going to go right over. She jumps back out of the way, grains of sand spurting into the air. There is something underneath but it's scuttling away, towards the akazia tree. She crawls after it. It stops dead and she peers at it closely. A shiny black body - skinny black legs, on its back a splash of red. Aiee! A blood spider! She springs back. 'Fede! Look! Fede!' But the children have gone. There are only grownups, a long way off, by the tents. The spider is moving towards the akazia tree. 'I can run faster than you, scary spider!' It scuttles across the sand towards the sleeping baby. 'Ama!' No – shh! She'll hit me for letting it out. I'll just smash it to pieces.

She looks around but there's no stick, nothing.' Where have you gone, scary spider?' She tiptoes closer. There it is, scuttling between the little stones.

Why doesn't the stupid baby wake up? It's going straight for his fat brown bottom that Ama loves to pinch till he giggles and she smiles back.

She tiptoes a bit closer. He is lying in the shade, still fast asleep. She stares at his chubby brown leg, the crease where his buttocks begin to swell. Ama is always crowing about how fat he is but that's because he is drinking all Ama's milk.

The spider is off again, going closer and closer. Aiee! The baby is too heavy to push out of the way and he can't even crawl. He would scream if the spider bit his fat bottom! He'd open his greedy gob and scream. No more giggling then.

She opens her mouth to shout but nothing comes out. Instead she starts to feel very tired. Too sleepy to go and get a stick. Too sleepy to find Ama. She watches, slow and sleepy and heavy, as the spider makes straight for his fat brown leg. Will he wake when he feels the tickly legs on him? The spider has stopped. Two of its legs are waving – trying to feel their way onto the baby's skin.

She leans in closer, watching, her mouth open, forgetting to breathe. Now the spider is moving slowly up his leg. It's enormous – as big as his knee - but he doesn't wake up. She puts out her hand to shake him but the blood spider scuttles across his hip, onto his buttocks. Now he's waking up, turning over. She jumps back as his mouth opens in a wail.

She doesn't want to watch anymore and she looks the other way. The grownups are too far away to hear the screaming. It doesn't last for long. When Ama comes at last, he is just grizzling, his fist in his mouth. Ama scoops him up with that smile she keeps just for him, and ties him to her front so that he can suck her milk. The blood spider is gone.

Though she is alone in the rockshelter, Ansa dares not

uncover her face. She remembers very well what happened later that day. She thinks about it often in the dark, when she is waiting for sleep to come. About running back, laughing with Fede, when it was time to eat, only to find no food and the women wailing. Ama with tears on her face. She was trying to make him suck milk, but he had gone stiff and his head wouldn't turn, and he kept puking up green, watery stuff all over her.

Alone on the mountain in the fading light, Ansa catches her foot on a stone and falls heavily. She gets up and stumbles on. Her knee is bleeding and her wrist aches from the fall, but she hardly feels the pain. She must get back to Ama Koru.

The blood spider. She had always known, somehow, that it was her fault that he had been so sick and had gone to sleep and never woken up again. That's why Ama had shaken and slapped her, asking her those questions, again and again. *Why didn't you watch him? Did you see him put something in his mouth?* She couldn't answer. Just closed her eyes to make the scuttling black legs, that frightening splash of red, go away. And they did go away.

But Ama was still angry, long after they buried him in the sand. When she climbed onto Ama's lap, Ama would hit her hard and push her off, even though *he* was no longer there to drink the milk. Ama's breasts soon grew slack and empty. Then, the next spring, Ama fell sick herself and died, leaving Ansa alone with only her father and his new wife.

Ansa's knee is stiffening and swelling up, giving her pain at each step. She stops to rest and get her breath. The night mountain is a stranger whose face she doesn't know. She should have come to the tortoise path long ago but the slope beside her rises steep and unfamiliar. Just ahead, the ground appears to fall away and the smell of buckthorn reaches her nostrils.

Balqa is nowhere to be seen and the sky seems to press down on her head, accusing her. She turns back, trying to retrace her steps, but it is too dark. Tears are rolling down her face. She tries to think of the mantis rocking his son in his arms, of Koru holding her hand. But the sky only bears down harder, its voice full of malice. *How can Koru love you now?* She sinks onto the wet ground, her knee throbbing.

After a time, a subtle change comes to the sky; the quality of the darkness is different. A thin blade of white appears above the mountain. He is too weak to give any light but he has risen and the black sky lifts a little. *Koru is not like Ama. She is kind.* Ansa remembers the magic Koru wove that morning when Hua was born. Perhaps she knows everything. Perhaps she already knows that Ansa killed her brother. Ansa drags herself to her feet, setting off again in what she hopes is the right direction.

Chapter 9

Bidari

While he is still a way off, Bidari hears the sound he has been dreading ever since the rains began: the high-pitched keening of the women. *Koru!* Breaking into a run, he reaches the cave and passes into the dark interior. The main chamber is unusually empty. He makes out a knot of figures around the passageway that leads up to his sleeping place. Pushing past old Bakar and the children, he thrusts his way through the wailing women. She is there, on the ground, propped up against the wall.

'Ama!' He is on his knees beside her, clutching her cold hand. Still he cannot think that she is gone. 'Ama! Wake up!'

He begins to chafe the icy hand between his warm palms. Frantically, he throws himself on top of her and, forcing the slack mouth open, breathes his own hot breath into her, again and again. There is no movement.

He pulls back and her jaw, with its folds of loose skin, drops lifelessly onto her chest. A terrible panic takes hold of him. *Don't leave me, Ama!* He sees her now, sitting by his father, sharing out the meat after a hunt, laughing.

Bidari stares at the pale faces of the women, tongues darting from side to side as they make the lament. The air is thick with horror and fear. He hears his brother's voice. The women make way and Koldo appears, dragging Nuno behind him, their figures filling the small space. The undulating sound falters and falls away to a silence. Nuno lowers himself awkwardly onto the ground beside Koru. His head wound is almost healed but still he has not come back to himself. The hand which reaches out to touch his mother's face shakes, his fingers struggling to find her cheek. There are tears in his eyes.

'Where do you want to make the circle?' Koldo asks. Nuno turns to look at him, blank. 'The circle,' Koldo repeats. 'Will you make it here?' Nuno's face remains empty.

Turning away from the corpse of his mother, Koldo pushes through the huddle of bodies and down the slope into the lower cave. Bidari follows him to the small hearth, Nuno shambling after them. Koldo has taken ash and is spreading it on the ground.

The sounds of mourning start up again and for the first time, Bidari thinks of Ansa. He doesn't remember seeing her face amongst those of the women. It is late for her to be out on the mountain alone. Should he go to look for her? More than anything, he just wants to sit, to stare at the flames and feel the warmth.

Koldo is busying himself, preparing the ground, ushering old Bakar over to the hearth. At last, all the men are gathered around the ash layer. Panic begins to rise again in Bidari's chest.

'What if she is only sleeping?' he blurts out. 'Let's wait till the morning.'

'No!' Koldo is adamant. 'Her body is cold. Balqa is approaching his death. It's the right time.'

Bidari glares at Koldo in the firelight. Can he never wait for anything, not even for their mother?

Koldo turns to Nuno, instructing him like a child. 'Brother, you must search for her in the place of the dead. When you have seen her, we can dig the trench.'

Bidari has been trying not to picture his mother's body, anointed in death red, disappearing little by little under the loose earth of the burial shaft. Now that Koldo has spoken, the picture will not go away.

Koldo gives Goi the drum and he starts the death beat, the slow, rhythmic thudding of bone on skin echoing around the walls of rock. Nuno is peering ahead, his face troubled.

'What is it?' Koldo asks, but his brother only looks puzzled. 'He needs something to draw with,' Koldo decides.

Tipi fetches a stick and Nuno holds it poised above the dull white ash bed. The drum beat grows more insistent and Bidari can feel his heart thumping in time with it.

'Start with the circle', Koldo prompts.

There is a glimmer of recognition in Nuno's eyes. Using the stick, he begins to describe a circle in the ash, but his hand trembles and the circle trails off into a straight line. Nuno tries again, tongue clenched between his teeth, but each time he starts from a different place till the ash is a mass of crossing lines which hold no meaning.

There is anguish in Koldo's face and something else that looks like fear. Bidari cannot bear it. He quickly rakes over the ash layer, then takes the stick from Nuno and draws a large circle in the ash, ignoring the gasps of disapproval.

'Now make the shape of our mother.' He gives the stick to Nuno and settles back on his heels. 'Let the drum beat take you to the place of the dead.'

Bidari closes his eyes. Everything will be all right. Nuno will travel to the far place and see Koru's spirit there, safe and happy. In the dark behind his eyelids, Bidari gives himself to the sound of the drum and the keening of the women. His breathing slows.

At last, he opens his eyes to find Koldo staring at him, dumb with pain. Nuno has drawn nothing inside the circle and the stick is lying discarded on the ground. He is staring out, through the cave mouth, at the night sky.

'Did you see her?' Koldo asks.

Nuno turns his head. 'Who?'

'Our mother, you fool!' Koldo's voice is sharp with fear. 'Did you see her in the place of the dead?'

Nuno's face crumples. 'Ama? Is she dead?' he cries.

Koldo turns away, spitting onto the ground.

The misery lying curled in the pit of Bidari's belly uncoils itself and strikes out at Koldo. 'Leave him alone!'

Koldo turns on Bidari, his face livid with rage. He picks up the stick and hurls it onto the fire. 'Don't you understand? He can't see for us any longer. He's no better than a child!'

The shocking, fearful words come at Bidari like blows, depriving him of breath. The drum beat stops abruptly, leaving only a throbbing silence.

'How can we bury her then?' he cries. He will die rather than let Koldo bury his mother like this. She might wake under the earth, unable to breathe. Fear makes Bidari reckless. 'Why did you shout at him?' he hisses at Koldo. 'He just needed more time. I could have made him see.'

In the shadows by the hearth, Bidari doesn't see the blow coming. The side of his face explodes with pain. He feels for his eye but the cut is below it, on his cheekbone. The first

99

drops of blood are gathering where the skin has slit. Koldo's anger has not abated.

'You think you can do something? It's your fault he's like this – that the Sakaitz attacked him. You were meant to be keeping watch.'

Koldo turns to Nuno, pulling him into an embrace, stroking the matted hair and the scar on his scalp.

'Look what they did to him,' Koldo cries. 'I wish it had been you, instead of him.'

Both Bidari's cheeks are burning now, with shame and rage. He stares at his brothers, locked together, weeping. He has never felt so alone.

Outside, morning is beginning to lighten the sky. Bidari stumbles up and wanders away. No-one tries to stop him. He crosses the floor of the cave and looks up to see Bo, standing in the shadows by the wall. His child, Hua, is asleep in her arms. The passageway which winds up to his sleeping place is narrow, but she doesn't move out of his way. Instead, as he passes, she reaches out and wipes away the blood from his face. The tenderness of the girl's touch brings tears to his eyes.

The women move back and Bidari sits beside his mother, but it brings him no comfort. Instead, the empty shell of her body begins to disgust him, as if it were the carcass of a beast, and he closes his eyes. There, behind his eyelids, he sees the mound of Bo's breast in the growing light, rising up as she reaches out to touch him, the nipple small and tight. Despite everything, he feels himself grow hard and he is ashamed.

Gashi approaches him uncertainly. 'Is it done?' she asks. 'Can we prepare the kho?'

Bidari shakes his head in despair. 'No. Nothing is done.

Nuno couldn't make the circle.'

There is a gasp from Esti and the smell of fear intensifies. The corpse of his mother seems to loom bigger and bigger in the small space. Bidari can sense how the women long to be rid of it.

'What can we do?' Gashi asks.

Before Bidari can answer, there is a scuffling noise in the passage behind and Ansa appears. She has been running and her body is streaked with mud; there is dried blood on her leg. When she sees the motionless body of Koru, she stops in her tracks. She opens her mouth and lets out a terrible sound, like the scream of a speared boar. The skin on Bidari's neck prickles.

He watches in horror as Ansa throws herself on top of his mother's body, clutching at her hands, stroking her cheeks, imploring Koru to wake up.

'Don't leave me,' she wails, again and again.

A hard bud of anger swells and opens in his belly. Koru is his mother, not hers. She should be comforting him, not shaming him in front of the women, with her wild crying. He goes to restrain her but Ansa is already pulling back from the corpse.

'She's gone where the dead go,' Ansa whispers. 'Just like Ama.'

Gashi reaches over to grasp Ansa's shoulder, a new light in her eyes. 'What did you say? Do you see Koru in the land of the dead?'

Ansa stares up at Gashi, uncomprehending. She turns back to Koru and takes her hand. She begins prattling to the corpse.

'Tell me about the mantis - the part where he wraps his son in the cloak. Tell me again, Ama.' She rocks forwards and

101

backwards on her heels.

Unsettled by Ansa's howling, the children huddle close to their mothers. Only Gashi seems to understand what is happening. She peers round at the others intently.

'Koru's spirit has reached the far place. Ansa can see her. Look! She's talking to her.'

Ansa is stroking Koru's cold hand. She seems not to hear Gashi. 'Please, Ama, tell me about the boy's eye. Will Zeru grow fat again like him, like Balqa?' She settles back and looks up expectantly into the pale, dead face.

Repelled, Bidari turns away from the sight of his wife, blabbering like a mad woman. But Gashi draws him away from the tutting of Esti and the frightened faces of the others. Her strong face is alive with hope.

'I will start mixing the kho, for the burial. Bidari - you must tell Koldo and the others.' Her hand is heavy on his arm, her voice insistent. 'Tell them there is no need to wait. Ansa has seen Koru in the place of the dead.'

Bidari is wary of approaching Koldo again but there is no need. As always, Koldo's anger, which flares up like burning twigs, has died down just as quickly. When he sees Bidari coming, he gets to his feet and, taking hold of Bidari's face, examines his swollen cheek. He gently cuffs the top of his brother's head.

'Ansa is talking to our mother - as if she can see her spirit,' Bidari says. Koldo steps back to think, his head turned to one side. 'Ansa doesn't see us,' Bidari continues. 'Gashi says she has gone to the far place.'

'Is our mother there?' There is hope in Koldo's voice.

'Yes – she is speaking to her.'

The fear begins to lift, chased away by the morning light

seeping into the cave. The spirit of Koru has left the Nose of the Antelope and made its journey to the far place. Now they can bury her body.

The women are heating the kho to make death red, but Ansa is not with them. Bidari climbs up to his sleeping place but it is empty except for the body of his mother, covered over with a skin. He is glad not to have to see her face. He runs down the slope, across the uneven floor of the cave, and outside. A fresh wind is blowing. Ansa is not with the children either. He climbs up to the spring to drink and catches sight of her back, disappearing up the path.

'Ansa! Wait!'

She turns and seems to see him, but then limps quickly away. Bidari catches up with her by a clump of buckthorn. She is panting, her eyes wild. He takes her hand and pulls her into the shelter of the trees, out of the cold wind.

'It's all right,' he says, 'don't be frightened. You need to rest.'

He helps her down onto the ground. Now that he is beginning to understand, all he wants to do is comfort her. His wife is a seer, like Nuno. That's how she knew about the calf. Why she is not like the other women. The strands of his thoughts are weaving together now, into something strong and sure.

Her knee is swollen and Bidari takes some wet leaves, gently wiping away the dried blood. *Ansa is a seer.* This thought is like a flower unfolding its petals and more thoughts come circling around it like bees. The Oak People have a new seer. What happened to Nuno up on the mountain top is his fault, as Koldo said. But he, Bidari, has brought Ansa to them and now the Oak People have someone new to journey to the spirit world for them.

Bidari wants to tell Ansa these thoughts but he doesn't know how to say them. Instead, he spits onto his finger and begins to clean the mud from her thigh. Touching her soft flesh, warm from the climb, makes him hard, ready to mate. The dark night of death, with its terrors, is fading and lust is building inside him, ready to burst. He helps her back onto the wet ground and starts to climb on top of her, the day young and new, the wind whipping through the buckthorn leaves.

Before Bidari can get in between Ansa's legs, he feels pain; she is tearing at his back with her nails. Astonished, he looks up to see her face, twisted with rage. Her lips begin to work and then she spits, the spittle landing on his nose and running down onto his lip. Now she is pummelling him with her fists, screeching at him to stop. Bidari pulls back from her and she sits up, her eyes wild.

'She's gone!' she screams at him. 'She's left me. Did you take her away?' Her fists flail out at him, one of the blows landing on Bidari's swollen cheekbone.

The pain is so terrible that everything goes dark for half a breath. When Bidari comes to, Ansa's face is close to his. Her lip is curled in a gloat and something inside him gives way. He grabs her by the shoulder and pushes her back down onto the ground, forcing her legs apart with his other hand. She tries to fight him but he is stronger. He lifts his arm and whips the back of his hand down hard across her face. He can feel teeth through her soft lips. For an instant, her face becomes Koldo's face: Koldo with eyes wide in surprise, his lip split and bleeding. Bidari grins, spit running down his chin.

'You're my wife, do you hear?' he shouts, beyond himself. 'Don't ever shame me again.'

She is shaking now and whimpering. Lust and rage spark through him like lightning. Pinning Ansa down with one arm, he forces himself inside her, thrusts twice, hard, and it is over. As he pulls out of her, his hand becomes caught up in her belt. Feeling the small bag tied there, he rips it away. He gets up and crosses to the path, where the mountain drops steeply down. With a yell, he throws the bag over the edge with all his strength. Frightened by the noise, a flock of bulbul rises from the treetops below. The tiny bag is not visible as it falls through the morning sky.

Chapter 10

Bo

'Ama Bo! Carry me!' wails Hua. She has flopped down in protest, in the middle of the path.

Bo turns round. 'Get up,' she calls. 'You're big enough to walk.' Hua's face creases up pitifully and Bo goes back for her, trying to keep the smile from her face. 'Come on then,' she grumbles, hoisting the little girl onto her hip.

'They've been here already!' Gashi says, when Bo has caught up with her. 'Why didn't they say?'

'Who?'

'The others - Ikomar and Sorne. It would have saved us a long walk. Every patch of peas here has already been stripped.'

'But surely we would have seen them coming back,' Bo muses.

Maybe they went further on, she thinks, with Nuno along to carry for them. It still doesn't seem right, a man foraging with the women, but picking peas is work he can still do. A smile comes to Bo's face. He can do one other thing, it seems, because his wife Ikomar is growing a baby in her belly at last.

'Eggs!' Gashi says suddenly. 'We'll go back on the tortoise path – there may be some eggs.'

'Eggs!' Hua crows. She clambers down from Bo's arms, happy to walk now.

amid the oak scrub, they find several scrapes, where the earth has been disturbed. Gashi tests the ground with her stick. She unearths eight perfectly round white eggs which had been completely hidden from view. Hua takes one and runs to find a rock with a sharp edge, so she can break it open.

Hua's face, covered in sticky yolk, reminds Bo of that strange day, last spring, when Ansa found the antelope calf. Bo quickly wipes Hua's face and hands. It is painful to remember Ansa as she used to be, before the madness took her.

Gashi has moved on, as far as the spring. Catching up with her, Bo sees a clump of nut grass, growing tall where the ground is damp. Gashi has started digging, to get at the tubers.

'Will they be big enough?' Bo is doubtful.

The roots are barely thicker than Bo's finger and the pungent smell is unpleasant, but Gashi seems glad to have found them. This spring, anything is better than nothing.

On the way back, Bo is quiet. When they reach the fork in the path, she takes a deep breath. 'Should we take Ansa a couple of the eggs?'

She waits anxiously for Gashi's reaction. The eggs are precious; perhaps they should go to the children, to Goi's son who is sick. Gashi is silent for a time, then she nods.

'I'll take them to her,' Bo says quickly, before Gashi can change her mind. After all, when Koru died and Ansa ran away to the shelter, it was Gashi who insisted they should keep feeding her. Some of the others wanted to leave her alone to die. But it's been so long and she's no better and they are all so hungry.

Bo takes two of the eggs from Gashi's bag. She squats down beside Hua. 'Go back with Gashi now.' She kisses the little girl's cheek.

'I want to go with you,' Hua says.

Bo exchanges a glance with Gashi. 'I won't be long.'

The older woman takes Hua's hand and starts back to the cave, while Bo takes the path across the face of the mountain and up to the rockshelter. It is the hottest part of the day. She stops to wipe the sweat from her eyes and to rub her back, low down by her buttocks, trying to ease the dull ache that has been plaguing her ever since she woke.

All through the winter and the spring, Bo has been taking food to Ansa. The winter rains and the spring flowers have long gone and now the days are growing hot. Bo reaches the shelter and calls from the path.

'Ansa! It's me. I've brought eggs.'

She is not surprised when there is no reply. Often, Ansa will not speak to her, not at first. Sometimes, on the coldest days of winter, she would sit staring out blankly, not seeming to notice that Bo was lighting a fire. Later, Bo would lie awake in the cave, worrying that Ansa would fall into the fire and burn herself.

'I'm coming up!' Bo calls.

She secures the bag with the eggs to her back and scrambles up the rocky cliff to the shelter mouth. Coming from the light of midday, at first Bo can see nothing in the dark gap beneath the overhanging rock. She climbs up over the ledge and crawls in, peering around her: dried bedding grass, skins they have brought to keep Ansa warm, the remnants of a fire. Something crackles under Bo's knee - acorn shells lie scattered over the rocky floor, amid the rat droppings. There is a strong smell of piss coming from the back, where the crack in the rock is nothing more than a narrow fissure. But there is no sign of Ansa herself.

Bo's heart is beating fast as she scans the path below. After a while, the figure of Ansa appears, coming back from the spring. She is hurrying, her head bent low, eyes on the path. Her gait is uneven. Bo gasps when she sees the swelling of Ansa's pregnant belly - her belt scarcely visible beneath it.

'Ansa!'

Ansa pauses, trying to locate the sound, then squints up towards the shelter. She often complains now about the bright light. There are wet splashes of brown around her mouth from drinking at the spring, but the rest of her body is caked with reddish dust. She doesn't return the greeting but climbs awkwardly up to the shelter.

Bo puts out a hand to help Ansa over the ledge and, for once, she accepts it. She is panting with the weight of her belly and murmuring under her breath.

'Has he come back?'

'Who?'

'Is he there?' Ansa jabs her finger in the direction of the opening.

'Balqa? You mean Balqa?'

'Shh …' Ansa hisses. 'He can't see us here, but he can hear us.'

Bo sighs. Balqa has been absent from the sky for three nights but it is no use trying to reassure Ansa. And, anyway, he will soon reappear, a fine crescent of white.

Back in the safety of the shelter, Ansa seems calmer. She

sits rocking in just the same way that Hua does when you sing to her. Tears prick at the back of Bo's eyes. She reaches out, but Ansa pushes her away and carries on rocking. After a time, she tries again, laying her palm flat on Ansa's taut belly. She waits, her mouth open. Soon, she is rewarded by a movement from inside: a tiny fist, or a foot perhaps.

'There! Did you feel it?' Bo is delighted. But Ansa just turns to her, blank eyes in a blank face. 'There it is again! That's your baby.'

Bo takes Ansa's hand and presses it down where the baby kicked but Ansa pulls her hand away.

'I'm hungry,' she says. 'What have you brought?'

Bo's pity is beginning to dry up, like a patch of piss under the eye of Eshtu. Ansa doesn't deserve another child. She never even asks about the one she has.

'I've brought something special,' Bo says. Surely she will be glad when she sees the eggs. 'Gashi and I found them when we were out with Hua.'

'Hua?' Ansa sounds puzzled.

'Yes, Hua. Your daughter. She misses you.'

Ansa shows no sign of having heard the edge in Bo's voice. She seems to be looking at something else, something far away. When she turns back to Bo, her voice is different – strong and clear.

'Ansa can't be trusted. That's what Ama says. Ansa can't be trusted. She didn't look after Zeru.'

'Zeru? Who is Zeru?'

But Ansa has turned away again and is drumming her fingers on the ground and muttering under her breath. It is no use trying to make sense of it. Instead, Bo opens her bag carefully.

'Look what I've brought.'

There is no response. Bo clamps her hand over Ansa's to stop the tapping, but Ansa wrenches her fingers free with surprising strength.

'Don't do that! Now I'll have to start again,' she protests.

Quickly, Bo holds out the eggs. 'Look!'

Ansa stares at them, then up at Bo. She edges away, hiding her hands behind her back.

'What's the matter?' cries Bo. 'They're fresh!'

Ansa holds her head still, as if she has heard something. Bo listens, but there is nothing.

'I'll crack one for you,' Bo says.

Ansa moves quickly and, with a deft movement, she knocks the egg from Bo's hand. It falls onto the rock and breaks open, the precious yolk spilling out, fouled by the dirt and droppings. Ansa recoils from the sticky mess and, snatching the other egg, throws it out through the mouth of the shelter.

Stunned, Bo watches as Ansa crawls back to the shelter wall, where she starts rocking once more. Anger pushes up from Bo's belly and out through her mouth.

'Why did you do that?'

The rocking stops.

'They're poisoned,' Ansa says then crawls close, peering into Bo's face, her eyes narrow slits of suspicion. 'Why did you bring them? Did he send you?'

Bo is beside herself. 'I brought you the eggs. What are you frightened of? I brought them because I thought you'd like them. It was me, not Balqa.'

Ansa flinches at the name and puts her finger to her lips.

'Stop it, Ansa! Stop all this stupid talk and come back to the cave with me.'

111

Bo is shaking but Ansa only turns her back and starts drumming again with her fingers. Tears begin to spill over and run down Bo's face, but Ansa takes no notice. After a time, Bo crawls towards the shelter's mouth. There is no point in staying any longer. The wasted egg lies smeared on the floor, food that could have gone to Goi's son or to Hua. At the ledge, Bo pauses, filled with an urge to punish Ansa.

'Hua thinks I'm her Ama now. Did you know that?' she says.

The drumming stops. Bo waits but Ansa will not turn to face her. Bo begins the climb down and, one last time, she peers through the gloom. Ansa has covered her ears with her hands.

As Bo scrambles down to the path, the dull ache seems to move round to her belly. Walking back, the pain grows worse but now the rest of her body is more comfortable, as if she were sitting around a warm fire, with food in her belly. Then, she feels it – something wet between her legs. She dabs at her puti and stares at the brownish red stain on her fingers. Blood! A woman's blood at last. She is proud but with the pride comes a heaviness. In time this will mean leaving the cave, living with a new people she doesn't know, sleeping beside a strange man.

Bo walks on slowly, her thoughts circling like flies around this new thing. She will need to gather moss and dry it, as the other women do, to soak up the blood. And now she will start to wear the belt that shows she is a woman. They will cut her hair, right back to her scalp. Bo's face colours with shame as she thinks of the men seeing her shaved head and knowing. *Bidari*. The thought of Bidari knowing races through her, tingling her skin.

Nearing the cave, she walks more and more slowly, but there is no going back. Esti is sat outside, chewing on a shoot of reed mace and watching the children. Keeping out of sight, Bo leaves the path, pushing her way amid the dense scrub. Soon, she finds what she is looking for – a hollow branch that will make a good clear sound. She snaps it in two and climbs back up till she is just below the path. Hiding from sight behind a bush, she beats one of the dry sticks against the other: once, then twice more in quick succession. She repeats the sequence then peers through the leaves, her heart thumping. Esti looks up at once, trying to locate the sound. Bo signals again and, this time, Esti gets up stiffly and comes towards her. Age has made her legs curve out from her hips, leaving a wide space between her knees. There is a look of excitement on her lined face.

'Bo? Is that you?' she calls, and Bo slides out from behind the bush, her face aflame.

'I thought I heard the signal. Has the bleeding come?'

Bo nods. There is nothing of the usual complaining note in Esti's voice. Her face breaks into a beam; for once, she will be the bringer of news.

'Stay back here,' she orders, 'I'll get the others.'

'Can't I come with you?' Bo asks, the strange new ache pulling at her belly. She doesn't want to be alone. 'Let me come and help with the grass peas,' she pleads.

'No.' Esti is full of her own importance. 'You must keep out of sight. I'll bring the belt – and a blade for your hair. We'll cut it here.'

The old woman starts off for the cave, then stops suddenly and turns back.

'What were you saying about grass peas? There aren't any

113

grass peas. Gashi came back with nothing. Just some eggs and a few measly roots of nut grass.'

'I know – I was with her. Ikomar had already picked the peas, with Sorne. Aren't they back yet?'

Esti stares at Bo. Perhaps her sense has left her along with the first blood.

'Ikomar and Sorne have been here all day,' she says. 'Now get behind the bush in case the men see you.'

She sets off for the cave, leaving Bo crouching out of sight. Bo is puzzled. She and Gashi went to all the places where peas grow. They had all been stripped, even the small ones that should have been left to grow. Bo sinks down to the ground, too tired to think anymore. Her body feels heavy and unfamiliar and it is a relief to leave everything to Esti. Later, the talking will begin and the planning. A man will have to be found for her. But not yet. For now, while the bleeding lasts, the women will keep her away from the men.

Bidari

Bidari is sitting in the shade of an oak. It is the middle of the day and too hot to be out in the open. He works a piece of bark free from the trunk, rubs it between his fingers and sniffs. The smell reminds him of when he was young, collecting bark for tanning. There were always hides to be worked then: antelope, goat, even deer. Thinking of meat sets off a growling in Bidari's guts. Soon, the drowsiness which seems to follow him now, like a shadow, creeps up on him again. He lies down. Sleep will take him far away from all his dark thoughts.

Bidari wakes to the sound of women's voices below him on the slope. He sits up, peering through the canopy of leaves.

It is Gashi and Ikomar and some of the children. They put their bags down under one of the pear trees. The children begin beating the lower branches with sticks, shrieking with delight when the pears drop to the ground. Hua is with them – she is running, squatting, waving the small, hard fruits in the air. Tears come to Bidari's eyes. His body soft from sleep, he watches Hua drop fruit into the bag that Gashi holds open for her, then run off to collect more. For her, it is not work but play, and the familiar sound of her laughter drifts up to where he sits, hidden from view. At least he still has Hua.

She has seen something. With a cry of pleasure, she drops the fruit and begins to run. Her high voice easily carries up to the oak tree where he is sitting.

'Ama! Ama! Come and see what I'm doing.'

Ama? Her mother has been gone all winter and spring, living in her own filth in that shelter. She must mean Bo. Bidari peers through the foliage and sees that he is right. Bo is climbing up to join the others, her gathering bag slung over her shoulder. Suddenly, he is straining forward to get a better view. He knows - all the men know - that her bleeding has come. The women have kept her hidden for days.

'Ama!'

Bo sweeps the little girl up into her arms and swings her round. Seeing them together, anyone would think that Bo was Hua's mother. She is a more of a mother than Ansa has ever been.

Bo kisses the little girl and puts her down. For the first time, Bidari has an uninterrupted view of Bo. She is squatting on the ground now and he can see the woman's belt, the deerskin flap that covers her genitals hanging between her thighs. His eyes travel up to her firm breasts and then up again, to her

115

face. They take in the forbidden sight: her shaved head, the newly grown hair a dark, exciting shadow over the graceful shape of her skull. No other man has seen her neck, her ears, her head, without the covering of hair. Every muscle tense, he watches as she takes up a stick to strike the nearest tree. Her back is towards him. Now that the woman's deerskin obscures her buttocks, the itch to uncover them grows, till it has become an insistent desire.

Careful not to alert the women to his presence, Bidari follows every movement of Bo's as Eshtu slowly moves across the sky. For the first time in many days, he is alert and full of energy, the misery of hunger and of what has happened to Koru and Nuno and Ansa, gone from his thoughts. Bo is not his woman to take, but there is no harm in just watching, imagining. Like the young boys when they stalk antelope for practice.

Hua and the other young ones soon grow tired of collecting fruit but the older children keep on till the bags are loaded down. They sit for a time in the shade, hunger forcing them to bite into the pears, though they are not sweet. When the other women start off for the path with the children, Bo stays behind. Bidari cranes his neck to see what she will do, but she just takes up her stick to rattle the topmost branches where a few pears remain.

After a time, she disappears from view. Bidari edges along the slope to a better vantage point. The lower branches of a pear tree heave and he realizes that she has climbed up to pick the fruit. She is sitting astride a thick, gnarled branch; he can see one of her legs hanging down. She reaches up to shake the branches and now there is a soft thudding as the pears fall to the ground. She tries to stand; he can see her back as she clasps the trunk, feeling for a foothold higher up. She moves on up the tree, till she is completely hidden amongst the leaves. Her movements startle a flock of tiny yellow birds in a nearby tree and they fly up, squawking.

Silence returns and Bidari begins to feel uneasy. Then comes a sudden swishing movement, a loud snap followed by a shriek, and a branch of the pear falls with a crash to the ground. He catches sight of a dangling leg and her foot reaching down for a foothold. Should he help? It is forbidden for a man to be with her – he should not even have laid eyes upon her yet. Suddenly, the shrill, bird-like danger call sounds from the tree. Still, he hesitates. Perhaps the women will hear and come back. He waits and listens, but there is no answering call.

Bidari scrambles down over the rocks. The branches sway but as he reaches the foot of her tree, they become still.

'Bo?'

Her face appears amidst the leaves and, again, he is shocked by its new contours. Why has he never noticed her beautiful eyes before? Her cheeks colour under the brown skin.

'I'll climb up,' he says, but she shakes her head. 'Don't be frightened. I won't tell Esti.'

Bidari grabs hold of the lowest branch, where the trunk of the tree has divided, and pulls himself up. The pear tree is old and the branch thick, easily strong enough to bear his weight, and hers too. He positions his feet securely in the crook of the branch and, clasping the trunk with one arm, reaches up to her with the other. She is too far above to grasp his hand, but her foot moves tentatively down the side of the trunk. He takes hold of her ankle, then has a better thought and lets it go.

117

'Work your way down till you feel my shoulders with your feet,' he calls up. 'It's not far.'

The branches above him creak and rustle. A few more pears thud to the ground and, for some reason, Bidari laughs out loud. An answering giggle comes from Bo and then a shriek, as her foot finds, then slips from, his shoulder. Bidari grasps the tree trunk tightly.

'Try again,' he says, and then he feels the weight of her, pressing him down, one foot on each shoulder. She is half laughing, half whimpering with fear. He steadies himself.

'Bo – listen now,' he says. 'You need to squat down – on my shoulders.'

'I can't!'

'Yes, you can. Keep hold of the tree and bend your knees.'

Her weight is a digging pain on his shoulders but then her knees are bumping against the trunk and her deer skin cloth is over one of his eyes and he is supporting her with one hand and clinging to the tree with the other, as she somehow clambers and slides down beside him. Bidari gives a whoop of triumph and pushes a branch away from her face. They are wedged together and she is giggling with relief; he can feel her body shaking. Both her inner arms are grazed where she burned them on the trunk. Without thinking, just as if she were Hua, Bidari brushes the sore skin gently with his lips. Realizing what he has done, he drops to the ground below. He turns to help Bo, catching her around the waist and lifting her down in his arms, her breasts against his chest. She is shorter than Ansa and softer to touch.

Bo's face is flushed but she looks up into his eyes without flinching or turning away. He kisses her lips, uncertainly, feeling his way. Astonishingly, there is no resistance. She is pushing her body closer to his, nestling into him. He tries to think clearly. If I take her, what will happen? Koldo will be angry and Bakar, her foster-father. But the thought fades as he kisses her again. It is like the first bite into melting honeycomb – the pleasure almost takes his breath away. He pushes her gently up against the tree and, as he bends to find her nipple with his mouth, he can feel her warm breath coming quickly in his ear.

Chapter 11

Bidari

Goi is bent low over something he has seen in the grass. Bidari chuckles, thinking how he looks like a huge tortoise, his back humped and shining with sweat. Then, suddenly, Goi's head is up and he is licking his finger.

'This way.' He springs to his feet. 'Antelope blood.'

Bidari and the others follow as he sets off in a loping run, his eyes never leaving the ground. The heat is sweltering. The grass on the plain is brown, the earth too dry to carry hoof prints, but Goi is like the eagles that circle over the plain; nothing escapes his sharp eyes. Bidari runs, sweat pouring down his back. *Blood!* If the antelope is injured, they might be able to run him down. Strength floods into his legs at the prospect of meat, after so long.

Goi has halted and is scanning the ground again. He straightens up and points toward the stream that flows into the Crocodile River. There are stands of reed and green grass on either side, where the roots reach down into wet soil. In the sky above the reeds, two vultures are circling. Perhaps the antelope is near death already. Goi puts his finger to his lips and they slow to a walk, following the blood trail. The antelope must have gone to the stream to drink. Koldo raises his spear to his shoulder and the others copy him.

The afternoon breeze brings the stench of stale blood and rotting intestines, dashing Bidari's hope of fresh meat. The antelope must be dead. But if a hunting cat took him in the night, there may be scraps of meat left. Goi signals and they spread out, approaching warily, though the air carries no scent of lion. Behind a thornbush, Bidari finds what is left of the animal, a full-grown male, crashed beside the reeds. The air is full of flies. The men gather uneasily around the carcass in the heat. Something is wrong. The guts still lie on the ground but the head is missing. A lion would not take the head.

The reeds close by have been flattened and Goi picks something up, sitting back on his heels to examine it: a blade, beautifully struck, but broken in two. There is dried blood along the edge. With darkness spreading over his thoughts, Bidari examines the bones closely. The flesh has not been torn from the haunches by lion teeth. The antelope has been butchered, and by skilful hands.

'Look at this,' Koldo says. 'It was in the grass.'

On the palm of his hand lies a strip of softened hide. It was once tied around an arm, perhaps, but one of the ties is missing. The middle of the strip has been pierced and the quills of two tail feathers forced through the hole. Bidari picks the strange thing up, the feathers with their mottled brown and grey markings still firmly attached. With a shiver, Bidari drops it back into Koldo's palm.

Goi is circling the bloody carcass, gently moving the trampled reeds to reveal the earth, softer here, by the stream.

'Don't move,' he barks and begins to weave to and fro, his eyes to the ground. He touches the earth with his fingers. 'I

121

thought so,' he says. 'These are not our tracks. And there's no mark here of a hunting cat.'

Bidari sees the puzzlement on Koldo's face. The breeze from the Salt Water gathers strength, playing on the surface of the stream, but the only sounds are the buzzing of flies and the call of the vultures overhead. The sense of darkness grows, like a magic silence but alien.

'What does it mean?' Tipi asks. 'If it wasn't a cat …'

'These are the tracks of men,' answers Goi.

'But who …?' Tipi sounds frightened. 'The Marsh People?'

'No.' Koldo sounds certain. 'They wouldn't hunt near our paths, and start the fighting again.'

Koldo takes out an axe and begins to chop at the antelope's ribs. There are scraps of flesh that can be eaten and, perhaps, marrow. 'Take what we can,' he says, 'then let's go back.'

The breeze has dropped and the air is sticky as they climb back up to the cave. Bidari walks with his nephew. Tipi is taller than him now and his chest is filling out but he is not going to be as big as Koldo.

'What did my father mean – about the fighting?' Tipi asks.

'Fighting?'

'The Marsh People. He said they wouldn't start it up again.'

'Oh – that was in the old days – when your grandfather was a child. In those times, if we went to the Salt Water to collect nefafa, they would ambush us.'

'Did we fight them?' Tipi sounds excited.

'Yes. They killed my father's uncle and we killed one of them. After that, we made peace and they let us follow their paths. There has been no fighting since.'

Tipi nods. 'And Ama says they have a man for Bo.'

Bidari stiffens; so it is already arranged. He glances keenly at Tipi. Why did he mention Bo? Has she told someone what he did? The young man's face shows no sign.

'So they wouldn't hunt on our land?' Tipi asks.

'No.'

'But then who took the antelope?'

Bidari can only shrug his shoulders. Tipi goes on ahead, leaving him to stand staring out across the plain. Beyond the plain the marshlands begin and somewhere there, beside the river, is a ring of huts. A boy, not much older than Tipi, sleeps in one of those huts. Soon the Oak People will be called to a gathering and Bo will be joined with that boy. His unknown hands will roam over her body and whenever he wants to, he will have her.

Bo

As darkness falls, the talk is all of one thing: the antelope lying amid the reeds, butchered and headless. Instead of sitting around their own fire, the women drift into the cave, to the central hearth. Bo is uncertain whether she should follow, to sit in full view of the men. The bleeding has passed and there is enough newly-grown hair on her head to grasp between her fingers. She glances nervously at Esti then finds a place to sit, keeping her eyes down.

The strip of hide is being passed around yet again. Ikomar holds it up to the flames, hissing at the sight of the feathers with their jagged brown markings. When it is her turn, Bo passes it on, scarcely touching the unlucky thing.

At last, she hears the voice she has been listening for. Bidari's figure is at the mouth of the cave, black against the fading light of the sky. He is carrying Hua. The little girl

123

sees Bo and scrambles to get down. Bo looks away to avoid Bidari's gaze, her heart thumping. The memory of his lips on her body races through her so fast that it is almost painful, and she feels her cheeks grow hot in the darkness. Opening her arms, she buries her face in Hua's neck.

Bakar is the oldest, now that Koru has gone to the ancestors, so he is the first to speak. His sight may be almost gone, but his voice is still strong.

'What news has been brought back today?'

Everyone understands what his words mean. The women draw the younger children close and hush them. There is no-one, from the oldest to the youngest, who has not heard about the antelope carcass but the story must be told nonetheless.

'My brother will speak it out,' says Koldo.

Bo cradles Hua in her arms, rocking her gently to and fro.

'As Eshtu climbed, so we followed the tortoise trail,' Bidari begins slowly, in the lilting voice of story-telling. 'Down to the toes of the mountain. In the heat of the day, we toiled across the plain, on the path that leads to the oaks. But there, our steps were turned. It was Goi, with the eyes of a hawk, who spotted the blood on the ground. He led us on to the reed stream, where the vultures were flying, high in the sky. We raised our spears, ready to strike.' Bidari lifts his arm and holds it poised, acting out what happened. 'There, amid the reeds, we came upon the antelope – a big male, in the prime of his strength.'

Bidari pauses and Bo can feel the tension growing. She holds her breath, straining for his voice, each word like a secret between herself and him.

'The stench of death stopped us in our tracks. The antelope had fallen, but not by our spearwork!'

124

A gasp goes up from the listeners, as they feel the shock over again.

'Was it lion?' Bidari places his palms flat on the floor, one after the other, like the paws of the cat. Suddenly he is upright again. 'No! The earth said nothing of her paws, of her tail.'

'What, then?' cries Goi's son, enthralled.

Bidari's answer comes in a growl, full of menace. 'It was the work of men, hunters with sharp blades.'

There is a sharp, hissing intake of breath. Then Bidari begins to chant.

'They stole our buck.

From the land that feeds us.

They killed him by the stream of reeds.

They stole his breath from him – he did not give it.

They stole his head.'

There are groans of outrage. A baby wakes and begins to cry.

'There is more!' Bidari calls out. When they are quiet, he begins again.

'They spoke to us by what they left behind. They left the marks of their feet in the soft earth.' His voice drops. 'And they left - this.'

Bidari holds something up. Bo cannot see it clearly in the flickering light but she knows it is the strip of hide that Koldo found.

'What kind of man would wear the feathers of the quail?'

Bidari has dared to name the poisonous bird and now the air is thick with horror. He leaves the question hanging, with the strip of hide, in the smoky air. There is an uneasy shuffling.

The telling over, discussion can begin.

Koldo turns to Goi. 'You saw their tracks. Was it the Marsh People?'

Goi shrugs his shoulders. 'Our footprints and theirs were mingled. It was hard to see what the earth was saying.'

'The Marsh People would not do this,' Koldo says, and there is a murmur of assent.

Now Esti gives shape to the dread that has been lurking in the cave. 'Sakaitz?'

Bo can feel fear spreading around the circle.

'Sakaitz have never been seen on the plain.' Gashi speaks calmly and the fear begins to lift a little. 'They live in the high places. They don't come down.'

Of course, she is right. Bo was not born on the mountain but even she knows that Sakaitz have never been seen on the lowlands.

Ikomar is the next to speak. Before Nuno was injured, she used to keep quiet around the fire, but not anymore. The wound on his head closed up a long time ago and yet still Nuno has not come back to himself. He cannot understand what she says to him. He is sitting beside her now, chewing on a piece of sinew, not at all troubled by the talk of Sakaitz.

'What can we do?' Ikomar speaks out, her voice brittle with fear. 'We must do something.'

Bo can guess what is in Ikomar's thoughts. The swelling in her belly is smaller than it should be. Every morning the men go to the watching place but it is many days since they saw antelope feeding on the plain. When they go hunting, they come back with only small meat or with nothing. If the antelope are being stolen from them, the people will starve.

'But what can we do?' asks Goi. His youngest son has been sick all through the last rains. Perhaps he will not live through another winter.

'We must send someone to the marshes,' Koldo says, after a pause.

'Are we strong enough to fight the Marsh People?' Bakar breaks in.

'No, Uncle,' Koldo replies respectfully. 'Not to fight. We will send someone just to talk – perhaps they have had meat stolen too.'

'I'll go,' Goi says at once.

'Yes!' Gashi has an idea. 'And you can take the news that Bo is ready for mating.'

There are murmurs of agreement. Feeling the eyes on her, Bo hides her face in Hua's hair.

Koldo looks relieved. 'Bo is the kinswoman of Goi's sister, so it's right that he should go.' He turns to Goi. 'And while you are with them, you can speak about the antelope.'

Bo can feel the people letting out their breath; a plan has been made. But then another voice breaks in.

'But you said yourself that it couldn't be the Marsh People!' It is Bidari. The cave becomes quiet again.

'What harm can it do to send Goi?' Koldo replies, puzzled. 'He will go alone and speak carefully.'

'They will be expecting someone, anyway,' Gashi agrees. 'With news of the joining.'

'I think we should wait.' Bidari sounds strangely urgent. 'The antelope in the reed bed will have females with him. How can we track them, if Goi goes?'

There is silence as the others take in what Bidari has said. The tone of his voice feels wrong, as if there is something hidden behind the words.

'Koldo is right,' Bakar says at last. 'We must try to find out who took the antelope.'

'And there is Bo to be thought of,' Esti says. 'She must go to them, now that she is ready.'

'No!' Bidari sounds desperate.

A new thought comes slowly to Bo, like the rim of Eshtu appearing over the tip of the mountain in the morning, filling her with pleasure. *He doesn't want me to go.* Her hands begin to tremble. The silence is full of unspoken questions.

'Why?' asks Goi at last, turning to Bidari. 'Why do you say no?'

Koldo holds up his hand. 'Wait!' he commands and jumps up, hauling Bidari to his feet. All eyes are on them as Bidari follows his brother to the mouth of the cave and out into the darkness. Hua stirs in Bo's arms and she rocks the child back to sleep. She can feel eyes turning in her direction.

When Koldo reappears at the mouth of the cave the noise subsides. He strides to the hearth, Bidari behind him, his head down. Koldo turns to Esti and Bakar, though he speaks loud enough for everyone to hear.

'It is as I thought.' He sounds angry. 'My brother objects to Bo going to the Marsh People.'

'Why?' Esti demands at once, her voice shrill. 'She is promised to them.'

Bo's heart seems to stop beating. She seeks out Bidari's face, but he is staring at the ground.

'Ah.' Bakar sighs, at last. 'I see it. Bidari wants her for himself, is that it? But you have a woman,' the old man peers ahead, unseeing. 'You have Ansa.'

Bo hides her face in Hua's hair. The circle has been silent, listening intently, but now someone lets out a cry.

'Wait – I want to hear it from him.' It is Goi's voice.' Is this true?' he asks Bidari. 'Do you want her for yourself?'

Bo shrinks back still further into the shadows, straining her ears for Bidari's reply.

'Yes,' he says, then again, more defiantly. 'Yes. I want her.'

His words seem to bounce back from the rock and she gasps.

'But Bo is promised.' That is Gashi's voice. 'And what about Ansa?'

There are murmurs of agreement. Bo closes her eyes only to see the image of Ansa, alone in the shelter. She is sick with shame.

Koldo puts up a hand for quiet. His eyes sweep around the circle of faces. This concerns them all.

'It's too late.' His voice is cold. 'Bidari tells me that he has already had her.'

'Is this true, Bo?' Gashi's voice rings out in the darkness and Bo is forced to look up.

'Yes,' she whispers.

'Did he force himself on you?' Esti demands, her voice cracking with anger.

She shakes her head. 'No!' They mustn't think that of him. 'He was kind to me – he helped me down from the tree.'

There is a giggle from one of the boys and Koldo spins around, cursing under his breath. 'This is not something to laugh about,' he growls. He turns back to address them all. 'How can we send Bo to the Marsh People now?'

He takes a step towards Esti and Bakar. 'What do you say?' he asks them. 'Bo is your kinswoman and my brother has spoilt her.'

For once, Esti has nothing to say, and Bakar keeps his silence. Koldo rounds on Bidari.

'Why did you do this?' He spits out the words. 'Now, when we have enough trouble?'

A small cry escapes from Bo but her voice is drowned out by young Tipi's.

'Stop it!' he shouts at his father.

Koldo strides across to his son and stands towering above him but Tipi doesn't shrink back. Instead he makes as if to stand up and face his father.

Gashi is on her feet in a breath. She takes her husband's arm, pulling him away. 'This won't do any good,' she says. 'We need to think carefully what to do. Let him speak. Let Bidari speak.'

'Yes,' agrees Bakar. 'What do you say for yourself, Bidari?'

Bo waits, holding her breath, willing the others to keep quiet. All eyes are on Bidari.

'It was wrong to take her, when she is promised to the Marsh People,' Bidari admits, at last.

There are sounds of agreement and Bo's heart seems to fall away within her chest. They will make her go after all.

'But Bo is not my sister or the sister of any of us. Why can't she stay here?' Bidari is standing tall now, his words taking on weight. He searches out Gashi's face in the firelight.

'She is a hard worker – you always say that.' He turns to Esti. 'You've taught her well, Aunt,' he says, 'she is already like a mother to Hua.'

The old woman looks pleased. Bo senses the air around them coming alive with new thoughts. Koldo is listening hard.

'Bo – what do you have to say?' It is Bakar's voice. 'Would you be willing to sit with Bidari?'

Bo's heart overflows to the old man, who saved her once

before. 'Yes,' she says quickly, before she can think of Ansa again. The tears that have been gathering begin to roll down her cheeks.

'It will muddy the waters with the Marsh People,' Koldo says, but his anger has lost its bite.

'They would rather we did not deceive them and pass her off as unspoilt,' says Goi.

Gashi seems to agree. 'I would like Bo to stay with us,' she says after a time. 'But what about Ansa? And the baby she is carrying?'

Whenever the Oak People try to discuss Ansa, a mist seems to roll down, making it hard to see which way to take. There are so many tracks of thought, crossing and recrossing. They have sometimes tried to bring her back to the cave, but she raves and kicks at anyone who comes near. Perhaps they should stop taking food to the shelter; there is little enough to eat. But then, she is the seer. She travelled to the land of death and saw Koru there. And she has given Bidari a daughter and there is another child in her belly.

It is Goi who ventures to speak first. 'Maybe Ansa will never come back. And Bidari cannot be without a woman.'

There are murmurs of agreement.

'She is very weak. Can she survive the birth?' Bo squirms at these words. Sorne has never liked Ansa.

The feeling of the people is becoming clear. They all like Bo. She works hard and learns quickly. But Gashi is determined that Ansa should be fed and cared for.

'We cannot leave Ansa to die. Koru chose her as seer. And she may come back to herself after the baby is born.'

There is acceptance of this. At the same time, it seems right that Bidari should take Bo as his wife. Koldo's temper has cooled. Now, as usual, he is the one to weave all the thoughts together into a rope that is strong enough to use.

'Goi will go to the Marsh People to explain about Bo and to talk to them about the killing of the antelope. If Goi takes Sorne with him, they will know he comes in peace.' Goi nods at this. 'They can ask about a girl for Tipi too. That will bind us close again,' Koldo continues. He turns to Bidari.

'You can have Bo as your wife,' he says. 'And we will carry on feeding Ansa. If she and the baby live, you must bring her back to suckle the child and you must help to care for it.'

There are noises of assent and Bidari nods. Bo's body feels heavy with the happiness that is beginning to seep through it. She will sit with Bidari and share his sleeping skin and feel his hands on her body again. A new picture, too, begins to dance around the edge of her thoughts: a picture of the tiny child growing inside Ansa's belly. The child is born healthy - a boy - and Bo is rocking him in her arms.

Chapter 12

Ansa

Ansa wakes in her sleeping place, far back in the shelter, the weight of her swollen belly pressing down on her bladder. She heaves herself over, grazing an arm against the rock. It is still night but the sky is not wholly dark. If she crawled to the entrance to relieve herself, she would risk the face of Balqa, hanging low over the Salt Water, his eyes reaching in to her. Instead, she lets the piss stream out between her legs, staining the red rock.

She lies down but her blood is throbbing with heat and thirst will not let her sleep. She thinks of the trickling water of the spring, cool even in summer: cold water on her dry lips, in her throat, splashing against her skin. I'll go to the spring when he has gone, she thinks.

As the last of Balqa's glow leaves the sky, Ansa crawls cautiously to the mouth of the shelter. She scrambles over the ledge, her feet searching for the familiar footholds. Dawn is beginning to sound and she stops to listen to the cry of a warbling bird. The bird is close, perched on one of the branches that struggle out from the sheer rock face. She listens intently to every trill, each sequence of notes. Has Koru given the bird a message for her? The scream of a hawk

133

up above startles the warbler and the song ends abruptly. As if her ears have been suddenly unstopped, here comes Ama's voice from its usual place, at the back of her head. *Why would she send you a message? She knows what you did. She knows all about you.*

Ansa feels with her toes for the next foothold. Ama's voice drones on, not loud enough to really frighten her, but too loud to ignore. Now that the slew of insults has started, it will be in her head all day.

Balancing the weight of her belly, Ansa reaches the path safely and turns toward the spring. The water runs with a clean sound, almost drowning out Ama's accusing voice. Stooping, she holds her face under the flow and gulps down mouthful after mouthful of the cool water. She lets the flow trickle over her head, in her ears, on her face, running down her body.

Sudden, heavy pain slams into her back. She is forced down onto the ground by the weight of it, struggling for breath. She can't move. The pressure eases on one shoulder and someone grasps her dripping hair and pulls, forcing her head back. Hot breath on her neck. There is movement at her side and she grabs out at something that feels like toes. She digs into the flesh with her nails and there is a howl in her ear. The foot wrenches itself free and she feels a painful kick in her lower back.

Her belly begins to ache unbearably and, whimpering with pain, Ansa tries to turn. She feels a shifting of the weight on her back and a sudden freedom but then her arm is grasped and she is being pulled up hard, into a sitting position. In his other hand, the boy is holding a short spear, just a blade hafted onto a length of branch. The edge is sharp and frighteningly close to her face.

The boy releases Ansa's arm and stands back, keeping the spear pointed at her. He walks in a circle then plants himself in front of her once more, the spear still poised for an upward thrust to her throat.

Ansa can see her assailant clearly now. Beneath the dirt, his skin is strangely pale, the colour of sand instead of earth. Is he a man or just a boy? He is the height of a child but the muscle in his spear arm is hard like a man's. With each breath, the ribs show clearly over the bowl of his belly. His hair hangs down over his face and his eyes are set deep under a jutting forehead. He has a wary, taut look about him and she senses that he would not hesitate to slice her throat. Ansa cowers, waiting for his move. Balqa has seen her huddling in the shelter and sent this boy to kill her.

The only sound is water splashing over the rock. Even Ama's voice has gone quiet. At last the boy opens his mouth and speaks two words, as if demanding something, but the words make no sense. Now comes a string of sounds – perhaps a question? His body is hard with muscle, but his voice is the voice of a boy and Ansa dares to take a breath. He moves closer, thrusting the spear towards her.

Ansa whimpers with fear and a hiss of surprise escapes the boy's mouth, but he steps back a little.

'Did he send you?' she whispers.

The boy stares at her. He pushes the hair from his eyes and Ansa sees a large nose, spread flat across his face, and an odd-shaped chin. A thought flits past Ansa but is gone before she can grasp it.

He speaks again, asking her something, but his words mean nothing. When there is no reply, he bares his teeth in frustration. Frightened, Ansa holds up her hands as if to push him away. He stands staring for a few breaths, then takes a step towards her. He is still pointing the spear but, with the other hand, he clutches at his belly, all the time looking intently into her face. The boy is pointing at her now, and then at his open mouth. He wants food.

Food. Ansa's thoughts are like the strands of a tightly tangled creeper. Memories of grubbing for tubers come back to her. Where is her digging stick? She is sweating. She must get back to the shelter; the morning light is hurting her eyes. Thinking of the shelter, she remembers that there is food there, some sort of small meat, but it's old and it stinks.

'Do you want meat?' she asks.

The boy grunts. He turns his head to one side, his eyes questioning. Ansa points along the path and up towards the shelter, but he doesn't seem to understand. She gestures towards her mouth. A light seems to come into his eyes and he motions to her to get up, then jabs with his weapon in the direction of the path. Ansa struggles to her feet and takes a few steps, then turns to see if he is following. The boy is still standing by the spring. He jabs in the air again with his spear.

Ansa struggles along the path, her belly aching and pulling. The heat is bearing down and the heel of her hand aches where she tried to break her fall. There is a sharp pain low in her groin. She feels sick. At the base of the cliff, she looks back, but the boy is nowhere to be seen. She rests, breathing heavily, then climbs steadily up to safety. There is no sign of the boy on the path below. She closes her eyes, listening to the way her breathing sounds. Once again, she feels the resolute heaving inside her belly.

Terror has left her very tired. That boy by the spring. Will he always be there when she goes to drink? Perhaps he will move into her head, like Ama, muttering his strange words there. She scratches at herself, trying to dislodge the fearful thoughts but they keep unfurling all the same: crawling up her arms, along her neck and into her head. There is no escaping from them and they are in her ears now, whispering the same words over and over. *He is your brother. He has come to kill you.* Whimpering, Ansa opens her eyes. Apart from the birds crying overhead the mountain is quiet. She feels sleepy and her eyelids drop.

The sound of stones, dislodged from the rock face, wakes her. Ansa opens her eyes and lets out a piercing scream. There, in the mouth of the shelter, is the boy's face, the haft of his short spear clenched between his teeth. She backs away but the boy has already hauled himself up and is on his knees in the shelter, the spear blade pointed towards her face. He peers around, his eyes adjusting to the dim light. He crawls forward, taking in the bedding grass, the food debris, the skins Ansa used in the winter.

His eyes light on the lizards that Gashi brought the last time she came. In the searing heat of summer, the meat is now becoming putrid. The boy snatches the lizards, shakes off the flies and crouches beside the wall. He stares at Ansa, then puts the spear down and falls on the meat. Ansa watches him tearing the charred skin away, trying to get at the flesh. The lizards are small and he growls with frustration, pushing his matted hair out of the way. He seems to have forgotten that she is there. His thick fingers are unable to do the fine work of teasing out the morsels of meat. Instead, he stuffs one of the lizards into his mouth, whole, along with the maggots. Ansa can hear the bones snapping under his teeth. The boy spits out the skin and bones and then picks at his chipped teeth.

He is giving all his attention to eating and Ansa forgets to be frightened of the boy. When he has finished, he doesn't pick up the spear again, or even look at her. Instead, he leans against the wall, resting. Now that his face is relaxed, it is clear that he is not yet fully grown. Maybe he will not kill her, after all.

After a time, the boy picks up his weapon and, clenching the haft between his teeth, he crawls to the edge of the shelter and turns, ready to climb down. He looks at Ansa and tries to say something, then he is gone. Ansa leans out to watch him climb down, agile on the cliff face. Back on level ground, he stands listening, then leaves the path, scrambling down the mountain between the scrub bushes. Soon he is out of sight.

Ansa stares out until the afternoon wind begins to breathe cooler air. The boy's face in the mouth of the shelter comes to her again and again, the blade of his spear glinting. Teeth tearing at the meat. Lizard bones cracking in his mouth. Slowly, the word that has been hiding in the shadows creeps out into the light, making the skin on her neck prickle. *Sakaitz.* Could he be a wild boy, like the people in the stories?

Eshtu drops below the Salt Water and the sky grows dark and still Ansa cannot forget the boy. But now he seems more like a shadow. Perhaps it was in a dream that he came to her. The darkness outside grows less dense – she can make out the shapes of trees below. Balqa is stalking the sky once more and Ansa draws back, away from the mouth of the shelter. She crawls to her sleeping place to settle but her back aches. A bitter taste keeps coming into her mouth and a burning pain and she has to sit up to relieve it. The living thing inside her belly heaves and kicks and Ama pipes up again, her voice full of cruelty. *What would you do with a baby? You'd only kill it.* Ansa covers her ears but now that Ama has started, she will be in her head all through the night.

Bidari

It will soon be growing dark but Bidari cannot bring himself to move. He is lying on his back under the oak, his head in Bo's lap. The pressure of her fingers on his scalp is soothing, as she teases out the tiny lice eggs from his hair. He begins to sing softly. After a time, Bo grows bored and her face appears, upside down, in front of him, lips parted in a smile. Her nipple brushes his ear and immediately he is hard again and he rolls over, pulling her down beneath him.

She pushes him away, giggling, and springs to her feet. Bidari laughs. Bo is quick and agile but he will catch her in the end and then she will be flushed and hot and ready for him. He lunges after her but she is away, running up the slope. He sets off in pursuit but, up ahead, he sees her stop dead still. He covers the distance between them easily and grabs her from behind but she pushes him away.

'Listen!' she says. 'Someone's coming.'

Bidari looks up to see Koldo on the path above them.

'Bidari! I've been looking for you. Goi's back.'

Bidari scrambles up to join his brother, signalling for Bo to follow. Koldo is already striding back along the path and Bidari has to run to catch up with him.

'What happened? What did the Marsh People say?'

Koldo doesn't answer. Instead, he turns to Bidari, his eyes narrowing.

'Did you lie with her – just now?'

Bidari laughs. 'Of course I did. Why – are you jealous?'

Koldo clicks his disapproval. 'It's not lucky. Tomorrow, you will have to kill.'

'Why, are we going hunting?'

Koldo only shakes his head and, all at once, a darker thought comes to Bidari.

'Not the Marsh People... Was it them? Did they steal our antelope?'

'No. It wasn't them. We've agreed to take one of their girls for Tipi. In return, her brothers have come back with Goi and they will fight alongside us tomorrow.'

Bidari comes to a halt, trying to make sense of his brother's words, but Koldo strides on.

'Hurry!' he calls. 'It'll be dark soon and we've got a lot to do. We must set off for the heights as soon as it's light.'

The heights. Bidari's heart seems to drop into his belly. He glances back at the figure of Bo. From here she looks very young and small. He feels his love for her as if it were a wound.

Bidari runs to catch up with Koldo. He shrinks from saying the name, but he has to be sure. 'Sakaitz?'

Koldo nods. 'It must have been them. If they've started coming down the mountain to hunt, we have no choice.'

Bidari understands now why Koldo's face is so dark. 'Are we strong enough?' he asks.

Koldo considers this. 'The longer we let them live and take our meat, the weaker we will become. Now is the right time, while Balqa is in his strength.'

They walk the rest of the way in silence. Bidari is thinking of the last time they hunted on the high mountain, but then it was only goats they were stalking. He shivers, remembering the monstrous figure he saw in the firelight. And Nuno, lying silent on the mountainside, blood seeping from the gash on his head.

Bo

It is growing dark by the time Bo rounds the bluff but she can make out the figure of Goi, sitting by one of the outside hearths, shaping a blade. She calls out to welcome him home. There is another man working beside him – a stranger. She climbs up to the cave mouth and hesitates. Everything seems different. There is a fire in every hearth and the flame light is making unfamiliar patterns on the walls of the cave. Everyone is at work, as if it were daytime, and the thought comes to Bo that perhaps they are preparing for a trek to the Salt Water. But there is no excited chatter and the drums are silent.

Bo begins to feel frightened. Bidari and Koldo are squatting beside a second stranger, talking quietly. Tipi goes to join them, dropping down to the floor, close to his uncle. There is a pile of spears on the ground beside them, as if they plan to go hunting. Koldo has taken one up and is showing it to the stranger. The heads of the men are close in talk and so Bo goes to the women's hearth where Gashi is grinding kho, but not the everyday brown one. A chill passes through her. Why is Gashi mixing death red?

'What's happening? Who are those men?' she asks.

'Two brothers, from the Marsh People,' Esti replies. 'And we have nothing to offer them to eat.'

Bo turns to Gashi, who sits tight-lipped, mixing the red powder with water.

'Why are you making that?' Bo asks. 'Is someone sick?'

141

Gashi looks up. 'For tomorrow,' she says, her voice sharp. 'The men are going to the high mountain.'

'To hunt?' Bo thinks of the succulent goat meat they brought back last winter.

'No. They are going to fight.'

Bo feels the strength draining from her body. No-one lives on the mountain ridge, where food is scarce and in winter there is snow. Only Sakaitz live there. A small whimpering sound escapes from her throat.

Gashi is picking her way across the cave floor to the knot of men and Bo follows. She feels the eyes of the stranger on her body and starts to blush, but Gashi ignores his presence.

'We must consult Ansa,' Gashi says firmly to the men. 'Before you go. What if it was not Sakaitz who took the antelope, and you provoke them for no reason?'

Koldo's face clouds over with anger at the interruption but she takes no notice. 'Bidari – will you go to her?'

Bo can feel Bidari squirming, like he always does when anyone talks of Ansa.

'It's late.' Koldo says. 'We have preparations to make.' Pointedly, he turns his back on Gashi.

She opens her mouth to argue, then thinks better of it. 'Bo and I will go,' she exclaims.

'Where? To the shelter?'

'Yes. We need Ansa to journey for us.'

'But how will we find our way? It's dark.' Bo is frightened. *Can Ansa really see things that are hidden? Does she know that I have taken her place beside Bidari?*

Gashi takes a long branch of firewood and places one end in the flames. Esti looks up from her grinding.

'What are you doing?'

142

'We're going to the shelter, Aunt. We need a torch – it's black dark outside.'

'You're going to Ansa? Has her time come, then?'

'Not yet, but we have something to ask her. Will you mix the kho, Aunt? Ikomar and Sorne can paint the men.'

Gashi turns to Bo. 'Hurry,' she says. 'We don't have long before the torch burns down.'

After the brightness of the cave, the night is very dark. Gashi holds the torch low and, coughing from the smoke, they manage to follow the path.

'How will we see to climb up?' Bo asks.

They reach the cliff face by the shelter, just as Gashi is forced to drop the branch. The last flames gutter on the path and then are extinguished. The sudden black is overwhelming. Terror creeps in Bo's belly but then the surface of the rising cliff begins to show itself. Fat and healthy, Balqa has begun his climb through the sky.

Gashi goes ahead, feeling for footholds. There is a scream from inside the shelter as they clamber onto the ledge. Inside, Ansa is cowering by the back wall, jabbering with fear. Gashi crawls toward her, but Bo pulls her back; it is better not to go too close.

'Shh, Ansa, don't be afraid.' Gashi tries to keep her voice calm.

'Don't be afraid, don't be afraid,' Ansa chants, rocking to and fro.

Gashi turns to Bo, her eyes pleading for help, and in a place beneath her fear, Bo's heart sings. She edges slowly forward on her buttocks, then waits before slowly putting out her hand. Ansa's hand comes out to meet hers and clings to it like a child's. Her skin is warm and tears begin to gather at

143

the back of Bo's eyes. Ansa is still muttering quietly.

'Is the baby growing?' Bo reaches out to touch Ansa's belly. It is hard and round as a nut, but when she presses her hand against it, Ansa squeals in pain.

'Shh…it's all right. It's all right.' Bo waits for a breath, then speaks again. 'Listen - Gashi has something to ask you.'

'Ansa.' Gashi has crawled forward. 'Ansa – can you hear me?' The muttering stops. 'Listen. This is very important. The men are going to the mountain top - to fight. Is it the right time?'

Silence. Gashi tries again. 'What do you see? Is it the right time for killing?'

Ansa's eyes stray to the mouth of the shelter and she shakes her head emphatically. 'Too strong,' she says, putting up her hands, as if to protect her eyes.

'What do you mean?' asks Gashi.

Ansa leans forward and speaks almost like her old self, her voice urgent.

'He is too strong – wait till he is weaker.'

Gashi searches out Bo's face, her eyes begging for understanding. 'Does she mean they shouldn't go?'

'I think she is talking about Balqa,' Bo whispers.

'Shh,' hisses Ansa. 'He'll hear you.'

Bo can feel rather than see Gashi's eyes on her. She must think of something to distract Ansa from her fear of Balqa.

'Are you hungry?' Bo asks. 'Did you eat the meat we brought?'

Ansa shakes her head but Gashi has found the remnants of bone and skin on the floor. 'She did eat it – look.'

Ansa reaches out to pick up a piece of charred lizard skin. In the soft light, Bo sees a look of wonder and fear come over her face. 'Sakaitz,' she whispers.

Gashi is excited. 'Ansa – can you see something? Can you see Sakaitz?'

Ansa's eyes dart to the mouth of the cave and back. 'With a spear – like this.' She clenches her teeth and holds two fingers like a spear shaft, across her mouth. She begins to whimper. 'Sakaitz.'

Gashi takes hold of both Ansa's hands and peers into her face. 'You see Sakaitz – with a spear? Listen, Ansa, was it them - did they take our meat?'

Bo holds her breath, waiting for the answer.

'Yes,' Ansa says, wonderingly. She shudders. 'Flies and maggots – everything.'

Gashi grabs Bo's arm. 'The carcass! She can see the carcass.'

'Everything - even the head.' Ansa is talking to herself. She seems horrified.

'That's right!' says Gashi. 'They took the head. And you're sure it's Sakaitz?'

Ansa is staring straight ahead and she begins to whimper again. 'Sakaitz. Waiting at the spring.'

'She means the stream – they took the antelope by the stream!' Gashi is triumphant. 'Come on, Bo. Let's go back and tell them.'

Gashi touches Ansa's forehead with her fingers, something like awe visible in her eyes. Then she edges back towards the mouth of the shelter and begins to climb down. Bo hesitates. She doesn't want to walk back alone but it hurts her to leave Ansa like this.

'Don't be afraid. I'll come again soon,' she says.

'Don't be afraid, don't be afraid...' chants Ansa.

Bo crawls away. Before starting to climb down, she takes a

last look back. Ansa is rocking herself once more, backwards and forwards.

Chapter 13

Ansa

It is getting late. The afternoon salt wind blows in, refreshing the stale air of the shelter for a time, but then it drops and the stifling heat returns. Ansa has been waiting and waiting, but there is no sign of the boy called Mul. She checks the vine leaves once more. They are there, in his place, and tucked inside them is the best thing of all, the precious spray of purple fruit she found. But the leaves are growing limp and soft.

Once Balqa's waning face has dropped from the sky, she will be free again to go to the spring. She prods her belly carefully. It has been sore ever since the boy jumped her to the ground. Her mouth feels as if it is full of dry sticks. One day, Mul took her bowl and climbed down to fetch water for her. She watched him carry it back along the path, pretending to spill it, his lips parted in a grin over his big teeth.

Ansa edges forward and starts tapping her fingers on the floor, one after the other, beginning with her little finger. She is trying to guess which is the finger for Mul. She stops and opens her eyes. Her pointing finger is touching the ground. Holding it there, she peers out one more time, scanning the path below. She has chosen the right one! There is the squat figure of Mul, loping towards the cliff face. But something is wrong. He is clutching at his arm, which hangs in an odd way beside his body, the hand turned outwards. At the bottom of the cliff, he is no longer in her view and she waits, impatient to see his smile when he finds the vine fruit. His face appears, creased up, in the mouth of the shelter. He is whimpering in pain.

'What is it?' she asks.

Mul's answer makes no sense and Ansa is irritated. Sometimes they can understand each other using signs and then they both laugh. Mul is pulling himself up onto the ledge with one arm and Ansa can see that the other one is useless. Rather than going to his place, he crawls towards her, pointing to his shoulder. He looks into her face intently.

'What?' she repeats.

'Onsa! Onsa!' No matter how many times she tells him, he cannot say her name properly. He is pointing at her now and pulling at his bad arm. She stares at him, puzzled. Then he lies down on his back and tugs her foot towards his armpit.

All at once, Ansa understands what he wants her to do. She has seen someone do it before. Leaning back against the rock she puts her foot into Mul's damp armpit. Then she grabs hold of his bad arm. Taking a deep breath, she pushes hard with her foot and pulls on his arm. Mul yells out in pain. Nothing happens and he motions to her to try again. Ansa braces herself, pushing and pulling as hard as she can. The tenderness in her swollen belly flames into a sharp pain but then, suddenly, she feels the movement in his socket, and the joint slides back into place.

Mul sits up, rubbing his shoulder. He is pale but he crawls to his place, grinning. The pain has not blunted his appetite.

He snatches up the leaves and stuffs them into his mouth then, with a grunt of pleasure, discovers the fruit underneath. Cradling herself and rocking, Ansa watches with satisfaction as he sucks the grapes one by one off the stem, oblivious to her now.

The effort of pulling his shoulder back into joint has tired her and the pain in her belly grumbles on. After a time, she feels something trickling from between her legs and, looking down, sees bright red blood on the rock. She glances out at the sky. Very soon now, Balqa will be gone and it will be safe to go down to the spring. When she gets back, Mul will be asleep.

Bidari

Bidari turns over on the rough ground and wakes, a cool early morning wind on his face. For half a breath, he is confused. Then the memory of why he is here on the high mountain thumps back, like a sudden sickening blow to his belly. He sits up. The others are still asleep, except for the two brothers from the marshlands, who squat in the shadows by the fire, keeping watch. They are speaking together in low voices. Now they turn and Apal acknowledges him with a nod. The younger of the two, Apal is the more talkative one, quick but small boned. Bidari has higher hopes of his brother, Eneko, who is as tall as Koldo, with broad muscular shoulders and a hard face.

Apal moves around the circle, waking the others, and soon Goi is squatting on the ground with the brothers, marking out a route. Bidari shivers as he thinks of the far face of the mountain, so different from their own gentle slopes. The ground falls away steeply on that side, all the way to a huge flat plain. It is said that there are small caves amongst the pines, just below the ridge, and that Sakaitz shelter there. Bidari wonders how many there will be. Just two or three males, perhaps, the rest females and children. He remembers the night the goat was stolen: the swarthy figure in the firelight, the bulge of muscle as he lifted his arm. Bidari feels his bowels cramp, then loosen, and he gets up quickly to find a place to shit.

When he comes back, Koldo is stamping out the fire. Tipi sits, arms clasped across his chest, his young face pale. Bidari wants to say something but his own fear is squeezing at his throat.

At last, Goi beckons them over. Bidari has tied his short spear to his belt and, once again, he tests the sharpness of the blade with his finger. He joins the others, nudging Tipi as he passes, but the boy does not respond. Suddenly, Tipi gets to his feet, lurching away towards the bushes, and soon there comes the sound of vomiting.

It feels better when they make the circle, sitting close and sharing the warmth of their bodies. The wind is cold at this height, even in summer.

'If we start out now, we might catch them sleeping,' Koldo ventures.

Goi goes to his pack and takes out some dried pear, but none of the others can eat.

'Take this,' Apal says and, opening the bag at his belt, he passes round some dry finger-shaped leaves.

'What is it?' Bidari is suspicious.

'It's gaat – it will give you courage.'

Apal brings the water bowl and places it in the centre of the circle. 'Sprinkle water on your leaf – just a little, to dampen it.' The men do as he says. 'Now put it in your mouth.'

Bidari watches the bulge in Apal's cheek as he works the leaf with his tongue.

'Don't eat! Just chew it,' he says and then, spitting onto his hand, he shows them the green foam. 'Swallow the spit, and soon you will be ready to fight.'

Bidari looks at Koldo uncertainly, but he is already chewing. Bidari puts the leaf into his mouth and softens it with his tongue. The taste is bitter.

'Remember,' says Goi. 'When we get to the ridge, keep silent - just like a hunt.'

Bidari closes his eyes, trying to see himself attacking the Sakaitz. No picture will come.

'How far – before we get to their cave?'

Goi shrugs his shoulders. 'Go quietly and watch for the smoke of their fire,' he replies.

Koldo nods. 'We'll split up. Tipi can stay above and throw rocks on them as they come out.'

'No! I'll fight them face to face,' Tipi protests, but then he notices that the big stranger, Eneko, is smirking. Colour spreads up Tipi's neck.

Koldo glances across at the slight figure of the younger brother, weighing up the risk of offending him. 'Will you attack from above, with Tipi?'

To Koldo's relief, Apal does not argue but just nods his assent. 'Eneko and I will go in first – then Bidari and Goi can follow,' Koldo continues.

'What about the females? And the children?' Tipi asks.

There is an uneasy silence. It is Apal who speaks at last, his voice low. 'If they were stealing from *my* people, we would kill them all.'

151

Goi seems to agree with Apal. 'The females are as strong as the males and they hunt along with them.'

'What about their young?' Bidari insists. He looks from face to face but only Tipi will meet his gaze.

'I think we must take them all,' says Koldo quietly, 'even the young ones hunt and use weapons.' He turns to Bidari. 'If we spare the cubs, they will only die a worse death.' His eyes pass round the circle, taking in each man in turn. 'Agreed?'

They all give their assent, but a picture has come to Bidari, a picture of Bo holding Hua against her soft breast. He feels sick.

A silence falls over them, too heavy to be borne. But then Koldo is up on his feet and yelling at the others.

'Come on! Get up!' He kicks out at Tipi, then turns on the others. 'Get moving! You're like old women huddled round the fire!'

Shaking his head so that the hair falls down over his face, he starts to tug and tear at it with his hands, till it stands up from his head in a tangled mess. The others are frightened but excited by the wild man who has appeared in front of them.

'What's wrong with you?' he yells. 'Are you afraid to fight?'

Apal springs up and copies Koldo, tearing at his hair. Bidari joins in and soon they are all on their feet, calling and whooping like a pack of hyena. Goi starts to laugh uncontrollably as, before his eyes, the others turn into madmen. Their skin is red with kho and now they are down on all fours, taking up handfuls of earth and smearing each other, grinding the fragments of rock into their skin till they draw real blood.

Liquid fire seems to be flowing through Bidari's limbs. He

will be the one to find the cave of the enemy, the first to spill their blood. He, alone, will kill them all. Taking his long spear in his hand, he thrusts it against the ground and springs into the air. The others form a circle around the spent hearth and join with him in the dance of death, jumping higher and higher. Bidari's voice rises above the shouts of the others.

'Kill them!' he chants. 'Kill them! Kill them!'

By the time they reach the ridge, it is light and Bidari's muscles are ready to burst with heat. He longs to get there, to crash through the trees at full pelt, screaming. To take them unawares, to thrust his spear into flesh and see the blood flow. It is becoming torture to creep along silently behind Goi.

At last, Tipi spots a coil of smoke between the trees to their left. The men stop dead. Bidari's heart is pounding so hard, he can feel it in his ears. Goi signals and they drop to a squat, though the trees on the ridge screen them from view. He creeps closer to the edge and scans the rocky decline, studded with pines, looking for a way down. Soon he rejoins them.

'It's very steep,' he whispers. 'We must move quietly. I can't see how they get to the cave mouth from here.'

Koldo's head is turned to one side. He is thinking. 'Goi – you go down and we'll follow. Look for a place with cover, above the cave.'

He glances round at Eneko and Apal, looking for their approval. Bidari sees the look and kicks out savagely at a pine cone. Why does he only care what the strangers think?

Tipi takes out his axe. He looks terrified.

'Not yet,' hisses Bidari. The boy is stupid. 'You'll need your hands to climb down.'

Tipi's face flushes with colour through the brown skin. His

153

eyes look strange: wide open and very black.

It is good to be following the familiar figure of Goi, just as if they were hunting antelope. He leads them from one pine to the next, half scrambling, half sliding down. Underfoot, sharp white rocks hide treacherously beneath the soft covering of pine needles. They move as quietly as they can but more than once Goi stops dead, hissing at the noise of their descent.

Further down, an acrid smell of smoke reaches their nostrils. Bidari's breath is coming fast. Up ahead, Goi raises his hand. A break in the trees reveals a steep path snaking down the mountainside to their left, following the easier slopes. They have climbed down on steep ground alongside the path and must have been very close to the cave without knowing it. Goi sinks to the ground, his body taut with danger. Lower down the slope, the tree cover is sparse and the mountain seems to drop down in steep steps - one rocky outcrop below another. Goi waits, listening. The silence confuses him. Eshtu is climbing fast; why can they not hear voices? Surely the Sakaitz are not still sleeping.

Koldo drops to the ground, easing himself down the slope on his buttocks. When he reaches Goi, they whisper together and Goi points down to the right, where the pines grow close. Koldo crawls back up to where the others crouch, under cover. They watch, their breath mingling, as Goi slowly moves off towards the trees, keeping close to the ground.

'He will be able to see the cave mouth from there,' Koldo whispers.

It is all Bidari can do to keep still and silent, while they wait. The smell of pine resin is in his nostrils and he remembers Nuno, crumpled on the ground, blood on his cheek. The urge to avenge him is like a living thing thrashing around in his guts, trying to find a way out. At last comes a crackling of twigs and Goi reappears beside the pines below. He is standing in the open, calling to them. Without stopping to wonder why he is not keeping cover, Bidari jumps up and is beside Goi in a few breaths, the others just behind him.

'What is it?' Bidari asks.

Goi's face is pale with shock and when he speaks, it is not a low hunting whisper. 'They're dead!'

The men look at each other, trying to understand. Koldo is the first to respond. 'All of them? How many?'

'I don't know... hyena have been here.' Goi tries to remember, using his fingers to count. 'There were skulls - maybe one hand of skulls – some of them were not full grown.'

'Did you go into the cave?' Koldo asks.

'No. Everything is quiet. They're all dead – outside. Bones lying there - the flesh is gone...' Goi shivers.

'Come on!' calls Apal, starting off through the trees with his brother.

'Wait! What about the smoke?' Tipi cries.

Koldo exchanges a silent look with Goi, then follows the strangers. They break through the pines, out into the open and the bright heat of Eshtu. There is a faint, sour odour on the air. They follow the path round a bend and Tipi suddenly pulls up short, so that Bidari slams into his back. The men stand motionless, silent, trying to take in what their eyes are telling them. It is hard to tell how big the cave is inside; the mouth is a long wide slit in the rocky outcrop. The stench comes again, stronger now.

On the steep rocky slope running down from the cave, handaxes and short spears lie where they were dropped, amid what looks like crumpled bed skins. Bidari edges closer to the nearest heap. Hooped white rib bones lie exposed to the sky, like the carcass of an antelope. Then he sees the head: a mat of hair lying across the cheek bones, flies clustering around the last vestiges of flesh which still cling there. The eye sockets are empty. Some tiny movement catches his eye. In the chest cavity of the Sakaitz, a number of fat white larvae crawl amongst a sea of black beetles.

Just then, two dark shapes, one after the other, swoop down from the blue morning sky and come to rest higher up the slope. Almost before their wings have folded, the curved beaks of the dirty white vultures are pecking at the remains of another white corpse, lying just outside the cave mouth. His eyes drawn to the flurry of the birds, Bidari catches sight of a wisp of smoke curling through the mouth of the cave. Fire! There must be someone still alive.

He turns to call the others but then comes a sound. He can taste the fear in his mouth as they all run back to the cover of the trees. Though muffled, there is no mistaking the sound - it was someone shouting. Now comes the clatter of stick against stone up near the cave mouth and the vultures reluctantly lift into the air, returning to their meal as soon as it is quiet again. The stick can only have been thrown from inside the cave.

The men squat amidst the pine needles, breathing heavily.

'Some of them are still alive,' gasps Koldo.

'What happened?' Tipi whispers. 'How did they die?' But Koldo only shrugs impatiently.

'Could it be sickness?' Apal suggests.

Goi is adamant. 'They were being attacked! Didn't you see the weapons?'

'Who attacked them? Who could it be?' Bidari asks.

There is no time to try to bend their thoughts to answer that question. For the first time, Apal's brother, big Eneko, speaks up. 'What are we waiting for? Let's go inside and finish them off.'

Bidari's guts seem to leap up into his throat. The time has come. The men climb up the slope, keeping to the steep ground off the path so as not to be seen. At the top, they press themselves against the rock, to the side of the cave mouth. Bidari unhooks his spear, adjusting its familiar weight in his sweating palm till the heavy blade tip is in balance. His other hand tightens over the haft of his thrusting spear. He looks round at the bodies of the others, smeared with dried blood, hair wild and matted with mud. He tries to rouse the killing lust again but now the fear is a heavy stone in the pit of his belly, weighing him down.

They burst through the opening, their cry desecrating the morning quiet. At once, they are enveloped in darkness. Close beside him, Eneko trips over something on the floor – another corpse – knocking Bidari's throwing spear from his hand. Bidari passes the haft of his short spear to his right palm, his eyes darting, trying to pierce the gloom. A thin trail of smoke rises from the dim glow in the hearth. He thinks that he can see Goi over by the wall.

'Nothing here!'

Bidari can tell from the sound that the cave does not extend far upwards – maybe not far back either. At last, his eyes begin to show him the shape of the space. There is something by the back wall and Bidari makes for it, his blade held out in front of him. It is only the ash heap, riddled with bones and debris. Koldo is somewhere behind him, shouting.

Just then, Bidari's eye catches movement in the ash heap. A rat? Pulling away some of the debris, he thrusts the blade of his hand spear into the pile. There is a loud cry and, suddenly, the whole ash heap is heaving.

'Koldo - here!' Bidari shouts.

His heart is drumming in his ears and he is suddenly full of strength. He grabs at something - a flailing arm – and pulls with all his might. A man's shoulders, a head, appear from the heap. The whites of his eyes shine out from an ash grey face. The mouth is open, twisted in pain. As the other arm goes up to protect his face, the flesh of the chest is exposed and Bidari draws back his spear hand, ready to thrust. But Koldo is beside him now, restraining him. Bidari fights to get at the Sakaitz.

'Wait!' shouts Goi.

Bidari can hear the man panting with fear. The mist in front of his eyes begins to clear and he realizes that Koldo is trying to loosen his grasp on the man's arm. Bidari lets go and Goi pulls the man's hands behind his back and ties them together at the wrists. He has no weapon. Together, they drag him clear of the ash heap and push him up against the wall. He cries out in pain. A trickle of bright blood is forming on one shoulder but, as soon as his right leg emerges, Bidari knows that this is the cause of his agony.

There is a gash on the top of his thigh – slashed perhaps by a hand axe. Through the layer of ash, Bidari can see that the wound is not new; the ridges of skin are beginning to reach together, but the leg looks bad. Swollen and hanging at the wrong angle, it is clear that the thigh bone is broken. The man's leg seems very long and the foot is slender. Bidari's eyes flash up to the man's narrow face, the fine, high cheekbones, the nostrils small like his own. Now he understands why Koldo stopped him. This is no Sakaitz. This is a man like himself, a man the colour of earth.

They are all crowding round now, peering at the man. His face is screwed up with pain but his eyes, birdlike, dart from face to face.

'Lima – ta?' he gasps, then waits, as if he is expecting an answer. The men look at one another, uncomprehending. He tries again. 'Nia a tas. Alacu?' His eyes shift desperately from face to face.

'What is he doing here?' Apal is the one to voice the question. 'He's not Sakaitz.'

'Sakaitz!' The man leans forward excitedly, nodding. Then he moves his head from side to side, rolling his eyes up, then down, taking in the whole of the cave. 'Sakaitz. Kill. Sakaitz.'

'He knows our words!' Tipi cries.

The man is silent but his eyes never leave their faces. It seems to Bidari that the fear in them is no longer quite so intense.

'Untie him.' It is Eneko who speaks and, when no-one disagrees, Goi loosens the sinew binding his wrists.

As soon as he has the use of his hands, the man points at his chest, saying 'People. Kill Sakaitz.' He peers up at them urgently, as if his eyes could bore a hole into their thoughts.

'His people!' Tipi says. 'They attacked the Sakaitz!'

The man turns to Tipi and nods, again and again. 'Yes, yes!'

Koldo is standing with his head to one side. Finding a man in the cave of the Sakaitz has unsettled them. That and the way he speaks, the way he looks at them as if he can see what they are thinking.

'Kep?' he says now. 'Kep?' He points at each of them in

turn, repeating the question. They look at each other, puzzled. Then he begins to trace his finger across his own forehead, right around the back of his head and to the front again. 'Head?' he asks. 'Head?'

Apal points to his own chest and speaks clearly to the stranger. 'Apal.'

'Apal?' the man repeats, excited, 'Head?'

Koldo breaks in. 'Don't give him your names!'

But first Goi, then the others, are pointing at themselves and saying their names. Koldo hesitates, scowling, but at last he does the same.

'Head?' the man asks once more but when the others just look blankly at one another, he shakes his head and smiles. When they have finished, he points to his own chest.

'Lotz,' he says.

Bidari is the first to give the sign of greeting: making a fist with his right hand against his heart, then opening his hand towards the stranger. The man – Lotz - copies him carefully, his mouth breaking into a wide grin. One by the one, the others greet the stranger. Tipi is laughing now and soon they are all joining in as they understand at last that they will not have to fight. Those who stole their meat are lying dead on the rocky floor or outside, under the morning sky.

'Water!' The man's voice is hoarse and only just audible among the laughter.

Goi passes the water skin to Bidari and he squats beside the stranger who takes long, desperate draughts. Some of the water dribbles down his chin and Bidari notices that, under the ashdust, the stranger's skin is darker than his own.

When he has finished drinking, Koldo tries questioning him again. 'Your people killed the Sakaitz?' Koldo points first

160

to Lotz, then to the corpse that lies near the cave mouth.

'Yes.' The man leans forward, trying to focus on Koldo, but he seems to be in pain. He counts the fingers of one hand and then two more from the other. 'Many days,' he says weakly.

'Where are they now?' asks Apal. 'Your people – where?'

The man lifts his head with an effort, and shakes it from side to side. 'Gone.'

'They left you behind?' Bidari asks, but the man only looks puzzled.

'You!' Bidari points at his chest, then describes the walls of the cave with his hand. 'Left here?'

Lotz nods, then points to his bad leg. He makes as if to lie flat on the ground, his palms facing up, his mouth open. 'Dead,' he says.

'They thought he was dead! That's why they left him behind,' exclaims Apal.

'How has he survived this long?' Goi whispers to Koldo.

Bidari walks over to the hearth. It is not wood that is burning, but a few pine cones and what looks like the remains of a cured skin. amid the ashes, he finds some small bones, perhaps those of a rat. He looks towards the cave mouth, to the rotting remains of the Sakaitz which lie there. Here, in the cool cave, the corpse still has a covering of flesh, though it is alive with ants and flies. Not now, but a few days ago, there would have been flesh worth eating there, if you were hungry enough. Bidari's gorge rises at the thought of it.

The man is tearing ravenously at some dried meat Goi has given him. Koldo and the others pull back and squat down together near the cave mouth.

'We'll have to carry him down the mountain,' Goi is saying. 'We can make a litter.'

'Wait,' interrupts Koldo. 'What if the bone doesn't grow together? He won't be able to hunt. Maybe he won't even walk.'

'But we can't leave him here, to die!' exclaims Tipi.

'He will die anyway,' retorts his father, 'if the wound goes bad. And he will be another mouth to feed.'

Bidari thinks about this. And about Nuno, back with the women, unable to fight or hunt. Is Koldo right? But they have given the stranger food and drink. And they have given him the gift of their names.

'Tipi's right,' he says quickly. 'We should…'

'Apal!' The voice of the stranger, calling from the back of the cave, cuts Bidari short. 'Apal!'

'Wait!' Koldo rasps. The voice falls silent.

'Eneko will help to carry him,' Apal suggests. They all look towards the big man and he nods his head.

'But it's our people who will have to feed and care for him, not yours,' Koldo breaks in, testily. He turns to Goi. 'What do you think?'

'His people think he is dead. They won't come back for him,' Goi answers. 'If we leave him here, it will be the same as taking his life.'

There is silence for a time, then Koldo takes a deep breath.

'You are right,' he says, at last. 'This man's people have killed our enemies. We will take him back with us.'

Chapter 14

Ansa

Climbing back up to the shelter with the pain twisting in her belly is almost beyond Ansa's strength. She stops to rest. The birds are calling overhead and she dares a darting glance up but Balqa has slunk away at last, leaving the sky clean and empty. Only his brother Eshtu remains, a stone of fire sinking into the great water, and he is harmless. Ansa reaches the ledge at last and hauls herself onto it. She calls out to Mul, but there is no reply. The shelter is empty. The spear twists cruelly once more and, with the pain, comes more blood from between her legs, forming a red pool on the rock.

Brushing her fingers across the wall in thanks, Ansa rests her aching back against it. Her body becomes quiet but a question twists in and out of her thoughts. Why is the pain different this time? She remembers leaning against the birthing rock all night, waiting for that other baby to fight its way out. She remembers Bo's face, peering up into hers. *It's a girl.* Ansa closes her eyes against the thought of Hua.

This pain is much sharper – a spear twisting again and again in the wound of her belly. It comes again, the mound under her stretched skin tightening to rock. She bites the end of each finger, one after the other: her left hand, then her

163

right. At last, her belly begins to soften but with the softening, more blood leaks from her puti.

Ama's voice is back. *You see?*

A dark mist of dread closes over her. But, this time, Ama is not talking to her, but to Gashi. *I told you this would happen. She's killed the baby. There's his blood, on the ground.*

An eagle flies past the mouth of the shelter, his outspread wings black against the soft gold of the sky. Ansa moistens her lips with her tongue. She has never known such thirst, not even in the desert. But then the pain comes again and she braces herself against the wall. This time she forgets Ama and Gashi and screams out, her voice folding back on itself in the small space, as if someone else were screaming at her. Ansa whimpers with fear as an answering sound comes from deep inside her secret parts. It is like the first heavy raindrop when it falls into the wadi and, sure enough, soon there is water gushing from between her legs onto the floor of the shelter. Ansa is so thirsty that she dips her fingers in the wet and sucks them. The water is red like the juice of vine fruit, but it tastes sour.

She feels sick, the child like a heavy stone in the pit of her belly, pressing down, always down. When the next pain comes, she tries to push the stone out but stars cross in front of her eyes and the floor of the shelter comes up to meet her. The weight inside doesn't budge but with each hardening of her belly, comes a trickle of blood. Straining to be rid of the stone, the throbbing in her temples grows worse. Now there is a weight outside too, pressing down on her head, as if the mountain itself is about to collapse and crush her. Sweat breaks out on her forehead. Her hands and feet are like ice – no longer attached to her body.

The hardening comes again and Ansa clenches her teeth and pushes with all her strength, the blood pulsing painfully in her ears. As she feels herself dropping down into a dark hole, there comes a loosening inside. She knows nothing until the next pain and with that comes a wet sound, as the child slithers out onto the rocky floor. There is blood everywhere. Ansa tries to pick up the baby but it is slippery and she is shaking. Its skin feels so warm to her icy fingers.

'It's alive,' she blurts out. 'It isn't dead.' But there is no answer. Perhaps Ama has gone away.

With a great effort, she manages to lift it up and lay it on her breast. It wriggles under her hand and makes small gulping sounds.

'Cry!' she whispers to it, with the last of her breath. 'Cry!'

Faint and weak, she leans back against the wall. *When will Bo come?* Slowly, steadily, the ice is creeping up from Ansa's hands and feet into her body. Her eyes close. The baby slides out of her hands, across her belly and onto the ground.

Ansa looks down at the hunched figure of the woman, her head resting motionless on her chest. The sky is growing light and the rocky floor of the shelter is slick with blood. Outside, birds are greeting the new day but, inside, everything is still and peaceful. The only sounds are the tiny breaths of the baby boy, who lies on his back beside the woman, his legs and arms gently weaving the air, his face working. He must be newly born, Ansa thinks, for the cord that comes from his navel coils across the woman's belly like a blue snake. She idly wonders why the woman does not pick the child up. Now down on the floor of the shelter, Ansa waits, watching the woman's chest, but there is no rise and fall of breath.

Curious, she looks up to see that the woman's face is her own. This is not troubling, just difficult to understand. She reaches out to touch the baby, but finds she has no hand. Yet she can feel the warmth of the child and the weak, unsteady beating of his heart. She can see the blood moving around in his veins.

Ansa listens to the birds calling to one another outside, the differing sounds coming from each soft, feathered throat. She marvels at the delicate strength of the hollow bones in each outspread wing. She floats back up, away from the mother and child. Way above, there is a chink of light, as if the day is reaching down through the mountain to find her. She longs to move towards the light and, as if in response to her wish, she is being lifted and drawn up through the darkness. The mountain has sheltered her, now it is releasing her. All is silence and soft darkness, as the patch of light above grows bigger. There is nothing and no-one to be seen, yet she does not feel alone.

Now Ansa is in daylight, way above the Antelope Nose. She looks down on it, on the plain with its thickets of oak like clumps of green fungus, and the Great Water, sparkling white under the fingertips of Eshtu. The vast unknown flat lands on the other side of the mountain stretch out beneath her like a skin pegged out for drying. But now the mountain, the plain, the Salt Water, are shrinking and soon they are lost to her. She is flying faster than any bird but there is no wind, no sound. She has never felt so safe.

The daylight fades and she is travelling through darkness once more, but always towards the soft white light, far away above her. Flashes of blue and red and yellow streak past her, like sparks when a firestone is struck. Way below, something hangs in the sky, perfectly round like Balqa but it does not glow a soft white, nor does it burn like Eshtu. Instead, it is deepest blue, with brown and green markings, wreathed in wisps of white gossamer.

Ansa is borne on towards the white light; it fills her vision and she drinks it in – long draughts that flood her with the sweetness of a half-remembered dream. How could she have thought the desert or the green mountain were her home? How could she have forgotten?

Now the light seems to swallow her up and she is one with it. She can feel the soft breath of a breeze caressing her right shoulder. She turns, but there is nothing to see. The wind becomes stronger, fresher, whipping playfully around and through her thoughts, teasing apart the black knots of pain. Only one dark twist remains, curling stubbornly in on itself, shrinking back from the reach of the light and the play of the wind. The limp body of Zeru in the pit of sand. The hatred in Ama's eyes. Nothing can take this away.

The brightness begins to fade, the wind drops, and suddenly Ansa is looking down on a river, winding its way along a wide valley floor. Her attention is caught by a crescent of lush foliage nestling within a loop of the river and, without seeming to move, she finds herself hovering above the reed tips, which sway gently in the afternoon breeze. There is splashing in the shallows, close to the bank. The wings and head of a young mantis emerge from the water. It is the story Koru told her in the cave; the father has placed the eye of his dead son in the river and the young mantis has grown again and is trying out his new wings. Where is his father? Ansa searches amid the reeds and catches sight of the hidden mantis, watching his son play in the water.

The peace of the scene begins to fade. Storm clouds gather overhead, the wind whips up and, at last, the first heavy drops begin to fall. Soon the rain is falling in torrents and the river becomes red-brown and swollen. An ugly snout breaks the surface but the mantis boy is still playing heedlessly, excited by the rushing water. He begins to swim further out, away from the river bank.

He will be swept away by the current. Why doesn't his father call and warn him?

The mantis is standing calmly now, on the bank of the raging river, his spindly body swaying rhythmically from side to side. He is not calling, but singing. His eyes are fixed on the small figure struggling in the torrent, and he is singing a love song to his son.

Surely the boy cannot hear, not above the tumult of the water and his fear. Surely he will be carried away by the current and drowned. Yet now his tiny head is turning towards the bank. His arms and legs keep disappearing under the water but, little by little, he moves closer to the shore. Once, twice, he grabs at the reeds but is sucked back into the swift, angry water. Now he gets a firmer grasp and pulls himself to safety. Shivering, he drags his weary limbs onto the bank and lies down to rest. The rain is still falling fast and the sky is dark with cloud. The father of the mantis boy is nowhere to be seen but the cool breath of wind is on Ansa's shoulder and a few words from the song are singing themselves, over and over, in her thoughts: 'don't be afraid... we are one... don't be afraid.'

Something stirs within Ansa, growing and swelling till she feels she will burst with happiness. There is no longer any shadow to this happiness, only a longing to know, beyond words and thoughts, to understand.

Quicker than thought, everything changes and Ansa is walking on a grassy plain. It is morning and the air is bright, with a tang of salt. In the distance, there is the soft rushing of waves across the sand. Her attention is drawn to a branch which has been thrust into the ground. It has been wrapped around with reeds in the familiar criss-cross pattern – a sign planted in the grass for others to see.

There are more waysigns, deliberately placed to form a circle.

The one closest to her begins to change shape, breaking open and swelling into a ball of reed. Now the colour is changing, green leaching from the sphere till Ansa finds herself staring into a cool white orb, the face of Balqa. Where is the terror she has known so long? Gone. Nothing but calm. The urge to explore races through her now, like a quick spark along a dry branch. She finds herself beside another of the waysigns. The woven reeds begin to unravel from the branch and wave this way and that. As she watches, they become the legs, the arms, the wings of the mantis. His body forms, then his face with the eyes wide apart. Last of all comes the pointed open mouth and now, suddenly, the morning air is full of the sound of singing.

The song seems to bring life to everything: awakening the grass, dissolving into the sparkling air, settling into every crevice. The mantis turns his head and Ansa follows his gaze. The neighbouring waysign has collapsed onto the ground, the branch swelling and thickening to become a log, then the trunk of a fallen tree. The tree trunk is bending in on itself, the reeds stretching and changing colour. Now it is the colour of sand and becoming malleable. A pattern of dark blotches is forming. Ansa watches as limbs begin to bud from the soft body. A long looping tail forms at one end and, at the other, the blunt head of a she-leopard. The leopard rises to her feet and stretches, arching her back and swinging her tail. Then she settles down on the grass once more and curls herself up to sleep. Without a qualm, Ansa climbs into the curve of the creature's body and rests against the warm fur. The deep throb of the leopard's purring is like her mother's heartbeat.

When Ansa wakes the plain with its ring of waysigns is gone and she is being whisked into the night. She finds herself floating above the entrance to a cave, the acrid smell of smoke rising up from it. It is the cave of the Oak People – on the Antelope Nose! Just by the cave mouth, old blind Bakar is hunched over a small fire, sharpening a spear point. Lying fast asleep, her head on his lap, is Hua.

Ansa comes down close but Bakar continues his work as if unaware of her; he stops now and then to feel along the edge of the blade with his finger. Ansa gazes at Hua, at every line, every curve of her body, the way her skin glows in the firelight. She is filled with wonder. How could she never have noticed the quick beating of Hua's heart, the way she sleeps with the tip of her thumb in her mouth? Fascinated, Ansa watches the blood flow along the fine channels inside her daughter's body, each pulse of her heart. Beneath the smooth skin, she can see the lungs swelling as Hua takes a breath, the intricate tracery of branches within the bowl of her ribs, the muscle filling the space as she breathes out. Ansa hovers beside the sleeping child, the same wind she feels on her own neck coursing through the body of her daughter, spreading life to every organ.

Hua is dreaming. She has found a tortoise in the undergrowth by the spring and wants to carry it back to Ama Bo. The harder she pulls at it, the more firmly it seems to be stuck to the ground. Ansa can see what Hua is dreaming, can feel the ridged shell under Hua's fingertips, taste her frustration and the ache of her empty belly. The little girl turns over in her sleep, and Bakar lifts his hands, waiting for her to settle again.

Now Ansa becomes aware of the overlapping bands of muscle beneath the scarred, leathery skin of the old man's thighs. But it is the fear clouding his thoughts that fills her awareness. The same fear is alive in the night air, mingling with the smoke, crackling through the space between the knots of people, as they make preparations for the coming fight. And beneath the fear, the

170

dull ache in every belly, the longing to feel full and satisfied and sleepy with food. Everywhere Ansa senses the dread of pain, of death, the horror of Sakaitz.

Ansa reaches out to Bakar but where her hand should be there is only night air and the flickering light of the flames. Bakar looks up, turning his head as though he has heard something, but then goes back to his sharpening. Ansa is still. Nothing can disturb the deep gladness that has settled inside her, yet she is filled with pity for the old man, for Hua, for all of them. What will happen to the men who are going to fight? When will the people find meat?

The firelight fades and she finds herself looking down on the cave from above, now from way above the mountain itself, moving smoothly and soundlessly through the night. She seems to be travelling a vast distance, though the journey takes no time and the sense of being caressed by the breeze never leaves her.

At last, a blue-white light, way down below, catches Ansa's eye. She drops downward, faster than an eagle, till an expanse of white stretches out before her in every direction. It seems to be a landscape of rolling hills, draped everywhere in a thick fur of soft white. Along the ridge of the nearest hill sits a line of oddly pointed trees, their unfamiliar outlines shrouded by a heavy coat of white. The grey air is full of countless small flakes of white, falling silently, unceasingly, to the ground. Then the silence is broken by the distant sound of yelping. The sound grows louder and then over the brow of the hill, from between the trees, come four hyena. They are running down the hillside, always the same distance apart, leaving tracks in the white snow. Ansa draws closer - there is something skimming over the ground, behind the beasts. It is flat and made of wood and there are skins piled on top of it. Now she can see that the animals are not hyena after all – their fur is not spotted but patched with black and white. Their faces are

171

different too - their ears pointed. With every breath, tiny clouds rise in the cold air.

Something like rope has been tied around their bellies and over their necks and this rope also ties them together and seems to reach all the way back to the litter. As the animals run, the litter glides across the snow on white runners made of bone. One of the animal skins is moving and Ansa sees the face of a man peering out from under the fur. He shakes the rope up and down and calls to the animals. Ansa longs to follow the moving litter but she feels herself being whisked up and away till the hills become a tiny patch of white, before disappearing altogether.

She is in bright daylight now, everything way below a lush green. Curious, she finds herself floating above a fluttering, swaying mass, the leaves of countless trees. But this forest is unlike anything she has ever seen. She follows one of the spindly trunks down to the ground, far below, where it becomes lost in a tangle of green ropes and foliage. On the forest floor, where the daylight can only pierce in narrow shafts, it is dark. The air is hot like desert air, but wet. She is surrounded by twisted foliage: plants with leaves as wide as a man's waist. There are ferns, three times the size of any fern she has ever seen, the points of the leaves as sharp as spears. But it is the sounds that fill Ansa with wonder. The air is alive with chattering and buzzing and calling and crying. There are bright flashes of colour between the trees. A bird – can it be a bird? – is perched on a branch overhead. It has a curved beak like an eagle but its belly is the colour of egg yolk and its wing feathers are the blue of a summer sky and the green of new spring grass. Ansa can hear every one of the myriad creatures moving in the trees, sense each tiny insect as it burrows into bark or crawls along a branch.

Long before Ansa is ready to go, she is rising up again above the green forest, higher and higher, till the light fades and nothing is visible. Once more, there is the sense that she is travelling a great distance, but there is no rush of air in the gentle darkness. A sound reaches up from far below, drawing her towards it: a long drawn-out clanging note, deep as thunder but somehow sharper. Ansa drops down into the softest evening light she has ever known. Eshtu is a ball of flame resting at the place where blue-grey hills meet the sky.

When she sees where the sound is coming from, Ansa is filled with wonder. Halfway up a hill stands a structure, formed from huge stones. A sort of shelter, perhaps? It is like a face with many dark eyes, each eye tall and coming to a rounded point at the top. Beside the great shelter is another, taller one that rises into the sky like a finger. Both have flat overlapping scales, the brown-red of kho, for a roof. Something large and heavy is swinging to and fro inside an opening near the top of the tall shelter. Each time it swings, the sound comes again. As she gazes at the marvellous sight, the figures of men begin to appear, swathed to their feet in black, hurrying along paths towards the mouth of the shelter. They pass beside straight rows of stunted trees, growing in naked earth with no undergrowth.

The last of the daylight is falling, a mellow red on the hillsides, the trees casting long shadows. The air is warm and still. High up, something moves in one of the eyes of the shelter. A bird? Immediately, Ansa finds herself there. A fine layer of something that looks like ice allows her to peer inside. She draws back. A man in black coverings is looking out at her, but he shows no sign of having seen her. Now he bends over a flat wooden surface and she sees that his hair, fine and the colour of sand, does not grow on the top of his head but only at the sides. Like the Sakaitz his skin has lost all its colour, but he is not Sakaitz. He begins to dab carefully with his pale fingers at something the colour of old men's teeth, which is laid out on top of the wood. It is covered with small black marks, like tiny drawings. The deep note is still sounding and now he turns and walks over to the wall. He grasps something and a part of the wall falls away. He disappears through it.

Suddenly, she is being drawn up and away, the hillside receding. The roofs are shrinking patches of red, the sounding note a faint echo. She is moving fast and, though there is no sensation of air passing by her, it seems to Ansa as if the breeze is still with her, bubbling up now from deep inside her own being, as a spring spouts from the belly of the mountain. Ever-changing landscapes are laid out below her, then are gone. There are gentle wooded hills and lush valleys: the black jagged peaks of a mountain range rising up from an expanse of green blue water: a great, flat plain of swaying golden grasses interrupted only by tiny moving specks like black beetles. Faster and faster she moves, passing right out of her understanding.

A flat, muddy plain by a winding river catches her attention. Smoke is rising from it and the terrible fighting cries of men, and sounds like thunder, and the snapping of twigs. There are the bodies of men lying on the ground, out in the open, where Eshtu and all the birds can reach them. Then comes the sound of hooves on stone and men appear, wearing clothes the colour of bright blood, sitting astride the backs of deer. One of the men lifts a stick and points it. There is a snapping sound and, some distance away, another man falls down into the mud.

Now the plain drops away from Ansa's view and she is travelling fast in darkness. Suddenly there is a light moving just below. Could it be a new star, from the nostrils of the Skyfather? But this light winks on and off, on and off. She drops closer, to see a red light to one side and a green light to the other.

The moving lights are coming towards her. Between them is the shape of a huge bird, darker than the surrounding night, its wings spread wide. She sees a row of tiny chinks of light along the side of the bird's body. A great reckless desire to see into the gutted belly of the flying starbird takes hold of Ansa. Immediately, she is moving at the same speed as the bird, looking through one of the chinks of light. There is no way to understand what she sees inside, yet somehow it does not surprise her. A woman's pale face is peering out and past her. She has shining black hair coiled around the top of her head and something smooth and beautiful and finely worked is hanging from her earlobe, catching and reflecting the light. The woman is sitting but not on the floor: on something high and soft that cradles her. Her clothing is the colour of iris flowers and she has crossed one leg over the other. Next to her is a man whose legs must be injured because they have been wrapped in dark coverings. Everything about the man and the woman is clean and smooth and seems to reflect the light. He is leaning his head back against his soft cradle and Ansa marvels at his chin which is hairless, though he is a full grown man. There are more people sitting, but not in a circle where they can pass the meat and sing together. Instead they sit in their nests, behind and in front, where they cannot see one another. And all this inside the body of a flying bird.

Suddenly Ansa seems to be rising so fast that the starbird becomes a tiny prick of light below her. The soft wind still breathes its calm within her but something is beginning to change. The darkness starts to take on a familiar sharp scent, as if she were back among the carobs on the Antelope Nose, on the first cool evening after the summer heat. Sounds and tastes, too, come rushing back. Crickets creaking outside the cave in the warm night. The crack of a deer's leg bone as it is broken in two. The taste of the delicious marrow on her tongue.

Life on the mountain is calling to her but how can she go back and leave behind this vast darkness, bursting with wonders? The wind is a sad, sweet sigh running through her as the voices of the mountain grow louder, more compelling. Must she go back? To pain and fear and not knowing?

No word is spoken, yet Ansa knows the answer to her question. She tries to hear again the song of the mantis, to touch the warm belly of the she-leopard, but she cannot quite remember the words, or feel again the spreading comfort. Even the picture of the starbird with people in its belly is fading.

She is falling now, her descent gentle and measured. The great flat valley on the far side of the mountain is spread out, way below. Now the ridge of high ground rises up steeply like a wall, dividing the valley from their own plain and the Salt Water. The light is morning light – Eshtu is climbing far above her. Now she is directly above the Antelope Nose, close enough to make out the pine trees on the higher slopes. As she descends, a familiar ache of fear takes root once more inside her, along with the sharp gnawing of hunger she had forgotten. Is there no end to the hunger?

As if in answer to her question, Ansa finds herself on the path beside the spring. She hears the familiar chuck-chuck of the chukar birds which roost on the craggy outcrops above. They are crowding together, greeting one another. The children used to try to climb up and chase them, but they were always too fast –fluttering just out of reach. She stares up at the small, bobbing heads, the bellies large and plump under the grey-pink feathers. Though she doesn't know how she got there, she is now way up on the ledge beside them. The chuck-chuck calling has ceased and the birds stand in rows, motionless and silent. She reaches out her hand slowly to the nearest bird, but there is no sudden movement, no squawking. Only a slight scraping sound as the splayed red toes edge a little closer to her fingers. The head of the nearest bird turns to one side and the black eye seems to be looking right into her own. Hope lights up her thoughts, like tinder bursting into flame. Ansa returns the bird's stare. The shining black bead of its eye seems to move towards her, swelling and growing, till before her there is only luminous blackness.

Without any awareness of having moved, she finds herself in an enclosed space. The smell seems familiar from long ago: damp, stale piss, droppings. Now the darkness is beginning to recede and, down below, on the bloody floor of the shelter, she can make out the slumped figure of the woman and, beside her, the tiny hump that is her newborn child. She is drifting slowly down to her own motionless body, as if drawn by invisible hands. Soon she and the woman will become one again. The figure is so still, so pale. A thought comes to her. Has she been, all this time, where Nuno and the seers go? Has she been in the place of the dead? If only she could have seen Koru, just once more.

Immediately, one half of the shelter shifts aside, revealing a bright light, while the other half remains dark, enclosed. The light has been there all along, waiting for her. It is like an early summer morning, full of promise. At first, she is aware of nothing but brightness. Yet the light has something like a taste – no, many different flavours – earthy, tangy, smooth, salty, tingling hot, savoury, sweet. The different flavours mingle, yet remain distinct, and now she begins to see what look like bodies of people, coming together, then drawing apart. The outline of the bodies is barely visible, as if they are themselves made of light and air. They are taking in the brightness and breathing it out again and Ansa can see that there is nothing inside them to restrict the flow of light.

Near to her, three of the bodies are forming a circle, their heads close together. One of them seems to sense Ansa's watching

177

presence and looks towards her. Koru! The same wise, kind presence and yet somehow more like Koru than ever. The other two figures turn. One of them is a woman. Memories come flooding back to Ansa: floating and stretching in a warm, dark place of safety for a time without end, that gentle whooshing sound always in her ears. The feel of loving arms around her. The smell of skin, the taste of spit on the rootmash. Ansa looks up into the face of Ama and sees no hint of anger or disappointment there, only a vast, clean love.

The third figure seems to be that of a young man. She remembers the plump, shiny body of her baby brother, Zeru; the face bears some of the same look. It is astonishing. She gazes into the face of the brother she could have known. The eyes meet her own: open, clear, with no trace of reproach. Zeru turns back to the others who have moved away, their arms opening to embrace the figure of a newcomer, who is joining them.

The walls of the rockshelter close together once more and Ansa is moving down to the littered floor. Close enough now to touch the pale slumped figure, she feels the breeze one last time, over her shoulder.

With a sickening judder, she is back. Back inside the suffocating narrowness, inside the all-consuming pain. She is shaking, and lifts her head weakly to look around. The afterbirth lies between her legs, in two pieces. With a great effort, she traces the blue rope with her fingers and reaches out to touch the baby lying on the ground beside her. There is still a faint warmth in the tiny body but there is no movement and no breath.

Chapter 15

Ansa

The flow of blood is less and the pain is like a blade that has lost its edge, but still her body will not stop shaking. Worse than anything else is the thirst. Water is dripping, cascading, splashing through Ansa's thoughts, torturing her with its sparkling freshness. Now and then, she can see past the pain long enough to look at the body of the baby. It is a boy, so small he would sit easily in her cupped hands but she doesn't have the strength to reach over and pick him up. It does not distress her to look at the still, empty shell of flesh. Why? In a rush of joy, she remembers. *The figures made of morning light – their arms open in welcome to a newcomer.* Ansa's eyes prick with tears, with the longing to follow him, to go home.

The fingers of Eshtu are reaching inside the shelter and now the shaking becomes less violent. She must have slept because she does not hear Mul climbing up. Opening her eyes, she finds his face close to hers, something like concern showing in his deep-set eyes. She tries to speak but her lips and throat are too dry. The boy's eyes travel quickly over the floor: the pool of blood, drying at the edges to mud brown, the afterbirth lying in two pieces between Ansa's legs, the tiny corpse. A groan comes from somewhere deep inside

179

Mul's chest, then he is crawling backwards to the mouth of the shelter and he is gone.

The water he brings from the spring is the most wonderful thing Ansa has ever tasted. She swallows again and again, her body crying out for the cold liquid. At last, she lies back against the rock, licking the last drops from her lips. Now that her thirst is slaked, thinking becomes easier.

Mul has picked up his handaxe and is turning away when the unsettled feeling begins to take a shape. She stares at the back of the boy's head, familiar now but strangely big for his shoulders. The fearful word hovers around the edge of her thoughts. She thinks of his flattened nose, the eyes widely spaced but deep-set, the muscles of his arms – so strong for a young boy. Another wave of dizziness sweeps down and she falls into a faint. When she comes back to herself, the terrifying thought has found its home. *Sakaitz*. Mul is not like us. He is Sakaitz.

Desperate to get away, she tries to move but her legs are too weak. She gasps as the boy crawls back. He is holding something out to her: a chunk of the afterbirth. Ansa dare not look up into his animal face. She cowers against the rock but he is murmuring something, over and over, pushing the blue-red meat towards her mouth. Ansa starts to shake again, and then to sob. Unable to move, she can only cry as the Sakaitz strokes her arm with long movements, all the time making his soft moaning. Her thoughts warn her to shrink back from his touch, but her body longs to be soothed and comforted. The sobbing begins to lose urgency and the words of the mantis father's song come into her thoughts. *We are one, don't be afraid.*

She gulps in a breath of air and looks up into the face of

the Sakaitz. The eyes are not those of a wild beast man but those of the boy, Mul. She remembers how he relished the vine fruits she gave him, the tears of relief when his shoulder slipped back into its socket, the funny faces he made, bringing water back from the spring. She feels faint again but Mul holds her up, the sour scent of his sweat in her nostrils. He is holding out the piece of meat and Ansa's tongue runs with spit. She is ravenous. This time, she lets him put it in her mouth. It is rich, like liver, and slides softly over her sore throat. She lets him feed her till every piece is gone.

When she wakes, the sky is tinged with red and Mul is not there. She is no longer faint and now the pain comes only in bursts. She sits, enjoying the heavy slowness of sleep, the feeling of food in her belly. For just a breath, it seems that she is back, curled up against the soft fur of the she-leopard. Tears prick at her eyes.

After a time, she rolls over onto her knees and slowly crawls towards the evening light, bracing herself for the touch of the baby's cold flesh. But there is no baby; the corpse is nowhere to be seen. She manages to piss near the ledge, then waits for the strength to crawl back. Hearing a scraping sound, she looks out to see Mul climbing back up. He has found some nut grass roots. Though the tubers are bitter, her belly is clamouring again and she is grateful to bite into them. She eats three and then offers the rest to Mul, but he shakes his head. He is not following her with his usual hungry eyes. As he turns away, she sees that there is blood on his cheek, close to his mouth.

Ansa sleeps, wakes as the light is finding its way in, then sleeps again. When she wakes once more, the shelter is stuffy with the still heat of late afternoon. She is no longer dizzy and it comes to her that she might be strong enough to climb down to the spring. Mul has been gone for a long time; perhaps he will not come back. Blood is still trickling from her puti each time she moves. Her breasts are aching and hard. She squeezes at her nipple and a little sweet milk sprays out onto her finger. The smell reminds her of suckling Hua in the cave at first light. At once, she seems to be back in the land of the dead, watching Hua asleep on Bakar's knee, seeing the blood run through her veins, sharing her dream.

She climbs down slowly and falls to her knees on the path, shaking. Her heart is pulsing in her ears. Glancing up, she sees Balqa, a thin curved blade of light against the darkening sky. His beauty takes away the last of her breath; there is no longer any fear. She kneels, gazing upward, wanting only to fade away into the darkness. Then, like young creatures nuzzling into the folds of their mother, words slip softly into her thoughts. *You will grow strong again, like Balqa.* Dragging herself to her feet, she goes on towards the spring. The mountain is settling into silence: the last strains of birdsong sound on the evening air. She drinks deeply and starts back for the shelter.

Bidari

The air is fresher here on the mountain heights, but Bidari is so exhausted he can hardly lift his feet. He has taken his turn at carrying the litter and now Eneko and Goi are shouldering the weight. They are stronger than the rest and have been making a better pace. Now it is growing dark and the stars throw no light on the ground. Balqa will not appear till the night is old.

The mountain falls away steeply to the right and more

gently on their own side. Just below the path, Tipi has spotted a wide platform of rock where they could sleep. Dragging his feet closer, Bidari recognizes the place. It is where they camped that fearful night when the goat was stolen and they found Nuno bleeding on the mountainside. The men are divided about what they should do. Apal and Eneko want to make camp there, on the rock; there are plenty of cones nearby for a fire. Bidari and Koldo are not so sure. There are leopards on these heights, and the place holds bad luck. They hesitate. If only Nuno were here, the old Nuno who could see hidden things. But it is growing dark and already Eneko and Goi are climbing down from the path, balancing the litter between them. They lower it gratefully onto the rock.

Once the cones are ablaze, lighting up the scrub bushes around them, the tang of pine scenting the evening air, Bidari feels better. It is enough just to be resting, after the terrors of the day. Closing his eyes, he sees again the stranger's arm coming out of the ash heap towards him. He steals a look at the man – at Lotz. His eyes are closed but his mouth is twisted in a grimace of silent pain. They have been surprised at his courage. In all the lifting and setting down, the jolting over rough ground, he has not complained once.

There is only dried pear left to eat, and the stabbing in Bidari's belly is constant. It seems that hunger is in Koldo's thoughts too. He is quiet for a long time but, when he speaks, Bidari's heart drops in his chest.

'When we get back, we should make plans to leave the cave.'

'Why?' Bidari's voice is sharp with anxiety. 'The Sakaitz can't steal our meat any more – they are dead.'

Bidari expects an angry response but when Koldo turns to

183

answer, his voice sounds uncertain. 'No. That's right. And perhaps when the rains come, there will be more antelope on the plain.'

Bidari tries to swallow, but his throat is tight.

'Where will you go?' asks Apal.

'Down to the Salt Water. We could follow the shore and see where it takes us. Perhaps if we walked on past the marshlands, there would be more meat.'

Goi's face is dark and closed. 'But where would we shelter? What about the people who hunt there?'

Koldo has no answer. None of them knows what lies along the shore. 'The rains will come,' he says, at last. 'And with them maybe the antelope will return to our mountain.'

Bidari takes first watch as he did that other night, but this time he has company. Lotz lies beside him, moving his good leg now and then, in an effort to ease the pain. Bidari fetches him some water and he sits up to drink. He looks grateful and there are tears in his eyes. After a time he whispers, so as not to wake the others.

'A cave? You sleep in a cave?'

'Yes. On the Nose of the Antelope.'

Bo, curled up under the bed skin, alone. The desire to feel the warmth of her body sweeps over Bidari in a fierce, sweet wave.

'All?' the stranger asks, indicating the ring of sleeping men around the fire. Bidari doesn't understand. 'All – sleep in this cave?'

'Not Apal and Eneko – they are from the marshes.'

The man nods, but says nothing more.

Bidari feels uneasy, tending to a man he almost killed. Once again, he sees Lotz, panting with fear, blood trickling where the hand spear had nicked his shoulder. Bidari shivers. There are many questions he would like to ask, but the stranger is very weak and his strange speech is not easy to understand.

Bidari cocks his head to listen, but there is only the hissing of the fire. From high up in a pine tree comes the harsh cry of a night bird. He pulls a stick out from the flames and places it ready in the embers. He wishes that the man next to him would lie down to sleep, but Lotz is struggling to speak again.

'No meat?'

Bidari looks round for his pack, but then remembers. 'No meat. Only pears,' he says and, catching the stranger's eye, he wrinkles his nose in distaste.

Lotz looks puzzled, but then his eyes light up and he bares his teeth in a grin. Soon they are both shaking with silent laughter, trying not to disturb the others. There is no mistaking the tears now – they are trickling down the stranger's cheek.

In a while, Lotz leans closer to Bidari, peering into his face. He is no longer laughing. 'Your mountain. No meat? No antelope?'

'No. Our people are hungry. The children are getting sick,' Bidari replies.

The man is quiet for a few breaths. 'Are there no…?' He pauses, then starts to flap his arms as if they were wings.

'Birds?' suggests Bidari.

'Birds! No birds, on the mountain?'

Bidari is puzzled. 'Yes – of course. There are many birds,' he says, pointing up into the top branches of the pine trees, above the path.

Lotz looks closely into Bidari's face, but then just nods slowly. He smiles once more and lies back down to sleep.

Bo

Bo opens her eyes to find that she is alone; Hua must have woken and gone to play with the others. Fear has been with her all night, darkening her dreams, and it is still here, leaving her sick in the pit of her belly. Three nights now, the men have been gone.

Esti is inside, tending the fire. The old woman returns Bo's greeting but has nothing else to say. At the mouth of the cave, Bo is assaulted by hot air, stealing her breath. It looks like being a khamsin day, when the wind will blow from the desert. She watches Ikomar, on her way to fetch water. In heat like this, they will be back and forth to the spring all day.

Bo stands, looking out at the bleached grass on the steep slopes below. The stretch of ground in front of the cave slopes more gently. The grass here has long since been trampled down and the mountainside is like a huge pink-grey bone, cracked and crumbling. Nothing seems to be moving and even the birds are quiet. It is difficult to picture the men coming back down from the mountain today. A huge, gaping wound of waiting opens up inside her.

She hears someone on the path. Gashi has been collecting wood, the sweat standing out on her forehead.

'No sign of them?' Gashi asks, breathing hard from her climb.

Bo shakes her head. She takes some of the branches and they walk back together in silence. By the cooking hearth, she looks up to find Gashi's dark eyes scanning her face.

'Will you go down to the river?' Gashi asks.

'What for?'

'Melez. In the soft ground by the bend. You remember?'

Bo thinks back to the start of last winter. A wet day. She

186

went down to the Crocodile River with Gashi, to dig up some long, white roots. They tasted surprisingly sweet.

'The flowers will be out now - tiny blue stars. Pinch them off – it will make the roots grow fatter.'

How can Gashi think of this now? The men could already be close - on the tortoise path perhaps – their voices soon carrying down from the slopes above.

Gashi arranges the wood in the hearth, before speaking again, her voice sharp. 'We will need the roots when the rain comes.'

On the lower slopes, the dull sickness rises up into Bo's throat. Without any warning, she finds the contents of her stomach spewing out onto the dry ground. Down on the plain, beside the river, she feels better, despite the biting flies that mass above the water. She finds a place where she can kneel on the bank, holds her hands under the cool water and bathes her face.

Gashi was right. Here, where the ground is soft, the tall green stems are growing in clumps, and dotted up and down their height are star-shaped flowers. She takes pleasure in pulling them off, one by one. She doesn't like to throw them onto the ground - they look so pretty. Cupping them carefully in her hands, Bo drops the blue stars into the river, watching them float away on the slow-moving water.

Climbing back up is hard in the cruel heat. There will be no cooling breeze from the Salt Water today. She feels faint but there is nothing to eat. All the time, there is the ache of fear. Will she sleep alone again when it grows dark, without the weight of Bidari's body at her back? Yet again, she tries to picture the men up on the mountain. They should have found

187

the cave of the Sakaitz the day they left – or the one after that. Where are they now? She does not let herself think of the cruelly sharp edge of a spear, the weight of an axe, cutting into Bidari's flesh.

Long before she rounds the bluff and the cave mouth comes into view, Bo knows that they are back. It isn't only the shouting that tells her; it is something in the air itself. She runs around the bend and there, in the cave mouth, stands Bidari. Her hungry eyes take in every part of his body. It seems unharmed. She feels her blood begin to drain away and then knows nothing more, till she comes to herself in the cool of the cave, propped up against the rock. Bidari is squatting in front of her, his smile showing the little gap between his teeth that she loves, the smell of him in her nostrils.

Although it grows dark and the heat of day hangs about the mountain, the cave seems to be light and full of air, as if nothing could ever frighten them again. All of the men who went to the far side of the mountain have come back. The Sakaitz are dead. Gashi has examined the stranger's leg and she thinks the bone will grow together. The mountain herself has smiled on them; the men surprised a young goat drinking at one of the high springs, so there is meat to cook tonight.

The women and children have been listening, rapt, as Bidari tells the story of how they found the cave with the corpses and Lotz, who had helped to kill the Sakaitz. Now Bidari is on all fours in the middle of the fire circle, butting his head out at them like the cornered goat, before the spear of Goi felled it. The children are jumping up and down. Esti laughs so much that tears are rolling down her cheeks, onto her sagging breasts.

As Bidari nears the end of the tale, a subtle change comes to the sky. Tipi points to the mountain top, where the first spear tip of light has appeared. A hush falls as they watch Balqa's half-face emerge from behind the dark mass. Then Bidari speaks again, still with the familiar lilt of the storyteller.

'When it grows light, Apal and Eneko will return to the marshlands. They climbed the mountain to spill their blood for us - they will always be our brothers. Their daughters shall sit with our sons, and our daughters shall sit with their sons.'

There is a deep murmur of approval and Bo can feel tears coming into her eyes. Then Bidari points to Lotz, sitting in shadow by the cave mouth.

'This man fought against our enemies.' Bidari crosses to Lotz and signs his respect on the newcomer's forehead. Then he turns back to the others. 'We carried him down to the place of the oaks, to sit and to sleep and eat with us. Today, under the hot hand of Eshtu, this man's blood boiled inside him with fever. His lips were parched, but he did not cry out. Our feet made patterns on the mountainside as we searched out water for him. At last, we found the spring and the goat there, waiting. It is because of this man that we have meat in our bellies.'

Once more, there are cries of assent. Listening to Bidari, a flame of lust licks through Bo's body. Spoken like this in the firelight, his words are like magic and yet the mouth that speaks them is the same mouth that explores her secret places in the darkness.

Suddenly, there is a movement on the far side of the circle. Koldo is on his feet. 'No!' he cries. 'No! It is not this stranger but Goi's skill with the spear that brought us meat.'

He turns on his heel and strides away, down the slope, into the darkness. There is silence for a few breaths and then the whispering begins.

Bo lies in the dark, her body warm and wet. Bidari fell asleep after their mating and she can feel his even breathing on her neck. He had seemed surprised that there was no blood. It is a long time since her last bleeding but Gashi has not bled either and she says it is because they have had no meat. Bo opens her eyes. She is remembering her sickness as she climbed down to the river – the tight soreness of her breasts. Could she be growing a child? A secret seed of happiness breaks open and begins to send out shoots. Will she be a mother like Gashi, with a tiny child of her own to suckle? If she bears Bidari a child, no-one can make her leave the cave.

Bidari stirs, interrupting her thoughts, and she waits till his breathing has become steady again. A calm sleepiness settles over Bo, as if she were a baby herself, wrapped around with soft kid skin. Not even the thought of Ansa, alone in the shelter, can give her pain tonight. In the morning, she will take some goat meat to the rockshelter.

Ansa

Ansa opens her eyes. Morning light is seeping into the shelter and she wonders if Mul will come today. Her breasts are swollen and milk is leaking from one of her nipples. She can almost feel a mouth, like a limpet, fastening itself to her body, but then she remembers the slack, blue lips of the tiny baby. There is an empty hole inside her and the milk dribbling onto her belly will be wasted. She sobs, each convulsion pulling and stabbing her body. At last, the crying subsides.

The child was no bigger than a tortoise – he could not have lived. Where is his body? Ansa remembers the blood on Mul's mouth and pushes the thought away with a shiver. Instead, she remembers the gentle touch of his hand on her arm, as he fed her.

She is very hungry, and thirsty again too. With every breath, the air in the shelter is growing warmer. Ansa's last thought before she fell asleep has remained; she will go back to the cave. She waits, half expecting to hear the mocking voice of Ama or Gashi in her head, but there is nothing: just the birds calling to one another. Like a tongue feeling its way carefully around a rotten tooth, she allows herself to picture Gashi's face, then the face of Ama. There is no pain, only a longing to sit once more in the cave at night with the others, to watch the dancing flames, listen to the soft thudding of the drums. She begins to sob again.

Climbing down the rockface takes a lot of strength and, already, the hot fists of Eshtu are beating down on her head and shoulders. Another khamsin day. She needs water but that means taking a detour to the spring. She hopes that Mul might have gone there to drink, but there is no-one to be seen. Only the flies seem to be moving – looping excitedly in the heat.

Ansa walks slowly, keeping in the shade of the larger bushes. After a time, the blood begins to drain down through her body and a vast weakness makes her stumble off the path. She drops to her knees and crawls through itchy grass, the dry red earth scratching her hands and knees. She lies down at the foot of the nearest oak. Even here, in the shade, the air is so hot that she can hardly breathe. Her heart is beating too fast and the branches above her begin to jump and jerk, then to fade away into the sky. A dark panic takes hold and her fingers grab at her belt for the little bag and the cool serenity of the Balqa stone, but it is not there. Then she remembers. *Bidari's twisted face, full of rage, ripping away the bag.* She feels herself falling - down, down, into the darkness. Just before the light disappears altogether, there comes a breeze, brushing gently over her shoulder and across her face. It is not the hot wind from the desert but a fresh salty breath and it reminds her of something. The frantic beating of her heart begins to slow. The breeze seems to linger and she takes in deep breaths of the cooler air, then closes her eyes and sleeps a while. She wakes, her belly crying out for food, and makes her way back to the path.

Bo

Softened by the heat, grease from the goat meat she is carrying dribbles down Bo's wrist. The strong smell of the food fills her nostrils and a wave of nausea rises up in answer. She waits for the sickness to pass, then her lips form a secret smile. The same sickness came to Ansa and to Gashi, when they were growing a child.

She walks slowly, her thoughts full of what is happening inside her body. Bidari wants her – she can tell by the way he reaches out for her when he is sleeping. If she has his child, surely they cannot make her go away? For the first time since the day, long ago, when Esti led her away from the still corpse of her mother, Bo feels safe.

She walks slowly for another reason too. It distresses her to see Ansa sitting in her own dirt, raving about Balqa. If the people stopped bringing her food, Ansa would die and, with her, the baby. At night, in the dark, Bo has been willing the child in Ansa's belly to grow strong. Perhaps it is a boy – a boy would make Bidari proud. Ansa cannot care for a baby so she, Bo, will look after him and he will call her Ama.

A small part of Bo knows something too shameful to say, something that makes her offer to take food to the shelter, again and again, that makes her more patient with Ansa than any of the others. What she knows is this. When Ansa's time comes, she wants Ansa to die but the baby to live.

Halfway to the shelter, Bo stops short as a new thought is suddenly revealed, like a blade emerging from a stone core. Everything has changed. It doesn't matter anymore about Ansa's baby, now she is growing a child of her own. Bo starts off again, at a quicker pace. Now, she cannot wait to give Ansa the meat, to cradle her and protect her.

Because she is thinking of Ansa, it is not such a shock when Bo rounds the bend in the path, and sees her there. Ansa gives a cry and staggers towards her. She seems smaller, her belly not so swollen. What has made her leave the shelter? Bo runs the last few steps and, putting the leaf parcel down on the ground, catches hold of Ansa, just as her legs are giving way.

'Bo…Bo…' she keeps saying, tears rolling down her filthy cheeks.

'Lean on me,' Bo orders, helping her off the path and down the slope towards the narrow shade of a mesquite.

Under the tree, it is a little cooler and Ansa seems to revive. She grabs at Bo's hand and peers up into her face. 'You came!' she says.

Hearing the gratitude in Ansa's voice, Bo's heart sings like a morning bird. 'Here – I've brought you something – look!'

She unwraps the leaf and watches as Ansa's teeth sink into

the succulent flank meat. She eats with relish, giving Bo time to look at her more closely. It is true – her breasts are bigger than before but her belly has shrunk. And there is dried blood on her legs. At last, Bo understands what has happened.

'The baby!' She cannot quite grasp it. 'But it's not time yet.'

Ansa looks up, her eyes filling again with tears. She swallows noisily.'He was too small,' she whispers. Cupping her hands, she shows Bo the size of the tiny corpse.

She has given birth, and with no-one to take the child and tend it. Bo thinks of last night's feast, the children laughing around the fire. Later, of coupling with Bidari in the dark. She should have been here - with Ansa.

'Ama and Koru will look after him,' Ansa goes on. 'I saw them take him.'

Bo stares at her, taking in the senseless words. So that is how things are. Gashi thought that, after the birth, Ansa's madness might pass, but perhaps it is better this way.

'Ansa.' She speaks slowly and clearly. 'Where is the baby?' It might still be alive.

Ansa wipes the tears from her face. She looks unsure. 'You mean the body? I think Mul took it.'

'What? Who took it?'

'The pale boy. His name is Mul. He brought me water.'

Bo sighs. She will have to go and look for herself. But is Ansa strong enough to walk back to the shelter and then to the cave?

'Bo - he's not like us - I think that he might be Sakaitz.' Ansa grabs her arm. 'Could we take him back with us? I think he has lost his own people.'

Bo gently removes Ansa's hand. 'You stay here and rest,' she says, getting up. 'I won't be long.'

At the cliff face, Bo looks around carefully but there is nothing to fear. As she climbs, the sickness makes her stop to retch but there is nothing in her stomach. At the top, she peers cautiously over the ledge and into the gloom of the shelter. There is no-one there. Clambering gratefully into the cool, her eyes become accustomed to the dim light. She finds the dark stains of dried blood but no baby, alive or dead. Perhaps Ansa has taken the corpse and hidden it in the bushes. Bo climbs back down and goes to the spring to drink.

Back by the mesquite tree, Ansa is awake and waiting. She is staring up at the feather-like leaves overhead, the patches of blue in between. Bo is worried that she will see Balqa, visible now as a thin blade of white in the sky. If Ansa sees him, she will be frightened to walk on the mountainside. Luckily, Ansa's thoughts seem to be elsewhere.

'There will be plenty of bean pods here, when the summer is old,' she says. 'Do you remember when we dried them in the sun? When Hua was growing in my belly?'

'Yes,' replies Bo. 'You told me about your brother.'

She looks at Ansa, lying quietly, gazing into the sky. How strange her madness is. It is like a mist that lifts from time to time, then falls again.

'Bo –what I told you was not true,' Ansa says now, sitting up. 'My brother didn't die like I said. I killed him.'

Bo draws away, as if a snake had suddenly crawled out of the long grass. This is a new kind of raving. But Ansa doesn't look mad – her eyes are alive in a way Bo has not seen before, even when Ansa slept in the cave with them. Her face used to be closed, now it seems open.

'You killed him? What do you mean?'

'When he was a baby, Ama told me to look after him. A

195

blood spider came from under the rock.'

Ansa sounds different too. She has never talked about her life in the desert before, or about her own people.

'What did you do?'

'I saw it.' Ansa pauses and hangs her head. 'But I didn't do anything. I wanted him to die so I didn't call for Ama. I let the spider bite him.'

Bo doesn't want to hear any more. She almost covers her ears but instead she stares down at her hands till they seem not to belong to her at all.

'Bo.' Ansa never uses her name but now she keeps saying it and it makes Bo want to cry. 'Bo - I went to the home of the dead and I saw him – my brother. And I saw Ama. She's not angry anymore.'

For an instant the air seems full of magic and a thrill of fear runs down Bo's neck, between her shoulder blades. Is Gashi right? Could Ansa really be a seer like Nuno? No. All this talk of a Sakaitz boy and a spider - it is the madness speaking.

Ansa's eyes have filled with tears which are falling freely down her cheeks. She begins to sob and reaches out to Bo. The young girl lets out her breath in a long sigh and puts her arms around Ansa.

'Shh... shh... It's all over now. It's all over.'

They stay under the tree till Eshtu loosens his fierce grip. Bo lets Ansa sleep. When they start for the cave Ansa is very weak and has to lean on Bo. Before starting the final climb up to the cave, they stop to rest. Ansa has not spoken for a time and she seems nervous. When she speaks at last, there is nothing deranged about her words.

'Will Hua be there? I am longing to see her. Has she grown taller, Bo?'

An uncertain fear stirs in the pit of Bo's belly. If she remembers that Hua is her daughter, she might remember that she is joined with Bidari.

'She's taller – but thinner too. The men have made no meat – not till the goat they brought back last night.'

Bo thinks of the preparations for battle, the terrible fear, Bidari returning unhurt. Ansa knows nothing of all this.

She is speaking again, more quietly. 'Do you think Bidari will be angry about the baby? I cried out with the pain. Perhaps that is why he died.'

Bo is stunned to silence. It seems that she does remember she is Bidari's wife. Is Ansa coming back to her senses? If so, what will happen to her, Bo? It is too late to take Ansa back to the shelter. Bo turns away and looks out over the plain, her new-found joy draining away.

Chapter 16

Ansa

Lotz is sleeping on his side, his good leg tucked under, his head cushioned by the pile of bedding grass she has laid for him. Ansa stands watching. From the time she first saw him, she has not been able to keep away. It is something about the way his eyes speak even when his voice is silent. And the way he sits within himself, alone, even when he is laughing with someone. She often thinks of that first day, when she came back from the shelter: the silent fear in the faces of the others. It didn't take long for her to understand what had happened - that Bo now sits with Bidari, that she is sick with Bidari's child. When the others saw that she had come to herself and was not grieved, they accepted her back and now even Bo sits with her sometimes.

Ansa drops down to a squat and peers closely at the leg wound, pleased with what she finds. Easing away the mallow leaf poultice, she withdraws, but the dead rat stench is gone. The last stubborn corner of the wound has stopped weeping. She leans back to look at the whole length of the leg. Gashi took the splint off many days ago, before she left with the others to go down to the plain. She said that the bone had grown together again, but the leg still lies stiff and a little crooked. Perhaps he will never walk without her help. When she came back to the cave, it was clear that someone must care for him. No-one told her to do it but they are glad that she does, she can see it in their faces.

Lotz stirs. She knows every movement he makes in his sleep, the way he flings his arm behind him. She used to think it must wake him, but it never does. His breath is coming evenly and his skin is a good colour. In the early days, his dry, flushed face was like a stone, heated in the fire for cooking meat. He would twitch and turn and moan in his dreams. Then the sweating would begin and his body would shake so much that it frightened her. Esti showed her what to do and she spent all day running to the spring for cold water to bathe him. After a time, the fever left him and he has been growing stronger.

Leaving him to rest, she goes out into the bright midday and sits down on the dry ground beside Esti. It is so quiet without the children. The others have all gone to the joining, leaving her behind to care for Lotz, with only blind Bakar and his wife. She has grown comfortable working with Esti. And soon the night of Balqa's fullness will come and, down on the plain, Tipi will be joined with his new wife. Then the others will come back to the mountain.

'How is he?' the old woman asks.

'Asleep. The mallow leaf has dried up the wound.'

They sit, enjoying the gentle autumn warmth, till a bank of cloud hides the face of Eshtu. Esti yawns, complaining that she is thirsty.

'I'll go for water,' Ansa says, getting up to fetch a container.

Back in the cave, Lotz has woken and is sitting hunched over a goatskin. For days now, he has been making a water bag. He passes the hide to her.

'Feel this.'

She rubs the skin, soft as the belly of a snake, between her fingers. 'But will it hold water?' she asks doubtfully. She had seen him rub goat brain and fat into it before the first soaking.

Now he laughs in that way of his that makes her want to join in. 'I hope so.'

'Is it finished? I'm going to the spring – let me try it.'

'Why not?' he replies. 'But only if I can come with you.'

She wonders if he is strong enough. The last time he tried to walk to the viewing place he fell, opening up the wound.

'You can help me,' he says, fixing her with his eyes.

Lotz is able to put more weight on his leg now and his arm does not dig so painfully into Ansa's shoulder. Once again, she is glad that she is tall and can support him. Perhaps, soon, a stick will be enough. He has not tried to walk this far before and has to stop. Ansa suggests that he should rest and wait for her, but he struggles on.

After a summer without rain, the spring is only a lazy trickle. Lotz bends, his leg splaying awkwardly, to drink. He tips his head back and lets the water run though his hair and down his cheeks. Then, grabbing Ansa's arm, he lowers himself to the ground. She pulls the goatskin bag from her shoulder and opens the mouth, holding it carefully under the flow.

'Look! It doesn't leak!' Her eyes are fixed on the water skin – her voice triumphant.

But Lotz's head is turned to one side, his forehead creased in concentration. 'Listen! Can you hear?'

Ansa cannot hear anything unusual. She ties the mouth of

the bag and sets it down on a flat rock.

'That call – *chuck-chuck-chuck!*'

She peers up at the rock face above the spring. She can just see the black and white head of a bird, perched on an outcrop, keeping watch. The rest of the covey is out of sight, roosting in hidden crevices in the warmth of the afternoon.

'You mean the chukar?' she says. 'They're always here – till the rains come. Then they disappear.'

'They stay here? All the hot days?'

Since he came to them, Lotz has learned many of their words but now he is excited and has forgotten the word for summer.

'Yes. Why? Aren't there chukars where your people come from?'

Ansa is thinking of her own childhood. They found a dead chukar once. Its meat was delicious.

'Yes – yes!' Lotz is leaning forward. 'But why don't you eat them?'

She looks at him, puzzled. 'How? If you climb up, they fly away.' Everyone knows you cannot catch chukar. The boys throw stones at them but only for the fun of seeing them hop and fly.

'You must put a trap for them.'

Ansa scans his face but, for once, he doesn't seem to be making fun of her. He clambers to his feet and leans heavily on her.

'Where are they?'

She points up to the ledges where the plump grey birds roost. The nearest one, the look-out, seems to be peering down at them. It turns its head and the gentle chuck-chuck becomes faster and more shrill: *chukka-chukka-chukka.* At the sound, Ansa senses some change inside her. A feeling of comfort, as if someone had stroked her shoulder; yet there is no-one behind her. Where has she felt this before?

The alarm call stops but the bird is still staring down at them; she can make out its red beak. A memory flits through her thoughts, trying to find a resting place.Didn't she dream once about chukar birds, lined up on a ledge? Not hopping away, not flying, just waiting. Or was it something she saw in the shelter, in her fever? Sometimes, pictures come back to her, in the dark, or when she looks out to the Salt Water. Could it be something in the land of the dead that she is remembering?

From the watching place, Ansa looks down to the thicket of terebinth, nestling at the toes of the mountain. Some of them are covered with red fruits that are darkening now to blue as they ripen. Bakar says the trees do not always fruit and the coming of the fruit is a good omen. She looks up to see a bank of cloud near the horizon and Eshtu dropping down towards it. There may just be time to go and pick some before the light fails.

She hurries back to the cave to collect her gathering bag. Lotz had been silent on the walk back from the spring, but now he calls her over.

'Where are you going?'

'Down to the terebinths - to pick fruit, before it gets dark.'

'Terebinth? What is that?'

She describes the tree to him and he seems excited.

'Take a sharp blade,' he says, 'go to the youngest tree. Cut the bark across, three times. Not too deep.'

He draws his finger across his palm to show her. Ansa

looks at him closely. Sometimes he says things she doesn't understand, and then laughs at her puzzlement. But there is no smile playing around his mouth now.

'Why? What for?'

'Just do what I say.' She can tell by his voice that it is important.

Now he does smile. 'You're hungry, aren't you?'

She nods. 'Bakar says the fruits don't taste good but they are filling.'

'Fruit?' His face is blank for an instant, then his mouth breaks open into a full laugh. 'Yes – you must go for the fruit. But don't forget the blade.' Once again, he mimes the cutting of the bark.

Ansa unties the blade from her belt. She has chosen the tree with the most slender trunk. Here, under the leaf cover, daylight is failing fast. She makes the first cut but the bark is thicker than she thought and she has to press harder with the sharpened edge. Now the bark is pierced through, showing the lighter wood underneath, but that is all. Why does he want her to do this? She cuts two more slits, as he said, then stands back to look. The trunk of the young terebinth looks strange, with three gashes in it. She touches it to find moisture gathering around the edge of the first cut. It is weeping, like the wound in his leg.

She climbs back up in the dusk, her thoughts full of Lotz. She knows his body well from washing and caring for him when he had the fever, yet his thoughts are hidden from her. He seems like a stranger all over again.

The bag of fruit is heavy on her shoulder and her legs are weak. Stopping to rest, she takes a handful of the dark fruits to eat. Bakar is right – they have an oily, unpleasant taste, but not the bitterness of something poisonous. Needing strength for the steep stretch of path, she forces herself to eat more.

Rounding the bend, the cave comes into view. Lotz is sitting outside with Bakar and she feels a prick of jealousy. Esti must have helped him. He could not have come out alone, unless he shuffled on his buttocks, as he has been learning to do. He beckons her over.

'You did it?' he whispers, miming the action of cutting the bark.

'Yes. But why?'

'Shh… Bakar has sharp ears,' he murmurs.

They sit around the fire, watching the flames. The nights are beginning to grow cooler. Balqa is high in the sky and Ansa peers up into his face, letting the calm settle over her. He is swelling now. In a few nights it will be the feast of fullness and, after that, the others will return.

Bakar was playing on his pipe but he has stopped and now there is only the buzzing of the night insects. Ansa is thinking of the wounded young terebinth down on the dark plain. Why does he not want the others to know?

'Uncle,' Lotz begins. He always addresses Bakar with respect. 'You lived on this mountain always?'

'Yes. I was a hunter when I was young. Like my son Goi.'

'Your son knows the tracks of the antelope - everyone tells me this.'

A smile crosses Bakar's face. 'And his spear arm is strong too. But the antelope do not come like they used to.'

They sit in silence, till Lotz speaks again. 'I'm thinking of a tree, Uncle. It is shaped like a pine cone, and has thin, spiky leaves – very small. It has brown fruit – round like the face of Eshtu, but not for eating. I don't know your name for it.'

'Does it lose its leaves when the rains come?'

'No. And if you hold a leaf in your hand, there are white lines – two – like this.' He draws them on his palm.

'The juniper, he means,' says Esti.

'Juniper. Does it grow on this mountain, Uncle?'

Ansa is listening carefully. Although he is blind, it was Bakar that Lotz asked about the tree, out of respect. These nights, with the others gone, Bakar has been more talkative than usual. He has never seemed so happy.

'There are juniper trees on the tortoise path,' Bakar replies now, without hesitation. 'I can see them, as clear as day.'

'Yes – that's right,' Esti agrees. She turns to Lotz and Ansa. 'You see? He remembers everything.'

The cloud has cleared and Eshtu burns in the morning sky, as if summer has returned. Ansa is climbing on the tortoise path and, already, there are juniper trees within sight, clinging to the steep hillside. *Find one that is growing by water.* He had said it three times so it must be important. It will mean scrambling over the rocks – closer to the spring.

From here, the voice of the water, falling away below, reaches her. The trees are not tall but they are growing close together and she is grateful for the meagre shade they provide. The one she chooses is young, its fibrous grey-brown bark not too rough and shaggy. This time, he wants her to cut away a whole piece, from right around the trunk. She works slowly, marking out a large shape with her blade, then pulling off the rough outer layer in strips and placing them in her pack. He seemed to want these too. Then she prises the

205

sheet of inner bark carefully, little by little, from the trunk. She hears his voice in her thoughts. *One piece. One whole piece.* It is like edging the hide away from the dead body of an antelope. Now the trunk of the tree is bare and yellow.

It would be quicker to go back to the path, but the water below is calling to her. Ansa climbs down, holding the sheet of bark high, to stop it snagging on the rocks. She tells herself that she has come to the spring only because she is thirsty but still she scans the hillside in every direction before drinking. She has been back many times but there has never been any sign of the boy. Was it all a dream?

She cannot rest till she has looked inside the shelter. Leaving the bark at the bottom of the cliff, she climbs up and crawls through the dark mouth, into the shade. The shelter is empty. She sits, looking out at the bright sky, then down at the rocky floor. The bloodstains are still there. Her body heaves with sobs and she rocks herself, groaning, till the pain begins to lessen: until it feels as if she is being held and rocked in the arms of another.

Lotz has been waiting, impatient for her return. He seems pleased with the bark.

'Now we need water, to soak it,' he says. 'And tomorrow, you must collect the sap – from the cuts you made.'

'What will you do with it?'

He screws up his face in a smile and shakes his head, teasing her. After a while, the smile drops away. 'Autumn is not the best time – but perhaps there will be enough sap.'

It is morning again and Ansa is setting off down to the plain.

'Not more of those blue fruit,' Esti complains. 'Go and get

firewood instead.'

Ansa thinks quickly. 'I'm going to dry some of them, for the winter.'

She makes her escape before Esti can answer and runs down the path, impatient to get to the young terebinth. She has her bag to collect more fruit and, hidden inside it, a bowl. Why doesn't Lotz want the others to know about the sap? He is so difficult to understand.

The cuts she made in the tree bark are seeping but the sap has dried to a soft, sticky mess. What can he do with this? She scrapes it into her bowl anyway and, stopping to pick some more of the oily fruits, starts the walk back.

Rounding the bend, her breath coming hard after the climb, she finds Lotz sitting beside Bakar, his bad leg stretched out in front of him. The two men are hunched together over the softened sheet of bark. She comes to a halt, staring. The bark was their secret – between her and Lotz - he didn't want anyone to know. There are blades and scrapers lying on the pink earth around them. Bakar has taken up his awl and, looking straight ahead with unseeing eyes, is boring holes along the edge of the softened bark, by feel. She has to pass close by them to enter the cave, but Lotz doesn't even look up.

After a time, Lotz appears in the gash of light at the cave mouth and drags himself towards her on his buttocks, across the uneven floor. She should go and help him but she is angry and makes no move. He reaches her at last and leans back against the wall gratefully, pain showing on his face.

'Where is the sap? Did you get it?'

She pulls the bowl from her bag and passes it to him. 'There's not much and it's dried up.'

He flashes her a smile. 'This is good. Very good. It will stick to the bird's coat. What do you call the coat of a bird?'

The coat of a bird? 'Feathers – you mean feathers?'

'Yes. We are making a trap – to catch the chukar.'

Ansa leans forward, her thoughts scattering in all directions. He had talked about catching the plump birds, when they were at the spring. Can it really be done?

'Is that what Bakar is doing? I thought you didn't want the others to know.'

Lotz gives her back the bowl of resin and shrugs.

'I have no awl. I need Bakar to make holes to lace the trap.' He cups his hands around Ansa's as they hold the bowl of sap and smiles up into her face. 'They will all know soon enough, when there is chukar meat cooking over the fire.'

Ansa and Esti squat beside the two men, watching as Lotz rolls the bark into a funnel shape, then begins to thread the strips of fibrous outer bark through the holes, to lace it together. When it is done, he calls for the terebinth resin and, taking a stick, smears some over the inside of the funnel. Esti's forehead is lined with concentration.

'How does it work?' she asks.

'You will see,' Lotz replies. 'We put some bait inside the trap. What do the chukar eat on your mountain?'

Ansa tries to remember what she has seen the birds pecking at, but Bakar answers straight away.

'Hawthorn berries.'

'Yes, yes!' Esti is excited. 'I will go and pick some.'

Thornfruit. Last time the berries grew red, Koru was with them. At once, in her thoughts, Ansa is back on the mountainside, picking the fruit for the old woman. *The last raindrops falling from the branches overhead. The sweet taste on her tongue. Listening to the story of Mina and the honeybird.* Warmth seems to spread up from the ground into her bones, into her deep belly. And now it doesn't seem to matter that Lotz has told the others about the trap, that it is no longer their secret.

He has finished tying the bark into a long funnel shape and now he is smearing resin over the lacing holes.

'Why?' Ansa asks.

'It must be dark inside. The bird goes in to take the berries. It is dark and she thinks it is night. She lies down to sleep.'

Lotz does not go himself to lay the trap; it is too far and he would not be able to climb up to where the chukar roost. So it is Ansa who goes, with Esti. The old woman waits on the path by the spring while Ansa scrambles up, then passes the trap to her and a bag of thorn berries. It is difficult to find a footing amid the rocks and the grey birds take flight amidst a flurry of chukking calls. Ansa finds a flat ledge covered in droppings where the rock juts overhead, and wedges the trap in place. She places a handful of the berries right inside and then, just as he said, lays a trail of the rest along the ledge, leading to the mouth of the funnel.

Later, Ansa lies awake, thinking about the trap. Twice, at dusk, she climbed up above the spring, scattering the birds, and twice she found it empty. The berries leading up to it have been eaten, but not those inside. Lotz doesn't seem surprised.

'We must put more berries and wait,' he says.

He seems so certain. Is he just trying to keep their hopes up? Sometimes she wonders if he is making fun of them.

Chapter 17

Ansa

Eshtu is slipping down behind a bank of orange cloud as Ansa clambers up once more to the ledge above the spring. Something is different; the trap seems to have shifted a little. She puts her hand inside carefully and there is scraping and a fluttering of feathers.

'Esti! We've caught one!' she calls to the old woman, waiting down beside the spring.

Her heart beating fast, Ansa feels for the feet of the bird, trying to draw it out, but there is resistance. The wing feathers are caught in the sticky resin. Grasping the bony feet firmly, she pulls the bird free and out into the light. The chukar gives a squeal of alarm and the grey wing feathers flap wildly.

'Have you got it?' Esti's thin voice from below.

It is hard to keep hold of the bird. The small head is twisted up towards her, its waxy beak opening and closing. There is a red ring all around its shining black eye. What did Lotz say she must do? Grasping the neck firmly between her thumb and first finger, she lets go of the chukar's feet. The flapping of wings becomes wilder. With her other hand, she pushes the red beak sharply up and back, towards her thumb. There

210

is a small crack and the bird's head drops, limp, onto the white throat. The fluttering continues for a breath, then stops. Ansa is shaking, still grasping the lifeless chukar as if it might fly away.

'Ansa! Have you got it?' Esti is calling.

'Yes. I'm coming down.'

It is only after she has handed the plump bird to Esti that Ansa remembers the bait. She climbs back up to lay another trail of berries, amid insistent calling from the slopes above – *chukka-chukka-chukka*. Beside the trap are several grey wing feathers. She picks one up, running her finger along its edge, smooth and perfect to the touch. Looking up to where the rest of the covey is hiding, she brushes the feather across her lip in thanks.

The night seems to ripple with magic. There is no darkness. As Eshtu drops below the Salt Water, Balqa appears on the horizon and hovers over the plain, swollen and perfectly round. He is no longer milky white but an earthy red, the colour of kho. Ansa draws in her breath. He seems to hang so close to the ground. Down on the plain, where the others are camped with the Marsh People, it must almost be possible to touch him. She thinks of Tipi and the girl he will be joined with tonight.

Bakar plays on his pipe while Esti plucks and guts the chukar. There will only be a small amount of meat for each of them but no matter. *The first of many.* That's what Lotz said, when they brought the limp bird to show him. And a good omen – that there is meat to eat on the night of Balqa's fullness. Lotz takes up the drum and beats in time with Bakar's piping. The old man smiles with pleasure.

Ansa watches the dancing of the flames and Balqa's steady rise. It hardly seems to be night at all. Lotz has his good leg curved around the drum, the bad one stretched out beside it. His hands move faster over the skin, throwing long shadows in the pale light. The aroma of roasting chukar reaches her nostrils and suddenly it doesn't seem possible to be still. She jumps up and grabs Esti's arm, pulling her to her feet. The old woman complains but soon she is joining in the dance, following Ansa as she snakes around the men and between the hearths. Ansa looks up to Balqa's open face, smiling down on them, full of hope and promise. She spins round, faster and faster. Esti collapses on the ground, laughing, but Ansa whirls on, a fierce excitement in all her limbs, the evening air cool on her sweating body. Now she can no longer stand upright and she staggers, the ground coming up to meet her. There is a warning shriek from Esti as Ansa almost falls into the fire. Suddenly, she is face to face with Lotz. His fingers are still on the drum but his eyes are fixed on her with a look she has never seen before. A shiver of excitement ripples from a place deep inside her body.

Ansa watches Lotz as Balqa nears the highest point of his climb. He sings the words of the greeting song as if he has always known them, as if he is now truly one of the Oak People. When the time comes, Ansa stretches out her arms and throws her head back to drink in the beauty of Balqa. The magic ripples across her scalp and courses through her body, again and again, like waves on the shore.

Now, at last, they can eat. The roasted chukar is not a fat meat but the flavour is good.

'Wait!' It is Lotz's voice, calling out in shock. Ansa drops the meat quickly back onto its leaf wrapping. 'The trap is mine,' he says. 'The bird is mine to share.'

Ansa watches Lotz as he crawls awkwardly around the fire. He stops in front of Bakar and bends low, touching the ground with his forehead. Bakar looks straight ahead, unseeing. Lotz reaches for the old man's hand and places it on his own head. Neither of them speaks. The women watch in puzzled silence until Bakar removes his hand.

'You eat first, Uncle,' says Lotz, placing the leaf package in Bakar's hand. 'Tonight, you are Kep among us.'

Kep? Head? What does he mean?

Lotz crawls back to his place and waits, his own meat in his hand. There is an uncertain silence. At last, Bakar puts some meat in his mouth and, seeing this, Lotz too begins to eat. Ansa is startled but Esti just gives a small laugh and begins chewing.

Lotz turns to the old woman. 'You have cooked chukar before, Esti?'

'No!' She giggles like a young girl. 'But now you have come, we can catch them whenever we want to.'

'This is the best I have eaten,' says Lotz, running his tongue slowly and luxuriously around his lips.

They are all laughing now. Bakar moves forward and, in the flickering firelight, Ansa sees that there are tears glistening on his cheek. Soon, the old ones are ready to sleep and Esti guides Bakar into the cave. The night is not cold but it seems to Ansa as if the long, dry waiting of summer is nearly over; it cannot be long before the first autumn rain falls. Lotz makes no sign of moving. She sits, staring at the last flames of the fire. The meat, small as it was, has brought a welcome fullness to her belly.

Something makes her look up to find that Lotz's eyes are

on her. For the first time since he came to the cave, she feels uncomfortable sitting alone with him.

'The others will come back from the plain now?' he asks.

'Yes. Now the feast is over, and the joining.'

'So. Tipi is a grown man - with a wife.' His eyes have not left her face. He continues in a low voice. 'Someone told me that you came to the cave to be Bidari's wife.'

Ansa looks down. 'Yes – but that was before ….'

'And now Bo is his wife.' It is not really a question, but he looks into her face as if waiting for an answer. She doesn't know what to say. She stares into the glowing embers, thinking of Bo and Bidari, laughing together, touching each other. The thought brings her no pain.

'I used to sit with Bidari and sleep under his skin,' she begins. Finding the words is like grubbing around in the soil for roots. 'But that was before.'

'Before what?'

Ansa looks away from the fire, out toward the invisible plain, towards the distant waves which rush onto the shore, then retreat, in an endless movement.

Before the dark night when Koru died. Bidari's face twisted with rage. His hands forcing her legs apart. Night after night, crouching in the acrid stink of the shelter – hiding from the face of Balqa. The weight of Mul on her back. His smile. Before the wracking pain in her belly and the icy cold spreading up from her feet. Before the soft light that called her home, the breeze playing on her shoulder. Koru and Ama and her brother all sheathed in light. Before the body of the tiny child on the floor of the shelter.

She looks up but cloud is veiling the light of Balqa and the face of Lotz is in shadow. She is not frightened but she remains silent. The words to speak about these things are hidden too deep for her to find them.

Tonight, for the first time, Lotz pushes her away when she tries to help him back into the cave. The laughter, the taste of the chukar meat, the greeting of Balqa – he seems to have forgotten all these. He crawls off into the darkness to piss and seems angry that she is squatting by the cave mouth, watching for him, when he comes back.

'Go to sleep. I don't need you,' he says roughly. He waits by the outside hearth till she turns and goes into the cave.

Ansa lies on her back, the rock hard against her shoulder blades, through the layer of bedding leaves. She listens to the faint growl of Esti's snoring, the scuttering of the rats in the ash heap. At last she hears small sounds – scraping and rustling of dried fern - that mean Lotz has come inside and is settling to sleep. Now her body begins to relax, but her thoughts are like the rats, running here and there. *The fluttering warmth of the chukar against her hand. Its head dangling over the white chest. Lotz kneeling in front of Bakar. The tear on the blind man's cheek.The dance!* Her face floods hot, remembering how it felt to twirl round in front of Lotz, his eyes on her body. Later - his hand on her arm, pushing her away. She feels again the grip of his fingers, fierce with something like anger. There it is again. The shiver of pleasure spreading like lightning deep inside her body.

When Ansa wakes, the sky is clear again, with no cloud to veil Eshtu's burning face. The slopes below are parched, bleached of all colour by the heat of summer. The first rain will not fall today, or perhaps for many days.

Esti is outside already and they walk to the watching place to look down on the plain. The old woman's face breaks into a grin, revealing a few yellowing stumps of tooth. They are both thinking of the others, camped way down below. Now that the feast is over, they will break up the camp and the Marsh People will return to their own land.

'Will they be back before dark?' asks Ansa.

Esti shakes her head. 'Tomorrow. Or maybe the day after that.'

Back at the cave, Lotz and Bakar are sitting close together. Lotz calls Ansa over. 'Where will you forage today?' he asks.

Ansa closes her eyes so that she can picture what is growing on the slopes above and below the cave. The colours and shapes of the leaves tell her what is going on under the earth: where there are roots or tubers good for eating, which trees are bearing fruit.

'The acorns are swelling now,' she says. 'I'll go down to the oaks.'

'Let Esti go for the acorns,' says Bakar. 'You should cut more juniper bark.' He turns to the man next to him. 'I am going to make more traps with Lotz. We will have meat for the others when they return.'

They sit around the fire, their bellies full of chukar meat. Esti is roasting acorns in the embers. Ansa remembers the vine fruits she found yesterday and fetches them from the high shelf where she had put them, safe from the rats. There are enough for each of them to have a spray of the grapes. Lotz smiles and drops them in his mouth one by one.

'Will you cut a stick for me tomorrow?' he asks, looking up into Ansa's face.

She squats down to look at the scar on his leg.

'It's healed,' he says, and he is right. The gash has completely closed and the ridged skin is dry.

Ansa leans back. The notes of Bakar's pipe rise and fall like the hunting birds above the plain. She is happy. Lotz will always limp where the bone has healed crookedly, but he will be able to walk alone. Tomorrow, he will make traps with Bakar and she will collect more hawthorn berries as bait. There will be meat for the others when they come back. She will see Hua again.

Later, when she lies down, sleep comes quickly and softly, carrying her away. After a time of no remembering, it seems that she wakes up in the warm darkness of the cave.

There is a splash of light at the open mouth of the cave, bright like the dawning of a spring day. The light grows in strength till it starts to hurt her eyes. A weight is lifted from Ansa, a weight that she didn't know she had been carrying. Across her shoulder, once more, breathes the soft breath. Now there is a figure in the mouth of the cave, dark against the light. There is something familiar about him.

She gets up and moves closer although her feet do not touch the rough floor. He is looking out into the light but, even from behind, she can tell that it is Nuno. He stands straight and tall, with no sign of the stoop he has had since that night on the mountain top. Nuno hears her approach and turns his head. He is silent but she can tell that he is the old Nuno, as he used to be before the blow to his head. Yet, somehow, he is different. If the old Nuno was a lick of flame, this Nuno is a blazing fire.

He turns back and, without warning, steps out into the brightness, disappearing from Ansa's sight. She gasps and lurches forward to follow him, but the brightness is already fading. All she can see outside is the smouldering hearth, the outline of bare rock and overhanging branches.

Ansa discovers that she must have got up in her sleep and gone to the cave mouth. She drops to the ground, crying out. By now she is awake but still she feels the passing of the light as if it were a loss of blood. The hard rock beneath her feet, the tang of smoke, the distant face of Balqa: these seem so pale, so empty now that the brightness has faded. She hears a sound and turns to see someone crawling towards her. Is this still a dream?

No – she is wide awake. Lotz is peering at her, curious. Without a word, he takes her face in his hands and tips it back gently, so that he can see the tears on her cheeks. His eyes seem to roam across her face for a long time, then he smooths her hair aside. She can smell the sleep on his breath.

He settles himself against the wall of the cave, then pulls her towards him till she is sitting between his legs like a child, her back against his chest, his arms wrapped around her.

'Why do you cry? Tell me.' His breath is soft in her ear.

Why? The tears fall again, faster now, and the words start to come. She tells him about the brightness and how she has seen it before and tasted it and swallowed it. And about Nuno, standing tall, in his right mind, stepping out into the light. About how much it hurts that she cannot follow him.

'Shh … shh…' he says. 'It is only a dream.'

He rests his head on her shoulder. At last, when there are no more tears to cry, Ansa looks down to his hands, clasped across her chest. She can see the white of his fingernails now, the creases of skin around his knuckles. Daylight is seeping into the cave and soon, the face of Eshtu will appear above the mountain. Back in her sleeping place next to Bakar, Esti is coughing her morning cough.

Bidari

Bidari's shoulders are aching and when he lets Hua down from her perch, she runs on to find her friend, Loza. Even these little ones are quieter than usual. They don't understand why Nuno is keeping so still on that litter. They don't like to look at his head hanging off the edge.

There is no strength in Bidari's legs: it is only will that keeps him climbing, step after step. Normally, he would be glad to reach their own path, the Nose of the Antelope outlined above them, just the same as when they left. He turns back to see Tipi, climbing alone. Tipi should be walking with his bride Lilura, laughing and happy, but she has gone ahead with the other women, to give the lament. Bidari pities the girl. Her first day in the cave will be a day of burial.

The path becomes steep and Koldo and Goi put the litter down, looking for an easier way up. Bidari turns away, struggling to get free of the grief that sticks to him like the web of a spider. *Nuno, lying in the dusk where he fell, his body convulsing, froth around his mouth.* Bidari thinks of Bo, of the child which is just beginning to show in the softness of her belly. He aches to touch her, but she is up ahead with the women.

They climb on – snaking their way slowly up the slope. It would be easier without the litter, but Nuno's body cannot be left behind. It must rest in the cave shaft, with their father and mother. As they come close to the cave, Bidari can hear the wailing of the women up ahead. The others, left behind on the mountain, will hear the lament. They will know by now.

At the last ascent, Bidari rounds the bend and the cave mouth comes into view. Everyone is outside. The trilling

219

calls of the women pierce the hot, dry air of midday. For the first time, he notices his thirst and the sweat that is trickling down his back. The litter is balanced awkwardly on the rocky ground, the women ranged around it. Esti is kneeling by Nuno's body, her face in her hands, rocking to and fro and keening. Ansa is there too and, seeing her, Bidari's heart makes its sudden, sick lurch of guilt.

Frightened and unable to reach Bo amongst the wailing women, Hua runs to her father and clings to his leg. He picks her up and holds her firm, warm body close to his chest. He gazes over her shoulder at the familiar patch of red earth, the working hearths. But everything is not quite as they left it; there are unfamiliar things. On the ground by the cave mouth is a pile of feathers, some grey, some striped in black and white. And, standing beside Bakar, leaning on a stick, is Lotz, taller than Bidari had thought. He has recovered. He is able to walk.

Koldo is beckoning to Bidari. He puts the child down and joins him and Goi, standing apart from the others. They are tired from the journey and there is pain in Koldo's face.

'We need to rest before we bury our brother,' he says. 'The women can watch with him for now.'

Bidari nods. Bakar has heard their voices and found his way towards them and Lotz follows, leaning heavily on his stick. It feels strange to have him standing there, amongst them. Bakar reaches out uncertainly for Koldo's arm.

'Will you dig a place for him now, beside your father?'

Bidari looks up and catches the eye of Goi, who looks away. They know that nothing can be done yet. As usual, it is Koldo who puts the thought into words.

'We must give Nuno's spirit time to find his way home.'

'To adar-so?' It is the voice of Lotz. He sounds excited.

There is a snort of impatience from Koldo and he turns to Goi.

'Adar-so? What is that? What does he mean?'

'Adar-so,' Lotz repeats. 'The place of the dead. Ansa had a dream - when you were gone. Your brother is there already.'

The men are silent, taking in what Lotz has said. Koldo spits onto the ground. Then Bakar is grasping at his arm again. 'Listen to him,' the old man urges. 'He knows many things.'

Bidari nods in agreement. 'Ansa is a seer – she saw our mother there – don't you remember?'

Koldo looks keenly into Bidari's face and then deliberately turns his back on Lotz, excluding him from the circle. When Koldo speaks, his voice is hard with anger. 'We will rest, as I said. Then we will bury my brother.'

The face of Balqa is high in the sky before they gather around the fire. Now that Nuno's body has been safely planted in the soft earth of the burial shaft, the people begin to feel their hunger. A hunger for food but also for laughter, for pleasure. Bidari turns his eyes away from the widow, Ikomar, who is sitting beside Gashi. Instead, he looks toward the hearth, where Esti is tending the chukar meat. The tantalizing smell of the roasting flesh makes his mouth water and he puts out a hand to squeeze Bo's arm, in sheer joy. She smiles at him as if he were a child. Next to her sits the Marsh girl, with her new husband. Bidari grins, remembering the day when Tipi was born. It does not seem so long ago. For the first time since they got back, Lilura is not looking rigid with fright.

Bakar clears his throat and they slowly fall into silence. Then the old man tells the story they have been waiting for,

221

the story of Lotz and the trapping of the chukar. Bidari leans forward, anxious not to miss a word. Ever since they got back, his eyes have been drawn, again and again, to Lotz. Now that he is walking, it is unsettling to think of him hidden in the ash heap in the Sakaitz cave, to remember him lying in the shade, raving in his fever, being tended by the women.

Bakar tells how Lotz sent Ansa for the bark, how he soaked and shaped it and laced together the funnel traps, leaving trails of bait for the chukar. The men nod, murmuring at how clever the traps are. What makes Bidari shiver with a kind of fascination is that the chukars have been close by all the time. All those nights and days they were hungry, when they could have been trapping meat.

When he is finished, Bakar calls for Lotz, who limps into the firelight. Feeling his way across to Lotz, Bakar makes the sign of respect on his forehead. Bidari springs to his feet to do the same. Back in his place, he watches the other men get up, one by one, till only Koldo is left sitting, his eyes fixed on the ground. It is only when Lotz begins to sway and lean more heavily on his stick that Koldo gets up and walks over. Keeping his gaze down, he makes the sign of respect, then turns and walks out of the firelight.

The warm night air is full of biting flies and most of the others have gone inside. Bo has fallen asleep across Bidari's lap – tired out by the journey and by the child who is growing inside her.

'Let's go in,' he says and she wakes, yawning.

By the cave mouth, Bidari feels a tug on his arm. Lotz is there, in the shadows.

'Come and sit with me,' he says. 'There is still some fire

left.'

Bidari follows Lotz back to the hearth, suddenly wide awake again. The cleverness of the traps makes him tongue-tied but he finds there is no need to speak. Lotz seems happy just to sit and watch the dying flames. After a while, he breaks the silence.

'The man we buried – Nuno. He is your brother, yes?'

'Yes. My younger brother.' Bidari stirs uneasily. 'Tomorrow - will you show me how to make a trap?'

Lotz smiles. 'You are my friend - I will show you. But tell me about your brother. He was sick?'

Bidari sighs. 'Many nights ago, we had a fight with Sakaitz on the mountain and they struck him on the head.' He stares out into the darkness. The next words seem to come out of his mouth unbidden. 'It was my fault. He heard them coming but I didn't believe him.'

'Ah.' They are silent for a few breaths, before Lotz continues. 'This is no shame to you. Sakaitz, they have - what is your word? – magic? They have bad magic that can stop your ears. That is why you didn't hear them.'

Bidari is listening intently, the words of reprieve welcome. He is amazed at the store of Lotz's knowledge.

'And their axe-blades have magic. Did the wound heal?'

'Yes. But he was not the same.'

'They stole his thoughts?'

Bidari sits back. Lotz is painting for him a new picture of what happened to Nuno, a picture that seems to be truthful.

'What happened when you were down on the plain?'

'He fell, on the way back – when we stopped to sleep.' Bidari shudders at the memory. 'He fell and then he began to shake, like this.' He jerks his legs and arms, miming how Nuno's body had looked, there on the ground. 'Then, he was still.'

'Ah. This is Sakaitz poison – it goes in through the wound and hides in the body.' Lotz touches Bidari's arm. 'You are not to blame.'

Bidari wipes away a tear with the back of his hand.

'But your brother is happy now, on the plains of the dead. He came to Ansa in a dream.'

Bidari nods, brushing away the thought of Nuno's dead eyes disappearing beneath the earth.

'Ansa – she has seen into the land of the dead before, perhaps many times?' Lotz asks.

Bidari nods again. 'Gashi says she is a seer, like Nuno.'

Lotz is silent for a time. 'It was good luck that you brought her to the mountain - to be your wife.'

Bidari is still. The flames have died down now – only the embers are glowing. So Lotz knows that he was joined with Ansa. She must have told him. There is tension in the air between the two men.

Lotz leans in close to him. 'Do you still want her?'

Bidari takes in a sharp breath. He thinks of the last time he was inside Ansa's body, the morning after his mother died. *Forcing her legs apart under the buckthorn. The blood from her broken lip on the back of his hand.*

'No!' He shakes his head, banishing the anguished memory.

Lotz leans back, moving his leg to ease the stiffness. When he speaks again, his voice is low and tight. 'Would you fight me if I mate with her? Would Koldo stop me?'

Bidari stares out into the dark night, thinking. He shakes his head.

Chapter 18

Ansa

Inside the cave, the air is still and clammy and heavy with threat. Clouds are gathering out above the Salt Water but they keep back the longed-for rain, instead of letting it go to the parched plain. How much longer before summer loosens its grip?

Ansa is not thinking of this, taken up instead with the sleeping child on her lap. Hua's hot cheek is resting against Ansa's chest, her eyes closed, her mouth a little open. Ansa curls strands of the little girl's hair, wet with sweat, around her finger. She watches the rise and fall of Hua's ribs, the flickering of the eyes beneath their lids.

In her sleep, Hua throws out an arm and the movement awakens her. She sits up, rubbing her eyes. Snuggling into the nest of her mother's lap, she leans back against Ansa's chest. After a few breaths, she takes her thumb out of her mouth.

'Ama Ansa.'

'Mmm?'

'Tell me a story.' Ansa shifts against the wall of rock, finding a better place for her shoulder blades, thinking of what to tell. 'A new story - about Mul,' Hua insists, turning to stare up into Ansa's face. 'About the magic boy.'

Ansa closes her eyes and begins. The stories always start the same way.

'In a cave, on the Nose of the Antelope, lives a little girl whose name is Hua, which means New Day. She is a very clever girl and very brave.'

'One day, Ama Bo tells Hua to go with the big children to look for eggs by the tortoise path. But Hua wants all the eggs for herself, so she goes on her own.'

Hua giggles. Tortoise eggs are her favourite.

'When she gets to the path, she finds a bush where the tortoise has made a scrape. Hua is very hungry so she digs into the earth.'

'She finds three eggs.' Ansa puts up fingers, one at a time. 'One, two, three.'

'One, two, three.' Hua copies her.

'She breaks open the first one and starts to eat it. Mmm.'

Hua licks her lips, copying Ansa.

'The eagle is flying low and now he sees something very bad.'

Hua cranes her neck to look into Ansa's face. 'What is it? What is it?'

'Wait and see,' replies Ansa. 'The eagle flies to the top of the sky and he tells the Skyfather what he has seen. The Skyfather calls for someone who has magic in his legs. Can you guess who it is, Hua?'

'Mul – it's Mul!' shouts Hua.

'That's right. Mul comes at once, running on his magic legs. He runs down the mountain, all the way to the tortoise path. Hidden behind the bush is a leopard snake. Hss…Hss… he is saying. Hua has eaten two eggs and now there is one egg left.

The snake wants to eat the last tortoise egg. What does the snake say, Hua?'

'Hss... Hss...'

'That's right. But here comes Mul – running on his magic legs. He reaches out with his long arm and grabs the leopard snake and throws him over the side of the cliff. Now there is thunder in the sky. It is the Skyfather clapping his hands.'

'Does Hua clap too?' The little girl asks but she knows the answer. It is the same in every story, when Mul comes to save her.

'Hua claps too,' answers Ansa and, laughing with excitement, the child begins to do just that. When she is tired of clapping, Ansa finishes the story. 'Mul runs back into the sky and Hua takes the last egg home for Ama.'

When they come out of the cave, Eshtu is dropping low. Hua runs off to play with Loza, Gashi's youngest girl. Ansa's eyes search for Lotz and find him sitting beside Bakar, in the patch of shade which appears late in the afternoon. Beside the cooking hearth there is a pile of chukar feathers and Gashi squats there, gutting the birds. Ansa wanders over to help, the sweat forming on her head and neck. It is so hot, even now.

Just then, Koldo and Goi appear at the bend in the path.

'Look!' Gashi calls to them. 'Three more chukar!'

Koldo stands looking for a while, then forces the air through his nose, wiping the slime from his nostrils with a finger and thumb. Neither he nor Goi comment on the birds. Ansa glances over at Lotz, who is watching intently.

'I am going to watch for real meat with Goi,' Koldo says at last. 'Not these little birds.' Though he is talking to Gashi, his words are for everyone to hear. He kicks the heap of grey feathers, sending the light downy ones flying into the air.

'It is good to go looking for antelope.' It is the calm voice of Lotz. 'Even a calf would make more meat than chukar.'

Koldo turns to Lotz, his eyes slits of suspicion.

Irritated, Gashi lays the gutted bird down. 'But chukar are better than nothing, Koldo. When did you last bring back antelope?'

Ansa gasps as Koldo drops down to a squat and slaps Gashi hard across her face. He gets up and strides away. Gashi's cheek is flaming but she is too proud to cry out. After a breath she turns to Ansa as if nothing has happened.

'We need more berries to bait the traps. Will you go?'

Ansa nods, anxious to be alone, but she feels a hand on her arm. Lotz wants to go with her. When they reach the place, Lotz drops to the ground to rest. The sky overhead is darker and she looks up to see clouds, running fast. A wind begins to lick the tops of the hawthorns and she feels a growing excitement. Could the rain be coming, at last?

She stands on tiptoe to reach up to a branch. Her fingers find the red berries but she squeals as the heel of her hand is stabbed by a long thorn. She pulls away, blood beginning to trickle down onto her wrist. Then she feels it – a drop on her head, another on her shoulder. At last!

The raindrops are huge and soon falling fast, wind whipping the branches. Already, the ground is giving off the warm, wet smell it had in last night's dream. She feels a hand at her waist and turns to find Lotz, propped up against the tree trunk. He takes her wrist and peers at the wound. The thorn has bitten deep, but the darting rain is washing away the blood.

He lets her hand drop, but does not move away. They

are very close, the raindrops splashing onto her head and then trickling down his shoulder. All thoughts fly from Ansa. There is only the joy of this first rain on her head, her face, her back. And the knowledge that, soon, he will touch her.

Lotz is looking at her as he did on the night of Balqa's fullness, when she danced. Keeping his eyes on her face, he puts out his finger and draws the tip of it slowly around the circle of her nipple. There is a leap of desire – almost a pain – in her secret parts. He pulls her towards him and begins to kiss her with his wet lips: her face, her ears, the skin of her neck, slick with the rain. Her body has never felt so alive.

But now Lotz is pulling away from her, groaning and clutching at his thigh. He drops to the ground and leans back against the tree trunk. He is trying to get his foot flat on the ground, but the injured leg is flexed straight in front of him and will not bend. The muscle has gone hard and the pain is bringing tears to his eyes. Ansa kneels down and begins to rub at his thigh to loosen the muscle. He pushes her away.

Knowing how proud he is, Ansa moves away to pick more thornfruit. When she returns, Lotz is still on the ground but the pain has eased. The rain is falling in a less hurried way now, after that first impatient rush to the earth. He tries to get to his feet, again rejecting her help. His lip is curled in a hard smile.

'I could hunt and run as far as any man. Now, I can't even stand up to take a woman.'

Ansa hears the bitter words but they leave no more mark than the raindrops on her skin. She is not frightened of him now. She pushes him back down onto the ground, the earth under her knees wet and warm as she caresses him. She feels

229

the muscle in his thigh begin to soften as she works it. He pulls her down on top of him and when they mate at last, his groan, the warm pressure of his hands on her buttocks, is just as it was in her dream.

The rain has stopped and they are still under the trees together. Lotz is humming a tune. It is not a song of the Oak People. A picture comes into Ansa's thoughts.

'Who did you lie with - when you lived with your own people?'

The humming stops. 'With Nahia.'

Ansa leans on the crook of her elbow. 'What was she like?'

He turns away but not before she has seen the loss in his face. 'She gave birth to my son.'

A son? She hadn't thought of him having a child. Suddenly, his eyes are closed to her and he seems to be far away, in a place she cannot reach. When he speaks again, it is as if he is peeling away his skin to show her the pain hidden inside his body.

'She thinks I am dead.'

Bo

Bo is gathering firewood with Ikomar when the rain comes. She runs out into the open, head thrown back, the water on her forehead, her cheeks, in her open mouth. For the first time since Nuno's death, Ikomar's face breaks open into a smile and Bo is glad. Her eyes move down to the woman's belly: flat again, since that night when the child growing inside her came away in a pool of blood. It frightens Bo to think of it. She cups her hands, the cool drops splashing onto her palms, then rubs the growing mound of her own belly. Will her baby live, to feel the rain on his skin?

230

When the rain stops, they move on to the pines. The dense cover here will leave some wood dry enough for burning. By the time they get back, it is late and Bo can tell that something has happened. Gashi and Sorne are whispering together behind their hands and the air feels thick with uncertainty. Bo seeks out Esti, emptying ash on the back heap.

'Have you heard?' The old woman grips Bo's arm. 'I saw him collecting bedding leaves. I wondered why.'

'Who?' Bo asks.

'Lotz! He laid them out – in his own place.' She pulls Bo closer and speaks into her ear. 'And Ansa's bed skin! He brought her bed skin.'

Bo's mouth opens in surprise. 'What – you mean they're going to be joined?'

Esti gives a coarse laugh. 'It's too late for that. They went to the hawthorns together. Ansa came to sit with me afterwards,' Esti is whispering now. 'I smelt it on her.'

Bo walks away, trying to make sense of the news. Relief grows with each step. If Ansa sits with Lotz as his mate, she will never be able to reclaim Bidari.

Outside, Bidari has returned and is sitting with Lotz and Bakar. Ansa is nowhere to be seen. The smell of roasting chukar mingles with smoke from the cooking hearth. Koldo is squatting beside his wife but now he gets up and comes over to the other men. The talking stops. Bo moves closer so she can hear what he will say. Koldo's eyes are fixed on Bidari's face, as if he were the only one there.

'Do you know what he has done?' Koldo's eyes flick across to Lotz and then back.

Bo holds her breath for the answer, but Bidari doesn't seem disturbed. 'I don't care. I have the woman I want.'

Koldo stares at Bidari, without a word. Then he shrugs his shoulders and walks away. Bo's face is burning. Bidari's words have made her heart take flight, soaring like an eagle across the face of Eshtu.

Bidari
Bidari's ankle aches where he twisted it, trying to keep up with Goi. They are toiling back up to the cave, empty-handed, the ground beneath their feet treacherous with mud. He thinks back to this morning, bright with the hope of meat. For the first time in many days, they had spotted a couple of antelope – females - on the plain.

It was a fearful thing to do, to make the circle under the oaks without Nuno, but squatting there with the others, he had still felt the magic. For the first time in many, many days, the air between them had been like clear, running water: Bidari, Koldo, Tipi and Goi, flowing together like one man. Out on the plain, Goi had spotted the tracks of the antelope almost at once. But then dark clouds had gathered again, hiding the face of Eshtu. More rain had fallen, hard and fast, splashing on the white rocks and washing away all trace of hoofprints.

They climb slowly in silence, dreading the disappointed faces of the women. Down on the plain, under the oaks, Koldo had seemed happy but now darkness hangs over him, spreading to them all. Nearing the cave, they meet Ansa coming from the spring.

'No chukar in the traps again,' Koldo tells them, after he has exchanged words with her. There is a bitter triumph in his voice.

The slope in front of the cave is deserted except for Bakar who sits sharpening a blade. He nods his head in greeting but has no need to ask about the hunt; if there had been meat, he would have heard them singing. Lotz appears in the mouth of the cave, leaning on his stick, his skin white with ash dust. His eyes take in the hunters – their faces blank, spears slung across their shoulders.

Suddenly Koldo is moving quickly up the slope towards Lotz. 'What are you staring at?' His voice is sharp as a newly-struck blade.

Lotz does not reply, but he lowers his gaze to the ground. Unease begins to grub at Bidari's guts. There is no way of knowing what Koldo might do when he is like this. He is within striking distance of Lotz.

'Your bird traps have been empty for days.' Koldo's voice becomes a sneer. 'But you wouldn't know that – you're too busy emptying the ash. Women's work!'

Bidari unhooks the spear from his shoulder and edges closer. Lotz keeps his silence, just stares at Koldo without blinking. The air between the two men grows tighter with every breath.

'What's wrong? Have you got nothing to say, now your birds have flown away?'

Goi takes Koldo's arm. 'Leave him,' he murmurs, but Koldo shakes him off.

'Leave him! That's what we should have done. We should have left him in the Sakaitz cave – one less mouth for us to feed.'

Bidari gasps as Lotz suddenly swings his stick, catching Koldo a heavy blow on his side, knocking him to the ground. But Koldo is up on his knees, his face aflame with anger.

'Come on then – let's see if you can fight like a man, at least.'

Disgust and shame for his brother rise into Bidari's throat.

What is he doing - fighting with a crippled man? But Lotz has thrown himself on top of Koldo and down at ground level there is not so much difference between them. The men move in close to see what will happen. Bidari's fists are clenched, but something holds him back from going to help Lotz. Somehow, he had always known it would come to this. Koldo and Lotz are thrashing out at one another, writhing on the wet ground, grunting with effort. Lotz is stronger than he looks. Now he has bent Koldo's arm behind his back and Koldo is roaring with rage. Lotz is shouting something that sounds like a curse. Goi cries out but now Koldo has broken free and rolled himself over. He raises his fist and aims at Lotz's jaw but the other man wriggles away and the blow smacks onto his shoulder.

Bidari hears noise behind him. The women and children are back. Gashi pushes her way through the ring of men, her second son, Iban, beside her. Koldo is sprawled astride Lotz's chest, pinning him to the ground. There is blood on Lotz's neck and they are both covered in mud. Lotz wrenches one arm free and reaches for Koldo's chin, trying to push him away.

Koldo catches sight of his wife and his son and now he seems ashamed and relaxes his grasp on Lotz. One of the girls begins to cry. The others watch as Koldo scrambles off his opponent and gets to his feet, slipping in the mud. Lotz sits up, moving his shoulder carefully. He puts his hand to his neck and finds blood, but there is no sign in his face that he is beaten. Koldo is walking away but Lotz follows him steadily with his eyes.

Bidari is watching his brother too, still fearful. The stick has rolled down the slope and Koldo goes to fetch it. He climbs back up and stands staring down at his opponent, a new respect showing in his eyes. He offers his hand to help the other man up but Lotz is suspicious, his face blank and unyielding. Then, to Bidari's surprise, he takes Koldo's hand, clambering awkwardly up. They stand together for a breath and a rueful grin spreads over Koldo's face. The crippled man stares but then begins to smile.

Bidari draws a long breath and turns away, looking out towards the plain. The thin gleam of distant water is no longer visible, but there is a new lightness in the air.

Ansa

After the heavy rain, the spring is bursting between the rocks and collecting in a pool, before finding its way down the hillside. Ansa reaches across, the cool water splashing her face and arms, and holds the bag under the flow. Carefully, she ties the mouth of the bag, marvelling once more at how it holds the water.

Back by the cave, her eyes seek out the figure of Lotz on the ground, resting. She traces the shape of his shoulders, taking pleasure in the way he holds his head, the movement of his hands when he speaks. Though she knows every line of his body, her eyes are drawn to him again and again.

Koldo is squatting in front of Lotz, nodding at something he has said. She smiles. Koldo's relaxed shoulders tell her that they are in agreement.

The women are dotted across the slopes, searching for bindweed, nutgrass, melez. Ansa heads up the path to find a tangle of earthnut stems she had noticed before the rains came. Climbing, she feels light and strong, her feet sure even on the steeper slopes. The red earth is giving off a wet smell of plenty. She finds the patch of earthnut, stops to rest for a while, then begins digging. It is hard work. The pear-shaped roots are deep underground, tucked in crevices between the rocks. The sweat runs down her neck when she stands back at last, satisfied with the good pile of tubers.

Thirsty, she scrambles down the ravine and up the other side, coming out by the spring near the rockshelter. Here, the flow is faster too - so different from the trickle of water she drank from all through those hot days, when the baby was swelling her belly. She takes the earthnuts from her bag and washes the soil from them. Taking a couple to eat raw, she bites into the starchy sweetness.

Ansa wanders along the path and climbs up to the rockshelter to rest in the cool. She sits, looking out at the sky. Her eyes stray down to the floor as she remembers all that happened during the fearful summer: the strange boy and the pain in her belly, the blood, the tiny corpse. But nothing can spoil the happiness of this day that seems to be washing the shelter clean of all that darkness. She notices a tingling in her hands. They are alive and now she watches as they begin to turn over in her lap, moving smoothly like the tortoise turns his neck, till they are palms up. With the tingling comes a peace that is full of power. The feeling of promise is familiar, drawing her back to that time when she was taken up from the shelter, travelling endlessly through the rich, still darkness. Was it a dream? She rests, hardly needing to breathe, till the tingling begins to fade. It is time to go back. Her thoughts turn to Lotz, like a flock of bulbul returning to their favourite roost.

Walking on the cave path, she hears voices from the slope below. Bo and Gashi are climbing up, with some of the children. She waits, listening to the excited buzz of their talk. The women's bags are full of food: acorns and roots and tubers, swelled by the heavy rains.

'What did you get?' Gashi calls to her.

Ansa opens her bag and there are shrieks of delight from the little ones; earthnuts are their favourite. Hua climbs down from Gashi's shoulders and runs to Ansa, who picks her up and swings her round, again and again. Giggling, Hua takes hold of Ansa's hand for the walk home.

Ansa falls into step beside Bo, glad that they are comfortable together again. Though it is Bo's first child, her belly is swelling noticeably. As they climb up the winding path, Gashi starts the song of the hare. Ansa's heart feels like it will burst. She opens her mouth and begins to sing.

It is black dark inside the cave, Lotz's body warm beside her. He is not asleep and she can feel that his thoughts are on her, as she hums softly. He turns over.

'What song is that?' he asks, his breath in her ear.

'The song of the hare.'

They lie for a long time but still Lotz's breathing does not settle into the slow rhythm of sleep.

'Where did you find the earthnuts?' he asks.

'On the edge of the ravine.' Ansa loves it that he is interested in what she has been doing. 'Near the rockshelter.'

'The rockshelter - where is it? Will you show me?'

She would like to take him there one day, but somehow she can't picture him in the shelter.

'When I was resting there today,' she says, 'something like lightning came into my hands. They began to move on their own.' It is easier to say things like this to him in the dark, even though he doesn't laugh at her so often now.

'How? Show me.'

She reaches for his fingers, placing them on top of hers, as she slowly turns her hands palm up. The tingling begins again, but more faintly. She can feel him smiling and then he is kissing her neck and everything about the day fades from her thoughts.

When Ansa wakes in the morning, Lotz is limping towards her, a bowl in his hand. She takes it from him, draining the water gratefully. He lowers himself down to the ground and she can see that he is excited.

'Who is the fastest with a throwing stick? Is it Goi, or Koldo? Or Bidari?'

She tries to remember. The men have not needed to go down to the plain to catch rabbits for a time - the chukar traps have been making enough small meat.

'I think Bidari is the fastest. Why?'

That smile is playing around his mouth, the one that makes her eager to know his thoughts. He is untying something from his belt – it's a throwing stick. She looks up at him, puzzled.

'Are you going to hunt rabbit?'

He laughs so loudly that Esti turns to stare from the cave mouth.

'Not with this.' He jiggles the stick in his hand. 'And not rabbit.'

'What then?'

'Hare.' He looks at her, the smile widening into a full grin. 'There is more meat on a hare.'

Ansa is doubtful. 'But hares run too fast.'

'Yes. And my stick will fly even faster.'

He strokes the top of her head then moves away, toward the cave mouth. She follows him with her eyes.

Chapter 19

Bidari

Bidari is squatting beside Bakar, watching him plane the lengths of pine. The wood is soft and sappy and Bakar uses his fingers to see. Earlier, he had taken up a blade to begin shaping the bulb at the end of the throwing stick, but Lotz had cried out to him to stop. Heavy rain has soaked the outside hearth so they are working inside, in the poor light. It is all the same to Bakar.

Lotz comes over, sweating from the effort of dragging hot rocks into the firepit. He picks up one of the planed sticks and measures it along the length of his arm.

'Good,' he says and brushes Bakar's forehead with his fingertips in respect.

When all four sticks are ready, Bidari takes them over to the firepit. He wonders how the sticks will spin without a club head.

'Put them in the fire,' orders Lotz. Bidari looks up at him, the surprise showing on his face. 'Don't worry. We will take them out before they burn.'

The smoke is blowing into Bidari's face. He turns away to cough and catches Koldo's scent. Goi is with him. They are standing a little way back, watching. After a time, Lotz takes up a hardwood poker and nudges the throwing sticks, one by one, out of the fire. He turns to Bidari.

'Now. They go in the pit – on the hot stones.'

Using the poker, Bidari rolls the hot sticks across the floor to the firepit and down onto the flat bed of stones. It makes no sense, but he has come to trust Lotz. He sits back on his heels, waiting. Lotz leans over the firepit, adjusting the position of the sticks. Now he indicates some heavier rocks he has kept to one side.

'These go on top – to make them bend,' he says.

Bend? The rocks are still hot and Bidari fetches a skin to wrap around his hands. When he gets back, he notices Koldo's blank face that probably means he is angry. Bidari lifts the rocks, one by one, and drops them down into the pit.

Taking the skin to protect his hands, Lotz rolls them along, till there is a heavy weight pressing down on the end of each stick. He wedges the hot rocks in place with smaller ones, then sits back, breathing heavily.

Next morning, the sky is clear and there is a gleam of excitement in Lotz's eyes as he and Bidari set off down the path. Bidari looks back to see that Koldo, Goi and Tipi are following behind. Eshtu is warm on his back and he starts to whistle under his breath.

They leave the path and cross the face of the mountain. She is changing; the autumn rains have coaxed the first green of winter from the dry earth. Ahead there is a slope, clear of trees. They sit down to rest and drink some water. Lotz gestures towards Bidari's pack and he takes out the four throwing sticks. They are pleasing to hold: smooth and tapered at the edges, each bent at one end. Bidari hands them round, but Koldo shakes his head. He has brought his own throwing stick. It is shorter than these new ones and has the familiar bulb shape at one end, to give weight in the air. Lotz shrugs and takes up the last of the new sticks.

Bidari helps him to his feet and the others stand watching, as he jiggles the stick, getting used to the feel of it in his grasp. Lotz chooses a flat place between two rocky outcrops, and plants his feet carefully, adjusting his stance till the weight is on his back leg, the good one. Over to his right, some distance away, stands a squat thorny shrub. In the spring it will have yellow flowers but the heat of summer has sucked it dry, leaving only the spiky thorns. Bidari is puzzled. Lotz seems to be eying up the shrub, judging its distance, but he will never hit the bush from this angle.

All eyes are on Lotz. Instead of raising the stick over his shoulder to throw it, he wraps his arm across his chest so that the stick is by his left armpit, then with a flick of his wrist throws the stick sideways. Bidari watches, open-mouthed, as the stick flies low, at chest height, through the air. It turns over in the air, side to side, and falls only just wide of the thornbush, breaking off one of its branches. Bidari and Tipi cheer.

Lotz moves aside for Bidari who takes up his position, eager to do even better. The stick feels too light but he is careful to copy Lotz's strange new hold. Bidari releases the stick and it spins fast and true, hitting the trunk of the thornbush with a loud thwack.

Koldo pushes forward, his own throwing club in his hand, and edges Bidari aside. He turns to face the thornbush, steadies himself, then lifts his hand high and throws his club overarm, in the way they have always done. It flies well –

arcing up into the air and then down, right into the body of the bush. A look of satisfaction crosses Koldo's face and Lotz nods his head, smiling. Koldo takes one of the new curved sticks from Tipi.

'Let me try with this.'

He places his arm across his chest but Lotz steps closer, moving Koldo's hand lower and turning the wrist to show him the flicking movement.

'Keep your arms close to your body,' he says, 'and the hare will not be alerted.' Lotz lifts the stick up and waves it above his head. 'Doing it your way, the hare will see and run.'

Bidari looks up quickly, but Koldo doesn't seem to be offended by the lesson. Instead, he is laughing. 'Hare? You think we can kill hare with these?'

'I know we can,' answers Lotz. He is smiling too. 'I have brought down hare with a bent stick like this.'

Koldo stares at him, then glances back at Goi. He shifts his weight onto the back foot and flicks his wrist. The stick leaves his hand and flies low, spinning over and over. It falls just beyond the bush but Bidari claps anyway.

The sky grows lighter with every step, as the four men wind their way down the mountain. They plan to reach the toes of the mountain just as dawn begins to break. This is when the rabbits run, cropping the new grass on the plain, and where they might just come upon hare, with his long ears and powerful hind legs. Bidari is in front; he always leads when they go to hunt rabbit. He has been practising the new sideways throw and his thoughts are full of the tricks that Lotz showed him. Koldo and Goi will be amazed.

The grass is wet under their feet from the dew. They go

slowly now, keeping silent. On the edge of the plain, they find a clump of oaks where they can watch for any movement on the lower slopes. Under cover of the trees, Bidari listens to his breath slowing down after the long descent. The sky is a soft pink and the leaves are becoming greener with every breath the men take. He settles down to wait.

It is Goi who spots something first, but the rabbit is too far away. They wait for one to come within throwing range, content that the young, tender grass will draw many out to feed. They stand motionless in the pale light of dawn, sticks poised. Now comes a low hiss from Tipi. He raises three fingers and then points over to the left. Bidari turns slowly and there, quite close, are three brown shapes in the grass, hunched over, feeding. There are two adults and one young rabbit. Their heads bob up and down as they crop the grass. One of them has lifted her head and is looking from side to side, her mouth moving, her ears pricked. Bidari puts a warning hand up to the others. They must wait till she is feeding again. Very slowly, he edges out from under cover and moves into position. He steadies himself, completely still, eyes on the brown hump of fur. Then, with a flick of his wrist, he sends the stick flying from his hand. It turns over, side to side, keeping low and fast. The rabbit hears nothing till the last breath. Her ears are up and her back legs spring but it is too late. The stick lands low, hitting her flank. The other two rabbits are bobbing away to cover but the felled rabbit lies, stunned, on the grass.

Bidari cries out to the others and sprints across. The rabbit's body is trembling but she cannot move; her hind leg may be broken. He kneels and strokes the fur around her ears to quieten her, then quickly twists her neck. The body continues to tremble for a breath or two, then lies still. Bidari slings the limp form over his shoulder.

'Get back to the oaks,' he orders Tipi, who has come to watch. 'Let's see how many more we can take.'

Back under the trees, Koldo acknowledges the kill with a nod and Bidari swells with pride. 'This new stick is better than the old ones.'

Koldo shrugs but Bidari knows that he is impressed.

'Keep still!' Goi whispers. 'There's another one!'

Their eyes follow the direction of his finger. There are three, no four, rabbits in the grass. This time, Goi takes up position and throws, but his stick falls a little short and the rabbits scatter.

The face of Eshtu slides into view above the mountain and soon the dew will be gone, but still the rabbits come to eat the fresh new grass. Bidari shows them the flicking motion and each one tries his hand. Goi brings down a buck and Tipi hits a doe, but she manages to spring up and run off to safety. Koldo has trouble in keeping the stick's flight low and he hits nothing.

The air is becoming hot and there has been no movement in the grass for some time. A blade of hunger twists in Bidari's belly; they should go back. He signals to the others, but Koldo's body is tense, his eyes on the slope to their right. Now he is creeping slowly behind the trees and out again into the open. Suddenly, Bidari sees it: a patch of brown, a head moving up and down, long ears. The others stand as still as the oaks, watching. Bidari holds his breath as Koldo takes aim. With a sudden, powerful flick, he sends the curved stick flying through the air. This time, the stick spins low. There is a flurry of movement and a shrill call as the ears prick up, the long back legs buck into the air. *A hare!* The creature springs to a run but the stick bends round in its flight, taking the hare by surprise. He runs into its path and is caught a glancing blow on the shoulder. Goi is up and away before Koldo, running the hare down. Injured, the hare cannot escape and soon the two men are on him.

Koldo strides back with Goi, his face alight. Bidari cannot believe the size of the buck's body. His ears lie spread over Koldo's chest, whilst his powerful hind legs dangle down Koldo's back, almost to his waist. Tipi is whooping with excitement. None of the Oak People has ever caught hare before. Awed by the power of the new sticks, Bidari lifts one of the back legs; there is meat for three men here. Only one thing blunts the edge of his joy. Why did it have to be Koldo? He should have been the first one to take hare.

Ansa

The women are crowding round, to get a view of the big buck. Ansa leans over Esti's shoulder, to watch the gutting. The hare's body lies arched across the flat stone, his head back and his long ears dangling, like the creature that can be seen in the face of Balqa.

They are excited. There are rabbits to skin after this; there will be plenty of meat tonight. Esti turns the animal over and makes the first slit along the length of his belly. Bo begins to giggle as she cuts away the bag containing the hare's stones. Esti waves the pouch around in the air. She turns to Ansa, a large yellow tooth visible in the midst of her grin.

'Nearly as big as your man's, I shouldn't wonder!'

Bo shrieks in delight. Ansa smiles and covers her face with her hands, knocking Esti's shoulder so that she drops the

246

bleeding bag into Gashi's lap. Now they are all laughing.

These nights, it grows cold as soon as Eshtu has slipped down behind the Salt Water. They are inside the cave, grouped around the cooking hearth, the smell of roasting meat everywhere. Bakar is playing his pipe and there will be dancing once their bellies are full. Ansa is sitting by Lotz's good leg, where he likes her to sit. Bidari is to his right and she can hear the excitement in his voice as he tells Lotz of the day's hunting. Lotz says little but Ansa can tell he is pleased they took a hare. This night will be a happy one.

At last, the juices dripping from the meat are no longer bloody and Gashi starts slicing the succulent flesh from the bones. Young Iban and his sisters are waiting to pass the meat around. Ansa watches them, warm and lazy from the heat of the fire. She feels Lotz's hand pressing down on her arm, as he hauls himself to his feet. He limps over to the hearth and speaks out.

'Whose stick was it that brought down the hare?' Lotz asks, his eyes searching the faces ringed around him in the firelight.

The hubbub dies down. They all know the answer but proper respect must be given and it is Bidari who gives it.

'Goi and I took the rabbits. But the hare – that was Koldo.'

A cheer goes up and Koldo lowers his eyes to the floor, grinning. Lotz takes a piece of the hare's hind leg and makes his way over to where Koldo is sitting. Ansa squints through the smoke, eager to see what he will do.

'Koldo felled the hare, so he must be the first to eat,' says Lotz, handing Koldo the meat.

He takes something else from the bag on his belt and gives it to Koldo. Ansa strains to see what it is in the flickering light. Koldo takes a look and shakes his head. Taking the thing back, Lotz turns to face the others. He holds it up in the firelight, turning slowly so that everyone has a chance to see. It is brown and knobbly, covered in fur. It looks like one of the feet of the hare, but a hole has been pierced through the middle and a cord threaded through. There is silence. The object reminds Ansa of something she has seen once before, but she can't remember when.

'Has any man brought you hare meat before?' Lotz calls out loud.

Bakar answers; they have come across injured hare before but no-one has ever brought one down.

'Then Koldo must wear the foot.' The words ring out strong and clear, in Lotz's strange accent.

Ansa glances at Bidari. He is frowning.

'Why?' asks Goi. 'What will it do?'

Lotz's face relaxes into a smile and there is tittering from the shadows behind.

'It will bring the Oak People good luck in hunting the hare,' Lotz replies. 'And Koldo will wear this sign of respect always.'

'No.' Koldo is shaking his head again.

Lotz looks to each of the men in turn. They are uncertain. The sign of respect is made on the forehead, by the fingers of another; it is not something tied on a man's wrist. But if he says it will bring them luck …

At last, Bakar nods and the others murmur their agreement. Ansa's thoughts dwell on the new picture Lotz has drawn for them with his words. The men carry the tooth of their prey when they go hunting. Perhaps wearing the hare's foot will make the same magic.

Lotz kneels beside Koldo, to fix the cord around his wrist.

Koldo is still unsure but the others are nodding and at last he holds out his arm for Lotz to tie the cord. The hare's foot now sits flat on the back of his hand. As soon as it is done, Koldo gets to his feet. He has something to say.

'Without Lotz's new spinning stick, I would not have made this meat.' He bends down and makes the sign of respect on Lotz's forehead. 'Now, let's eat.'

There are cheers from the young boys but Lotz is struggling to his feet again. 'Wait. There is one more thing you must know.' The noise dies down. 'Your fathers and mothers who sit in adar-so, on the plains of the dead, it is they who have sent us this meat. They spoke to my woman, Ansa.'

Ansa's heart seems to stop beating.

'They sent life into her hands so that they turned over, just as the throwing stick turns in the air. They put the song of the hare into her mouth. She brought this message from your ancestors. I only made the sticks as they said.'

Ansa is astonished. What is he saying? Could he be right? The cave is silent, except for the spitting and cracking of burning wood.

At last, Gashi speaks out. 'When he was with us, Nuno used to see things that were hidden. Now it is Ansa who sees them.'

The others are nodding. All around, Ansa can feel their good will, like arms embracing her. She looks at Lotz, at his clever, beautiful face. He is smiling and a wave of love rises up inside her, washing everything else away in its wake.

Chapter 20

Ansa

Ansa wakes to darkness. Winter is creeping closer and a damp cold rises up through the bedding leaves. She pulls the bed skin up to her neck, turns onto her back and listens to the deep, steady breathing of Lotz. All around in the high, wide space, there are night sounds: rats scurrying in the ash heap, the rhythmic gasp of Esti's snoring, a whimper from one of the children. But now it comes again, the muffled sound of a man's cry, coming from higher up the slope where Bo sits with Bidari. She huddles in closer to Lotz, the warmth from his body gradually seeping into her own.

In the morning, Ansa goes to the cave mouth. The stars have been chased away by the growing daylight. Lotz is already outside, the fingers of Eshtu reaching between the branches to paint bright patches on his back. Koldo is sitting with him again and their heads are close, bent over something in Lotz's lap. She is glad that they are no longer like hyenas fighting over the same piece of meat.

Ansa hears noisy breathing behind her and Bidari brushes past, his cheek cradled in one hand. He is clearly in pain. He sees the men sitting in the morning warmth and turns away towards the spring, a guttural sound escaping from his throat.

Gashi is working on a rabbit skin. She looks up and beckons Ansa over. It seems strange to Ansa now that she used to be frightened of the older woman.

'It's for Bo – for when the child is born,' she says, handing her the skin. It stinks of rotting brain, but it is already soft and Ansa rubs it against her cheek, smiling. She remembers the moaning she heard in the night.

'Bidari has toothache. Is there anything that can ease it?'

Gashi screws up her face, thinking. 'Terebinth,' she replies. 'There may be a few berries left on the trees.'

Hua comes running up, just as Ansa is starting off. 'Where are you going? Can I come?'

Ansa's face lights up and she drops down so that her eyes are level with Hua's. 'Yes – you can help me. We're going to get some medicine.'

'For me?'

'No – for your Ita. He has a bad tooth.'

Hua takes Ansa's hand and skips along beside her. They do not need to go all the way down to the plain. Perhaps there will still be fruit on the terebinth that stands alone, close to the path. A wind has blown up, sending white clouds scudding across the sky. They sing Hua's favourite song as they walk, the crocodile song. Hua pretends to be the crocodile, opening and shutting his mouth.

There are just a few curled, reddish brown leaves left clinging to the branches. Here and there, clumps of the small fruits remain, some puckered and too dry to use. Ansa climbs up to reach a spray of brighter red berries. They must contain some juice.

'Let me see!'

Ansa shows Hua the fruits, then tucks them in her bag. As they start back, the first drops of rain fall. She looks up; it will only be a shower, but a heavy one. Taking Hua's hand, she runs for the nearest oak, whose leaves have not yet fallen. Hua is shrieking with delight.

They huddle together, laughing, then Ansa lowers herself to the ground and takes Hua onto her lap. The child puts out her palms to catch the drops of rain that find their way through the leaves. She is still humming the crocodile song.

Soon Ansa feels her daughter's body relax in sleep, the weight slumped across her chest. Ansa leans back, waiting for the rain to stop. Hua's breathing is shallow but even. She looks down at the child and a memory begins to stir. *Hua asleep, draped across Bakar's knee. The blood pulsing around the veins in her body, the heart squeezing.* She feels again something of the wonder of that other place where she could see so much more. In that place, she had been able to look deep inside her daughter's body. Now she sees only Hua's hair against her cheek, one arm on her chest, her leg dangling. Once again, she recalls what Lotz said to everyone by the hearth. Did the ancestors give her a message, as he said? Could it be true that she visited the land of the dead again and has, perhaps, forgotten?

Rain is no longer spattering on the leaves. The grey clouds are parting, to reveal the face of Eshtu. The wind whips fresh between the oak branches, across her back and shoulders. Now it plays around her face and she gasps as the breeze seems to enter her open mouth, pass through her body and Hua's then on, up the trunk of the oak, along the branches, into the leaves. The berries in her bag, the ground under her buttocks, even the deep earth itself: everything is alive with the wind. A thought comes to her, as gentle as a caress. *Breathe the wind.* She sits, filling her belly with breath, then blowing the wind out through her mouth. She is like the oak, with roots that go deep, with sap that flows freely. How could she have forgotten this?

Soon Eshtu is blazing down on the oaks, the wet earth giving off a warm smell. Hua wakes, hungry, and they start for home.

Ansa longs to sit and talk with Lotz but he is nowhere to be seen. Instead, she goes to find Bo, squatting by the inside hearth with Esti. The young woman's belly is swollen and tight above her belt. Ansa unslings her bag and takes out the sprig of berries.

'Gashi said these will make medicine – for Bidari's tooth.'

Esti takes one of the fruits, screwing up her eyes in the poor light. 'Terebinth? Yes. Tell him to chew on these. It will ease the pain.'

Bo takes the berries and looks up at Ansa, grateful.

'Take them to him now,' old Esti says. She knows only too well the agony of a rotting tooth. 'I can see to the fire.'

But Bo only stares down at the ground. 'I don't know where he is,' she says.

Esti stares at her. 'The men took the throwing sticks. They've gone to practise.'

'I know, but Bidari didn't go with them.'

Ansa can feel the disquiet in Bo.

'He's gone walking, I expect,' says Esti. 'To deaden the pain.'

Sitting in the dark beside Lotz, Ansa can't stop laughing. Lotz has told her the story of his brother and the bees before, but every time he adds something new, something funnier. She loves listening to him talk about when he was a boy: the valley with the river running through it, the baskets they wove to catch fish.

Later, they are lying close, Ansa pressed against Lotz's back. Her hands begin to tingle and she can feel the life inside her pulsing in and out with each breath. She puts her hand on his arm and breathes the wind, feeling it flow through her body and into his. The air around them seems still and heavy with life.

Lotz turns towards her, his voice gentle. 'Koldo wants to speak to his brother.'

'Bidari?'

'No. The other one – Nuno.'

Ansa is puzzled. 'You were there when we dug a place for his body.'

Lotz nods but just stares into her eyes. She stares back at his quick, beautiful face. He is waiting, waiting for her to see something. He reaches out and pushes the hair back from her face.

'He wants to know if Nuno is free from the Sakaitz poison, now that he sits on the plains of the dead.'

'But how?' Ansa has stopped breathing.

'You saw Nuno – after his spirit flew from his body. You can search for him again. Perhaps he will send a message for Koldo.'

Ansa turns over onto her back. The peace she felt has faded. Her thoughts are looping, round and back, like flies in the heat. What does he mean? She didn't go searching for Nuno. He showed himself to her.

'I don't know how,' she says at last.

Lotz takes her hand and strokes it with his fingers. He looks past her into the darkness and speaks as if he is telling a story. 'Among my people is an old man who can journey to the place of the ancestors, whenever he chooses. He prepares himself, and then he flies from his body.' Lotz turns back to her. 'He always returns. With healing and messages from the dead ones.'

Ansa remembers what Bidari told her about the hunt magic: about the chanting, about the drumming when Koru died.

'How does he prepare himself?' Ansa's voice is a whisper.

'He dances - like you danced on the night of Balqa. And he cuts his arm – here and here – with a blade.' He touches both sides of Ansa's wrist.

She looks away from him, her thoughts becoming entangled. *A man who flies from his body?* The thought fascinates her but there is also a mist of confusion. Lotz's eyes are on her. His body is taut, waiting for her to answer.

Ansa takes a deep breath and the looping thoughts begin to slow their pace. She pictures herself under the oak tree, breathing the fresh, clean wind and now she feels it again, here in the cave. It is blowing over her, through her, into the rock beneath and above, into the heart of the mountain herself. There is nowhere that the wind cannot reach.

Lotz is staring at her, puzzled. What was it again that he wanted from her? She puts out her hand, as if to calm him.

'There is no poison in Nuno.' She feels certain of this. 'Nothing can trouble him anymore,' she whispers.

Lotz hauls himself up onto his elbow but the sudden movement disturbs Hua, sleeping close by. She turns over, opens her eyes, and begins to whimper. 'Ama! Ama!'

Ansa scoops her up, holding her tight and rocking her till

the whimpering subsides, but she is still awake.

'Ama – tell me a story,' she whispers. 'About Mul.'

'Who is Mul?' Lotz asks.

Hua's thumb comes out of her mouth. 'The magic boy. Ama saw him at the spring – on the mountain.'

'I don't know that story,' says Lotz. 'Who is this Mul?'

It sounds from his voice as if he is smiling but somehow Ansa feels uneasy. She lays Hua down on the bedding.

'It's just a story,' she says to Lotz, 'to make her laugh.'

She kisses Hua. 'Go back to sleep now.'

Bo

The cold nights have come and gone and now it is good to sit outside again, enfolded in Eshtu's warm embrace. The lower slopes of the Antelope Nose are dotted with reds and yellows, pinks and white.

Bo sits, suckling the baby she gave birth to in the winter, gazing out toward the Salt Water. The men are out on the mountain but Bidari is not with them. He is somewhere down on the plain, hunting rabbits. He left while it was still dark, two throwing sticks slung across his back. She was awake but he would not speak to her; maybe he is still angry with her. She looks down and strokes the dark fuzz on the infant's head while he pulls at her teat. He is small but he feeds well and seems to be growing.

Ikomar comes out into the daylight, her arms full of old bedding, and Bo quickly reaches for a skin to cover the child. Since her husband Nuno died and the swelling in her belly bled away to nothing, Ikomar has been bitter. Sometimes, when she stares at Bo's baby, there is a longing in her eyes that frightens Bo. Ikomar passes, wandering over to join the other women, who are parching the first of the grass peas.

Bo wriggles on the ground, trying to ease her numb buttocks. She has been hungry all winter, what with suckling the child. Soon, the mountain will make more food for them. She tickles the baby's cheek, to wake him up.

'Suck,' she whispers. 'Grow big and strong.'

She hears loud, animated voices as Koldo and Goi return from the watching place. Have they sighted antelope? She strains to hear what is being said. Koldo is looking back along the path and soon Lotz appears, leaning on his stick. There is something in his hand that looks like a bird.

From over by the women comes a shriek of terror. What's happening? Bo pulls the sleeping child gently from her nipple and, binding him close, gets to her feet and goes to join the others. Lotz is seated on the ground, plucking the bird. *Aiee!* The feathers which lie all around him have striped brown snake-like markings which speak of poison and danger. Quail feathers! She shudders and covers the baby's head with her hand. How does Lotz dare to touch it?

'Koldo – where are you? What is he doing with it?' old Bakar demands.

'He says it is safe to eat, Uncle,' Koldo replies. 'His people eat them.'

'No!' Esti shakes her head. 'If you eat quail – you will die. Everyone knows that.'

Lotz takes no notice and carries on plucking the bird, the hint of a smile at the corner of his mouth. A breeze blows up, scattering some of the feathers, and the children jump back.

Bo hears a noise and turns to see Bidari appearing on the path. She forgets about the quail. He is striding along like the old Bidari, smiling so broadly that she can see the gap between his front teeth. There is a bundle of meat strung over his shoulder. Hua goes running to him and he squats, letting her stroke the fur, the long ears of one of the limp bodies.

Bo nudges Gashi. 'Look! Bidari has brought a hare!'

Gashi glances across but then turns back to Lotz and the poisonous bird. Everyone wants to see what he will do with it. He has taken a blade and cut off the head and now he is crawling towards the hearth with it. Esti climbs to her feet and stands between Lotz and the fire. Her face is screwed up in distaste.

'Goi!' she appeals to her son. 'Stop him!'

Lotz shrugs and smiles, as if Esti is just an old woman who knows nothing. Bakar has been murmuring but now he speaks out. 'Esti is right. We do not eat this bird.'

Bo feels Bidari's hand on her arm. He has come across to see what is going on. 'It's a quail,' Bo whispers to him. 'He wants to cook it to eat!'

Bakar is peering around the ring of people, trying to sense where Lotz is. When he speaks he sounds distressed.

'You say your people eat the flesh of the quail? We have always known that it brings sickness.'

Goi breaks in, impatient. 'Yes, Ita, but Lotz's people have more knowledge than we do. Didn't he show us how to bend the throwing sticks?'

Bo is listening carefully. Lotz knew how to trap the chukar, she thinks. Perhaps he is right and the old ones are wrong. But the bird has such a dirty look. Even its feathers seem to reek of danger.

Bidari pushes past Bo and elbows his way into the circle. He throws the rabbits and the hare down onto the ground and looks round at them all.

'Look! While you were all sleeping, I went down to the plain and hunted real meat. Why waste breath arguing over that thing?' He nods in the direction of the small bird in Lotz's hand.

The others go quiet: hunters should not boast about their own skill. But then comes a chuckle from Tipi and he ventures into the middle of the circle and brushes his fingers across Bidari's forehead. He bends down to examine the pile of meat. The children are edging closer but Gashi pushes them back, away from Lotz and the foul bird.

Lotz speaks out, loud enough for them all to hear. 'Let me cook this bird,' he says, 'then I will eat the meat and you will see that it is safe.'

'Last spring, I was with my people,' Lotz continues. 'Travelling by the Salt Water. We came on other men with nets - these birds were dropping from the sky. We ate till we were full and no-one was sick.' A sadness seems to fall over his face and Bo can only just hear what he says next. 'But if you are too frightened...'

'We're not frightened.' Goi breaks in. He looks round but Koldo is staring at the ground, uncertain.

Even Bidari seems to have forgotten about his kill now. Ansa has dared to pick up one of the feathers and is looking at it carefully. Suddenly, Bo remembers the strange thing the men found last summer, beside the remains of the antelope. A quail feather on a thong.

'Could it be that some quail are poisonous and some are good to eat?' Ansa asks.

Lotz shrugs. 'It could be. This has the same markings as the birds I ate last spring.' He gives a small laugh. 'We shall

259

know when I have eaten it.'

There is a titter of laughter and the tension begins to lift, but Bidari stands his ground. 'We have plenty of meat now – why dirty our hands with this quail?' His voice is bitter. 'We don't have to do everything Lotz says.' His eyes roam around the faces in the circle, looking to Esti, Gashi, Tipi, for support. 'Bakar, you have lived more winters than any of us. What do you say?'

Bo wills Bidari to keep quiet. *Why can't he see how the land lies?* He was all for Lotz at first and the other men have come to respect the stranger. Why is Bidari questioning him now?

Old Bakar clears his throat. 'It may be that we have been wrong. If Lotz wants to build a fire of his own and cook the bird, who should stop him?'

'But the smell of it cooking,' protests Gashi. 'Maybe that will poison the little ones.'

Lotz laughs again. 'Oh well. If you are frightened of the smell of a bird on the fire, I won't cook it.' He smiles at Bidari and shrugs his shoulders. 'You have won. You and the women.' He starts to move away from the hearth, then suddenly spins round. 'But what do you say, Koldo? We've heard no word from you.'

Even the children are quiet now – everyone wants to hear Koldo's answer. To Bo it seems that the dispute is no longer just about the dead bird. Koldo looks troubled. He sees Bidari staring at him but he turns to Gashi.

'Light a new fire over there,' he orders her, pointing away from the cooking hearth. 'Lotz will cook the bird and I will eat it with him. Our people are not afraid of the stories of old women.'

Bo is lying alone in the dark, suckling her child, wondering where Bidari has gone. Her belly is full but she is wretched. It should have been a happy night: Bidari telling the story of the hare, making them laugh. But instead all the talk was of the quail and how Lotz and Koldo shared it between them and how nothing bad happened. She thinks of them joking together and Lotz lifting up Koldo's hand to show them all. He had added one of the ugly striped feathers to the hare's foot that Koldo wears on his wrist.

'This is the man who dares to eats quail! The bravest of you all!' Lotz had called out, between bursts of laughter. Even Koldo was grinning. Then Lotz had started to chant 'Kep Koldo! Kep Koldo!' and the others had joined in.

Now that the two men have eaten the bird and they are not sick, it seems foolish to have been so frightened of the quail. Bo wonders at Lotz's knowledge - he has seen many places, known other men. And why does he keep calling Koldo *Kep*? How can a man be a head?

Bidari comes inside at last, picking his way across the floor to lie down beside her, but he doesn't speak. Hatz has finished feeding and his eyes are fixed on Bo. Now his tiny mouth curves into a smile. She prods Bidari and he turns to face her.

'Look! Your son is smiling.'

She thrusts the child into Bidari's arms. Sometimes he will play with the baby and be happy for a time, but not tonight. He stares blankly and Hatz screws up his face and begins to cry. Bidari hands the child back and turns over to sleep.

Chapter 21

Ansa

Eshtu's touch is hot on Ansa's head and she longs to feel water on her hair, on her face. She threads her way between the children, past the men's hearth where Koldo and Lotz are flaking stone. On the path to the spring, she hears the dull thud of Lotz's stick behind her and she turns.

'Where are you going?'

Surprised that he has left the company of Koldo, Ansa tells him. He falls in beside her and she slows down, reminded of last autumn, when he was first learning to walk again. With the others down on the plain, she and Lotz were alone then, with only Bakar and Esti. Now, he is always with the men.

At the spring, Ansa can feel the eyes of Lotz on her as she holds her head under the flow. The water soaks slowly through the hair to her scalp, running down her back.

'Come with me.' His voice is thick with lust and he grabs her hand.

She laughs, feeling the secret place between her legs begin to swell, and he drags her off the path, pushing her on down the slope till they reach the hawthorns. Ansa gasps at the beauty of the branches, thickly padded with white blossom. He has brought her to the place where they had their first mating. She lies on the ground for him and, before long, they are trying to catch their breath and laughing.

It is good to lie resting in the shade under the hawthorns. Lotz reaches over to smooth Ansa's wet hair from her face. Through his fingers, she catches sight of something in the sky.

'Look!' She pulls Lotz's hand away and points upward.

'Where?' He stares up, shading his eyes from the glare.

'Balqa! There – can you see him?' In the cloudless sky above them, the faintest, hairbreadth curve of white is visible against the blue. 'He has come back.'

That first sight of Balqa, after the dark nights of his death, always brings a shiver to Ansa's scalp. Now, she finds herself taking a deep breath and as she breathes out the life inside her seems to dance up through the air to greet and merge with the newborn Balqa. Lotz is smiling at her excitement but there is no ridicule in his eyes and she is content.

They lie back, sleepy in the spring heat. An afternoon breeze stirs and the white-clad hawthorn branches wave gently above. Gazing at them, Ansa remembers the strange pointed trees she had seen in that other place: the cold blue-white that had settled over everything, like a covering of white fur. She gasps as, for a breath, the vision seems almost close enough to touch. If only she could share it with Lotz – make him see it.

'Is there snow, where your people come from?' she asks, getting up onto one elbow.

'Snow? Like on the mountain tops? No. It is hot where we come from. In summer, the river in our valley dries up, and the ground becomes cracked and hard.'

'Is that why you left? Where were your people going?'

263

He grins up at her. 'You're full of questions. We needed a place with more meat to hunt, and fish. We walked to the ocean and then walked on, beside it.' There is sadness in his eyes. 'Who knows? They are still walking, perhaps.'

Ansa tries to picture them: men, women, old ones and children, walking along the seashore, camping at night on the sand. She does not like to think of the woman called Nahia, with a boy who looks like Lotz.

'The men you found, netting the quail. What were they like? Did you fight them?'

'No. Kep Zorion sat with their Kep and traded with them. We camped with them for two nights, then we walked on.'

Kep. He is saying that word again. How can a man be a head? Suddenly, Ansa understands. It is a man's head that decides where the man should go, what he should do. Is it the same with a whole people?

'Tell me about your Kep Zorion – how does he know what should be done?'

Lotz's eyes dart towards her face and then away. He shrugs his shoulders. 'He wears the band on his head. He is Kep. Like Koldo.'

Koldo? Is Koldo the head of the Oak People?

'But when the men go hunting, Goi leads the way, not Koldo,' she says. 'And it's always Bidari who tells the hunt story afterwards.'

One man speaking for everyone, deciding what to do; grasping what this means is like trying to catch a butterfly in your hand. Ansa goes on.

'And Koldo can't make medicine when someone is sick – Gashi has that knowledge, and Esti. And what about Bakar? He is better than anyone at making new tools.'

'But if a leopard has many heads, with eyes looking in many different directions across the herd, how can she pick out the weak antelope who is falling behind?' Lotz is looking keenly into her face. He speaks slowly but his eyes dance with the thoughts that lie behind them. 'If everyone speaks, there is only quarrelling. And fighting.'

Ansa remembers Koldo and Lotz rolling on the ground, Koldo's fist crashing down onto Lotz's bare shoulder, and she shudders. Perhaps he is right.

'Koldo doesn't always speak out.' Ansa is remembering nights around the fire. 'But he listens. And we all wait to hear what he will say.' Then she has another thought. 'But now you have come, we listen to you.'

Lotz puts his finger to her lips, as if she is a child who must be kept quiet. 'No.' He shakes his head. 'I am not Kep.' His eyes drop down to his bad leg and then up to her face again. 'Koldo is Kep.'

Ansa lies flat, staring up at the moving branches and the sky beyond. She loves hearing the thoughts that race behind Lotz's eyes, watching his face for the new words and meanings.

'Koldo should wear the band,' he says now, 'around his forehead. To show that he is Kep.'

She thinks of the others: Bakar and Esti, Goi and Sorne, Gashi, Ikomar. Would they laugh if Koldo put a band around his head? Would they understand? She is sure that Bidari would be angry.

'Bidari is always miserable now. Why don't you sit with him anymore?' Ansa has wondered about this many times. Surely Lotz is not jealous that Bidari mated with her first.

'Bidari?' Lotz's face is blank.

'Yes. When you first came to us, Bidari was always with you. Don't you remember? It was Bidari you taught - to bend the throwing sticks.'

Lotz shrugs his shoulders. 'But his brother Koldo is Kep – not Bidari.'

He turns onto his side to face her. She can feel him deciding to say something important. 'Ansa. There are not enough antelope on the plain. We may have to move away. Or join with another people – to trade with them.' He speaks more quickly now. 'Like my people did with the quail men. But not just once - a pact of trading.'

Ansa pulls herself up on her elbow and looks into his face. *Move away? Join with another people? A pact of trading?* His words flit and dive like swallows and she cannot follow them. She is uncertain, excited.

'When we meet up with others, someone must speak for us. It should be Koldo.' His voice is calm now and there is no trace of doubt in it. His thoughts seem to turn to something new. 'You told me about the wise old woman - Koldo's mother. What was her name?'

'Koru.'

'Koru sees everything, now that she sits on the plains of the dead. She must be happy that her firstborn is Kep.'

Ansa thinks of Koru, here, under the hawthorns, telling her the story of Mina and the honey badger. She can almost hear the old woman's voice.

Lotz goes on. 'The others would listen to Koldo if she told them to.'

But Koru is gone. Ansa closes her eyes, frightened that he will start talking again like he did before, about journeying to the land of the dead. She tries to turn his thoughts to something else. 'When you ate the quail, by the sea, did the children eat it too? Was anyone sick?' she asks.

Lotz turns over onto his back. He sounds irritable. 'Of course not. Was Koldo sick last night?'

She remembers the men joking around the fire – the quail feather Lotz had put in Koldo's wristband. A question that has been troubling her takes a shape at last.

'Last summer,' she says slowly, keeping her eyes from him, 'when the men were hunting down on the plain, they found an antelope carcass. There was a quail feather on a thong, left in the grass. It was by a reed bed, near a stream.' She gazes up at the sky. 'Did your people hunt on our land?'

He is silent and his breathing seems to have stopped. She turns to seek out his face but he looks away.

'We thought it was Sakaitz,' Ansa continues. 'That's why the men went to the heights to kill them.'

Lotz sits up straight, a wariness in his eyes.

'Ansa. We didn't know about your people - that you hunt on the plain. How could we know?'

She frowns, trying to make sense of it. So it was not Sakaitz who hunted and killed on their plain after all. It was Lotz's people.

'The children were hungry,' he says.

A picture of a small boy, the son of Lotz, comes into her thoughts. He is right. They were not to know. To Lotz's people, it must have seemed as if the antelope gave himself to them.

He leans over and starts to kiss her shoulder. He speaks quietly, close to her ear. 'It's better if you don't tell the others.' His lips are on her neck. 'If the bee's nest is left alone, then no-one gets stung.'

267

He speaks so cleverly but there is something else she doesn't understand. 'You said your people were following the shore. But it was you who killed the Sakaitz. What made you climb up to the top of the Antelope Nose, to their cave?'

He laughs as if this, at least, is easy to explain. 'Filthy animals! We saw their trail – further along the plain there.' He points west. 'We hunted them all the way up the mountain.' There is pride in Lotz's face and a cruelty that makes Ansa want to turn from him. 'We caught them, like rats in their hole! Only one of their young escaped but he wouldn't last long, without the rest of the pack.'

A thought comes to Ansa with the sickening, winding force of a blow. 'A boy? Was it a boy who got away?'

'Yes – a young male.' Seeing her pale face, Lotz wraps his arms around her. 'There's nothing to be frightened of – the hyena made a meal of that cub long ago.'

Weaving her way up between the rocks on the steep hillside, Ansa can feel the heartbeat in her ears. Her palms are sticky with sweat. She stops to get her breath and turns to see the lower slopes stretching out below, dotted with the pinks and yellows and whites of spring. The mountain is turning her mild face towards them, like a mother bringing out toys for her children. Ansa is climbing up to the tortoise path to see if she can find the first egg, as a treat for Hua. Yet still she feels troubled.

The first of the scrapes, not far from the path, has nothing in it. Further on, she finds what she is looking for: two tortoise eggs, then three more. Smiling at the thought of Hua's face when she sees them, Ansa scoops up the eggs, wrapping them carefully in leaves before placing them in her bag.

She is thirsty and crosses the face of the mountain, to the high spring. Twisting her head to catch the flow in her mouth, she glimpses something and pulls back. There, amid the rocks beside the spring, is a tall stem wrapped around with fibres. At once, she remembers the waysigns in that other place, the place of the dead. *A ring of waysigns pointing in toward the centre. The wind blowing over her shoulder.* With a beating heart, she moves closer, but it is only tendrils of bindweed that have twisted themselves around a stem of charlock.

She squats to piss then, looking up, notices the clouds forming above the Salt Water. Eshtu is dropping fast but there will be time to get back if she takes the steep path down by the rockshelter. She turns in that direction and here it comes again – the sigh of wind on her shoulder, like the caress of a mother's hand. Her eyes fill with tears.

Walking by the cliff face, Ansa finds herself wanting to climb up to the shelter. To sit, once more, and look out to the sky. She wonders if the blood stains are still visible on the rock. But then she remembers Hua, waiting for her eggs, and she walks on.

From above, she hears the sharp crack of stone hitting bedrock. She looks up and another stone comes flying down from above, this time catching in a broom bush. She retraces her steps and peers up, but the dark mouth of the rockshelter gapes silently down at her. Perhaps it was a bird landing on the ledge. She turns to go but then comes the cry. It is not the cry of a bird, or the bleat of a goat. The skin on her neck prickles. Which way to run? The call comes again, hoarse and cracked, urgent. A face appears in the dark mouth of the shelter. Mul!

The blood seems to drain from Ansa's head. The boy is

alive. He is not just a shadow in her dreams. Fear pounces onto her shoulders, trying to pin her to the ground, but the breeze seems to whisper in her ear that she is safe. Hasn't she always known somehow that this would happen?

Now he is calling her name in the old way - *Onsa!* His voice is weak.

Ansa doesn't stop to think. Her feet find footholds as she climbs up, her ears full of the piping of tiny birds that flit across the face of the rock. Clambering up onto the ledge, she finds that he has crawled back to the wall and is crouching there, clutching a handaxe. Even in the dim light, the sight of him is a shock; bare patches are showing on his head, his lips are cracked. The hand holding the axe is so thin, the wrist bones sharp. His arm twitches.

'It's me – Ansa.'

She crawls towards him, making soothing noises as if he were Hua. She kneels back, showing him her palms. He drops the axe onto the floor but his eyes continue to watch her warily. Is it safe to go closer? The axe edge looks viciously sharp. She remembers the gash on Nuno's head that took away his thoughts. Ansa peers into the face of Mul: thinner and weaker, but still the boy who brought her water, who stroked her arm. Something wet is shining on his cheek. She moves closer and now there are small moans coming from his mouth. She wraps her arms around him, taking no notice of the foul smell. Shutting her eyes, she breathes deep from her belly, letting the life flow from inside her into the body of the emaciated boy. She feels the life within him flicker in answer.

She breaks open three of the eggs and watches as he sucks the food greedily. His gums are bleeding; there are streaks of blood mixing with the yellow of the yolks. Ansa searches in the debris at the back of the cave and comes upon the tortoiseshell bowl she used to fill with water from the spring. She shows it to him.

'I'm going to get water,' she says.

She climbs down to the spring. The sky is grey with cloud but there is a band of red above the Salt Water. Back in the shelter, Mul drains the bowl. 'Onsa,' he whispers, as if he is remembering too.

She peers into her bag, then back at his thin face. Amid the dirt, she can see a rash of red blotches on his pale skin. She takes out the remaining two eggs and places them in his hands.

'I'll come back - with more food.' She mimes eating and he nods, as she crawls back to the ledge.

By now the trees are dark growths on the grey face of the mountain. With every breath, the half-face of Balqa glows whiter and sharper in the sky. Ansa trusts her feet to find their own way, her thoughts back in the shelter with Mul. He is very weak – perhaps close to death. She will go back tomorrow and the next day, to take him water and food. She walks on, pictures filling her thoughts, one after the other. *Mul, squatting beside Bakar, watching him shape a tool. Hua, crouching behind him, her little arms around his neck.*

The pictures fade as a cold voice breaks into her thoughts. *They will never let you bring Sakaitz back to the cave.* She remembers Lotz's face - how ugly it became when he spoke of killing them like rats. But if they could only see Mul for themselves. Lotz is clever - he would understand there is nothing to fear.

Before she has rounded the bend, Ansa smells smoke and

hears the crackling of the flames. A complaining rumble sounds in her belly. She must keep back some food for Mul.

Gashi is returning from the dungheap. 'Where have you been?' she asks Ansa. Without waiting for a reply, she goes on, in a low voice. 'They've got it.'

'What?'

Gashi's voice drops even further, to a whisper. 'What Koru told you to dig for.' She sounds frightened, but her eyes are shining with excitement. 'Come and see.'

Ansa is confused but the older woman pulls her into the firelight. Everyone is sitting on the ground – even the children. Despite the fire, Ansa shivers; there is something wrong. Lotz is holding something up beside the flames. Now it is being passed from hand to hand, around the circle. Lotz looks pleased. His eyes turn to the shadows where Koldo squats, away from the fire.

Whatever it is has reached Bidari and he is staring at it in horror, but seems reluctant to let it go. The excited murmuring fades as he puts it to his lips. Next to him, Esti becomes impatient and pulls it away then, after a quick glance, places it in Bakar's hand. He traces its shape with his finger before passing it on. At last, it is Ansa's turn and she holds the object up to catch the firelight. It is only a small piece of bone – shaped like a tree with a thick trunk. Puzzled, she hands it on to Ikomar.

Bakar has started drumming. The bone is passed back to Lotz and everyone falls silent as he takes a thin lace and seems to tie it around the bone. Now, suddenly, he is walking towards Ansa. She looks up, questioning, but he just meets her gaze, giving his sudden smile. He leads her over to the hearth where Koldo is kneeling, his head bowed.

Lotz thrusts the little bone on its lace into her hand and whispers in her ear. 'Tie it round his head.'

Ansa shrinks back. The excitement in the air feels dark to her and troubling. Lotz's breath is warm on her neck. 'Tie it around his forehead.'

Koldo looks up – he seems to be waiting. She bends down and does as Lotz said, tying the cord at the back of Koldo's head. The tree-shaped bone sits on Koldo's forehead, half-hidden by his hair. Lotz limps over to Bakar, whispers something, and the drumbeat slows to a steady pulse. Now Lotz kneels down in front of Koldo. He bends low, till his forehead is touching the ground. Ansa remembers the night they caught the first chukar. He bowed like that then, in front of Bakar; now he is doing it to Koldo. He gets up and moves aside for Goi, who kneels and bows in the same way. One by one, the others are doing the same.

Ansa goes back to her place. Lotz is clapping and calling out, to the drumbeat: 'Kep! Kep! Kep!' Other voices join in and the chorus grows loud and raucous. Koldo sits silent beside the hearth, watching the figures kneel before him in turn. He looks dazed, but doesn't try to stop them. Ansa tries to bend her thoughts to understand. Why are they doing this, making Koldo their head? Something must have happened while she was on the mountain. She looks up to see Bidari bowing, his forehead low to the ground. Lotz was right; even Bidari is agreeing to Koldo as their head. Perhaps it is a better way.

When it comes to her turn, smoke stings Ansa's eyes as she kneels but the rock floor is cool on her forehead. She goes back to her place and takes up the cry with the others, losing herself in the drumbeat, like on the nights of Balqa's fullness.

The strength of the Oak People folds around her – a new strength, greater than ever before. Lotz is right. Now they are one man, with one head.

Bakar is weary. Sorne takes the drum from him and Koldo begins to lead them all in the snake dance. He weaves in and out, faster and faster, the children shrieking happily as they try to keep up the pace. At last, the snake begins to rupture into pieces. Ansa collapses onto the ground, pulling Gashi down with her. They roll apart, laughing and panting for breath.

Suddenly, Ansa remembers Mul, alone in the rockshelter, with no fire to warm him. She will go back tomorrow with more food. Another troubling thought comes to her and she turns to Gashi.

'What was it you said before - about Koru telling me something?'

'Don't you remember?' Gashi takes in Ansa's blank face and looks away. 'You fell into a deep sleep when you came back.'

'Came back? What do you mean?'

'From the place of the dead,' Gashi whispers.

Now it is Ansa's turn to look puzzled. Gashi falters, not wanting to speak it out.

'Lotz told us that you saw Koru. She was pointing to Koldo.' Gashi's voice drops still further. 'He warned us that you would not remember.'

Ansa stares, dark fears circling around her, like hyena scenting a kill.

'You don't remember her words?' Gashi looks down at the ground. 'She said that Koldo must be headman.'

The darkness closes in as Ansa begins to understand. It

makes her sick. She thinks of the tree-shaped bone, hanging down from Koldo's forehead. It is probably the right size and the right shape for a forefinger, a pointing finger, but how did they get it? An ugly picture crawls into her thoughts. Koldo and Bidari, digging in the soft earth of the burial shaft for Koru's body.

'Koldo is wearing his mother's finger?' she whispers.

'She said he should. You must remember.' Gashi sounds worried now. 'She wanted us to take the bone. She isn't angry with us.'

Ansa gets up and runs into the darkness, away from the noise and the firelight. Cloud is covering the half face of Balqa and she dare not go any further. She drops to the ground and squats there, covering her face with her hands. Using all her strength, she searches in the darkness, trying to remember, to understand.

Ansa lies alone on the bedding leaves, turning first one way then the other, and still Lotz does not come inside. She hears something and her heart starts to beat faster, but it is only Gashi and the young girl, Lilura.

The palest light of dawn is showing at the cave mouth when she wakes to feel Lotz crawling alongside her, his hair reeking of smoke from the men's fire. The troubling thoughts crowd in at once: Mul, lying weak in the shelter, Koldo with the finger bone tied around his forehead. Lotz yawns and settles down beside her but she rolls over to face him. The sick dread has returned to the pit of her belly.

'Did you dig up Koru's body and take her finger bone?'

Lotz smiles a tight smile. 'Go back to sleep,' he says, soothing her like a child. His fingers slide down her neck to the small mound of her breast and start to fondle it.

Ansa pulls his hand away, her heart beating fast. 'Tell me. What made you do it?'

'You did. You said that's what Koru wanted. She chose Koldo to be headman.'

Ansa peers at him in the gloom, but his eyes are saying nothing.

'But I didn't see Koru. Only before, in the shelter...' Ansa tries to remember. *A bright morning place. Three shapes of light, three flavours, mingling and separating.* 'She didn't say anything to me. She didn't point to anyone.' Speaking it out, Ansa is growing more certain. 'If she had given me a message – I would remember.'

Thoughts are racing behind Lotz's keen eyes. He takes her hand. 'Perhaps, but it makes no difference. Those who have passed to the plains of the dead see everything. They see that Koldo must be the head of your people. Our people.' He yawns again and turns away from her. 'Now let me sleep.'

Ansa sits upright in the early morning light. Her thoughts are like muddy streams of water, cascading down cliff walls after heavy winter rain. First in one place, then another, they find their way down, down to the lowest place, the dry bed of the wadi. Lotz stands on the far side and her thoughts are like the roaring, churning water, filling the river bed, cutting Ansa off from him.

Perhaps she has forgotten, like he said. She clutches at his arm. 'Did I tell you that I saw Koru? Did I tell you that?'

Lotz shakes her off, impatient, then reaches for her hand. 'Ansa. I told you before - Koldo must wear the band. Now he wears it and we have a headman.'

'You said that Koru gave me a message but she didn't. You

lied to the others.'

Lotz's eyes are closing. 'It's what the ancestors want.'

His breathing slows and deepens, as he drifts into sleep. His grasp of her hand relaxes and she turns onto her back, staring up at the rock, high above her. She looks at his sleeping body, so close she can touch him. Yet it seems to her now that he is far away, across a wide chasm, and there is no crossing place.

Ansa's guts twist with hunger and her thoughts turn to what she can take for Mul to eat. Outside, the birds are singing in the growing light and with the new day comes a clear, cold knowledge. She can never bring Mul back to the cave. She must never speak to Lotz about the boy – not to Lotz, not to anyone.

Chapter 22

Bidari

Bidari is striding downhill, the day's burning heat already a threat in the air. Soon he will reach the plain and the shade of the oaks where he can watch, unseen. A part of him knows that there will be no movement on the slopes – this scratchy summer grass will not draw the hare. He has seen nothing for days – not even rabbit. But still he comes down every morning, then toils back up in the fierce heat, empty-handed.

If hare does venture to come, he will not match the speed of my stick, thinks Bidari. Not one of them – not Goi nor Tipi nor Lotz, not even Koldo, who wears Koru's bone - can throw as well as he can, with this curved stick. He has been practising every day.

Bidari waits in the pale dawn, now leaning against an oak trunk, now squatting so that his eyes are level with the tips of the grasses. There is no ripple of movement. Come out hare, he begs, show me your back. Once Eshtu becomes a burning stone above the Nose of the Antelope, he will know for sure that hare is not coming and he will start to climb back. It is then that the question stalking his footsteps will overtake him once more. *I was my mother's favourite. Why did she choose Koldo?*

But it seems that today will be different. There is movement on the plain, not down amidst the grass, but above it. Two dark heads bobbing, wavering in the heat haze. Two men, one taller than the other, making their way steadily through the long dry stems, towards the toes of the mountain. Bidari drops to the ground and crawls behind the tree, his palms suddenly wet, his heart thumping. Tucking the throwing stick into his belt, he catches hold of the lowest branch and hauls himself up, till he is crouching where a branch forks from the main trunk.

Behind the cover of the glossy leaves, he watches the men approach, his breathing shallow, sweat stinging his eyes. They seem to be making for the path onto the mountain. Close to each head, he can see the tall shaft of a spear reaching skyward. He takes the curved stick from his belt but the closer the men come, the more certain he is that they have not seen him. They are side by side, as if talking together, and the sound of laughter reaches him across the shimmering expanse. They do not seem wary.

Now they are close enough for him to see their faces. The smaller man stops to take something from the bundle on his back and, suddenly, Bidari recognizes the line of his nose, his forehead. It is Apal from the Marsh People! And the taller, bigger man is Eneko, his brother. Bidari clambers down from the oak, calling out. The two men spin round and Eneko takes aim with his spear, but Apal has seen him and holds up his hand.

The men jog over to the oak tree where Bidari waits, grinning with relief. Because this is Oak People hunting ground, Bidari is the one to make the greeting. He clenches a fist close to his heart, opening his palm to each in turn, then embracing them both. As always it is Apal who speaks but even the big man, Eneko, is smiling.

'We have come to visit our sister.'

Climbing up the mountain, Bidari takes them to the lower spring to rest and drink. Apal asks about Bo's child, keeping his eyes averted from Bidari's face. It was autumn when the Marsh People and the Oak People camped on the plain together and Bo's belly was heavy. Everyone knows that winter is not a lucky time to be growing a child. The brothers are relieved when Bidari's face breaks into a smile.

'She gave me a strong, healthy boy,' he announces proudly, 'before the spring rains came.'

Apal exclaims and reaches over to brush Bidari's forehead with his fingers. 'And Lilura, our sister?'

'No sign of a child yet, but I'm sure my nephew Tipi is working hard at the task.' Bidari chuckles. 'She is a beautiful girl.'

The brothers from the marshland laugh, gratified.

When they reach the cave only the old couple and Ikomar are there, with the young children. Bakar greets the brothers and Esti fusses around them, bringing something to eat and drink.

'Go!' she instructs Ikomar. 'Go and fetch Lilura.'

There is no sign of the men so Bidari sits with the brothers, swapping news and enjoying the afternoon breeze.

After a time, they hear the women coming down the slope. Lilura appears first; she has been running, her face flushed with excitement, but now she comes to a stop, suddenly shy. Apal calls out a greeting but it is Eneko who wraps his huge arms around his sister. Bidari looks on; there are tears on her cheek. Now she is dragging him by the hand towards the watching place. Apal shrugs and smiles.

'You could not part them when we were children.'

The women are chattering, full of the arrival of the visitors, but Bidari is quiet, wondering what it would be like to have a sister who longs to see him, instead of brothers who show him no respect. Apal's voice breaks into his thoughts.

'Our mother wants to know that my sister is being treated well. Is Lilura happy?'

Bidari thinks back. Until today, he has never seen her weeping, not even when she first came to the cave.

'Tell your mother we have made her welcome. If my nephew were ever to mistreat her, he would have his father to answer to. And me.'

Apal looks out towards the Salt Water. He seems satisfied.

'My brother died on the way back from the joining,' Bidari goes on.

Apal turns back, shocked. 'Your brother? Koldo?'

'No. My brother Nuno.'

'Ah.'

Apal looks down and Bidari knows what he is thinking: that it is not much loss to bury an injured man who cannot hunt and whose thoughts have been stolen by Sakaitz magic. Anger flickers in the soft place below Bidari's ribs but he says nothing. Apal is right.

It is growing late but still the men have not returned. Perhaps they have gone after game. It will be good if they come back with meat to offer the visitors. Now Bidari feels Apal stiffen beside him and turns to see Lotz, standing in the cave mouth. Lotz has been sitting inside for days now, patiently working at a lump of stone. No-one knows why. Apal is staring with suspicion and Bidari remembers that the last time the brothers from the marshes saw him, Lotz was a stranger, lying half dead on a litter.

Lotz limps down the slope towards the two men. Apal gets to his feet and Lotz makes the gesture of greeting.

'Apal and his brother have come up from the marshes to visit their sister,' Bidari explains.

'You are welcome,' Lotz says quietly.

Just then, Eneko and Lilura come back and Apal beckons to his brother. Lotz reaches out to grasp Eneko's broad shoulder, his face breaking into a smile. 'You are very welcome. I have reason to be grateful for your strength. You carried me here.'

The brothers seem tongue-tied by the sight of Lotz standing tall, by the sound of his voice. He speaks like one of the Oak People now, with hardly any trace of an accent. Apal bows his head in acknowledgment.

'Come with me to the watching place,' Lotz suggests to the brothers. 'The others have gone hunting – they'll be back soon.'

The Marsh men turn to Bidari and he gives a small shrug and nods.

It is growing dark when Koldo, Goi and Tipi return, exhausted. The women and children crowd around but their packs are empty and Tipi's shoulder is badly grazed from a fall among the rocks. Bidari can sense Koldo's shame that there is no antelope meat to offer the men from the marshes. Lotz sends Gashi and Bo to the spring and soon they come running back, their hands full of limp chukar bodies. Apal and Eneko stare at the birds.

'What are they?' Apal asks.

Goi chuckles. 'Chukar. The women will cook them.'

282

Apal seems astonished. 'But how did you catch them?'

Koldo grins with pride. 'The chukar roost on the rocks above the spring. We lay traps for them.'

The brothers are silent. They do not want to appear ignorant, but Apal is unable to contain his curiosity. 'How?'

Goi laughs. 'Lotz showed us. Before you go back, we will teach you how to make the traps.'

Eneko is staring at Koldo's forehead, where his hair has parted to show the finger bone, but Apal has not noticed. He is looking round at the faces of the men.

'We have come to see our sister,' he begins. 'But we also have news for you.'

The men hear the gravity in his voice and they all, except Lotz, head down the slope to the men's hearth, settling themselves on the ground. Goi takes out firestone and the others wait while he strikes it to start the fire.

Apal clears his throat to begin, but Koldo puts up his hand. 'Wait.' He turns round, beckoning to Lotz.

Apal's face darkens. 'This concerns only our people and yours,' he says quickly.

Koldo looks surprised, a hard edge coming to his voice. 'Lotz needs to hear it. He is one of the Oak People now.'

Leaning on his stick, Lotz makes his way down the slope. Koldo moves to make a space for him and he lowers himself awkwardly to the ground. The two brothers from the marshes are sitting close together, cross-legged. Koldo's eyes flicker between the two.

'What is your news?'

Apal frowns uneasily at Lotz, but he begins to speak. 'When Balqa was strong, some people came to the marshes, as night was falling. Men, women and children.'

283

Bidari's neck prickles with thrill of the unknown.

'Who were they?' Goi asks.

It is Eneko who answers. 'New people. Strangers.' His eyes are on Koldo's face; they keep straying to the band around his forehead.

'What did they want?' asks Koldo.

Apal takes a long breath. 'Nothing, at first. Just shelter for the night.'

Lotz is leaning forward and Bidari can suddenly smell his sweat.

'How many were there?' Lotz asks. His voice sounds tight - higher than usual.

Apal moves his head from side to side, remembering, counting. 'Four men – more women – some children.'

Bidari is eager to know what happened. 'Did you share your fire with them?'

Apal nods. 'We have never seen people like them. It wasn't just the kho paint. The women had woven their hair into ropes. And they had shells and feathers around their arms and legs – the men too. We could only understand part of what they said. They agreed to give us their weapons for safekeeping.'

It is like the night of a hunt when the story is being recited. Bidari edges forward so as not to miss a word.

'We let them make their shelters close by. They shared the food they were carrying and they danced our dances with us. We thought they would leave the next day but they stayed another night and then another and another.'

'What were they like?' Goi asks.

'The men came with us to fish and they watched and then copied us. They were quick with their hands. The women didn't know the marsh grasses but they listened to my mother and they learned quickly. They stayed four nights.' Apal looks across at his brother. 'After that, we wanted them to move on. But we had given them shelter and exchanged names with them.'

Tipi speaks for the first time, echoing the question in Bidari's thoughts. 'Why did you want them to go?'

Apal screws up his face, trying to find words that will paint a picture.

'Around the fire, they showed us respect. But when our backs were turned, we heard them laughing, and talking quickly in their own speech so that we couldn't understand them.' Apal's eyes travel around the faces in the circle. 'And they were not like us.'

'What do you mean?' Koldo asks.

'It's hard to say. They had no fear of us. And yet they were like children too, frightened of one of their own men. They wouldn't eat till this one man had tasted the food. And another thing. On the second night we heard the old man screaming in one of the shelters. My mother went to help and she saw blood on the ground, but they pushed her away and told her to go back to sleep.'

Bidari shivers, though the heat of the day is still in the air. The last of the daylight has gone and the flames dance in the darkness. Apal continues speaking, his face now lit, now thrown into shadow.

'When they had been with us for one hand of nights, the man they called Kep said he had something to discuss with us.'

Bidari feels Lotz's leg brush against his knee as he edges forward. 'What was his name?' Lotz asks. 'The one they

285

called Kep?'

'Zorion. Kep Zorion, they called him,' Apal replies. 'He was the one they were afraid of. He wore a band around his head, with a tiger's tooth.'

For the first time, Eneko speaks out. 'Like that,' he says, pointing at Koldo.

Koldo's hand goes up to his forehead to touch the object that is hanging there. 'This is magic,' he murmurs. 'My mother told me to wear it.'

Apal exchanges a glance with his brother, but Koldo urges him to go on. 'What happened then? Tell us.'

Apal takes a breath and continues his story. 'They kept asking us: 'which one of you is Kep? Who is your headman?' In the end, we said that we would all speak with this Zorion around the fire.'

Bakar has been listening in silence but now he speaks up. 'What did he want?'

'He wanted our people to join with his people to make one big ta-uma.' There are murmurs of surprise. 'We went back and spoke to my mother and the other women, but we knew that they would not agree. There would not be enough food for all of us. The women would have to walk too far to dig for roots.'

There is a nodding of heads in assent. Bakar turns aside and, gathering the spittle in his mouth, spatters it onto the ground, before Apal continues.

'We told him – this Zorion – what we had decided.'

'What did he say?' Tipi asks.

'Nothing, but he looked angry. He went to his shelter to sleep. But when we woke in the morning, the strangers were packing up, ready to go.'

Bidari realizes that he has been holding his breath and now he lets it out. 'So. It ended well.'

Apal shakes his head and peers round at the faces in the firelight. 'They hurried away – without saying the proper words of thanks. They didn't even ask for their weapons back.'

Eneko breaks in. 'Tell them about Gutshi.'

Apal nods. 'I'm coming to that. When darkness fell that night, after they had gone, we went to the place where we had hidden their weapons but it was empty. And our young cousin Gutshi was gone. He has not returned.'

There is silence, except for the crackle of the flames and the voices of the women, higher up the slope.

'What happened to your cousin?' Goi asks, at last.

Before Apal has a chance to answer, Lotz breaks in. 'What happened is clear. This cousin of yours went with the people by his own choice. Did he know where the weapons were hidden?'

'Yes.' Apal looks down at the ground. 'He was there when we dug the hole. And, on the fourth day they were with us, my wife saw him in the dunes with one of their girls.'

'Ah.' Lotz nods. 'So there it is. Did he already have a wife?'

Eneko shakes his head.

'Then he has found one now.' Lotz smiles a broad grin. 'The day they came was a lucky day for him.'

Apal stares at Lotz suspiciously and then turns back to the others. 'We wanted to warn you – in case they come this way.'

Apal sits back – he has said what he came to say. Lotz has pulled Koldo aside and is whispering something in his ear. The two of them turn their backs and speak together. Bidari shifts uneasily on the hard ground.

'We are grateful for your visit,' he says to Apal while they wait, and there are murmurs of agreement.

At last, Koldo and Lotz turn back and rejoin the ring of men. Koldo addresses Apal and Eneko. 'I thank you for coming,' he says. 'But Lotz tells me that there is nothing to fear from the people who came to you. They are not strangers after all. They are Lotz's people.'

All eyes fly from Koldo to the man next to him. The flames dance in the cool night breeze, throwing light on Lotz's face, and on the tears that are trickling down his cheeks.

Ansa

Ansa pinches the seedhead gently between her finger and thumb so that Hua, her tongue poking out between her teeth, can pick off the last of the petal strands. Ansa shows her how to break off the case, without spilling any of the precious qartam seeds.

'Be careful!' Hua's fingers are straying close to the sharp points of the leaves.

They work their way through the patch of thistly plants.

'Look! There's more.' Hua points above them to another patch of blue and they scramble up, but the thistles are still in full bloom.

Ansa shakes her head as Hua starts to pull off the petals. 'They're not ready. See? The leaves are still green.'

Hua is disappointed. She pulls at Ansa's arm. 'I'm thirsty!'

Ansa looks around, gauging how far they are from the cave. It is very hot and they have drunk the water she brought with them. The tortoise spring would be closer but Ansa shakes her head. The boy no longer seems to be using the shelter to sleep in, but the food she leaves there is always gone when she returns.

'Let's go back,' she says, but Hua is already climbing down to the path. Ansa watches her; the brown legs scrambling across the rock are thin but they look sturdy. Hua is already as tall as Gashi's youngest girl and she was born before Ansa came to the cave.

'Ama Ansa!'

Ansa picks her way down the slope to find Hua squatting on the path, intent. Only her head is moving, as she looks from one side of the path to the other.

'What is it?'

'Listen!'

Ansa drops down beside Hua but there is nothing to hear, or to see. Then comes a low drone and Hua grabs at her mother's arm, as another bee flies across the path, low to the ground. They watch as it rises then disappears among the rocks, back up the slope they have just climbed down.

'Honey! Ama - let's follow them!'

Ansa gets to her feet. 'We should go back,' she says. 'it's hot and you said you were thirsty.'

'I'm not thirsty anymore,' Hua pleads. 'Look, Ama!'

Another bee passes in front of them, heavy with its load. They cannot be far from the nest but even if she can find it, the bees will be angry. Ansa cannot decide. Thinking of breaking off a soft chunk of honeycomb, her mouth fills with spit.

Ansa.

The voice is soft but it has a warning tone. It seems to come from behind and she spins round, but there is no-one in sight.

'Did you hear that?' Ansa asks, but the little girl looks up at her, puzzled.

289

She scans the hillside in every direction, listening, her head to one side. All is quiet except for the faint piercing call of an eagle, high overhead, and the hissing rattle of the leafhoppers. Fresh sweat breaks out on her head and, suddenly, Ansa longs to be sitting in the cool of the cave. She calls to Hua, who has started climbing again.

'I saw the bee, Ama! He went up there.'

The little girl is off again, her agile feet finding the way. It is steeper here and snakes could be sleeping between the overhanging rocks.

'Come down!' Ansa calls, but Hua ignores her.

Ansa toils up, sweat trickling down into her eyes. Hua's excited voice reaches down to her. 'It's here, Ama! It's here!'

'Don't touch it!' Ansa calls. 'Wait for me.'

Hua is on a patch of flatter ground, almost hidden amidst the long dry grass. A wall of white rock rises steeply above them. The air is full of the buzzing of bees, coming and going from a dark crevice between the rocks, just above the height of Hua's head.

'Keep away!' Ansa shouts, her voice cracked with fear.

'Is there honey, Ama? Is there?' Hua cries, jumping up and down.

Ansa reaches inside her bag for her digging stick. Then she ties the bag up once more and drapes it over her head, for protection.

'Keep back,' she commands Hua.

She edges slowly towards the rock face, moving the bag aside just enough to see. She begins to be hopeful. The crevice widens out lower down and she can see the edge of a waxy mass inside, covered with crawling bees. The buzzing is so loud, it seems to fill her ears. Her heart thumping, she brings the stick slowly forward, then quickly jabs it into the gap. The frantic noise of the bees becomes louder still. They angrily swarm around her hand, her arm, but Ansa has managed to hook the end of her stick around a part of the comb. All she has to do is hang on and pull a piece free. She closes her eyes and sets her teeth against the sharp pain of the stings as they come – one on her hand, her arm, her shoulder. A chunk has broken off, lodged in the bend of her stick. She staggers back from the rock and away, along the ledge, holding up the honeycomb triumphantly. She can still hear the raging of the bees. A few have followed her but the rest are massing around the crack in the rock. The pain of the stings is nothing.

'Look, Hua! Honey!'

Hua is clinging to her leg, shrieking with delight. Ansa breaks off a piece and pops it into Hua's mouth. The little girl sucks and chews, her eyes shining.

'Is there more?' she cries, licking her lips. 'Can we get some more?'

Ansa is savouring her own mouthful of honey and doesn't notice Hua, dancing closer and closer to the bees' nest in her excitement.

'Come away!' Ansa calls, but Hua is already squealing with pain. She runs back to her mother, screaming now, covering her face.

'Shh… shh … The pain will pass.'

Ansa prises the hands away and tips Hua's face up to hers. There are tears on her cheeks and she is sobbing.

'Ama! It hurts!'

Soon, a red lump appears close to her eye and another beside her nose. Hua shrieks as Ansa brushes the skin with her finger, to get rid of the poison.

Ansa takes her daughter's hand and picks her way through the long grass towards a spindly oak, growing out of the rock face. They sit in its shade and Ansa holds Hua close and rocks her. Hua's swollen cheek feels hot to the touch, but it will soon subside.

Ansa hears the crack of a falling stone. It hits the rock twice before rolling into the grass close beside her. She stiffens and, pushing Hua off her lap, crawls out from under the low hanging branches of the oak. The stick! She left it near the bees' nest. She scans the slope above but the overhang of rock restricts her view. There is a scraping sound from above, and her mouth goes dry. Then a face appears, over the edge of the rock.

The blood seems to rush through Ansa's body in a warm flood of relief. Mul's legs are over the side and he is shinning down the rock face towards her, his face alight. He drops onto the ledge and crouches in the grass, croaking her name. Now his lips are parted in a huge grin. There is more flesh on him and he looks stronger. Moved by the sight of him, Ansa reaches out her hand.

'No food,' she says, shaking her head. 'I don't have any meat for you.'

Hua has stopped crying and is clinging to her leg, staring at Mul in wonder. Ansa smiles at her rapt face but then a cold space of fear opens up in her thoughts. She must get the child away quickly. It isn't safe for her to see the Sakaitz boy.

She gestures with her hand for him to go but Mul has noticed Hua and is looking at her intently. Ansa takes Hua's hand and walks away, along the ledge, towards the bees' nest. She looks back to see him staring after her, his mouth open. His lips shape into a grimace but whether of fear or anger, she cannot tell. She shakes her head, trying to make him understand. Ansa pulls Hua along but she is dragging her feet.

'Ama! What's the matter with him? Why is he that colour?'

Ansa ignores her. 'Quickly! We must find the way down!' she says.

'I know! I know!' Hua begins to crow. She pulls away from her mother's grasp and begins to clap her hands together. 'It was Mul, the magic boy!'

The cold patch of fear is spreading, deep into Ansa's belly. 'Shh... You go down first. I'll follow you,' she urges.

Hua needs both her hands and feet to scramble down the steep slope back to the path. But when they are walking on the level, she starts up again.

'Ama Ansa! It's just like the stories. The bees made my face hurt but the magic boy came and made it better!'

Ansa reaches for Hua's hand and holds on to it firmly, while she tries to think. 'He was only a boy, Hua. The bee stings got better on their own.'

Hua is quiet for a breath, then she begins to cry. 'It was Mul. I know it was. I heard you say his name.'

Ansa comes to a stop and squats down beside Hua, wiping the tears from her face.

'Listen, Hua! You must never tell anyone that you saw the boy. Do you hear me? We must pretend we never saw him.'

Hua opens her mouth to ask a question, then closes it again. Ansa takes her hand once more and they set off towards the cave. They walk in silence, till Hua pipes up again.

'Ama! Why did he call you Onsa?'

Ansa stops and slaps the child across the face. 'Be quiet! Remember – we must never talk about him.'

Hua's face puckers up, her eyes filling with tears. Ansa reaches down to wrap an arm around her. 'Did you like the honey, Hua? Maybe we can go back with Gashi tomorrow and get the rest of it. Would you like that?'

Hua nods and smiles through the tears. Before long, she is skipping along the path. The heat is fierce and Ansa's throat feels scratched and dry. As they near the cave, Hua complains again that she is thirsty and they make for the cave spring. When they have drunk all their bellies will hold, Hua sits with her legs crossed under the flow, squealing as the cool water runs over her shoulders.

Ansa hears a thudding sound and turns to see Lotz walking towards them. His shoulders are broader than those of the other men. Looking at the swell of muscle in his upper arm, the old desire flickers in Ansa but then she feels herself tighten and become wary. He is scowling.

'We found honey!' Hua calls out to him.

Lotz looks down at her blankly.

'I got stung! Look!' She shows him her red cheek. 'But then we saw...'

Ansa breaks in quickly. 'The nest is low down – easy to reach. We can go back and get the whole honeycomb tomorrow.'

The scowl remains. 'Now you've disturbed the nest, it'll probably be gone.'

Ansa shrugs and turns away. Then she remembers that Koldo and Goi have been away for two days now, looking for the tracks of Lotz's people.

'Are they back?'

Lotz nods tersely.

'Did they find them this time?'

Lotz looks into the distance, shaking his head.

Bo

The child, Hatz, is asleep but as soon as Bo tries to pull him away from her breast, he starts up sucking again. It is cool in the cave, but her belly is damp from the heat of the baby's body. She strokes his head and leans back, waiting for Bidari. Surely the men's fire will have burnt down by now. The drumming stopped a long time ago, before the baby started to feed.

At last, she hears him. Bidari crawls onto the bedding leaves beside her.

'Is it decided?' she asks.

'What?' Bidari sounds tired, but she wants the news before he falls asleep.

'About the gathering with Ansa's people. Are we going?'

She hears Bidari's long breath out in the dark. 'Yes.'

Bo hunches forward, clasping her knees in excitement. A trek, all together, down to the plain: dancing, feasting. She can show her son off to the others. When they last met with the Desert People, she was still a child herself.

She shakes his arm. 'What did they say about it - Lotz and Koldo?'

Bidari grunts, pulling his arm free. 'What should they say? We will meet when the days are cooler - when Balqa turns red.'

Bo takes this in. Balqa must grow and die and grow again another time before they make the journey. Hatz will still be small enough to carry on her back.

'But what did Lotz say about it?'

'Why does that matter?'

The familiar impatience stirs in Bo again. Why does he pretend to be stupid? The messenger who came to call them to a gathering in the desert said that strangers had come to live with them: a man called Zorion and his people.

'Are the strangers Lotz's people? They must be.'

Bidari does not reply. Whenever he has been sitting with the men, Bo can feel the anger coiled inside his body, though he doesn't shout or strike her. Why is he so angry with Lotz, and with Koldo too? It makes her frightened. Koldo is headman now.

Bo turns her back on Bidari but he doesn't go to sleep straight away. Soon, his hand has crept onto her belly and between her legs. He turns her over and mates with her quickly and fiercely, like the hunting cats do. Lying back, he gives a small moan and Bo feels his body go soft. Now he will sleep, she thinks. But, instead, he seems to want to talk.

'A bee was buzzing around Hua's face today. Every time I brushed it away, it came back.' He turns to Bo, chuckling. 'Do you know what she kept saying? That a magic boy would come and save her.'

Bo smiles in the dark. It is good to hear him laugh.

'Mul. That's what she called him. A magic boy called Mul.' He yawns. 'How did she make up a name like that?'

Mul. Suddenly, Bo remembers where she has heard that name before. When Ansa came back to the cave, after the dead baby, she kept talking about a Sakaitz boy and she called him Mul. But she was raving.

'It's only Ansa, telling her stories,' says Bo.

Bidari is quiet for a breath. 'Yes, it must be – Hua kept saying something about Ansa having no food for him.' Bidari turns over to sleep. 'I don't like her filling Hua's head with her stories.'

Bo listens to the sound of his breathing as it settles. Her thoughts begin to drift like seedheads, blown this way and that. She has noticed Ansa taking a lot of meat to eat, but she is still as thin as a reed. Often, when the women need her, she is not there and then later she reappears, climbing down the mountain. Could there really be a Sakaitz boy, sleeping on the mountain? Bo snatches at the thoughts but sleep is creeping up on her now and they drop away.

Chapter 23

Ansa

Ansa stumbles in the dry grass but manages to keep hold of Hua's hand. Down here on the plain, the fingers of Eshtu are loosening their hot grip, and the light is fading fast. She stops to look back. It is becoming difficult to make out the shape of Bakar and Esti behind, walking so close that they seem like one figure, his hand resting on her shoulder. From up ahead she hears someone call, then the sound of angry words.

When she catches up, the others are standing around in groups. The children, who were noisy and excited when they left the cave at first light, are quiet now. Bo's baby begins to cry and she unties him and puts him to the breast. Why is it so dark? Ansa looks up but the face of Balqa is all but hidden behind a bank of cloud. The summer is coming to an end.

She searches out the figure of Lotz in the gloom. She can tell from the way he is holding himself that he is in pain. His thoughts are often closed to her now, and she is careful to keep her own hidden from him. Yet still she can feel in her own body the strain that every step puts on his back, the aching in his leg.

Goi is frowning up at the dark sky but Bidari is sure the cloud will clear and there will be enough light to keep walking.

'Three nights before Red Balqa -that's what we agreed. The Desert People will be waiting for us.'

The old couple catch up with them at last and Esti drops to the ground to rest. Bakar's breath is coming in soft moans. Ansa wishes they had stayed behind, but Koldo insisted they must be at the gathering. In the old days, they would all have had a say around the fire.

Despite his leg, Lotz wants to go on. There has been a hunger in his face for days, a tight waiting. He longs to see his own people, Ansa thinks, and wonders again why she doesn't feel the same way about those she grew up with. A dark mist seems to settle over her whenever she thinks of the gathering. There will be so many, now that Lotz's people have joined her Desert People. She tries to picture the woman, Nahia, and the boy who is Lotz's son. Will Lotz go back to the desert with them, after the gathering? Surely, after all this time, Nahia must sit with another man.

Koldo's eyes are taking in the terrain and the people grouped around him: the old couple huddling together on the ground.

'We will sleep there.' He points in the direction of a stand of oaks, the last before the plain opens up and the ground becomes swampy. 'We will go on to the two rivers tomorrow.'

Ansa can sense the impatient tightening in Lotz's body but when Bidari starts to argue, Lotz speaks up sharply. 'Koldo has spoken.' He limps away in the direction of the oaks.

All cloud has passed away overnight. The air is already hot when they spot the first signs of the camp. Last night, Hua fell asleep under the trees beside Bo, and did not stir all night. Now she is full of life and skipping beside Ansa.

299

'When we will get there?' she keeps asking.

Ansa feels more tired than ever. She had lain awake, listening to Lotz and Koldo, whispering together into the night. With every step, the weight pressing down on her seems to grow heavier.

To reach the meeting place, they have to cross the smaller of the two rivers. Now that the summer is old, the river is shallow and they can wade through it. The children splash, wanting to stay and play, but Gashi herds them on. The cool water swirling around Ansa's waist is welcome, but it brings her no ease. She has a sense of dark clouds forming, billowing with menace, yet the morning sky above her is clear blue and tranquil.

Scrambling up over the bank they walk on and, before long, a cry of greeting goes up, as they are sighted. The tents litter the flat ground between the rivers like discarded flints. The children come running to meet them and, among the faces, Ansa sees that of Garoa's son, her half-brother, Elori. He was not much more than a baby when she last saw him and now he is a wiry boy, running and shouting with the others. He does not seem to remember her.

Holding tightly to Hua, Ansa hurries toward the tents. Her eyes are on Lotz, just ahead with Koldo and Goi. He leaves the others behind and walks, in his lop-sided way, toward a group of men, beside a working hearth. The men are strangers to Ansa and she gasps as she draws closer. They are all tall, like Lotz, and they are as beautiful as women who have been painted for a joining. Their dark skin is covered with swirls of colour. One of them has shells around the top of his arm, where the muscle begins to swell. Another – the shortest of the three but broader and stronger than the others – has a huge curved tooth hanging down from his forehead, giving his face the look of an eagle. The other men come forward to embrace Lotz and make the sign of greeting. She can hear their laughter. The man with the tooth stands back, waiting, and now Lotz drops awkwardly onto his knees in the dry grass. The eagle man stands, legs apart, hands behind his back. He is not smiling like the others. As Lotz struggles to get up, Ansa sees in his face something she has never seen there before: fear.

Gashi and Ikomar have caught up with Ansa and now women begin to crowd around them, trilling a greeting. Ansa is searching for familiar faces from her childhood, but it is the strangers, Lotz's people, who have come forward first. Like those of the men, the women's bodies are decorated and yet Red Balqa is still two nights away. Shells and feathers hang on strings around their wrists and necks. But it is their hair that Ansa is staring at: black like her own, but somehow smoothed and twisted into ropes, like the tail of a hunting cat. She is remembering something: a woman she once saw in that other place, a shining woman with hair coiled around her head. The women smile at the travellers in welcome and behind their eyes run the same quick thoughts that show on the face of Lotz.

One of the women cups her hand and makes a long low call. Ansa turns to see two figures emerging from the scrubby brush that lines the river bank. The shape of one head is familiar. As the woman staggers closer, her arms full of branches for the fire, Ansa sees that it is Garoa, her father's wife. She looks so old.

'Take it over there,' orders one of the Painted women, pointing to a big hearth in the space between the tents.

301

Garoa has been staring at Ansa in recognition but she doesn't stop to speak, just moves off in the direction the woman indicated. Ansa swallows, trying to moisten her mouth. Garoa was unkind to her, back in the desert, but still it is troubling to see her being given orders, like a child, when this young woman with braided hair stands idle. Ansa peers toward the tents, looking for the figure of her father. All this time, Hua has been clinging to her leg, shy in front of the strange new women. Now Ansa takes her hand and they set off after Garoa, in the direction of the fire pit.

The older woman is bent low over the hearth, arranging the brushwood in criss-cross patterns and, suddenly, Ansa is a young girl again, dreading the harsh words and the blows. She approaches, her heart beating fast, but when Garoa straightens up, her hand in the small of her back, all Ansa sees is an old, broken woman. Ansa meets her eyes, expecting the familiar contemptuous look, and is surprised to see tears on Garoa's cheek. She moves forward, clutching Ansa in a quick embrace, and reaching out her hand to Hua.

'Is she your child?'

Ansa nods. 'Her name is Hua.'

Garoa holds Hua at arm's length to look at her. She smiles, but the smile only shows how wrinkled her face has become. There are only two or three teeth visible in her mouth. It is difficult for Ansa not to stare.

'Where is my father?' she asks.

Garoa shakes her head and her shoulders seem to droop. 'Gone. To the old ones. It was last winter, before…' She falters.

'Before what?' Hua is hiding behind her legs and Ansa picks her up. The little girl rests her head on her mother's shoulder.

Garoa glances over her shoulder at the Painted women. 'Before *they* came,' she replies, with a slight movement of her head. Ansa can hardly make out the words. 'There was sickness – your father was not the only one. There weren't many of us left. We couldn't fight them.'

Dread slices through Ansa's thoughts, quick and clean, like a sharp blade through flesh.

'Fight them? But why would you fight them? They are clever,' she says. 'Lotz is one of them and he has taught us how to trap the grey chukar and now we have meat.'

'Lotz?' The older woman's voice wavers with uncertainty. 'Is it true then? That one of them has been living on the Antelope Nose - with you?'

'Yes. His leg was broken but we cared for him. I sit with Lotz now.'

Garoa stares at her. 'But the man you were joined with – Bidari. Is he dead?' she asks at last.

'No.' Ansa takes a deep breath. 'Not dead. You will see how things are.'

Garoa and Ansa retrace their steps to join the women and the children, each step a greater effort for Ansa. Eshtu is high in the sky and the plain is shimmering with heat. She longs to go and find water, but it will cause offence if they do not join in the welcome dance that is just beginning. The air is full of trills and whooping as the women shuffle forwards, then sideways, then forwards again.

Ansa bends down to whisper a question in Garoa's ear. Her father's widow points toward one of the tall, decorated women. Her face is long, with delicately shaped eyes. Though she is a grown woman, her full breasts are still firm. In front of her is a boy of perhaps ten summers, jumping with the other children. She rubs his hair and he pulls his head away, laughing.

Bidari

Bidari stands uncertainly in the long grass of the plain, looking at the tent shelters, the hearths for cooking and for working already in use. The people from the desert must have arrived some days ago. His eyes scan the male figures, searching anxiously for the face of Ansa's father. Perhaps he will not care which man his daughter sits with, as long as she is well treated? But most of the figures are unfamiliar to him: tall and very dark, like Lotz.

Tipi catches up with him and they weave between the shelters to join Koldo and Goi on the edge of the clear central space. Together with the others, Bidari feels stronger. Koldo's eyes are darting in every direction, gathering knowledge. Lotz is already there, in the centre of the ring of meeting, standing beside a broad-shouldered man. He is shorter than the other strangers but covered, like them, with red and white markings. It is hard to see his face – there is something dangling from his forehead.

Lotz calls to them but now he puts up his hand, gesturing for Koldo to come forward alone. There is a twist of anger in Bidari's gut. Who is Lotz to forbid him to do anything? Koldo strides forward, his gaze calmly fixed on the man beside Lotz. The man moves his head and Bidari gasps in surprise. The thing hanging down over his face is a curved tooth: the eye tooth of a wild hunting cat, perhaps. He stares at it, a thrill of fear running along his spine. How has he won the right to wear such a thing?

The stranger must be their headman. He is looking Koldo

up and down and his eye rests for a full breath on the bone that is hanging from Koldo's own forehead. The man's mouth is a hard, tight line. He stands, legs wide apart, as unmoving as a wall of rock. But now, at last, he makes the sign of welcome and, more than that, he lowers his head to Koldo. Bidari watches Koldo's shoulders relax as he returns the sign of respect. The man with the tooth is leading Koldo to a patch of shade thrown by one of the shelters, bigger than the rest. He squats on the ground. Koldo glances back at Bidari and the others, then drops to the ground beside the stranger.

Bidari turns to Goi. 'What's happening?'

He shrugs in answer and now Lotz is limping towards them, a smile breaking his face open. 'Let's go and drink,' he says. 'And find something to eat.'

'Who is he?' asks Tipi. 'The man with the tooth?'

'He is Kep Zorion,' Lotz replies. 'But there is nothing to fear.' He seems relieved. 'Look – he is sitting with your father.'

Something in Lotz's words, or rather something behind them, is troubling Bidari, but he cannot give it a name.

Some of the women are already back from foraging and there are nut grass tubers baking in the embers. Bidari and the others eat and drink some water, then wander over to join a small group of men, squatting on the ground, away from the tents. Bidari recognizes one as a cousin of Ansa's, but the others must be Lotz's people. The red and white lines painted across their chests and around their limbs are vivid against the near-black skin. Bidari looks down at his own body and feels its plainness, as unadorned as the antelope on the plain.

The Painted men look up when they come near and move a little to make room for Bidari and the others. Lying in the grass at their feet are some lengths of hollow cane of the kind that grows in the marshland. One of the strangers opens a pouch strung to his waist and takes out several sharpened spear points. He takes a cane shaft and fixes a point to it, wrapping it tight with spliced tree root. Then he lifts it to feel the weight, as if it were a spear, and passes it carefully to his neighbour.

Bidari looks at Goi who cannot conceal the guffaw rising in his throat. The cane is light and springy in the man's hand. No one could bring down an antelope with a cane! Even Tipi smiles but the strangers do not seem to notice. They are tying a second, lighter spear tip to a second cane shaft. Bidari sits back on his heels, a smile escaping his lips. It pleases him to know that Lotz's people are not so clever after all. The man next to him is bending low and Bidari notices that he has a scar running over his shoulder and down his back.

Now one of the men takes the flimsy spears, one by one, and holds them up to his shoulder. Goi can no longer keep his thoughts hidden.

'They are too light to throw!' he exclaims. 'The shaft needs to be made of wood.'

The eyes of the men turn on him, their faces blank for half a breath. Then it is their turn to laugh. The man holding the spear puts it down and goes to his pack, taking out a short length of oak branch. It has been cut just past a joint and the side branch has been cut right down, leaving only a short spur. Bidari leans forward, fascinated, as the man wedges the spur into the hollow end of one of the flexible spears. He gets to his feet and holding the branch and the cane close together with his fingers, he holds them up to his shoulder, takes aim, brings his arm back and throws the spear, flicking his wrist forward. The oak branch stays in his hand, but the flimsy spear is released and springs forward, so fast and so far that Bidari cannot believe what his eyes are telling him.

The blood rises to Goi's face but he gets to his feet, full of wonder. He takes the oak branch from the stranger and examines it carefully. His thoughts are written on his face. With this throwing tool, think how fast a spear could be made to go. A spear made of cane could even bring down an antelope.

Next morning, Bidari wakes in the shelter that Bo hastily put together for them the night before. He pulls back the flap of skin and crawls out. Eshtu is rising in a clear sky, but there is a bank of cloud at the horizon. Not tonight, but tomorrow night, Balqa will be fullface and hanging low and red over the plain. Hopefully, the cloud will clear by the night of the feast.

He walks a distance away to piss, then wanders back among the tents. It is mostly women who are moving about: there are no Painted men to be seen. He finds Bakar, sitting on the grass, and Goi and Tipi come to join them.

'Where are the men?' Bidari asks.

'They've gone hunting,' Goi replies. 'Ikomar heard it from their women.'

Bakar shifts on the ground, flicking away the flies. 'There should be meat for the feast – if it can be caught,' he murmurs.

'Yes, Uncle,' replies Goi. There is quiet for a time, then he voices the question that has been hanging between them in the morning air. 'But why did they go without us?'

A new thought comes to Bidari. 'Did they take Koldo with them?'

Goi shakes his head. 'Look,' he says, pointing over to the

grass behind the big tent, where it seems that Kep Zorion sleeps with his woman.

Three men are standing, their heads close together, talking. Bidari recognizes the broad shoulders of Zorion and the tall, slightly bent figure of Lotz. The third man, standing between them, is Koldo.

Bakar listens to the silence. 'What is it?' he asks. 'What can you see?'

'It's only my brother,' Bidari answers, turning away. 'Talking to Lotz and their headman.'

'Wait!' Tipi cries. 'He's coming over here.'

Sure enough, the knot of three has come apart and Koldo is walking towards them. He seems to be in no hurry.

'What did he say?' Tipi calls, as soon as his father is within earshot. Koldo doesn't answer at once but, instead, he signs a greeting with his fist, almost as if they were strangers.

Goi stares in surprise, then reaches out to grab Koldo's arm. 'What is he like, this Zorion?'

'Kep Zorion,' Koldo corrects him. 'He is a clever man. There is a lot I can learn from him.'

Bidari stirs uneasily. Again, there is something troubling behind Koldo's words that he can't quite grasp. They hear shouting from over by the tents.

'The hunters are back!' exclaims Koldo and sets off through the dry grass.

Following him, along with the others, Bidari is shocked to see Koldo's back. A pattern, in red and white, has been painted on it.

In the central ring, the hunters are laying out the meat they have caught. Only small meat, Bidari thinks, but then he sees what is causing the excitement: the body of a female antelope.

The men stand proudly while the women and the children gather round to admire the kill. There are tall hunting spears on the grass, but Bidari can also see cane spears and the strange new throwing tools. Was it one of those that brought down the antelope?

The men look dusty and spent. They must have gone out very early, while it was still dark. Soon they drop to the ground and the women bring water for them. Bidari moves closer. One of the hunters calls him over and sits grinning as Bidari squats beside the antelope, his fingers stroking the swell of her flank. She is fully grown and will make plenty of meat. The hunter touches Bidari's arm.

'You want to butcher her?' he asks, pointing to the animal. He signs with his hands, miming the act of pulling the hide away and slicing the flesh.

Bidari springs up, gesturing towards the shelter where he slept last night. 'I'll get my tools,' he says, setting off at a loping run.

Bo is sitting outside the tent, feeding the child. 'What is it?' she asks, but he just grabs his pack and turns back.

When they see Bidari sharpening his blades, Tipi and Goi venture over to join him. The women and the children crowd around, but the Painted men lie back on the grass and rest, chattering. After a while, the hunter who had spoken to Bidari comes over. The animal has been skinned and Goi and Bidari are jointing the meat. The hunter clicks his tongue in approval. He grasps Bidari's arm and gestures in the direction of Bo, who stands watching.

'Your woman?' he asks, his eyes moving up and down her body.

Bidari nods.

The man's face breaks into a lewd grin. 'You are a lucky man,' he says.

They are smashing the bones to get at the marrow, when Lotz appears. Bidari puts down his hammer and wipes the sweat from his neck. Lotz is leaning on his stick, brushing away the flies; the long trek to the plain has taken its toll. Somehow he seems smaller here, surrounded by his own people.

'Where is my brother?' Bidari asks, realizing that he hasn't seen Koldo since they started work on the carcass.

'Kep Zorion asked for him,' Lotz replies.

The morning of the third day on the plain – the day of Red Balqa - dawns clear, without a trace of cloud. Bidari wakes early. Bo's deerskin has ridden up in the night, revealing the curve of her buttocks. Remembering the admiration in the eyes of the hunter, he reaches across for her.

He cannot sleep again after they have mated, and goes out of the tent into the sparkling light. He watches two women clearing ash away from the blackened hearths. There is no pattern painted on their backs but then they are not dark newcomers but women from Ansa's people. Thinking of Ansa, he feels a flicker of guilt, as usual. At least, he no longer has to face her father; it had been a relief to learn of his death from Ansa's cousin.

Bidari decides to walk to the place where they crossed over the river. The water is shallow there and he can clean himself and even swim, perhaps. This far from the camp it is quiet, except for the distant cry of an eagle, far overhead. He thinks of Koldo sitting with this Zorion, their heads close together. What does the headman say to him? Sometimes, the two of

310

them even send Lotz away when they talk. Bidari's lip curls with satisfaction, thinking of Lotz being shown disrespect.

The summer river is shallow and slow-moving. He climbs down the bank and into the water, scooping it over his chest and head. He hears movement further along, in the belt of tamarisk growing along the river's edge. The sound comes again: branches cracking, brushing across the ground. Is it the children collecting firewood? Now he hears laughter and two figures crawl out from under the spindly branches. Bidari is about to shout a greeting, but then he sees who it is. Taking a deep breath he dips down under the water. When he ventures another look, Lotz is standing on the bank, pissing into the river. The tall, dark-skinned woman has climbed down and Bidari watches the bounce of her breasts as she cups water in her hand, splashing it between her legs. Climbing back out, the woman glances in all directions then starts off, walking alone along the river bank. Lotz has turned and is heading back to the camp.

Chapter 24

Ansa

Gashi empties her bag onto Ansa's pile and the two women begin to sort through the tubers, cutting them free of the trailing roots. When Ansa asks if she should start the fire, Gashi looks up, but Eshtu is creeping slowly across the sky like an old man. She shakes her head.

Ansa swallows, trying to rid herself of the lump stuck in her throat. The air is heavy with excitement. Tonight Balqa will be fullface, hanging huge and low and stained with blood to show that summer is coming to an end. At a hearth nearby, some of the Painted women are working the skin of the antelope. Ansa's eyes scan their faces but the beautiful woman that Garoa had pointed out is not there. Nahia sleeps beside a different man now; Ansa has seen them coming out of a tent together. But still the darkness she has felt ever since they left the Antelope Nose refuses to lift. Instead, it seems to grow thicker and heavier. Gashi, too, seems subdued.

'Has Lotz told you anything?' she asks.

Ansa shakes her head.

'They are hiding something.' Gashi puts down her blade and wipes the sweat from her forehead. 'Zorion - all the time Koldo sits with this Zorion.'

Ansa shakes her head again. Lotz was not beside her when she woke this morning, and she hasn't seen him since. Dark thoughts have been swarming around her all day, like black bees, and she cannot seem to brush them away.

The sound of a child's wailing reaches them and, recognizing the cry, Ansa springs up. Bo is hurrying across, Hua balanced on her hip.

'She's crying for you,' Bo explains. 'She's hurt her head.'

Hua reaches out with her arms and Ansa takes her. Now she has seen four summers, she is heavy to hold. Tears are running down her face and a lump like a tortoise egg is already visible above her left eye. The skin is broken too and a few drops of blood are forming at the slit. Ansa hugs the girl close and turns on Bo, her voice high-pitched.

'What happened?'

'I didn't see. The boys were throwing stones – she must have been in the way.'

'Why didn't you do something?' Ansa shouts. She feels herself beginning to shake with anger.

Bo stares at her, then turns and walks away.

Gashi parts the hair to examine Hua's head. The cut is not deep and the child's tears are beginning to subside but now, for no reason, Ansa begins to cry herself. At last, she puts the child down.

'Stay close to me!' she calls, but Hua runs off, the lump on her head already forgotten.

Eshtu is sinking into the Salt Water and the smell of cooking meat begins to spread through the camp. The children are watching the sky, waiting for the first glimpse. At dusk, the cry goes up for RedBalqa.

Ansa is restless and she goes in search of Lotz. When his

313

figure finally emerges from the skins draped across Zorion's shelter, Lotz walks past her without a glance. She catches up with him, grasping at his arm. He stares at her in the fading light as if she were a stranger, then pulls his arm away roughly. She feels as wretched as if he had struck her. Although she knows it would be better to keep quiet, the question makes its own way out of her mouth.

'Will you come back with us – after the feast?'

She already knows the answer. Why would he return with the Oak People when his own people are living in the desert? But the thoughts which move like lightning behind his eyes surprise her once again. He glances towards Zorion's tent and his lip curls in a bitter half smile.

'I am to go back with you.'

Ansa looks down, unable to bear what is staring out from his eyes. Is it disappointment? Anger? More than anything, it feels like hatred.

The stars have gathered together in a clear sky and are dancing already. Balqa hangs low: a huge circle of light, stained as if someone has painted his face with kho. The young ones are weaving their way between the hearths, whooping with excitement, and all around is the high trilling of women's voices. But, to Ansa, the drumming that echoes across the plain sounds like the beat of death.

An urge to have Hua close by sends Ansa searching among the shelters. She passes by one of the smaller hearths but something makes her go back. Some of the Painted men are there, squatting beside a figure who sits cross-legged, close to the flames. He is an old man, his hair not grey like Bakar's, but white. She has noticed him sitting outside Zorion's shelter in the day, unmoving, from dawn till dusk. Under the paint, his skin is creased and leathery.

Moving back into the shadows, Ansa watches as the old man steadily stretches his hands out, right into the fire. Ansa gasps. He holds them there, the flames licking his palms. The watching men do nothing, only draw back a little. Ansa's heart is beating so loud she is frightened they will hear it. The old man lets out a long screetch of pain, like the night birds, but still he holds his hands in the flame. There is a loud hissing from the men as the old man crumples, collapsing towards the fire. Now they pull his sagging body back, laying him down on his side.

Ansa feels sick. She turns away towards the cooking hearth, where most of the people are gathered. The drum beat is faster now and Gashi and Ikomar and the others are dancing. Perhaps they didn't hear the scream. She finds one of the Painted women and pulls at her arm.

'The old man has fallen in the fire!'

The woman is quiet for half a breath. 'The white-haired one - Itzal?'

'Yes - he's not moving.'

The woman hisses. She pulls Ansa close. 'He will come back to us,' she whispers, 'when he has the names.' She turns back to the fire.

Ansa's heart is thumping, her thoughts scattering in different directions.

Esti catches sight of her. 'Come and dance!' she cries. 'For RedBalqa!'

But Ansa's feet feel so heavy, she cannot dance. The night itself is heavy - the sky weighing down on her so that drawing in each breath feels like an effort. She stands back in the shadows, looking anxiously for Hua, only to see her tucked safely between Bakar's crossed legs. The Oak women are dancing in front of the cooking fire. Ansa has never heard drumming so loud. She watches Bo and Gashi, Lilura, Ikomar, Sorne - even old Esti – twirling and jumping higher and higher. Why do none of the Painted women dance? Even the few of her Desert People who remain are only watching, not joining in. They seem anxious. Now and then someone looks up, as if tracking Balqa's path through the sky. Some of the Painted men are leering at Lilura's young body. The hand of one is moving up and down under his belt and the others are laughing. Do they have no shame? She peers around for Tipi but he is nowhere to be seen.

The dancers slow down and, one by one, drop to the ground to rest and to wait for Balqa to reach the highest point. Lotz's people are quiet now; they seem uneasy. The high wailing of the bone pipe drops away, leaving only the beat of the drums. Ansa stares up at the huge stone that is Balqa - hanging over them. If he were to fall from the sky, he would crush them all and the plain would disappear into the Salt Water. A wave of terror rises up inside her.

There is a commotion on the far side of the big fire and now the Painted People are pulling apart to make the shape of a great ring. Those sitting are dragged to their feet and Ansa is pulled into the circle. The flickering firelight reveals face after face; no-one is left outside. She catches sight of Garoa, Tipi, Koldo, of the beautiful woman, Nahia.

There is only one drum still sounding, the hollow, deep one that they beat when someone dies. The heaviness is spreading now; Ansa can feel fear all around her. And lust too, but not the clean lust to mate, something new and dark that makes her afraid. Ansa senses some movement on the far side of the circle, away in the shadows. A child whimpers. Then a loud scream of pain slashes through the silence and a figure drops to its knees.

She turns to the Painted woman next to her, but the woman only stares straight ahead.

More sounds from the darkness. Something is moving behind the backs of the people, hidden in the shadows. Another cry goes up, closer this time. It is high-pitched, the voice of a woman. Ansa steps back, but a hand drags her forward again roughly, so that the circle is not broken.

The flames crackle and dance, revealing the face of Tipi, only ten paces away from Ansa. He is staring at the fire, his fists clenched by his sides. Now, there is movement beyond him and Ansa catches a glimpse of something white, moving slowly in the air behind the waiting people. It is the hair of the old man. Itzal is in the shadows, outside the ring. He has something in his hand – something that looks like a long blade of stone. Why does no-one turn? Can't they see him? Instead, they keep their eyes firmly on the fire.

A low moan comes from somewhere and Ansa feels a lurching in her guts. The white hair has come to a stop behind Tipi. Itzal is raising his arm. There is a shout and the sound of running and Bidari streaks across the grass towards Tipi. The drumming halts, leaving the silence itself throbbing with the beat. A child begins to cry, but the Painted People keep the circle closed and face straight ahead, their eyes on the flames.

Now someone else comes running past the hearth. Though his body is painted, he is not as dark-skinned as the others - it's Koldo. Ansa lets out her breath in relief but instead of

317

grabbing the old man, Koldo orders Bidari back to his place in the circle. He goes to Tipi, who is shaking with fear.

'Tonight is the night of Red Balqa,' Koldo calls out, looking round at the faces in the firelight. 'He will be angry if we let him bleed alone.'

There are murmurs of agreement from Lotz's people and the drumming starts up again. Koldo stands resolutely in Tipi's place, drawing his son in front of him and exposing his own back to the old man and his blade. Ansa watches the bony arm as it rises up high in the air. Then comes Koldo's grunt of pain, as the sharp stone edge bites into his shoulder and down his back, slicing through the flesh. Ansa's legs turn to water beneath her but Koldo stands firm, gazing straight ahead.

The patch of white that is the hair of Itzal moves on slowly, behind the backs of the people. Will he stop and strike again? Ansa remembers what the Painted woman said about names, when Itzal was lying like a dead man by the fire. The words of Lotz come back to her: *an old man who journeys to the place of the ancestors.* Do the ancestors give him the names of those who must bleed? Her whole body begins to shake. She can no longer see anything white and listens for the sound of movement behind her. Is the old man there? Perhaps that is his breath she can feel, warm, on her ear. Have the old people chosen her to bleed? Terror holds her rigid, facing the leaping flames of the great fire. Surely that rush of cool air is Itzal raising his arm to strike.

Almost as if someone has cupped her chin, gently tilting her head back, she finds herself looking up into the sky. There, above her, is the face of Balqa, swollen and stained with colour. There is no terror in it. She feels a familiar peace:

feels herself being drawn up, away from the circle, away from the plain, into the brightness. There is only calm now, and the steady pulse of the drum becomes the heartbeat of the Skymother, the warmth of the night like soft leopard fur. She is travelling closer and closer to the face of Balqa but there is no anger in him, as Koldo fears. It is not blood that has stained his face but drift after drift of red flowers amidst the lush grass of a plain. The flowers are waving their heads, the long stems bending in the breeze. She hears the chattering of split-tailed birds as they swoop down close, then up again into the blue sky.

A roar of pain breaks through the birdsong, chasing away the vision of red and green, and Ansa is back in the frightful dark, hearing only the spitting flames and the dry pulsing of the drum. Further round the circle, to her right now, the headman Zorion bends over, clutching at his shoulder. The light catches something dark and shiny oozing from the gash, mixing with his body paint. She touches her own neck but there is no pain, no blood. The old man has passed on without cutting her, and gone to Zorion.

Now a great roar goes up. Itzal staggers into the centre of the circle and collapses onto the ground. He has completed the task given him by the dead ones. There will be no more letting of blood. More drums start up and the circle is broken as people cluster around those who were chosen. Women surround the girl who was cut, clicking their tongues. Someone is prodding the wound with her finger. Ansa is surprised to see Lotz break through the knot of women.

'Come.'

The girl gets to her feet. The blood is still trickling down her back towards her waist.

319

'Quickly,' he says, taking her by the arm. 'Kep Zorion is waiting.'

The girl goes with him. She looks back at the women with something like pride showing in her eyes.

Since the bloodletting, the stain on the face of Balqa has begun to clear. An eerie light spreads over the plain as the smell of roasted antelope fills the still night air. Now, at last, the Painted People begin to dance. The unfamiliar movements seem to carry a meaning but, confused and frightened, Ansa cannot make out what it is. She watches until the red and white markings on their bodies blur into one in the firelight.

Kep Zorion appears in the meeting ring. He walks over to the cooking hearth, the tiger tooth swinging from side to side with each step. There is dried blood on his chest and back. When everyone is quiet, he calls out, his voice clear and loud.

'Where is Kep Koldo?'

Koldo appears in the firelight and drops to his knees. The headman puts out a hand to help him up.

'Remember this night of Red Balqa,' Zorion proclaims. 'Watch me.'

He touches his shoulder and shows the people his fingers, red with blood. Ansa hears Koldo's hiss of pain as the headman turns and rubs his fingers into the wound on Koldo's back. He nods and waits while Koldo takes some of his own blood and works it into the gash on Zorion's shoulder.

'We are Zorion and Koldo,' Zorion's voice rings out. 'We have bled for you, our people. You have seen our blood become one. From this night, the Oak People will call themselves by a new name: Zorion-uma.'

It is the day of parting. The shelters have been taken down and the People of the Oaks have begun their journey back to the Nose of the Antelope. They walk for a long time, the plain stretching away in front of them, shimmering in the heat. By the time they reach the toes of the mountain, Esti and the children have no strength left for the climb up to the cave. Clouds are gathering again. There is no choice but to sleep under the oaks, near the clearing where the men make the hunt circle, and then make the ascent in the morning. The women make their own fire away from the clearing. One by one, the children fall asleep.

Bidari

The men gather silently in the magic clearing. The air is tight with echoes, memories of the night before: the bleeding face of Balqa, the dancing, the great fire, the screams of pain. Bakar is the first to voice the question they all want answered.

'Cousin Koldo, what passed between you and Zorion?' The old man keeps his voice respectful. 'Have you made an agreement with him?'

Bidari watches Koldo's face carefully as he flicks his hair away from his eyes, revealing the white bone at his forehead. Koldo has been striding ahead of the others all day, with Tipi beside him, showing no sign of tiredness. Now he answers impatiently, his fingers drumming on the ground beside him.

'Kep Zorion's words were for my ears alone.'

The silence has an edge, sharp like a blade. Bakar turns his head a little to one side, but he says nothing. Bidari looks to Goi, but his gaze is fixed on the ground. Bidari can no longer keep quiet.

'What did he mean?' he blurts out. 'Zorion-uma! We are

321

not *his* people.'

Koldo hisses through his teeth in anger. 'We are honoured that he has given us his name.'

Bidari feels the hot blood rising up his neck.

'But they are not like us.' He glances at Tipi. 'That old man was going to wound your son! And look what they did to you.'

Koldo snatches a burning branch from the fire. Bidari flinches but does not move back.

'Be quiet, little brother,' Koldo growls. 'You don't know what you are saying. I am Kep, not you.'

Koldo is on his haunches now, the burning brand lighting the space between himself and Bidari.

Tipi leans forward, but when he speaks, it is to side with Koldo.

'My father is right.'

Bidari stares at him, then looks around for support. He reaches across to Bakar.

'Uncle - you don't want to take their name, any more than I do.'

'Koldo must have his reasons for making an agreement with these people,' Bakar says quietly. 'No good will come of us fighting.'

Koldo nods, settling back onto the ground, and now Lotz speaks for the first time. He looks straight at Bidari.

'You should trust your brother. The pact Kep Koldo has made with my people will bring more meat to us all.'

'What do you mean?' asks Goi, the hunter.

Lotz nods toward Koldo. 'He will tell you when he is ready.'

'Tell us now,' Goi insists.

Koldo looks proudly around at the circle of faces. He gives

a small smile.

'You saw the new throwing tool they have, that can make a spear fly far and fast. A spear like that can bring down an antelope before he has even caught our scent on the wind. Zorion's people have agreed to teach us the skill of this tool in return for our oak wood. They need hard wood for this thrower and they don't have it in the desert. If we work together with them, none of us need go hungry.'

Goi nods his approval, his eyes shining in the firelight. Tipi is gazing at his father in admiration. Bidari, too, feels the power of the picture Koldo has drawn with his words. The flame of his anger dies down, and now he feels again like the stupid boy his brothers would laugh at and disregard.

Lotz turns to Bakar. 'What do you say to that, Uncle?' he asks, with a chuckle. 'Do you object to our agreement now?'

Bakar is silent for a breath, then he shakes his head. 'Soon, I will be leaving you to join the ancestors. It is for young eyes to see the path ahead.'

Chapter 25

Bo

Bo tucks the goatskin more tightly into her belt against the wind. Esti and Gashi are further down the slope, an antelope hide stretched out on the ground between them. Esti is laughing as the children take it in turns to piss over the hide. One boy points his skinny worm up, so that the spray arcs into the air then down onto the antelope skin. Bo smiles as his careful aim is spoilt by a gust of wind and the droplets shower Esti's head instead. The old woman shrieks and tries to chase him but Poz is much too fast for her.

Bo coughs, her throat pricking as the chill wind blows smoke from the fire towards them. Hatz toddles towards her, rubbing his eyes and crying. She catches him up and moves round to the far side of the hearth. Ansa is leaning across a wooden frame, braving the smoke to turn the strips of lean meat. With this wind, they are drying well.

Though it has been a cold winter, the people are fatter now than they were in the summer. No one has been sick, except blind Bakar, who fell ill and died soon after they got back from the gathering on the plain. Now, as often as not, the women are greeted by the sound of singing when the huntsmen return. The man whose spear brought down the animal leads the way, holding high the power of Zorion, the carved wooden tiger tooth that Lotz made.

A new gust of wind tugs at Bo's shoulder and she feels first one raindrop, then another, splash onto her face. She puts Hatz down and, ignoring his howling, moves quickly to help Ansa. Together, they snatch the strips of meat from the frame and run, laughing, into the cave. By now, the wind is driving rain across the cave mouth. Esti labours up to the cave mouth, water pouring in rivulets down her face. She has abandoned the antelope hide. The rain will do it no harm.

Inside, the women do as Lotz's people showed them, hanging the strips of antelope on sinew cords from the roof, out of reach of the rats. It makes Bo feel good to see the dried meat hanging there, no longer succulent but still full of flavour. One thing puzzles her, though. It doesn't look so much now it is hung up. There seemed to be a lot of meat when it was drying outside.

Hatz is grizzling and stretching out his arms to be picked up. Bo sits to suckle him, waiting for the rain to pass. She notices, with surprise, that Ansa is missing. Surely she is not out foraging in this driving wet. His belly full of milk, Hatz's eyes begin to close and his warm weight on Bo's lap is comforting. Soon she drifts off to sleep.

When she wakes, it is still to the whining of the wind. Her son is playing and she stands by the cave mouth, thinking of the men. They are down on the plain and will have to climb up with the wind on their backs. A bedraggled figure rounds the bend in the path but it is Ansa, not the men. She is dripping wet and shivering.

'Where have you been?' Bo calls.

Ansa jumps at the sound of her voice and looks up, her face

full of secrets. The bag slung over her shoulder seems to be empty. She hurries into the shelter of the cave, keeping close to the wall, her face turned away.

'Did you get anything?' Bo asks.

Before Ansa can answer, a high-pitched wail comes from behind. Hatz has tripped and fallen, his face screwed up in pain. It is only his knee, scraped and bleeding. As she jogs him up and down and his crying becomes less, Bo thinks about Ansa and her empty bag. Why would she go to forage in rain like this when there is plenty of meat? Suddenly, little things she has noticed all winter seem to come together and find their place, but it makes a troubling picture. Bo is almost certain now. Ansa has been taking meat away from the cave. But where has she been taking it and why?

Bidari

The men wait at the foot of the mountain, under the oaks, but there is no sign of the Painted men from the desert. Bidari moves uneasily, begging the wind to blow the clouds from the face of Eshtu. He longs for the spring that must soon come, to throw off his itchy clothing and be warm through to the bone. Iban, Koldo's second son, has climbed down with them. He has lately grown tall and soon, perhaps in the summer, he will hunt for the first time. Bidari scans the horizon. Who will Zorion send this time to collect the oak wood? Fear stirs in his guts but, so far, the headman has never come himself.

At last, movement is spotted on the plain. It is the third day after Balqa's new birth, the day that was agreed, and they have come. There are two men this time. As the figures move nearer, Bidari recognizes one of them as Odol. He squirms with shame, remembering the gathering on the plain for Red

Balqa. He had thought Odol was honouring him, allowing him to butcher the meat. Since then, he has learned many things about Zorion's people and he fears they were only using him to labour for them.

The visitors reach the shelter of the oaks, tired from their journey. Odol bows to Koldo and, the greeting over, Lotz comes forward.

'We have cut the wood and the cane – it is waiting for you in the cave,' he says quickly.

Odol nods. He and the other man accept the water that Goi offers them. They sit down to rest under the oaks and gesture to Koldo and Lotz to sit with them. Bidari and the other men stay back, watching. The heads of the seated men move close together in talk and it seems to Bidari that their eyes slide, just for half a breath, in his direction.

Zorion's men will stay with them in the cave tonight and maybe another night, before they return to the desert with the oak and the lengths of cane. Bidari feels a sudden cramping, low down in his gut, and he moves away from the others, to shit. When he comes back the men are on their feet, ready to start the climb up. They are half way when the wind starts to batter their backs and the first raindrops fall. They climb on, water dripping down Bidari's neck, inside his antelope skin. The skin grows heavy and rubs his shoulder, forming a sore red weal. They round the bend at last and hurry for the shelter of the cave.

Inside, Koldo gestures to the women to move further back, where the chamber narrows. The men sit around the central hearth and soon the stink of wet hide fills the cave. Odol's companion notices the meat drying on the frame and he nods, approvingly.

327

'You have made meat?'

'Four antelope!' Koldo answers. 'Two females and two males, since you came last time.'

Goi leans forward. 'And plenty of small meat. The cane spears fly like birds from a bush.'

Bidari frowns. Goi is right. The oak spear throwers give them far greater range but the new, light spears do not last and already they have cut down all the cane that grows by the river. This time, to have enough to give Zorion's men, Koldo sent him and Tipi as far as the marshes. They had to work quickly in case any of the Marsh People were near.

'Tomorrow,' says Odol, 'if there is antelope on the plain, we will go with you to hunt.'

Bidari has learned to keep quiet when Zorion's men are here, but he hopes that there will be no antelope on the plain and then they will leave in the morning after all. Whenever they are here, Koldo sits alone with them, hanging on every word. Then, when they are gone, there is always some new demand for Koldo to pass on.

Night has fallen and the wind is still howling but the rain has stopped. The women bring the last of the fresh meat and some thistle root. The flames blaze up, throwing shadows which dance across the walls. Bidari looks up from his meat to see Odol's companion gazing across at Bo, bent over the cooking fire. He turns and says something to Lotz, in a voice too low to hear.

The men eat in an uneasy silence. Yet again, Bidari wishes that Bakar was still with them but instead he sits with the old people on the plains of the dead, leaving them only his bones, rotting in the soft earth. The food and the fire are warming him and Bidari throws off his skin, hissing with pain as he catches the blister on his neck. He looks up to see Odol staring at him, at the small shell that is all Bidari is permitted to wear around his neck. Odol's eyes flick up into Bidari's face with a look of contempt. Bidari swallows, covering the shell with his hand. Odol looks straight at Bidari and speaks, loud enough for all the men to hear.

'When we return to the desert, we will need someone to carry the cane and the oak. Your woman will come with us.'

Bidari stops breathing, fear building inside him as he tries to understand what this means. He hears the voice of Lotz from across the hearth. 'It won't be for long. Bo will come back.'

Lotz turns to Odol, his eyebrows raised in a question. Odol shrugs. 'Perhaps she will come back. Perhaps she will stay.'

Bidari finds his voice. 'No! You can't take her.'

Trembling, he searches out the face of Koldo in the gloom. Koldo frowns, then lets his gaze fall to the ground.

Odol is staring across at Bo, sitting with the women. He exchanges a laugh with his companion. 'Bidari says no and I see why. If she was mine, I wouldn't let another man take her.'

Odol turns to Koldo. 'He says no to me, but he can't say no to his headman. What do you say, Kep Koldo? Will this Bo come with us?'

Koldo lifts his head, then looks away, towards the mouth of the cave.

'Koldo!' Bidari's voice is hoarse, pleading.

His brother meets his eyes for half a breath, then glances toward Zorion's men. 'She is a good forager. We cannot spare her,' he says quietly.

'I am sure she could be spared,' Lotz breaks in. There is

fear in his voice. 'You and Goi are making more meat than ever before.'

Koldo's anger suddenly erupts and he turns on Lotz, the tree-shaped bone bumping against his nose. 'I am Kep, not you! I say she stays.'

Further back in the cave, the women go quiet, wondering about the raised voices. Bidari is shaking with rage and shame, but he dare not speak out. Odol looks at his companion, then turns to Koldo. When he speaks, his voice is cold.

'We will sleep now and when it is light, we will go back. Kep Zorion will be angry that you have refused me.'

The two men get to their feet but Goi intervenes. He wears the tail of a lizard around his neck and has the right to speak out. 'Koldo - I will go with them, to carry the cane.'

The men take no notice and, as he brushes past, Odol spits on the ground in front of Bidari. Lotz is whispering urgently in Koldo's ear.

'Wait!' says Koldo.

Odol and his companion turn and walk back to the hearth, exchanging a chuckle.

'We can spare you Ikomar instead,' says Koldo.

The smile leaves Odol's face. He stares at Koldo for a full breath, his eyes like slits. 'Which one is she?' he asks.

Lotz gestures with his thumb to where Ikomar is sitting, beside old Esti. 'Her husband is dead,' he murmurs, 'but she is still young.'

Odol peers across till the firelight falls on Ikomar, showing her face and her smooth hair. She has learnt to brush it like the Painted women do. He nods his assent.

Koldo stands up. 'I will show you where to sleep. The

women have brought fresh bedding.'

Next morning, while it is still early, Bidari crawls away from Bo and creeps down the slope, between the sleeping bodies and out into the mountain air. The sky is beginning to lighten. His limbs heavy with misery, he follows the path to the place where the rock drops steeply away, watching the mist rising from his warm piss as it streams out into the air. He is reminded of something: flinging Ansa's Balqa stone away in his rage, the morning after his mother died. Bidari groans with pain.

He drinks at the spring. No-one else is stirring and he climbs up, away from the path in the growing light, going wherever his feet take him. He will not go back until Odol and the other one have gone. He doesn't want to see the look on Ikomar's face when she leaves the cave with them.

Eshtu has appeared above the Nose now and the air is growing warmer with every breath. He finds some shade and sits but the picture is there, waiting for him, behind his eyelids. Odol, staring across at Bo, lust in his eyes, contempt on his face. *Your woman will come with us.* At last, the heaviness of sleep steals over him and he drops into emptiness.

Bidari is woken by the sound of Bo calling. She is climbing up towards him, Hatz strapped to her back.

'Where have you been?' she cries, gasping for breath. She stands in front of him, one hand reaching over her shoulder to soothe her wriggling son. 'They've gone and taken Ikomar with them!'

Bidari cannot look up into her face.

'They said it was to help carry the wood – but why did they take her and not one of the boys?'

331

Bidari shrugs.

'She didn't want to go – she was crying. Will they bring her back next time they come?'

'How should I know?' Bo's questions buzz and sting, like biting insects.

'And I heard Koldo shouting at Gashi – he has given her a black eye.'

Now Bidari looks up. 'What were they quarrelling about?'

'I don't know. I asked her about Ikomar, but she said there is nothing to be done.'

Bo unties Hatz and puts him down on the ground, where he goes toddling off. She is staring down at Bidari. He motions to her to sit down, but she shakes her head.

'Gashi said something else. She said that I am lucky.'

Bidari looks away to where Hatz is squatting on the grass, trying to catch a beetle perhaps.

'Bidari!' Bo always sounds angry when she is frightened. 'What did she mean – that I am lucky?'

All at once, Bidari wants to tell her: to vomit out all the shame and the fear. The women will whisper together anyway and she will find out soon enough.

'He wanted to take you.' Bidari looks up into Bo's face, still young, her cheeks rounded now from eating meat. He sees the blank look of shock turn to horror. 'There was nothing I could do. They don't let me speak.'

He reaches out, trying to pull her down beside him, but she steps back. 'He wanted to take me?'

Bidari nods. Something in him wants to make things worse, to hurt her if he cannot protect her. 'And not just to carry wood for him.'

Now she drops to the ground and grabs his arm, her eyes

searching his face. 'But you refused him – you wouldn't let them take me.'

He avoids her eyes but it is no use. She will find out.

'Koldo is Kep. He made Koldo decide.' He laughs bitterly. 'It was my brother who saved you.'

'What do you mean?' she asks.

'He let Ikomar go.'

'Ikomar went instead of me?'

'Yes. This time.' Bidari's face is aflame with colour. She knows it all now.

'But why did Koldo let them take anyone? He is Kep.'

He turns on her savagely. 'You're a woman. You don't understand.'

Bo is not cowed by his anger. 'It's you who is stupid, not me!' she flashes straight back at him. 'When Lotz first came, it was you he chose to sit with. But you let Koldo and Goi worm their way close to him and you went off sulking. And now you're nothing more than a turd under their feet!'

Chapter 26

Ansa

Hua is trying to make Hatz sit down quietly so that she can tell him a story, but he keeps running off. When Hua chases him, he giggles with excitement. Ansa watches them, smiling. Usually, Hua plays with Gashi's youngest, Loza, but today Loza is complaining of pain in her belly. The air is full of the freshness of rain and the slopes below are lush and green, dotted with the colours of spring. It reminds Ansa of the day she gave birth to Hua. Using her fingers to count, she guesses that there have been one hand of summers since Hua was born.

Soon after midday, the hunters come back with nothing. There is still dried meat to eat but the men are silent when they return, their faces dark. Goi seems fearful and Iban is hanging his head. Koldo let him go with the men, to carry the tiger's tooth made of wood that brings them luck. It appears that, running on the plain, he dropped it and they could not find it in the grass.

Gashi puts her arm around her son's shoulder. 'Lotz can carve us another, when he gets back from the meeting.'

Koldo flashes her an angry look. 'What do you know, woman?'

Goi is frowning. 'We could make a new one, but unless Zorion touches it, it will have no magic.'

It troubles Ansa to hear the men speak like this. But now the talk among the women turns from the lost carving to the other question. When Lotz returns from meeting the Painted People, will he bring Ikomar with him? When he left the cave yesterday to walk to the meeting place, Lotz's face was full of eagerness. She had been astonished because the news he was carrying to Odol was likely to make him angry. There is no cane left on the plain and the Marsh People are not willing to trade theirs.

Lotz returns in the half-light of evening. Ikomar is with him! Her face breaks open with joy as she embraces Esti, but she is thin and there are marks on her neck. When she wraps her arms around Ansa in greeting, Ansa can sense the shame she is carrying. Holding her, she sends healing into Ikomar's bruised body.

Lotz does not look like the same man who walked away from the cave at first light the day before. No doubt his leg is aching from the journey but there is a heaviness in his shoulders that speaks of something else. When he discovers that the carved tooth is lost, he curses Iban loudly and Ansa watches fear creep across his face. Does he think the hunters will not be able to make meat without it? As the last light leaches from the sky, Lotz sits alone with Koldo, their heads close. Loza is very sick now, soiling her clothes before she can reach the dungheap.

When it is time to eat, the women gather around their fire and Gashi finds the choicest pieces of dried meat for Ikomar. They tell her the news, but no-one dares to ask the question that really matters. *What happened to you in the desert?* Instead,

335

Esti asks about the journey back.

'Did you camp on the plain? Did you hear any hunting cats?'

Ikomar shakes her head. 'We made a big fire. Nahia brought firewood on her back.'

'Nahia?' Ansa asks quickly. 'Was she at the meeting?'

The colour rises into Ikomar's face and she bites her lip.

'Did she come with her husband?' Ansa insists.

Ikomar looks down. 'No.'

Later, Ansa carries a sleeping Hua inside and lays her down on the bedding. She lies beside Hua, troubled. At last, threading her way between the sleeping bodies, she goes to the cave mouth. Only Lotz is left by the men's fire, hunched over the small flames. She joins him, shivering in the night air, but he makes no sign.

'What happened to Ikomar?' she asks. 'I saw the marks on her neck.'

Lotz shrugs. Ansa stares into the flames, waiting, but he neither speaks nor gets up to go inside.

'Loza is sick,' she says at last.

Suddenly he turns to face her and she catches the unmistakable sweet-sour smell of coupling on his body. The slender face and firm breasts of Nahia flash into her thoughts and now she is certain. Lotz knew she would come with Odol. No wonder he was so eager to set off for the meeting place.

His face is closed to her, his voice bitter. 'You say Loza is sick, so why don't you help her?'

Ansa feels her heart begin to race.

'Why don't you journey to the ancestors and find out why she is sick?'

Ansa reaches out to touch him but behind the jeering voice,

336

he is like a wall of stone.

'You could go back to your people,' she gasps, 'back to her. Why don't you go?'

Suddenly, like water spilling over a precipice, the hatred pours from out from him. 'Because he won't let me.' He grabs her wrists. 'Because Kep Zorion needs me here.' He is pulling her towards him. 'Because you are stubborn and you won't fly to the old people and bring back their words to us.'

She tries to fight him off but he is stronger. The thought she hardly dares to think escapes from her mouth. 'You don't care what the ancestors say – only what this Zorion says!'

He slaps her hard, then drags her close to the fire. 'You are a seer, so go,' he hisses. 'Let the heat of the fire take you as it takes Itzal.'

He is thrusting her arms out over the fire, his thumbs biting into her wrists, so tight that she cannot pull them away. The searing flames begin to lick her palms.

At dawn, Ansa stumbles down the path, all the way to the plain. It is enough to be moving, the chill air on her swollen, blistered hands, cries like those of a wounded animal escaping her lips. She has only one idea: to get away from Lotz, his body and his thoughts, which do not belong to her any more. Away from the cruelty behind his eyes, from the darkness that is spreading over her people.

She can still see the flames, flicking up to scorch her hands, then dropping back. Rage rips through her chest as she feels again the imprint of his thumbs, holding her there, against her will. She doesn't remember how it came to an end. She only remembers lying curled up in the cave, riding the throbbing waves of pain all through the night till, with the first light, she left him sleeping and fled.

On level ground now, she runs on through the green spring grass, on and on, till the only thing she knows is the need for water. Cool, running water for her parched mouth and her swollen throat and her burning hands. She comes to a halt, sniffing the air like a beast, slowly becoming aware of how far she has run. The oak thicket where the men make hunt magic is way behind her, a small green hump by the toes of the mountain. Suddenly she feels alone and outside of her knowledge. She peers around for any sign of water, but the face of the land is hidden under a mass of green. The wind catches the grass tips, blowing them this way and that, so that the plain is a living, swaying thing.

There is a patch of darker green stems ahead and now she sees a string of them, forming a gentle curve across the plain. Reeds! Ansa starts to run again and soon the ground becomes soft underfoot. Water begins to seep into the holes left by her feet. Pulling herself free of the sucking ground, she struggles on till the reeds start to form borders on either side of a running stream.

Whimpering with pain and thirst, she finds a place where she can get to the water. It is bliss to plunge her hands into the cool flow and she squats in the mud, tears rolling down her cheeks. Now she scoops some water to drink in her red, weeping palms. Perched on the bank, her thighs shaking, she still cannot bear to leave the stream.

Sobs begin to build and course through her body. The cave, the whole of the Antelope Nose, seems dark to her now. How can she ever lie beside Lotz again? Dread beats in her heart as she remembers the secret in Ikomar's eyes and the bruises on her back. It is as if a poisonous mist is spreading from the

Painted People in the desert, all the way to her mountain.

The fingertips of Eshtu play on the smooth skin of the sparkling water, as it laps gently against the reeds, cool and clean and comforting. She could sink into it and let it take her. She would only need to stop fighting the slope and to slide down. There, under the water, she might find herself travelling once again into the light, as she did before. How she longs to be back there, drinking in the peace. And yet still her toes grip the mud.

Gradually, she begins to notice the sound of a voice, crying. Someone is crying with pity and love and sadness for her, just as she sobbed for the baby boy who was too small to live. Perhaps it is only her own crying she can hear but now it begins to change and there is hope in it too. *Soon*, the voice cries, though there are no words. *Soon.*

Ansa crawls back up through the reeds and onto firm ground, the heat in her palms already gathering itself again. She turns for home but soon her empty belly is bleating and she is too exhausted to go on. She lies on her back, not caring about hunting cats or snakes lying hidden in the grass. Small clouds are scudding across the sky above her, blown by the same wind that sighs and hums through the grass tips.

She closes her eyes and thinks of water, first of the still water among the reeds, then of the great Salt Water far off, crashing over the shore. There is no shadow there, no spreading poison, only the vast cold flow of life. She remembers being in the waves that day with Bidari and now she begins to feel the tingling again, but this time it seems to be coming from deep inside her own body, as if the great rushing Salt Water were alive inside her. It comes in waves, the flow of life, spreading up from her toes to the top of her head. She is being flooded with life, even her thoughts are being washed clean of fear. There is still pain in the wasted skin of her hands but inside they are tingling with life. She reaches up with her fingers towards the sky, sharing the joy of the dancing clouds.

There comes a whirring and then a thud as something lands in the grass not far from Ansa. She sits up, surprised, but not fearful. The sound of running and then the figure of a man comes into view. *Bidari!* For half a breath Ansa is confused, thinking they are back on the shore together, but the waves are not outside, they are inside her.

Bidari is standing, open-mouthed, his eyes narrow with fear. 'What are you doing here?' he gasps. 'Aren't you afraid? This is a bad place – it's where we found the carcass.'

Ansa is puzzled.

'The antelope.' His voice drops to a whisper. 'The one they took - the Sakaitz.'

It hurts her to hear the distress in his voice, when there is no need. 'It wasn't Sakaitz, it was only Lotz's people. There is nothing to fear from Sakaitz. They are like us.'

He steps back from her, aghast. Ansa peers at the throwing stick in the grass and, at last, her thoughts gather themselves into familiar shapes again. Bidari has been hunting rabbit. He must have seen her in the grass. She gets up and walks over to retrieve the stick.

'How can you say Sakaitz are like us?' Bidari asks. 'Lotz says they leave poison behind, even in the air.'

As Bidari speaks, Ansa can feel the shadow gathering once more. Perhaps she has said too much to him. Bending to pick up the stick, she winces with pain. Her fingers are swollen and she drops it. For the first time since the death of Koru, he comes close to her, examining her palms. He swears under his breath.

'What happened? How did you burn yourself?'

Ansa cannot decide how to answer. It is not safe to speak without thinking first. One thought frees itself from the tangle.

'It's only the skin that is burnt,' she says. 'The pain inside has gone.'

Still feeling the life rippling through her body, Ansa looks into Bidari's puzzled face and, suddenly, it is as if she can see inside him: the helplessness, the shame, the guilt, writhing there like snakes in a pit. She stands, intent, picturing clean waves of salt water coursing through him, sweeping away the pain.

Bidari looks at her, his head turned to one side. Then he drops her hands and busies himself with stringing the stick across his shoulder. He shows her the rabbit he has caught, and offers her some dried meat. They start back across the plain together, walking in silence. After a time, she catches an old familiar sound. Bidari is humming under his breath.

Bidari

Bidari is walking behind the other men. His guts have been clenching and loosening all day and he keeps having to squat down by the path. He is not the only one. Back at the cave, Goi's boy, Poz, is the same and little Loza is still complaining of belly pain. She has been hanging round her mother for days.

It is past midday and they have been walking since dawn. Bidari loves the fresh salt wind and the crying of the gulls here in the marshland. He wishes this was only a trip to

341

collect nefafa, with the children laughing and excited. He watches the others ahead, their spears bobbing beside them. Bidari catches sight of the broad shoulders of Zorion and his guts grumble again. Up till now, Zorion has always sent messengers to their mountain to discuss trade, but this time he has come himself. And he has brought Odol with him and that other man Bidari has never seen before. He is not tall, like the Painted People, and his skin is more the colour of Bidari's own. Around the fire last night, Zorion said that Koldo must deal with the Marsh People. So why has he come?

Bidari envies the Marsh People, living only a morning's walk from the Salt Water, with its wide sky and its cool wind in summer. He stops to pick a frond from one of the low shrubs and laughs to himself. It stands up stiff, with a knob at the end, like a tiny man ready to mate. There are tamarisk trees on both sides of the path, their spindly branches dotted now with pale flowers.

Before long, the huts of the Marsh People come into view, beside the river that flows down from the mountain. Bidari catches up with the others but keeps well away from the eagle face of Zorion. Odol looks at him with mocking eyes. Now that they are close to the huts, Bidari can sense the growing tension. The Marsh People are our brothers, he reassures himself; they will welcome us. And, anyway, there are seven of us, with spears and axes.

Koldo and Zorion are talking and now Tipi dares to break in. He sounds anxious. 'What will we do if they still refuse? Do we have anything to give them in return for the cane?'

Zorion frowns at the interruption but then the frown is replaced by a wry smile.

'That's a question for your father.' He turns to Koldo. 'Well?'

Koldo's shoulders move a little and his voice does not carry with its usual strength. 'I could teach them how to make the spear throwers.'

Tipi nods, relieved.

'That is a fair exchange for the right to cut their cane,' says Goi.

Bidari is not reassured. He is watching Koldo closely. He knows the meaning of every movement, every look on his brother's face. There is something hidden, something being held back.

A Marsh woman is out collecting wood. When she sees them she runs back, calling to the others. By the time they reach the circle of huts, thatched with reed, the women are clustered inside, shielding the children. The men have come forward to meet them, beside a hearth where fish are drying on a frame. There are only four of them: Apal and Eneko and two others, and another who is no more than a boy. Though they all open a fist in welcome, each one has a short spear or axe in the hand by his side and they do not speak.

Koldo gestures to Tipi, who steps forward. 'Greetings, brothers,' he calls. He turns to Apal and Eneko. 'Lilura is well and sends you this.'

Eneko walks over to take the handful of curly hair that Tipi is holding out. He nods. An old woman is peering out from one of the huts and now she gives a shriek and comes running towards them.

'Gutshi! My son!' she cries, struggling to free herself from Eneko, who is holding her back.

Bidari follows her gaze to the third man who came from the desert with Zorion and Odol. Suddenly, he remembers what the brothers from the marshes said that day they came to visit. About their cousin who had left them to go with the strangers.

Reassured by the familiar face of Gutshi and news of Lilura, the women have left the safety of the huts and are creeping closer, to hear what is being said. But the men are still grasping their weapons and have not asked the visitors to sit. Their eyes keep returning to Zorion.

Koldo comes forward to join Tipi. 'We have come as friends,' he says. 'Will you not share your fire with us?'

Apal answers, ignoring the question. 'You didn't send to say you were coming.' He turns his gaze to Gutshi. 'Are you returning to us, Cousin?'

The old woman, Gutshi's mother, is still being restrained by Eneko. She waits in silence for his reply. Gutshi is looking troubled. When he shakes his head, she starts to keen, as if someone has died.

'If you will not welcome us, we must stand here to talk,' says Koldo. Bidari can hear the icy edge in his brother's voice. 'I speak for my people. Who will speak for you?'

The men from the marshes exchange looks. Apal moves forward. He is a head shorter and smaller boned than Koldo but he looks him straight in the eye.

'When we made agreements with you before, it was always around the fire and every man had his say. But for now, I will speak for my brothers.'

'We have only come to talk,' Koldo begins. 'We have learnt a new way of making spears that fly fast and, for these, we need cane.'

Apal interrupts him. 'We have seen you cutting cane from our land without agreement. So far, we have let you return unharmed.'

Koldo makes an effort to swallow his anger. 'There is plenty of cane in the marshes, enough for us all. Why did you send to say that you won't trade with us?'

'Because you have nothing we need,' Apal's answer comes back quickly. 'And because we do not trust these people you have joined with.'

Zorion steps forward at this, his face dark with rage. Big Eneko lets the old woman go and moves to stand beside his brother.

Bidari takes a breath, his chest tight with anxiety. If Apal knew Zorion better, he would not have dared to say those words

Koldo clears his throat. 'Your sister sits with my son, as his wife,' he says to Apal. 'Don't be hasty in your decision.' He continues, keeping his tone smooth. 'If you let us cut cane, we will teach you how to make the throwing tool for these new spears.'

Gutshi steps forward, fear showing in his face. 'Listen to him, Apal!' he urges. 'Agree to what he says.'

Apal turns to the other Marsh men and they whisper together. Bidari notices Eneko's fingers running along the blade of the axe in his hand. After a short time, Apal turns back to Koldo.

'We live close to the salt water and our river has plenty of fish. We do not need faster spears than we have. As for the cane, our women rely on it for food.' His eyes show fear but he keeps his voice strong. 'If you come to cut it again, you will not return to your mountain.'

There is a sudden movement behind Bidari. Odol and Gutshi push past him. Zorion is striding across the grass. He is not much taller than Apal but he looks huge beside the smaller man.

'Enough!' Zorion growls. 'I will not listen to the yelping of this pup any longer.'

Gutshi grasps Apal from behind, an arm around his neck. Odol takes hold of Apal's jaw, forcing his mouth open. Bidari is struggling to understand what is happening. Apal's eyes are bulging in terror.

'So no-one must cut your cane,' Zorion says, breaking into a laugh. 'You want to eat it instead. Let's see how much you can eat without that busy tongue of yours.'

The other Marsh men seem rooted to the ground but Eneko flings his bulk at Gutshi, in a bid to release his brother.

Zorion swings round to Tipi and Bidari. 'What are you doing, standing there like women?' he barks.

Before he has had time to think, Bidari is launching himself at Eneko with the others. Together, they pull the big man off and wrestle him to the ground. He struggles wildly till Goi takes the hammer stone from his belt and strikes him across the forehead. At last, he is still.

Bidari gets to his feet, gasping for breath. Seeing the blood lust on their faces and Eneko lying stricken on the grass, the other Marsh men back away. But Zorion withdraws from the trembling figure of Apal, still held fast in Odol's grip, his head back, mouth gaping. Zorion takes a long blade and holds it out to Koldo, his eyes on Koldo's face.

'This is your business.'

Bidari can see the battle in Koldo, in the twitching of his shoulders, the grimace of pain on his face.

Zorion sighs. 'Do I have to do this for you, as well?'

Bidari watches, horrified yet excited, as Koldo takes the blade and bends over Apal's mouth. Suddenly, the air is full of screaming and sprayed blood and a terrible gurgling sound, and Bidari's bowels have opened without him knowing.

Chapter 27

Ansa

The night is very dark. The mountain, the plain, the great
Salt Water are waiting for Balqa to be reborn. Ansa lies awake
beside Lotz, her hands itching terribly as the burns heal. She
thinks of the other men, far away below them, sleeping in the
huts of the Marsh People. Lilura is missing her mother and
had begged to be allowed to go with them but Koldo refused.
Lotz, too, is silent and surly, left behind with the women so
as not to slow the others down.

Ever since the dealings with Lotz's people began, dread has
been Ansa's fellow traveller. Tonight dread is very close by,
breathing darkness into her thoughts. She thinks of Loza, so
weak now that she lies curled up against Gashi to keep warm.
Most of what they give her to eat seems to come straight from
her body. Little Poz is sick, too, showing the same signs.

It is not only the pain in her hands which is making Ansa
restless. She has an uneasy sense that she should be doing
something, but what is it? She gets up, making her way to
the cave mouth where she stands, feeling the rain on her face.
Her thoughts keep returning to the marshes in fear, and yet
the Marsh People are their brothers. What can be the danger
there? She waits till the cloud has passed and the curved

thread of light that is the newborn Balqa appears. Instead of making her heart leap with joy, the sight only makes her tremble. Balqa seems so weak and small, like the baby she gave birth to in the shelter. The thought comes that Balqa will never grow full and round again, that he is dying.

As the shapes of trees, below, begin to be visible in the dawn light, she turns to go back into the cave, feeling that she might sleep. But someone else is stirring now. She hears a scream from the far side of the cave and Sorne is on her feet, clutching the limp form of her little boy. Ansa runs to her, stumbling on the rock-strewn floor. Sorne thrusts the boy's body into her arms and throws back her head, the sound of death escaping from her mouth and echoing through the cave.

Ansa climbs back up from the plain with Lilura, a lump of pistacia resin carefully tucked into the bag at her belt. Six nights have passed since sickness took the son of Sorne and Goi, and the men have returned from the marshes. Loza, who was the first to become sick, is still very thin but she is beginning to play again. But now Sorne's daughter, Amuna, has cramping pains and she is spewing her food. Some of the adults have had pains too but they have been mild, all except for Esti. Ansa draws in her breath as she thinks of the old woman, lying groaning in the cave. It is too early for reed flowers to make medicine and the vines have not yet sent out their curling tendrils. It was Lotz who suggested pistacia resin. His people know so much - perhaps it will help. They will make a drink from it for Amuna and Esti.

Ansa pauses to get her breath and notices the sudden tingling in her hands. Is it the burns again? But now the tingling is spreading throughout her body. With it comes a thought – a kind of knowing – that Esti is beyond the reach of any medicine. She looks out over the plain as a picture comes to her of Esti's sick body curling up into itself and disappearing into the light.

'Come on!' Lilura's voice breaks into Ansa's thoughts. 'It's going to rain again.'

The clouds are gathering and the two women quicken their pace. Lilura has been quiet all day and she seems troubled. Is she frightened of getting sick herself? But it is the children who are most affected. Ansa thinks of her own daughter and her fists clench with fear, though so far Hua has been well.

'Let's hope the resin will stop the sickness,' Ansa says, but Lilura's eyes only grow bright with tears. At last, Ansa coaxes from her what the trouble is.

'Why won't Tipi couple with me? Since they came back from the marshes, he turns his back on me.'

Ansa tries to comfort the young girl but dread is slipping back into step beside her. Since the return of the men, she has felt a new darkness swirling around them, something different from fear of the sickness. Why does she feel this darkness? The men brought a great haul of cane back with them and they say the dispute with the Marsh People is settled.

The rain holds off. Back at the cave, the men are gathered around their hearth, working on a new batch of spears. They take no notice of Ansa and Lilura.

Amuna is lying beside her mother, knees hunched up in pain, crying. There is a bowl beside her.

'I have been making her drink, but nothing will stay inside.' Sorne's voice is sharp with fear.

350

A gust of wind blows across the cave mouth and the first drops of rain fall. Gashi is helping Amuna inside, when they hear the sound of Goi's voice, shouting. He appears on the path.

'Deer – a female! I saw her hoofprints in the mud! Are the spears ready?'

Koldo and Bidari get to their feet, a new energy in their movements. Tipi is up too, leaving only Lotz on the ground.

'Hurry!' calls Goi. 'Before the rain covers her tracks.'

Sorne runs towards her husband, a cry escaping from her lips. 'How can you go hunting? The sickness took your son and now it's taking your daughter.' Her hands twist together, over and over, her voice is shrill with anger. 'And your mother is lying, too sick to move!'

Once again, the picture comes to Ansa's inner eye. *The wrinkled body of Esti, curling up, fading into itself, disappearing.*

'She's dying,' Ansa blurts out to Goi. 'She will be gone when you get back.'

Silence. Except for the raindrops, falling hard now and fast. Goi turns away, the look of a trapped animal in his eyes. Ansa can feel the power of his urge to flee. Slowly and deliberately, Koldo hands a spear to each man. He calls for his son, Iban, then walks to the path with the others, pushing Sorne out of the way.

'We are going to hunt deer. No words of women will stop us.'

The drink made from the resin only makes Amuna vomit. Taking some inside the cave, Ansa crawls to Esti's sleeping space. The stink is acrid in her nostrils. Hua runs into the cave after her, dripping with rain, and Ansa shouts at her to

351

keep away. She lifts Esti's head and holds the bowl to her lips but the old woman cannot open her eyes. Her face seems an odd, dark colour and her breathing is quick and shallow. Her skin is hot and dry, shrivelled like an old grape.

Bo and Ikomar return with a bag of grass peas, Hatz fastened to Bo's back. She will not let her son out of her sight. Even the older boys, who usually roam free on the mountain, have been staying close to the cave since the sickness came.

After a time, the rain stops. Even the thought of deer meat brings the women no joy. To Ansa's relief, Lotz has disappeared somewhere. It is hard to think there was a time when just the sight of him could bring her pleasure. Taking a deep breath, Ansa senses a subtle change and looks up to see if the face of Eshtu has emerged from the cloud, but the grey of the sky is unchanged. She wanders into the cave, with each step more certain of what has happened. She is right. Slumped by the wall, she finds the lifeless husk of a body, already losing its heat. Esti has gone. Kneeling there, amid the stench, tears come coursing down Ansa's cheeks. They are tears of sadness and a longing to follow where the old woman has gone.

Ansa gathers herself to go and tell the others but then she hears a woman's voice from outside, shouting for help. She hurries out to see Gashi, an arm around her daughter, Ula. She has shown no sign of sickness before but now she is bent over by the path, spewing the contents of her belly into the bushes.

Little Loza begins to cry and Ansa goes to comfort her. At least Loza has started to eat again now, though her ribs are all too visible.

'Is it my fault that Poz died?' she whispers in Ansa's ear. 'I was sick first - then

Amuna and Esti.' Her sobs start to come faster. 'And now my sister is sick.'

'It's not your fault,' Ansa says, rocking her to and fro. She peers over Loza's shoulder, to where Hua sits safely, playing.

Strains of the hunting song die away as the hunters come close enough to hear the women keening. The men file along the path in silence, reluctant to face the news of death. Tipi and Bidari busy themselves with the doe, turning their faces from Goi and his tears. When Koldo hears about Ula he berates Gashi, as if it is her fault that another child of his is sick. Suddenly, Ansa realizes that Lotz is beside him. He must have gone to meet the hunters on their way back.

Frantic with grief and fear, Gashi shouts back at her husband. 'Why did you go? Ansa said that Esti was dying.'

Koldo lunges forward at his wife, but Lotz restrains him.

'Kep Koldo,' he says, as if they are around the fire at night, 'let me speak.'

Koldo nods. The others edge closer to hear. Her heart sinking in her chest, Ansa joins them.

'Gashi is frightened by this sickness. We are all frightened,' Lotz says. He looks around at the ring of faces. 'Bidari was sick, and Ikomar, but they have recovered. For those of us who are full grown ...' He spits on the ground. 'It is just that. Nothing. But for the children ...'

'And now my mother,' Goi breaks in.

'Yes. Your mother.' Lotz makes the sign of respect in the air. 'But she was old and weak. It is the children we must think of.' He turns to face Koldo. 'You must send for help, before there are more deaths.'

353

'What do you mean?' Koldo asks.

'You must send for Itzal,' Lotz replies.

There are gasps of horror. Since the summer gathering on the plain, they have spoken about the old man with the white hair and the sharp blade only in frightened whispers.

'When Itzal journeys to the land of the dead, he brings back healing,' Lotz continues. 'If Kep Koldo decides to send for him, he will journey for us and find out what has brought this sickness and what will send it away.'

Koldo stands, his head to one side, thinking.

Gashi speaks up. 'But Ansa sees into the hidden places for us. She saw Esti's spirit leaving her body.'

Lotz's laugh feels to Ansa like the twist of a blade in a wound. 'So – Ansa sees. But what good is that?'

He is limping towards her now. He takes her hand and pulls her into the centre of the ring. His fingers are tight on her wrist, like they were on the night of the flames. 'So Ansa is your seer. What do you see, Ansa?'

She has stopped breathing. He is hurting her. Her thoughts become like chukar birds caught in a trap, in darkness.

'Do you see Loza dead?' he asks. 'Do you see Amuna dead?' There are gasps and one of the girls begins to wail, but he goes on. 'Do you see Ula dead? Perhaps you see all the children dead.'

The others are staring at her but Ansa cannot speak. Dread is beside her now, so close that its dark breath is in her face, her ears, her mouth.

'Well? Tell us what you see,' jeers Lotz.

Ansa lifts her eyes, seeking out the face of Gashi, but she cannot find the strength. At last, Lotz lets go of her hand and now her legs will not hold her and she slips to the ground on her knees. Lotz steps in front of her.

Koldo takes a step forward. 'I will send my son to the desert for Itzal,' he says.

Yet more rain clouds are gathering out above the Salt Water. Ansa takes a water skin and starts off towards the spring. The space in front of the cave mouth has changed. The women no longer chatter around the fire, as they work. Instead Sorne sits with Amuna or with her son, Ortzi. The sickness has come to him too, but he is strong so perhaps it will not steal his life, as it took the life of Ula. Since they buried her, two days ago, Gashi has sat weeping, unable to do anything. The women used to pity Ikomar that she has no child. Now they envy her.

Ansa feels a cramping pain in her gut and makes a detour. The stench of the dungheap takes away her breath. Like the other adults, the sickness has touched her only a little and, once again, she wonders why it is the young who have been weakened by it. The only children untouched are little Hatz and her own Hua.

After all the rain, there is food to be found on the mountain, but while there is still deer meat in the cave no-one has the heart to go and gather. Returning from the spring, Ansa finds the men sitting together, quarrelling. She is surprised to hear Goi's voice raised to Koldo in anger. There have been whispers among the women, too. Koldo is headman - perhaps he has brought this on the Oak People. It was his daughter, Loza, who was sick first. Why didn't she die? So far, she is the only child to regain her strength. Ansa hears the whispers but they only add to the darkness resting over the people. Lotz is speaking now – asking how they dare to question Koldo. Itzal will be here soon, he says, and he will know what to do. Ansa shivers at the sound of that name.

She notices the small figure of Hua standing in the mouth of the cave. There is something about the way she is standing. Ansa puts the water bag down and runs the last part of the way. Hua is calling for her, her cheeks are wet.

'What is it, what's the matter?' She snatches the child up into her arms. Perhaps she has only fallen or someone has spoken harshly to her.

'My belly hurts,' Hua moans, her voice in Ansa's ear.

'No. No!'

Ansa clutches her close as if to stop the words coming but now Hua is squirming and a fixed look comes into her eyes. Her body begins to arch and Ansa runs awkwardly with her towards the dungheap. She is too heavy and Ansa has to put her down and let her vomit into the bushes.

Sorne hears the noise. She brings a bowl of water to Ansa who squats on the ground, wiping Hua's mouth with the palm of her hand.

'She must drink, even if she doesn't want it,' Sorne says.

As Ansa lifts the bowl to Hua's mouth, a flash of cold runs through her like a warning. She stops, uncertain. But there is no harm in water and the sickness leaves the children dry. She puts the bowl to Hua's lips and watches her swallow. Sorne is down on her haunches beside them. There is pity in her eyes.

Hua seems more cheerful now and she runs off to find Loza. Ansa sits on the slope above them, her fists clenched tight. Hua's face is turned towards her friend and she is laughing. Perhaps, for Hua, the sickness will be mild. Ansa watches every movement of her daughter's body, for signs of discomfort. There is nothing to see but she cannot break free of the fear. Now Ansa understands why Sorne and Gashi sit alone and do not talk. Her eyes take in only the two girls, playing below. Then comes the sound Ansa has been dreading. Hua is looking round for her, her face screwed up in pain.

'Ama!'

Ansa is beside her daughter in half a breath, pushing the hair back from her face. The little girl is clutching her belly. 'I can't help it!' she keeps saying as the foul-smelling green liquid rolls down the back of her leg. Ansa rushes her to the dungheap, reaching round for leaves to wipe her with.

Fear is roaring in Ansa's ears like a huge wave, breaking and rushing to engulf her. But even in the midst comes a familiar whisper. *Let it come.* She fights back at the voice, struggling, thrashing about in terror. But the cool breath is in her ear, calm and sure, steadying the beating of her heart. She holds Hua close and now it seems to her that the oncoming wave teems with life and power – the power to lift them and hold them up and carry them.

Bidari

Since the angry words of the morning, Koldo and Lotz have pulled away from the other men and are talking together, their voices low. Bidari is glad. He doesn't want to hear about the old man from the desert. He gets up and wanders towards the watching place. If he were to see something on the plain, there might be enough light to go hunting.

Bo is sitting there, suckling Hatz. Bidari strokes his son's head, but Bo flinches away.

'Why can't I touch him? I'm not sick.'

357

Bo smiles, something of the old softness in her face. He touches the top of her shoulder, feeling the warmth of her skin, but when his fingers slide down her breast, she nudges him away and offers the nipple to Hatz instead. Bidari feels a sharp pang of jealousy.

He sits beside Bo and stares out, till they hear footsteps on the path – it's Goi. Bo edges closer to him, as if she is frightened to hear of another death. But it is not news about Goi's son or his daughter.

'It's Hua,' says Goi, 'she has it now. The same as the others.'

Bidari scrambles to his feet, but Bo tries to pull him back. 'Don't go,' she wails. 'You can't do anything.'

Back at the cave, Bidari finds Ansa leaning against the wall where she sleeps with Lotz. Hua is lying across her lap. There are tears on her cheeks. Bidari is torn between wanting to take Hua in his arms and wanting to run far away, to escape what is happening. He squats down and strokes her hand. Ansa moves along, making room for him to sit. She is humming gently to soothe her daughter.

'Hua,' she says, when the little girl is quieter. 'Do you ever think about your name? The name Ita gave you when you were born?'

Hua looks up, puzzled. 'Hua. New Day,' she replies. 'Did you give me my name, Ita?' she asks.

Bidari nods, afraid that he will weep like a woman.

'It's a good name,' Ansa goes on. 'You know when you wake in the night and it's dark and you're scared?'

Hua nods, the corners of her mouth trembling.

'What happens?'

'You cuddle me,' Hua whispers.

'And then what?'

358

'I go back to sleep.'

Bidari leans back, listening. He is surprised to see that Ansa is smiling.

'And then what happens?' she says.

Hua is chuckling at all the questions. 'Then I wake up again,' she choruses.

'Yes!' says Ansa. 'And the darkness has gone and it's …. what is it?'

'It's me -Hua!' the little girl exclaims. 'A New Day!'

Another night passes and still Tipi has not come back from the desert with the old man. Amuna is very weak now. Hua is still complaining of cramps and everything Ansa gives her to eat or drink leaves her body in spew or shit. Bidari goes to the spring for water to wash her and hearing someone on the path behind him, finds that Bo has followed him, her eyes dark with fear. It is strange to see her alone.

'Where's Hatz?' he asks.

'He's with Ikomar,' she replies. 'Come with me.'

She gestures towards the carob trees in the distance. Bidari looks at her. Her fingertips are resting in the dip at the bottom of her neck and now they are tracing a path through the gulley between her breasts and down to her belly. He sees what is in her thoughts and is instantly ready to mate with her. Putting the water down, he pulls her towards him.

'Not here,' she says. 'Under the carob trees.'

Bo takes Bidari by the hand but his foot touches the bulging waterbag and he remembers that Ansa is waiting.

'I have to take this for Hua,' he says. He gestures towards the bushes, just off the path. 'This is a good place – we can be quick.'

Suddenly, her voice sounds high, ugly. 'No! Come with me. Don't go back to her.' There are tears in her eyes.

Bidari shakes his head, his lust dying as quickly as it came to life. Leaving Bo by the spring, he picks up the water and carries it to the cave. He watches while Ansa washes Hua and gives her a drink, though she can only manage a few sips. Her eyes look sunken in her face. She falls asleep, her head in Ansa's lap.

Bidari leans back and closes his eyes. It is comforting to sit beside Ansa in silence, listening to Hua's quick breathing. He wishes he had not shunned Ansa all this time, since she regained her senses and came back to the cave; it seems that she doesn't hate him after all. Being with her feels easy now, not like those first days after they were joined. More and more, sitting with her reminds him of sitting with his mother.

Sleep takes him and when Bidari opens his eyes, he finds that Hua has woken and Ansa is telling her a story. He closes his eyes again, to listen. It is a story of the old people, like those Koru used to tell around the fire. It sounds as if the story is coming to an end.

'The Skyfather has been singing to Hua all along,' Ansa is saying, in a storytelling voice. 'And can you remember what he is singing to her? Can you remember the words?'

Hua smiles, as if she has heard this many times before.

'Don't be afraid,' she answers. 'That's what he always sings. Don't be afraid.'

Still half in the land of sleep, words keep drifting in Bidari's thoughts. *Don't be afraid. Remember your name.* Bidari opens his eyes, wondering about the meaning of his own name: Bidari - the acorn. How often he has wished for a better name, like those of his brothers. An acorn is small and bitter – it is nothing. When he was a small boy and there was no meat so they had to roast acorns in the fire, his brothers always teased him. He would run to his mother and she would comfort him, saying that Bidari was the right name for him. Inside the acorn, she used to say, lives a seed so small that no-one can see it. But if someone treads on the acorn and it breaks open, then the seed will fall into the ground and drink the rain and perhaps it will grow into a mighty oak tree.

Chapter 28

Ansa

The doe is thirsty. She turns her head, sniffing the air, then picks her way down the slope to the pool beside the spring. Her flanks brush against the rockface, her hooves clipping the stones, then sinking into the mud at the edge of the pool. She stands, craning her neck in each direction. There is nothing to worry her and she lowers her head to drink. As the water touches her nose, the sense of danger returns. The water doesn't smell right. She feels a movement in her belly and greenish liquid spurts from under her tail, running down her back legs, mingling with the mud and the water. Though something is not right, she is thirsty and lowers her head to lap the water again. When the ripples fade, she catches sight of the bones again, lying at the bottom of the shallow pool. She knows them. They are the bones of her calf and, once again, she feels her womb tugging. She lifts her head and peers across the face of the mountain, her ears twitching. She opens her mouth to call.

Ansa jerks awake, the sound of the doe's bleating in her ears. She can still see the soft snout, the open mouth, the movement of the deer's tongue. There are words too. *Come now. Come quickly.*

In a panic, Ansa reaches across to touch Hua's warm body,

rising and falling with each breath. Still, the dream stays with her. The wet brown eyes of the doe seem to watch her, full of purpose and pleading. Getting up and skirting round Lotz's sleeping body, she picks her way to the cave mouth. Bo and Ikomar are there, clearing ash from one of the hearths. It is quiet and Ansa takes a deep breath in relief; each morning now, she dreads waking to the sounds of death and grief. She goes to the spring and still the dream is with her. There is no pool here, at the cave spring, the water runs away over the cliff edge and down the mountainside. Yet, as she stoops to drink, she feels again the doe's unease.

Walking back, it comes to Ansa that the spring in her dream is the tortoise spring, near the rockshelter, where Mul jumped onto her back. But there is no pool there either, just a muddy wet patch. The eyes of the doe have not left her and now she hears the words again. *Come quickly.* A cool breath of calm that feels familiar now is playing on her neck. Her hands, her feet, pulse with a need to answer the doe's call.

Ansa goes back into the cave, climbing up the slope to her old sleeping place. Bidari wakes and when he sees her, fear crosses his face.

'It's all right - Hua is sleeping. Sit with her and try to make her eat. I will come back soon.'

He nods, relieved.

Ansa snatches a water bag and, seeing the remains of the dried deer meat on the shelf, she thinks of Mul. She has not been to the shelter since the sickness came. She puts some meat into another bag and strings them both across her back.

A wind is blowing up as she crosses the face of the mountain and a heavy rain begins to fall, but she pushes on. At the cliff face she climbs up to the shelter, almost losing her footing on the wet rock. Nearing the top, the same foul smell that surrounds the dungheap reaches her nose and there is something else too, that even the rain cannot hide: the stench of death. A wordless sound escapes her lips at the sight of Mul's body, rigid and swollen, stretched out towards the back of the shelter. Tears gather behind Ansa's eyes as she thinks of him lying alone, whimpering in pain. The shelter reeks of sickness. A dull despair settles over her and in a kind of panic she tries to reach the calm place, deep inside her, which cannot be touched by any sadness or pain. Filling her belly with breath, she slowly comes to peace and now Mul is there in the shelter with her. Not the empty shell of his body, but Mul himself. She can feel his laughter bubbling up, as if he is jumping in the high waves of the Salt Water, calling her to come and play with him. She is filled with a longing to go and the soft breath of hope is on her neck. *Soon. Soon.*

The presence of Mul begins to fade. Ansa would like to bury his body but all she can manage is to drag the empty corpse closer to the mouth of the shelter, so that the vultures will find it.

She climbs back down and goes on to the spring, the urgency of her dream returning. As she comes close, it is the sound that strikes her first. Mountain water is streaming down the rocks, gurgling as it drops into a pool that has formed below. It is just like in the dream except that, now, darts of rain are slanting onto the surface. There are hoof prints in the soft ground at the edge of the pool. The deer must have been coming here to drink for many days. There is a strong sense of danger and Ansa looks over her shoulder but there is nothing. Forcing herself closer, she squats at the water's edge. There, in the mud, her nose picks up the telltale foul smell and she pulls back.

Where it is deepest, the pool looks clear and fresh, like the water from their own spring but, suddenly, Ansa is afraid to touch it. A new thought is unfurling in her mind, like the petals of a mallow flower. The Oak People have always drunk water from the mountain without fear, as a baby drinks milk from his mother. Could this water be making them sick?

Ansa remembers again the bones in the pool – the doe's sadness. Did she come in a dream to warn them that the water is bad? Ansa breaks off a branch, using it to stir the water in the pool. The hair on the back of her neck stands up as it touches something hard. Hooking it with the stick, she lifts from the water the ribcage of a small animal.

She drops it back, more sure with every breath that the water is poisoned. Still at its centre, the pool water trickles over the cliff edge, down the mountain, to join the stream that feeds their own spring. She pictures Ikomar, Gashi, fetching water from the spring and giving it to the children to drink, and her whole body begins to shake.

Bo

It is the morning of Ansa's dream and Bo is outside the cave. She sits Hatz on the ground, tired of trying to keep him away from the children who are sick. He plays for a while but soon he has rolled onto his knees and is stumbling to his feet. Bo retrieves him with a sigh, then looks up to see Ansa leaving the cave. She is not making for the spring or the dungheap. Instead, she crosses the slope to join the path that leads up and across the mountain. Bo follows with her eyes. How can Ansa leave Hua, when she is so sick? She kisses her son's head. If he were sick, she would never leave him to go foraging.

The gathering bag on Ansa's back has something in it already. What can it be and where is she going? Bo watches till the figure of Ansa has disappeared, glad that she will have Bidari to herself today, though no doubt he will be caring for Hua now. And then, tonight, he will smell of the sickness and will want to play with his son and mate with her. If he does, she will push him away.

Hatz begins to grizzle but Bo's breasts are soft and empty. She goes into the cave and takes down a piece of deer meat. She puts it into a bowl with some water and pounds it to make a paste. When the food is ready, she smears some onto her finger and feeds him.

There is not much meat left and she wonders when the men will go hunting again. Fear seems to have sucked away their strength and they sit, quarrelling, waiting for Itzal to come. Everyone is waiting.

The rain starts to fall heavily again and everyone goes into the cave for shelter. Bo tries to shut out the sound of Amuna's quiet crying. She is too weak to walk anymore and lies beside her mother. The bigger boys, Iban and Ortzi, are almost unrecognizable – their ribs sharp, their eyes large in their thin faces. And that awful sour stench no longer hangs only around the dungheap; the cave itself smells bad.

Bo sits close to the entrance, glad to feel the spatter of fresh rain. Hatz is lying still for once, his head in her lap. Bo strokes the tight curls on his head, filled to bursting with love for him. Soon, he is asleep and she lifts him into the space between her legs and leans back to rest. After a while, feeling something wet and warm on her leg, she is instantly awake. There is mess all over her leg and the ground. The sour smell she has been dreading. Her son is wriggling and crying.

Bo stumbles up and staggers outside into the rain with Hatz, tears trickling down her cheeks. She cleans him as best she can at the spring and runs back to the cave. Sorne looks up and calls to her but Bo takes no notice. She strides with the dripping child to where Bidari is sitting with Hua in his lap, her thumb in her mouth. Bo stares into his shocked face.

'Come away from her!' she shrieks. 'Hatz is sick – you've made him sick!'

Bidari closes his eyes as if to fend off her words. The colour leaves his face. Bo tugs at his arm but he resists and Hua begins to cry, turning to nestle closer to her father.

'Let her go. Come and sit with your son!' cries Bo.

'Be quiet!' Bidari shouts. 'Take him away and give him some water. I have to stay with Hua.'

Beside herself with anger, Bo lunges at Bidari, but he grabs her arm and pushes her away. She backs off and catches sight of Lilura, watching them. 'Stop staring at me!' she screams.

After a time, the face of Eshtu appears from behind the clouds. Bo is sitting on the wet ground by the path, away from the others, suckling Hatz. Her son must drink milk and keep up his strength. She looks up at the sound of footsteps. At last! Tipi has returned and the old man is with him. They are both wet through. Bo shrinks back from Itzal, his long white hair hanging down in rats' tails. The two pass her and begin to climb the slope. When Koldo and Lotz come down to greet them, it seems to her that even Koldo is frightened.

Lotz helps the old man to sit and Lilura brings water and the last of the deer meat. She looks ashamed to bring so little and runs back into the cave, where Sorne and Gashi and the children are hiding. Bo is not close enough to hear what the men are saying. She keeps her head down, only daring a quick glance in the direction of the old man. The long stone blade is lying on the grass beside him - the same one he wielded down on the plain. She shivers with fear. But something must be done to bring healing for her son and the others.

Suddenly, there is movement in the circle. Itzal has picked up the blade and now he runs it down the inside of his arm, from his inner elbow to his wrist. There is a low moan and he topples over onto the ground. Bo gasps but neither Koldo nor Lotz move to help him; they just watch in horror.

Bo's heart beats in her ears like a drum. Eshtu begins to drop down in the sky and still Itzal lies motionless on the ground and still Bo does not dare to move. She remembers that Balqa will be shining fullface tonight, the time of his greatest strength. Surely this must be a good sign.

At last, the old man stirs and Lotz and Koldo help him up to a sitting position. They talk for a while and then Bidari is sent into the cave, bringing the women and the children back with him. They come out slowly: Amuna and Hua too weak to walk without help. Ansa is not with them – she must still be on the mountain. Bo gets to her feet, settles her sleeping son on one hip and goes to take her place in the circle.

Sticky blood is trailing from both sides of the slit in Itzal's arm. The oak people wait, hardly daring to breathe, but he sits in silence, looking frail and tired. Instead, it is Koldo who speaks.

'Itzal has journeyed to the ancestors on our behalf,' he says. He turns to the old man and makes the sign of respect in the air but Itzal doesn't appear to even notice. He is staring straight ahead.

'They told him what is causing this sickness,' Koldo goes

on. Every eye is on him now, every ear straining for his next words. 'This is Sakaitz magic. The Sakaitz are trying to steal our children.'

There are gasps from all around: naked fear as if a hunting cat has bared her claws. But there is puzzlement too and Goi gives it a voice. 'There are no Sakaitz left on the Nose of the Antelope. The mountain is clean.'

There is silence for a breath and then Itzal beckons to Koldo and speaks quietly in his ear.

'The mountain may be clean,' Koldo continues, 'but he says the People of the Oaks are not. One of us has been poisoned by Sakaitz breath. This is how they are stealing our children.' Koldo's face has gone pale and now he calls out in anger. 'Which one of you is it?'

The people look down, not daring to meet Koldo's eyes. The men who found the corpses at the Sakaitz cave are frightened. Did they bring the sickness back with them? But that was long ago.

Bo sits motionless, the weight of knowledge growing heavier inside her with every breath. Women are no longer permitted to speak in the circle and she is frightened of Itzal. But if she doesn't open her mouth and let the knowledge out, the weight of it will crush her from within. Ignoring the stares, Bo sits her son down on the grass and walks around the outside of the circle to Bidari. Koldo is frowning, but she takes no notice. She pulls at Bidari's shoulder till he turns.

'Tell them,' she says, not caring now if people hear. 'Tell them it's Ansa. You remember what she said - when she was sleeping in the shelter. About a Sakaitz boy.'

'Be quiet,' Bidari says, trying to pull her down onto the ground.

'No!' she screeches. 'Tell them. She takes food to the Sakaitz – I've seen her.'

There are gasps and then silence. Now Itzal clambers to his feet and stands, stooped and unsteady, in the centre of the circle. He does not look at Bo; his eyes are fixed instead on Bidari's face.

'Tell us,' he says, his voice cracked but still strong. 'What does your woman have to say?'

Bidari's face is dark with struggle and pain. For one awful breath, Bo is frightened that he won't tell them.

'Answer him!' Lotz says. He is on his feet now.

Bidari stares blankly at Lotz, then at last he speaks. 'Bo thinks that Ansa is the one.' His voice is low and strangled, as if there is not enough air in his throat.

Heads turn, searching for the face of Ansa, but she isn't there. The only sound is that of the birds, singing after the rain.

Koldo walks over to Bidari and stands in front of him. 'What do you know about this, Brother?' he asks, his voice blade-sharp. 'Have you heard Ansa speak about the Sakaitz?'

Bo clenches her fists by her sides, willing him to speak. She watches the doubt, the horror, crossing his face. He stares wildly at the faces all around him. 'She hates this sickness,' he says, 'her own child has it!'

'So why did she leave Hua this morning?' Bo cries. 'To climb the mountain with a bag of meat for the Sakaitz?'

There is a terrible silence. Then Itzal simply nods his head. He says something to Koldo, then turns to climb up towards the cave, an old man with a bent back. Koldo stoops to pick up the long stone blade from the grass. He places it carefully beside the hearth and raises himself to his full height.

'Itzal has gone to rest,' he announces. 'When Ansa returns, no-one is to speak to her.' His eyes travel around the circle of faces, as if daring them to oppose him. When he speaks again, his voice has never sounded so full of power. 'The Sakaitz poison must be cut out. The old ones have spoken.'

There are gasps and whimpers of fear but no-one speaks out against him. 'We must obey the old ones in order to save our children,' he says, his voice more gentle now. 'And tonight, Balqa will shine on us in all his strength. It is a sign of healing.'

Ansa

The rain has stopped and Ansa sits down to rest, but she can still hear water tumbling into the poisoned pool and then over the edge, finding its way down the side of the mountain to soil their own spring. She feels suddenly as weak and exhausted as an old woman. How can she go back now to Hua, and give her this poisoned water?

Ansa begins to cry. If only Koru were back in her old body. Then she would rest in Koru's arms and lean against her chest. She closes her eyes, remembering that day together under the hawthorns. It was a day like this when they went to pick thornfruit: the fingers of Eshtu caressing her face with warmth, the ground wet from the first showers of autumn. Ansa thinks of the place where the hawthorns cling to the edge of the cliff face. The ground there must be sodden now after the heavy winter rains- where can the rain water go? She opens her eyes. Might it not run off over the edge in a stream?

At once, she feels her strength return. Her hands begin to tingle, life is pulsing through her limbs. She starts off quickly.

It is a long walk, down as far as the ridge above the cave, across and down again. But Eshtu is smiling on her and in the steep places, the mountain seems to delight in showing her the easier ways. At last, she reaches the patch of carob woodland that gives way to hawthorn. The ground slopes down here, soft and squelchy underfoot. She threads her way through the carobs, her ears pricked for just one sound.

She is under the hawthorns when she hears it: the voice of rushing water, louder than she had dared to hope. She runs on beside the stream, through the clearing where she sat with Koru and right to the edge of the precipice. The water has channelled out its own course, dislodging rock and exposing tree roots, and is spilling at last over the edge and down the side of the mountain. She laughs out loud with the joy of it. The water is clear and sparkling and it smells good. No hoof prints here. Clambering down, Ansa takes the water bag from her back. She unties it, empties out what is left and, rinsing the bag, fills it with fresh, clean water. She takes a long draught and laughs again. Her body has never felt so full of life. Now she must go and tell the others.

Ansa toils back up between the trees. Stopping to catch her breath, her eye is drawn to a young plant in the grass; an oak seedling has managed to push its way through the earth. She wonders how it was that an acorn came to be here among the carobs, where no oaks grow, and whether the seedling will survive to become a sturdy tree. She climbs on, eager to get back to Hua. She must warn the others not to drink from the spring. If the women are quick, they can climb down to the hawthorns and fill all the water bags before nightfall.

She rounds the bend at last and the cave slope comes into view. Lotz and Goi are standing on the path, as if looking out for someone.

'I've got clean water!' she cries, but instead of answering her, they only pull back to let her pass. She hurries up the slope, panting from her climb, and peers around for Hua, but she is nowhere to be seen. Sorne is on the slope, sitting with her sick daughter.

'Give her some of this!' Ansa calls out, unslinging the bag from her shoulder. 'It's clean water, from down by the hawthorns. Don't use the spring - it's poisoned!'

When she offers Sorne the water bag, Sorne backs away, pulling Amuna close, her eyes wide and watchful.

What has happened? The air hangs heavy with something new - not just the familiar dull worry of this sickness. It smells like death. *Hua!* Fear clutches at Ansa's guts. But Hua has been getting stronger, and the women would be lamenting if someone had died. She runs across to Gashi, laying wood for the fire.

'Where's Hua?'

Gashi looks up, her face full of pain. Ansa's eye catches sight of something lying flat across the boulder stones that ring the hearth. It's the long, thin blade that she last saw down on the plain, in the light of Balqa.

'Where is she?' Ansa repeats.

Gashi opens her mouth to answer but then a voice rings out. 'Don't speak to her!'

Spinning round, Ansa sees that Lotz and Goi have followed her up the slope and are standing just an arm's length away. Goi is grasping something so tightly in his hand that his knuckles are white.

What is happening? Ansa searches Lotz's face for any sign. She moves towards him, holding the water bag out in front,

373

but he steps back.

'It's only water,' she says. 'From a new stream by the hawthorns.'

Goi raises his hand and now, beneath his fingers, she can see the edge of a handaxe. Ansa begins to shake. She turns back to Lotz, desperate to make him understand.

'The water up at the tortoise spring is foul - that's why the children are sick! We must take our water from this new stream, by the hawthorns.'

His eyes rest on her face for an instant and then, with a shock, comes the knowledge that he is afraid. Afraid of the water, afraid of her. With a quick movement, Lotz lifts his stick and knocks the water bag from her hand. She cries out and bends down to save it, but then staggers back as the end of his stick comes thrusting hard into her belly. There is a sick pain and she cannot breathe. The precious water is spilling onto the grass and draining away. She looks up into his face but he is backing away now, his eyes fixed on something above and behind her. Ansa turns to see Koldo at the mouth of the cave and, beside him in the fading light, bent shoulders and a patch of white. *Itzal*. She gasps as the two men start down the slope towards her.

Goi has crept up behind and now he grips her arm tightly, and Gashi is wailing, and she can smell Lotz and feel his breath quick in her ear. Now his fingertips are digging tight into the flesh of her other arm. Itzal is bending down over the hearth. He walks towards her, his old man's eyes staring past her, at something that no-one else can see. Like a flash of lightning, understanding comes and her thoughts scatter, up and away, taking flight from what she now knows and from the long, thin blade, resting in Itzal's hand.

There is no more pain and the confusion is clearing. The ice where her legs and arms used to be has melted and she is warm and at peace. Down below, the old man is still bent over the body by the hearth but now he stands up and throws the blade away from him, into the grass. There is blood on his arm and spattered over his chest and face. She can feel the fear of Sakaitz race through his body, as he calls for water to wash the blood away.

There is horror all around, rising up into the gathering darkness. It is rising up from Bo, where she sits, her back to the cave, stroking the tight curls on her son's head so hard that he begins to cry. Rising up from the women who stand huddled together, not daring to start the lament. From Bidari, crouched inside the cave and up the slope, his hands over Hua's ears to keep out the sound of screaming.

Looking down from her place of peace, Ansa can feel the waves of terror but they are somehow distant, like tiny lines of white foam on the calm blue expanse of the Salt Water. Joy is breathing on her shoulder and, way above, the soft light is calling and she knows that, this time, there will be no return to her body. She delays, reaching out to Hua and Bidari, to Bo, to Koldo, to the old man. She tries to comfort them, but they cannot see her or feel her touch.

Still she waits, wondering, and now the night seems to slide away and she is looking down on the floor of the cave and it is day and the rain is falling fast outside. It's not terror that is rising from the people now but the ache of grief. Sorne is clasping the body of her daughter close and the sound of keening fills the air. Tipi sits by the wall and curled up beside him in pain is the figure of Lilura. Ansa looks through the wall of Lilura's belly to see the mass of seed-like creatures, swimming and feeding inside the red loops of her gut. Ansa senses movement underground, at the back of the cave. She watches Goi ease himself through the hole and

375

down the shaft to the burial place, to make a space for his daughter in the soft earth.

Now her attention is drawn away, to the slope in front of the cave. Gashi is half way down, a water bag slung across her shoulder, but she is not making for the spring. Instead, she starts on the path that leads to the carob woodland and the hawthorns. Ansa feels the sudden leap of fear in Lotz, who is sitting at the entrance with the other men. Now Koldo is on his feet and running down the slope after Gashi. He knocks her to the ground.

Bidari appears at the cave mouth. He stands, watching, and now, at last, Ansa sees the seed of courage inside him split open. He strides out into the rain. She watches as he turns off the path to the birthing rock and clambers up to the ridge above, where her own bones lie scattered, picked clean by the hyenas and the vultures. Ansa can feel his heart beating fast as he takes hold of her skull.

The rain has stopped and he is back on the slope outside the cave, holding the skull up for everyone to see. There are cries of fear. Koldo is backing away, his eyes wide with horror. Ansa can feel the confusion as the people gather at the mouth of the cave, whispering. But now Gashi has gone to stand beside Bidari, and the children start to edge nearer. The heaviness begins to lift, as if the wind had changed direction. Lotz is screeching at Koldo but Koldo's gaze is fixed on the skull in Bidari's hand and he pushes the crippled man away. Unsteady on his feet, Lotz crashes back onto the ground, but no-one goes to help him. Everyone is watching Gashi. She has picked up her water bag again and now Ikomar joins her and they set off together to gather water from the stream by the hawthorns. This time, Koldo stands back to let them go.

The white light above Ansa is growing, filling her vision, beckoning to her, but still she is reluctant to leave the Antelope

Nose. Days and nights on the mountain seem to pass and she knows them one at a time, yet all at once, and everything is clear to her and close at hand, yet somehow distant. There is Hua, fat and strong again and playing with Hatz in the afternoon shade of a thornbush. Now it is early light and Bidari is sitting with his brother and with Tipi and Iban, making spear tips, and Lotz is not there: not in the cave nor on the slope, nor anywhere on the face of the mountain.

There are times of terror and times of happiness. Fighting with the Painted men, down on the plain. Fearful days of waiting for the wounds to heal. More bloodshed and the tearing grief of Sorne as Goi's body is carried up the mountain on a litter. A night of great joy when Balqa smiles fullface and Lilura gives birth to not one but two strong boys. A winter of hunger, when the antelope do not come. A spring day when the brothers climb up from the marshes and Koldo kneels before dumb Apal and begs his forgiveness, and Eneko sits their sister's twins on his knee.

Ansa is content now but as she feels herself being drawn upwards into the light, still the pictures come, one folding into another. There is Hua filling her water bag at the spring: a grown woman, with a child on her back. And Bidari, old and wrinkled, acting out stories around the fire. No – it is not Bidari, but another old man with the same gap between his front teeth. Ansa waits to listen to the tale. It was taught to him, he says, by his grandmother, whose name was Hua. It is the story of the sickness that came during the dark days of Zorion and of the boy called Mul who showed Hua's mother where to find water that would make the people well.

Ansa is high above the mountain now and looking down onto the plain, but the landscape seems different. Curious, she finds herself beside a dense wood of oak, where the hunt thicket used to be. Beside the wood there is a circle of round sunken shelters made

377

of stones and brushwood. A young boy opens a door and steps up out of one of the huts and, behind him, she glimpses a fire burning in a hearth. The boy has an animal on a rope that she has never seen before. It is something like a hyena, but the boy is stroking and patting it and the animal looks up into his face and she can feel the love there is between them.

The women are a little way off, working in a patch of tall yellow grass with long blades, hafted into wooden handles. They are swinging the blades to and fro, slashing the grasses so that they fall onto the ground. They bundle the grasses together and take them back to the shelters and Ansa watches, fascinated, as they beat them against the ground to release the small grains, letting the husks fly off in the wind.

Now the picture changes and she watches as the people leave their shelters on the plain and climb up, a trail of ants, among the toes of the mountain. The path they are using is not one that Ansa knows but she watches as it winds round and brings them up, at last, to the mouth of the cave. Everything is different here too. There are rocks strewn across the slope and pistacias and thornbushes have grown there and the entrance to the cave is much smaller. She can feel fear coming from some of the people. Now one of the women takes a basket with some of the grains in it and begins to pick her way across the rocks towards the cave mouth. While the woman climbs up and disappears into the darkness, the others begin to sing in memory of their dead, whose bones lie buried in the cave, and of the ancestors from long ago. The words of the song are unfamiliar to Ansa, yet she finds that she can understand them. The words accompany her as she is drawn up, at last, into the light.

About the Author

Ruth Mohrman has a PhD in Medieval English and lives in the Welsh countryside, close to the border with England. She has always been drawn to mysticism and has a lifelong fascination with the past, so it is perhaps not surprising that the two come together in her writing.

You can connect with me on:

[f] https://fb.me/ruthmohrman

🖉 https://medium.com/@ruthsmith453

Also by Ruth Mohrman

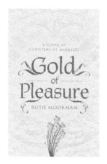

Gold of Pleasure: A Novel of Christina of Markyate

Ruth's first novel to be published was *Gold of Pleasure: A Novel of Christina of Markyate* (2021). https://viewbook.at/goldofpleasure

It tells, in fictional form, the story of the historical twelfth-century English visionary, Christina, who refused the sexual advances of a Bishop and later escaped from a forced marriage. She was hidden for years in the hermitage of the renowned holy man, Roger of Markyate. At Roger's death, she was hidden by another cleric, only to find herself entangled with him emotionally and perhaps sexually. Yet another important man - Geoffrey, the Abbot of St Albans - found Christina compelling and it was through his patronage that she eventually became a Prioress with a community of her own.

Ruth also writes articles on literature and spirituality under the name Ruth Smith, which can be found on Medium. https://medium.com/@ruthsmith453

Printed in Great Britain
by Amazon